"Stay far, far away from me."

With unexpected speed and grace he whirled on her. He loomed over her, so close she could see the lines around his eyes, but not so close he was touching her. "Amiable," he whispered. "We will never be amiable."

"Why n-not?" she stammered.

He smiled, but there was nothing light about it. "Because I am a wicked man, Miss Weston. Don't you listen to the gossip? Madness runs in my family. My estate is utterly ruined. People call me a thief. They even say I killed my father."

She frowned. "I doubt it."

"But you don't *know*. That should warn you to run away."

She stared at him. "You intrigue me."

He leaned closer. "And you intrigue me," he replied, his breath stirring the hair at her temple. "That's why I avoid you."

By Caroline Linden

CAROLINE LINDEN

It Takes a Scandal

AVON
An Imprint of HarperCollinsPublishers

This is a work of fiction. Names, characters, places, and incidents are products of the author's imagination or are used fictitiously and are not to be construed as real. Any resemblance to actual events, locales, organizations, or persons, living or dead, is entirely coincidental.

AVON BOOKS
An Imprint of HarperCollins*Publishers*
10 East 53rd Street
New York, New York 10022-5299

Copyright © 2014 by P.F. Belsley
ISBN 978-0-06-224490-1
www.avonromance.com

First Avon Books mass market printing: May 2014

Avon Trademark Reg. U.S. Pat. Off. and in Other Countries, Marca Registrada, Hecho en U.S.A.
HarperCollins® is a registered trademark of HarperCollins Publishers.

Printed in the U.S.A.

10 9 8 7 6 5 4 3 2 1

For Lyssa Keusch, editor nonpareil

Prologue

1816

He came awake with a start, heart racing. The French were upon him—the *tirailleurs* leaping over the barricades, their long muskets gleaming in the hazy light as they tried to sweep his brigade from their position. His ears rang, deafened by the first shot that had shattered his knee. For a moment he struggled to breathe, waiting for the second shot that would end it all.

The deafness persisted; no second shot came. Belatedly he realized there had been no first shot—not tonight. He was not on the battlefield in Belgium, trying desperately to beat back the Emperor's troops from a sunken lane. He was home in England, sleeping in a chair by the dying fire with his ruined leg splinted in front of him.

Sebastian Vane slumped back into the worn leather, exhausted, as his heart still beat a frantic tattoo against his breastbone. With a trembling hand he wiped the cold sweat from his face. There were no French here, only laudanum nightmares of them.

A soft bang made him start again. He looked toward the door, but it was closed. Another door had slammed, downstairs from the sound of it.

The housekeeper must be up and about. Mrs. Jones was running herself ragged nursing her husband, who'd been sick in bed for the last week, as well as caring for a madman and a cripple. The poor woman. Sebastian groped for his watch; it was late, after midnight. He'd been asleep for two hours, and now felt as though he wouldn't sleep again tonight, which was a shame.

It had been a relatively good night thus far. His father's madness seemed to have receded a bit, leaving him more like the parent Sebastian remembered and less like the deranged lunatic he'd found on his return from the war. Michael Vane had eaten a few bites of his dinner tonight before hurling the platter aside and muttering about poison. When Sebastian helped him out of his clothes, he hadn't kicked, only cursed. And when Sebastian put him to bed, his father had gone as docilely as a child, wrapping his hand around the ragged strip of fabric that had once been Sebastian's mother's nightgown. That nightgown had been a godsend; with it in his grasp, Michael grew calmer and more manageable.

Well. That wasn't really the father Sebastian remembered—calm and docile, soothed by a worn-out nightgown—but it was a far sight better than the screaming madman he often was. Sebastian shifted his weight, trying to stretch his leg without reopening the wound. His father had kicked him the previous day, splitting open the scar over his knee and leaving him so faint with pain, Mrs. Jones had run for the laudanum. Nasty stuff, laudanum. He'd almost weaned himself off it, before the kick, and hated that he had to take it again.

The wind howled past the windows, rattling the panes of glass, and the door below banged again, harder. He raised his head and frowned. That sounded like the heavy front door. "Mrs. Jones," he called. Perhaps she'd had to step out and failed to latch it on her return to the house. There was no reply from below, only a slightly softer thud from the door. Mrs. Jones must have gone to bed, and she wouldn't be able to hear it from her rooms behind the kitchen.

He sighed. He could ring the bell and wake her, but he wasn't going to sleep anytime soon. Didn't he want to be independent again? Gingerly he eased himself forward in the chair, setting his left foot on the floor. With a hard shove he was on his feet, unsteady until he got his crutch set.

The corridor was dark, only a faint light bleeding up the stairs. As he reached the head of the stairs, there was another great thump from below, with a gust of cold air. Alternating between cursing and holding his breath, he hobbled down the stairs to see the front door, unbarred and unlatched, swing slowly open as the wind caught it.

Puzzled, Sebastian propped his shoulder against the door frame and caught the door as it blew toward him again. The heavy bar that should have held it closed lay across the threshold, preventing the door from slamming closed. Normally it fit across the jambs, to prevent the door being opened from the outside. It was as if someone had removed the bar and simply dropped it.

The back of his neck prickled. Only one person in the house would do that . . . but Michael Vane was securely locked in his room upstairs. Sebastian did it himself, every night, for his father's own good.

Still, he pushed the door open and peered out. The

moon was a thin crescent, and the cold wind whipped the shrubbery and trees into frenzied waving. But the sky was clear of clouds, and there was enough light to see that the grounds were deserted. He shook his head; it must have been the housekeeper, who was no doubt exhausted to the point of delirium. He closed the door and dropped the bar into place before limping up the stairs to his room again.

He had barely settled into his chair, though, when there was another thumping from below. This time it wasn't the door itself, but someone pounding on the door. "Vane!" cried a familiar voice over the moaning wind. "Damn you, Vane, wake up!"

The pounding continued as Sebastian made his way back down the stairs, cursing all the while this time as his knee burned. He wrestled the bar up and away, whereupon the visitor threw open the door and surged over the threshold.

"Where is she?" demanded Benedict Lennox. "So help me, Vane, if you've touched her—"

"Who?"

"Samantha," spat Benedict.

Sebastian's eyebrows shot up. "Why would your sister be here, at this time of night? She's only sixteen—"

"Which is probably why she's gone and done such an idiotic thing!" Benedict lowered his voice. "If you just produce her now, I'll take her home with no questions or arguments. No one else knows she's missing yet—"

Sebastian's mouth thinned. "She's not here."

Benedict glared at him. "No? She told me she's in love with you, and has been for years."

"Schoolgirl infatuation," Sebastian said in a low voice.

"But a headstrong, impulsive schoolgirl could easily be persuaded to throw her lot in with a—"

He stopped abruptly, but Sebastian could fill in the rest: *a madman's son, crippled and destitute.* "How flattering," he said evenly. "I never guessed my personal charms would be strong enough to persuade an earl's daughter to throw herself away on me, bankrupt and lame though I am."

Benedict's eyes flashed with fury. "You know she would elope with you if you asked," he snarled.

"But I didn't," Sebastian pointed out. It made no difference. Benedict had already headed down the corridor, opening each door he passed. Sebastian stood listening to the search in impotent humiliation. He knew Samantha had once fancied herself in love with him, but it was calf love. Even if it wasn't, she had to know that her father, the Earl of Stratford, would never allow her to marry the son of Mad Michael Vane. Everyone knew it. And it had made Samantha's infatuation, once something amusing and flattering, into yet another source of mortification as her family made certain everyone knew such a match was utterly unthinkable.

And now Samantha's brother, who had once been his dearest friend in all the world, thought he'd schemed to elope with her. Sebastian limped to the bottom of the stairs and rested against the newel post. Benedict was making a very thorough effort; he knew the house well. He'd practically lived here as a boy, fleeing the strict air at Stratford Court for the woods and hills of Montrose Hill. One upon a time, Benedict's arrival in the middle of the night would have filled Sebastian with elation and excitement, and the two of them would have stolen off into the woods for a night of illicit adventure.

But that had been a very long time ago.

Benedict came back to the hall, his expression grimmer than ever. "I'm going upstairs."

"I can hardly stop you," Sebastian said under his breath. Benedict was already headed up the stairs, and this time he followed.

As expected, Benedict took more care up here. He opened the door at the top of the stairs, pausing when he saw the bottle of laudanum on the mantel. He gave Sebastian a wary glance, seeming for the first time to take in his splinted leg, his crutch, the dressing gown he wore. "You could help me look," he said in a somewhat calmer tone.

"She's not here." Sebastian leaned on his crutch, still winded from going up and down the stairs so many times. "Whether I look or not, you won't find her."

Benedict set his jaw, and continued to the next door. He made his way quickly down the corridor; all those rooms were empty, even the linen cupboard. Everything in them had been sold. Only at the far end of the corridor did Sebastian stop him.

"That's my father's room," he said as Benedict reached for the knob. "It's locked."

But it wasn't. The door opened an inch under Benedict's hand.

His former friend looked at him. Sebastian stared at the door in shock. He'd disabled the lock on the inside of the door himself. He stumped closer, clumsy in his haste, and reached up. The key hung in its usual spot on the wall, next to the door in case of fire. He was sure— *certain*—he'd locked it just a few hours ago. And yet the door opened, creaking softly as Benedict pushed it open.

It was as dark as pitch in the room. No fire or lamp of any kind was allowed, not since Michael Vane had tried to set himself ablaze. Sebastian hobbled to the window and threw open one of the shutters. Benedict made a noise of quiet shock at the sight of the bars crossing the windows, too closely to allow even a hand through them, but Sebastian was staring at the bed.

The empty bed.

He grabbed Benedict's coat. "Why are you here?"

"To—to find my sister." Benedict seemed rattled as well.

"Why the devil did you think she was here?" he demanded.

Benedict stared at him. "Because she said nothing would stop her from marrying you."

Sebastian cursed again. "If her father wouldn't—and I strongly assume he would—*I* would." He thumped his crutch in illustration. "But why did you think she was *here* tonight?"

"I— She went missing," said Benedict, finally appearing to grasp how thin his logic had been. "I couldn't find her . . ."

"She's not here—she never has been." Sebastian limped from the room, the crutch digging into his arm. "And now, neither is my father." His brain still felt a bit fuzzy from the laudanum; damn it, he must have forgotten to lock the door. How long had it been since Michael escaped? Between the cold and the darkness, time was of the essence in finding him.

He turned back toward the stairs. Behind him he could hear Benedict opening the last few doors, all of which led into rooms that were completely empty. Benedict caught up to him in the hall below, as Sebastian was putting on his hat and coat. "Where else could she be?" he asked, only slightly subdued.

"I've no idea. She's your sister." Sebastian pulled open the front door and gestured. "Go home, Ben. She probably went to the library for a book, or to the kitchen for some warm milk."

Benedict scowled, although with real worry this time. "I looked there. I looked everywhere. She was gone, I tell you. And you—and she—"

Sebastian shrugged. He was fond of Samantha . . . as a brother or a cousin might be. With her promise of beauty and her father's position and wealth, she would marry much better than he, a crippled soldier whose father had laid waste to his estate because he thought the devil was after him. Sebastian himself had told Samantha that he wouldn't be a good husband; he'd only meant to let her know, gently, that her affection for him was misplaced. He was needed at home to care for his father, and now he'd been proven negligent even at that.

"Why were the windows upstairs barred?"

Sebastian raised his eyebrows at the hesitant question. "Because he's gone mad—hadn't you heard? He's a danger to himself and must be locked in every night."

Benedict glanced up the stairs. "But the door was unlocked. Perhaps Samantha . . ."

"Crossed the river, in the dark, climbed the hill, found a way into the house, unlocked his door, and then left, without anyone seeing her?" Sebastian finished when Benedict didn't. "How likely is that? And what would it gain her, in any event?" He shook his head, fumbling with his buttons, cursing the laudanum that made him clumsy—and forgetful—tonight.

"No," murmured Benedict. "I know that even if she thought . . . That is to say, there would still be . . ."

He flushed, stopping short of saying what they both knew.

"Even if he died, it wouldn't change anything?" Sebastian gave him a hard look. "I suggest you go home to find your sister."

Benedict hesitated, then jerked his head in a single nod. He went out and untied his horse from the post. With a quick, easy motion that gave Sebastian a pang of useless envy, he swung into the saddle and wheeled his horse around. "Good luck," he said after a moment's pause.

Sebastian nodded once. "And to you."

Benedict disappeared into the night. It would take him close to an hour to get home on horseback. He would have to ride through Richmond and rouse the ferryman, although perhaps he'd paid the man to wait when he came across the river the first time. He'd be cold and stiff by the time he reached home—which must say something about how strongly he feared his sister had been persuaded to run off with Sebastian. Just another bit of proof that their friendship was irrevocably over.

Sebastian glanced longingly toward his dark and empty stables, wishing he, too, had a horse. It would make searching for his father much easier, if he had to go into the woods. Of course, he couldn't ride anywhere. Thanks to his ruined knee, mounting a horse would be agony, and thanks to his father's delusions, they didn't have any horses anyway. He went to rouse the Joneses, unable to answer their alarmed queries about how Mr. Vane had got out. When a quick search of the house and stable revealed nothing, he struck out for the woods.

As he limped down the uneven path, the echo of his

own words followed him. *Even if he died, it wouldn't change anything.* That wasn't quite true. If his father died, he wouldn't have to sleep in his chair, ready to spring into action if another fit seized Michael. He wouldn't suffer any more injuries trying to keep his father from harming other people. He wouldn't have to watch his once intelligent, practical parent become a distorted shell of himself, filthy and insane and raving about the demons pursuing him. In many ways, Sebastian knew it would be a mercy when death finally claimed his father.

But it wouldn't make him any more eligible. Samantha had to know that as well as anyone. Benedict would find her safe at home, and feel like an idiot for rushing to Montrose Hill. For a moment Sebastian wondered if his onetime friend would apologize for his accusations, and then he shrugged it off. The odds were highly against it, and if not for Benedict's visit, he wouldn't have known his father was missing until morning. Perhaps he should thank Benedict for being so suspicious. He raised his lantern higher and tried to think where his father might have gone.

At dawn, Mr. Jones found Sebastian and half carried him back to the house for a few hours of sleep. Together he and Mr. Jones combed the meadow and dragged the pond, an exercise which put Mr. Jones back into bed with chills and a cough.

Two letters arrived that day. One was from Benedict, apologizing for troubling him. Samantha had indeed been safe at home. The other letter was from Samantha herself, urging Sebastian to call on her. He supposed Benedict had told her what happened, and she also wanted to apologize. He hoped that was all she wanted to say; the sooner she redirected her affections, the better for all of them. Sebastian threw both notes on the fire.

But no trace of Michael Vane was ever seen again. And instead of making anything better, his father's disappearance only made everything much, much worse.

Chapter 1

1822
Richmond-on-Thames

"**W**ell, my dear, what do you think?"

Thomas Weston stood in the center of the main hall at Hart House and spread his arms wide, beaming.

"What's wrong with a house in London?" his wife asked, casting a dark look on the dust motes floating in the sunlight that streamed through the open door and tall flanking windows. The estate agent who had brought them to view the house waited discreetly outside.

"London is London. A country estate is what sets a man apart and makes him a gentleman."

"It's also what squanders his fortune and incites him to spend ever more, redecorating and building and entertaining." His wife tipped back her head. "That plaster is already cracked. You'll be a pauper within the year, fixing every little thing around this house."

"A bit of cracked plaster," he scoffed. "The house is sound, Mrs. Weston! It's within a day's drive of town, so you can go back and forth if it pleases you. You'll never be apart from your dressmakers and bonnet shops and all those furbelows you don't seem to mind spending my fortune on."

"A new bonnet is nothing to the cost of a new house," she replied tartly. "To say nothing of landscaping and furnishings and staff."

He put his hands on his hips and sighed. "But think of the parties you can throw here, in the finest gowns from Bond Street," he cajoled. "Mrs. Weston of Hart House! It will be the most coveted invitation in all of Richmond, I've no doubt. And think of the girls—picture our daughters gliding down these stairs, also in splendid new gowns, dancing with the gentlemen of the neighborhood, forming friendships with the daughters of the nobility." He put his arm around her and drew her into the very center of the hall. "Imagine it: you and I, standing right here, welcoming our genteel and noble guests. My lord, my lady." He made an extravagant bow to an imaginary couple. "What an honor to have you grace our humble home. May I present my wife?" He swept her hand up to kiss it, giving her a sideways, hopeful glance. Mrs. Weston pursed up her lips, obviously trying not to smile. Encouraged, he went on. "Why, yes, my lord, she is the most beautiful lady in all of Surrey, and the most gracious hostess. Indeed, my lady, her gown is the very latest fashion; I'm sure she would be delighted to commend you to her dressmaker." Mrs. Weston rolled her eyes at her husband's antics.

From the top of the curving staircase overlooking them, Penelope Weston leaned closer to her sister. They were watching their parents' little drama from there, after exploring the upper rooms. "He's laying it on a bit strong, isn't he?"

"Just wait," murmured Abigail in reply. "You know what's coming . . ."

As if he could hear her, her father clapped one hand to his heart. "And you must meet my daughters! Two lovelier, sweeter girls you've never met, and every bit as beautiful as their mother. What's that? You have an unmarried son and heir? A gentleman in search of a bride? A bride whose family is refined and respectable, with property in London and Richmond?"

"There it is," said Abigail with a wry smile. Penelope gave a quiet snort.

"Stop, Thomas!" Mrs. Weston finally burst out laughing and swatted his shoulder. "You're too ridiculous—as if buying this house will guarantee a match for one—or both!—of our girls!"

"Well, it can't hurt, can it?" He gave her a winning smile. "Come, Clara; what say you? It's a fine house, isn't it?"

"Yes, it's very fine," she agreed. "Exceedingly fine! It must cost the earth, and how much time do you expect to spend out here in the wilds?"

"Wilds!" He threw up one hand. "It's less than ten miles from London."

"We're settled in town," she went on. "We're comfortable. You're ignoring how disrupting it will be to pack up and move house, even a mere ten miles."

"But once we're settled here, it will seem a mere trifle. We can journey by river. I shall buy you a barge with ten Egyptians to sail you back and forth, like a modern Cleopatra." He sidled closer. "What will convince you, my love?"

She gave him a stern look. "We both know you aren't really asking my approval. I expect you've already bought it, haven't you?"

"But I still want you to be pleased," he answered, not bothering to deny it.

Upstairs, Abigail stifled a laugh. How like her father. So this would be their country house. She looked around it with new consideration. It really was a lovely building. Mama would come around once it was time to choose carpets and furnishings, if by some chance Papa didn't manage to win her over sooner. He usually did, though.

"I'm going to go choose my room now," whispered Penelope. "As far away from Mama's as possible." She disappeared toward the bedchambers.

Abigail went down the stairs and walked past her parents, her mother still pretending outraged disapproval and her father still cajoling her, and out onto the gravel drive. The house itself wasn't enormous, but it was well proportioned and handsome. The landscape was peaceful and beautiful, and the air was certainly clearer here than in town. Yes, Mama would come around. Within a year, she'd probably prefer it to their house in Grosvenor Square.

Her brother, James, came around the side of the house. He'd probably been off inspecting the stables. "What do you think, Abby?"

"Papa's already bought it."

He nodded, squinting in the sunlight. "I know."

"What?" she exclaimed. "He told you, but not Mama?"

A faint smile touched his mouth. "If he bought it before he showed it to her, she couldn't argue him out of it, could she?"

"That's cheating!"

James laughed. "All's fair in love, I suppose. Father's had his heart set on a country property for some time now, and this is a good one; the house is sound, only in need of decoration and a few minor modernizations. The prospect is ideal, as Mama will agree when she can plan picnics and boating trips. And the price was reasonable."

Abigail shook her head. "He's in there now, telling her Pen and I are likely to meet titled gentlemen because of this house."

"I shouldn't doubt it. The Earl of Stratford's seat is nearby, and there are dozens of villas and small estates where the nobility come for the fresh air."

"The Earl of Stratford!" Abigail snorted. "Now you're as fanciful as Papa."

"I never said any of them would marry you," he pointed out. "Just that you're likely to meet them—fat, gouty, senile, or lecherous though they may be. Besides, Lord Stratford is Papa's age, and already married. He's got a son, but I believe he's away in the army. You and Pen are out of luck there; perhaps the Marquess of Dorre, who owns Penton Lodge near Kew, will bring his sons. Although I hear rumors the middle one is someone to avoid."

"How do you know all that?"

He shrugged. "I pay attention. Don't you?"

Abigail bit her lip. She did pay attention to gossip about gentlemen, titled or otherwise. Still, even she hadn't known about Dorre's middle son; what had he done, that people ought to avoid him? "Perhaps you'll meet a young lady now that we have a country property. In fact, since the house will be yours one day, it's far more likely to snare you a bride."

Her brother's lips twitched. "Don't you know I'm hopeless? Penelope told me so herself."

"No, she said you were dull and unimaginative, and

no one wants to marry a dull man." Abigail grinned. "I myself find it far more likely that you'll marry an aristocratic girl than that some viscount or earl will appear out of nowhere to call on me or Pen."

"Don't wager your pin money on it," he said shortly.

She laughed. "Believe me, I won't. Haven't I learned after all these years that you usually beat me?" Together they walked through a covered walkway to a very pleasant lawn overlooking the river. The house was set on the head of a gently rolling slope toward the river, and one could probably go punting right into the heart of London from here. Even if Mama didn't come to like it here, Abigail thought she very well might.

Still, her father's reasoning was somewhat daft. "They must know it's not terribly likely for any of us," she murmured. Her brother shot her an unreadable glance. Abigail flipped one hand. "Aristocratic husbands—or wife. Everyone looks down on us as nouveau riche tradesmen."

"Noblemen," said James, staring down at the sparkling river, "have married actresses. Mistresses. Americans. Some lord somewhere has probably married a scullery maid. Believing a pretty girl with a handsome dowry could catch one isn't too much of a stretch. They don't put up much of a fight, when enough money is involved."

"*Could* catch one," she repeated, laying heavy emphasis on the first word. "Not necessarily *will* catch one. And what if I don't like any that might deign to take me? Mama chose a humble attorney's son, and she seems happy enough. Perhaps I'm destined to be a butcher's wife."

"Your friend's marriage raised her hopes." He gave

her a sideways glance. "To say nothing of Father's hopes."

Abigail grimaced. Her dear friend Joan Bennet, who had been every bit as ignored by the gentlemen of London as Abigail and Penelope, had recently married one of the most eligible, and elusive, men in London, Viscount Burke. It certainly had caught everyone by surprise—even including Joan, if she could be believed. But Mr. and Mrs. Weston had indeed been very pleased by the news. "You'll recall that began inauspiciously," she reminded her brother. "She hated him at first, and he tormented her."

"He tormented her?" James raised his eyebrows. "I recall horrid tales of him dancing with her, and even a cruel report that he took her ballooning. Dear sister, if any eligible, wealthy viscount torments you so, do let me know at once. I'll rush straight to the betting books and wager my entire fortune that you'll be married to the fellow before the end of the year."

"Stop it." She scowled at him. "Obviously he stopped tormenting her. But even so, Joan's father is a baronet; her uncle is the Earl of Doncaster. She has connections, and we don't."

"Take heart, Abby." He gave her one of his rare, sly grins. "I'm sure the butcher will treasure you with all his heart."

"He'd better," she retorted, before giving in to the urge to laugh. Her brother joined in a moment later.

"What's so funny?" Penelope joined them, looking a little grim. "Jamie, did you know Papa already bought this house?"

"Yes."

She made a face at him. "And you didn't tell us! You're utterly worthless as a source of gossip."

"Being able to hold my tongue is a useful skill. You might try it some time."

Penelope huffed. "Where would be the pleasure in that?" She faced Abigail. "There is one absolute failing of this house, and I'm sure you know what it is."

"Ah . . ." Abigail darted a look at her brother, who shrugged.

"You know," repeated Penelope meaningfully. "We're all the way out here in Richmond, away from the shops of London."

"There are shops here as well, you know," said her brother.

"Not the right shops," she replied without looking at him. She seemed to be trying to bore a hole in Abigail with her bright blue gaze. "How shall we ever get the right lotion, and rouge, and hair pomade? We'll look like Druids camping out on the moors."

"Buy plenty in London and bring it with you," suggested James. "A little planning will solve nearly every problem."

Penelope gritted her teeth, still staring fiercely at Abigail. "But we may run out. And what if I put on weight, with so many fewer balls to attend? I shall need a new corset—perhaps one of those with the extra gussets under the bosoms, you know, the sort that hold each side separately—"

"I regret underestimating your suffering," said James hastily. "You'd best ask Mama's advice." He was already edging away, and disappeared into the house in a minute.

"Poor Jamie," said Abigail in amusement. "How will he ever marry, when the mere mention of a corset makes him turn green?"

"How will he ever marry, when the only things he

talks about are horses and money?" Penelope flicked one hand, dismissing their brother. "You know what I meant, don't you?"

"I believe so." Abigail turned and strolled a little farther from the house. Who knew when her parents might come out to see the view? Her mother seemed possessed of supernatural hearing at times, and unlike her sister, Abigail had the common sense not to test it.

Penelope followed her. "How are we to get new issues of *50 Ways to Sin* all the way out here? It took weeks to discover the bookseller in Madox Street. For all we know, no one will be selling it in Richmond."

"Perhaps we ought not to look for it at all." Abigail gave her a stern look. "You're still in Mama's black books over that, you know. Querying every broadsheet seller in Richmond will make it worse."

Fifty Ways to Sin was the most notorious pamphlet in all of London. Each issue recounted one of the author's amorous encounters with prominent gentlemen, in lush and explicit detail. The author, calling herself Lady Constance, concealed her lovers' names, but wrote of them in such terms that made everyone desperate to unmask the gentlemen involved. The true identities of the men, to say nothing of Lady Constance herself, were hotly debated by most of London, and the pamphlets were highly coveted. The erotic nature of the stories meant they had to be sold rather discreetly; one had to know which booksellers to ask, and since the pamphlets were published irregularly, one had to ask at the right moment, or they would be all sold out. No one was a more avid fan than Penelope, although Abigail was nearly as engrossed.

Together with their friend Joan—now the Viscountess Burke—they had analyzed every issue in great detail. *Fifty Ways to Sin* had provided a remarkable education on topics normally forbidden to young ladies. The lure of that forbidden fruit had been Penelope's downfall, though. In her eagerness to read one issue, she'd been caught by their mother, and was now under strict watch. So far Abigail had escaped that scrutiny, and she meant to keep it that way.

Her sister's face wrinkled up in frustration. "I know! Oh, blast and damn. Why did you have to give all our copies to Joan?" When their friend had recently married, with a whiff of hushed-up scandal, the Weston sisters had agreed she needed them more, and they gave her all the copies they could find. With a husband of her own, Joan might actually be able to test some of the more incredible acts described, and—presuming she was a very good friend indeed—report back on the truth of them. The only trouble was, her new husband had taken her off to his family estate in the country, and the issues had gone with her. Or so Abigail supposed; if she had a handsome husband, she would be sure to take every issue with her, for helpful suggestion and instruction.

"You agreed," Abigail reminded her sister.

"I know!" Penelope put her hands on her temples. "I thought there would be a new issue, or three or four, by now. How could it be a month without even *one*?"

"Perhaps Lady Constance retired to the country for the summer as well."

"Don't say that!" Penelope kicked at the ground, sending a stray pebble bounding into the grass. "Papa's already decided we shall have a ball. He intends to impress everyone in Richmond right from the start."

"Already?" Abigail felt a stirring of interest. "We haven't even taken possession of the house. When does he propose to have it?"

"In a fortnight. Just enough time for Mama to order

a new gown," Penelope finished in a gruff imitation of their father. "He might ask us! Joan won't be there, we shan't know a single soul in the room, and now Papa will be expecting all sorts of noblemen to appear magically in front of us, begging every dance of the evening." Her tone expressed what she thought the odds of that were.

"We shall have to endure as best we can," murmured Abigail dryly.

Her sister just scowled.

"It might be a wonderful change," she pointed out. "We've had plenty of chances to meet gentlemen in London, with no real luck. Perhaps in Richmond there are more men of taste and good humor, and less pride and condescension."

"Perhaps," Penelope begrudged. "But it's so quiet! Why would anyone interesting want to spend time here?"

"It's one summer." Abigail laughed. "You make it sound like eternal exile. And I shall tease you to no end if you end up meeting the man of your dreams here."

"I highly doubt it. You can have the gentlemen farmers and country squires." Penelope nudged her shoulder with a small grin. "I shall save myself for an exciting, mysterious man of town who would kill and maim for the chance to spend just one night in my arms."

"That's a very short-lived marriage," Abigail observed. "To say nothing of what Mama would say about it." She knew Penelope was wildly irked about being so closely watched.

Her sister gave a gusty sigh. "Mama! As if I'd even have a chance at a clandestine kiss with her trailing around behind me everywhere! Abby, you must help me—I swear I'll run mad otherwise. I will owe you the greatest favor in the world if you promise."

She thought about it. There was no finer conspirator than Penelope, if one wanted to sneak around. Such a favor might come in handy at a future date. Besides, she was sure she knew what her sister wanted, and it would certainly suit her as well. "Very well. I'll help you track down any copies of *50 Ways to Sin* that might have escaped London."

"Thank you!" Penelope seized her hand and squeezed it near to pain. "Bless you, Abby!"

"And in return you must not pester me to death about it." She pulled free of her sister's fervent grasp. "I mean it, Pen. I'll try to find it, but if you nag—"

"Not a bit!" Her sister looked wounded. "I'll merely help."

Abigail had suffered Penelope's help before. She put up one hand. "Only if I ask for your help. Otherwise you must hold your peace."

Penelope rolled her eyes. "Very well."

"And one more promise . . ." She fixed a stern eye on her sister. "I get to read it first."

Chapter 2

Mama must have been more resistant than usual to Papa's persuasion, for when the Westons reached Hart House a week later, baggage in tow, there was a surprise waiting in her new dressing room. Abigail and Penelope came running when they heard their mother cry out, but when they burst into the room, they saw it had been an exclamation of delight. Mrs. Weston held a wriggling ball of black and brown fur up to her cheek. From the tiny pink tongue flicking frantically toward her face, the girls deduced how their father had schemed to win her over.

"Isn't he darling?" cried their mother, holding up the puppy. He was a tiny thing, easily held in one hand. Penelope gasped in excitement and ran forward to see.

"A country lady needs a dog," said Papa from the other side of the room. He stood in the doorway to the adjoining bedchamber looking very pleased with himself.

"Oh, Thomas, you shouldn't have," replied his wife, her beaming smile negating her words. "What a darling little creature!"

"I hope the sight of him gamboling about the lawn makes you more fond of Hart House." Papa winked.

"You're a shocking manipulator, Thomas Weston." Mama let the puppy lick her face once more before handing him to Penelope, who cooed over the animal as much as her mother had done. "But for once I whole-heartedly thank you." She crossed the room and kissed his cheek.

"For once!" Papa threw up his hands in mock exasperation. "If I'd known a little vermin catcher would steal your heart, I'd have got one years ago."

"Vermin catcher! No," protested his wife, hurrying back to stroke her pet's ears.

"He's too adorable for that," added Penelope, laughing as the dog nipped at the ribbon on her dress.

Papa just shook his head. "What shall you call him, my dear?"

Mama gazed lovingly at her new baby. "Milo."

Milo quickly became the center of life in Hart House, for better and for worse. Mrs. Weston took him with her everywhere, but he was as wily as an otter and needed only a moment to escape her sight and vanish into some dark cupboard or closet. More than once a day, a cry would go up to find Milo. After the first frantic search, Mr. Weston declared it was a dog's duty to find his own way home and he refused to lift a finger to hunt for him. James seemed to develop sudden hearing difficulties whenever Milo was mentioned at all. Penelope doted on Milo almost as much as their mother did, but somehow she was never around when Milo went missing and had to be found. Abigail, as usual, was caught in the middle, reluctantly drawn into every search by her mother's pleas. The puppy was a sweet little dog, but he was also a great deal of trouble, in her opinion.

That trouble came to a head the night of the ball.

Papa had planned it for a week after their arrival, which was a shockingly short time to pull together such an event. Mama managed it, as she always did, but at great expense to household peace and harmony. And sure enough, in the confusion, Milo disappeared.

"Where's he gone?" fretted Mrs. Weston, meeting her elder daughter in the front hall, now decorated with all manner of greenery and silk ribbons. "I told Marie to lock him in my room but she let him get out. Have you seen him, Abigail?"

"Not since this afternoon."

"Oh dear." Mama put one hand to her lips. "I hope he hasn't got outside. He's so small, he could be crushed by the horses or the carriage wheels."

"I'll go have a look," Abigail offered. "I'm already dressed, and you have other things to see to." Like getting Penelope out of her sulks; Abigail wanted no part of that. She'd had quite enough of her sister's bad humor since they arrived in Richmond, and for some reason Penelope was in an especially cross mood today.

"Thank you, dear." Mama pressed her hand gratefully. "Don't go far, though. If he's not to be found near the house, I'll get James to go after him, since he refuses to attend the ball," she finished darkly. "What I ever did to deserve these men in my life . . ." She shook her head, looking irked.

"I won't," Abigail promised. "I'm sure he'll be nearby. His legs are too short to have taken him far."

Her mother smiled and threw up her hands before hurrying off. Abigail went outside. With the servants rushing around getting ready, more than one door had been left open, and a small dog could have easily slipped out without notice.

She walked along the gravel path, keeping a keen

eye out for her mother's pet. It was lovely to be outside, where it was quiet and cool, and where she didn't
have to listen to Penelope grumble. In a week's time
Penelope had found a long list of things to dislike:
the sounds of boatmen on the river, the lack of shops
nearby, the way the door of her bedroom squeaked.
But to Abigail, the hardest thing about life in Richmond was enduring her sister's disgruntlement; otherwise she thought Papa had done tremendously well
in his choice. As much as she liked the bustle and
activity of London, there was a peace out here that
couldn't be found in the city. The air was different as
well, warmer and softer somehow without the smells
of town, even before one encountered the path lined
with flowering shrubs and trees. It smelled utterly
divine on this walk, which was one of Abigail's new
favorite spots on earth. Without hesitation she turned
down it and took a deep breath in appreciation. Hart
House suited her remarkably well.

She reached the end of the sweet-scented path,
and stopped to look around. "Milo," she called again.
"Where are you, silly dog?" There was a rustle in the
shrubbery ahead. She walked forward, whistling a
little tune. "Come here, Milo. Your mistress is worried
about you."

Obediently, Milo trotted out of the bushes onto the
path, tail wagging and head held high. And, to Abigail's
horror, there was something in his mouth—something
squirming.

"Milo!" she gasped. "Put it down!"

The puppy saw her and gave a little bound, his eyes
shining joyfully. Oh no; he thought this was a game.

"Milo," she said sternly, "drop that rabbit!" For it
certainly looked like a young rabbit wriggling franti-

cally between his teeth. Her stomach lurched at the thought of having to carry the dog back into the house covered with the blood of a baby bunny.

He shook his head, almost as if in reply to her command, and the rabbit made another desperate squeal. Abigail put one hand over her mouth; she hadn't known rabbits could make a noise like that.

She crouched down, taking care to keep her skirt out of the dirt. "Milo," she said gently but firmly, "come here." She had no idea how she would get the rabbit away from him, but somehow it seemed an easier prospect if she had hold of the dog first. "Come, boy."

He backed away, stubby tail still wagging from side to side. Abigail pressed her lips together; she should have brought a treat of some sort to tempt him. "Come," she said again, scooting forward on her tiptoes. "Come here."

For answer he turned and loped away, still holding his prey in his teeth. Abigail scrambled to her feet and ran after him. "Milo, you wretched little pest, come here!" He only ran faster, every now and then giving his head a shake, before he veered to the left down a wilder path, little more than a dirt track through the trees.

She paused, clutching her skirt with one hand. Her mother had said not to go too far. Abigail had no hope of finding the little brown dog in the woods, with twilight rapidly encroaching. The wise thing would be to go back to the house and let her mother send James out into the thicket after the miserable little rabbit killer. "I'm not chasing you in there," she muttered after the dog, whom she could still hear rustling in the underbrush even though she couldn't see him any longer. "It wouldn't hurt you to spend a night in the woods." She didn't think about what harm might befall the small animals of the wood.

But as she turned to go back, there was a sharp yip—Milo—and then the deep, menacing bark of a much bigger dog. There was another yip, this time higher and sounding pained, before Milo began whimpering. Abigail whirled back around, her pique forgotten. Mama would be devastated if anything happened to the puppy.

"Milo!" she cried, plunging into the woods. "Where are you?" She warded off branches and vines as best she could, but she could feel her hair snagging and slipping from its pins. She pulled her skirt tight around her and went deeper into the woods. "Milo!" She could hear something—hopefully her mother's pet—struggling in the leaves and branches up ahead, still whimpering loudly. If he was caught in something, he'd be easier to catch. As to what dog was making that sonorous barking . . . she didn't want to think about that.

She almost fell in astonishment when a large black beast appeared in front of her. He lifted his square, jowly head and regarded her with calm eyes, then let out another deep, echoing bark. It sounded like the hound of hell was baying at her, but the animal himself looked peaceful.

"Don't mind him," said a voice. "He won't hurt you."

The sound of someone so near almost sent her leaping out of her skin. It took her a moment to locate the speaker. He wore a brown coat that blended with the trees, but took off his hat as he approached.

"He startled me," she managed to say.

The stranger's mouth quirked. "He does that sometimes. Sit," he said to his dog, who obediently sat. "Is that your dog in the bracken?"

"Yes. I mean, it's my mother's dog," she replied.

"Milo. He's only a puppy, but he ran off and I think he might have a rabbit in his mouth."

He looked toward the whimpering sounds. "A terrier?"

"Yes, a small golden-brown one."

He nodded. "I'll fetch him." He glanced at her dress. "You aren't dressed for walking in the woods."

She blushed, and realized she was still holding her gown in a death grip, pulling the fabric tightly around her hips and exposing her legs almost to the knee. "I didn't plan to walk in the woods. The cursed dog ran away, and I was chasing him." She released her skirts, fluffing them a bit.

His gaze flicked downward for a moment, following the descent of her skirt. "It looks like a very elegant party you're attending. I don't want to keep you from it." He hung his hat on a branch just over his head and headed into the thicket of bracken and fallen trees, whistling between his teeth as he went. Only when he had to step over a tree branch did she notice he used a cane, pressed tight to his left side.

"Thank you, sir," Abigail called after him self-consciously. It was very awkward to be left standing in the middle of the woods with that giant dog watching her, even though the dog hadn't moved since his master commanded him to sit. She also didn't know what to make of his comment. Obviously it wasn't his fault she was late for her parents' ball; it was Milo's, and her own, and that flighty maid Marie's fault, if one was honest about it. She wondered who he was. Her parents had invited every last person in Richmond, it seemed, and most of them had accepted. Clearly he had not, or else he wasn't from Richmond.

But he was retrieving Milo for her, which she deeply

appreciated. By straining her eyes, she could see him go down on his knees and disappear behind a shrub, only to emerge a few minutes later with Milo in his arm. Slowly he tramped back through the brush toward her, occasionally using his cane to swish some bracken out of his way.

"Thank you," she said again as he drew near. "I cannot tell you how little I wanted to go in there myself." She put her arms out for the puppy.

He held up the dog by the scruff of his neck and studied him. Milo wiggled and whined, but lapsed into silence at a curt "Shh!" from the man holding him. "He's filthy." Again his gaze skimmed over her. "He'll ruin your gown."

Abigail pursed her lips. Even she could see the mud matting the puppy's fur, which would indeed ruin her fine pale silk gown. "I can change it."

"I'll carry him home for you." He lowered the puppy and tucked the dog under his arm. "Hart House?"

She stared. "Yes, how did you know?"

Not a trace of smile touched his lips. "You can't have come far, and Hart House is the closest house from here. In addition, Hart House was recently taken by a man with two beautiful daughters. I presume you are one of them."

"I am Miss Abigail Weston," she said slowly, uncertainly. Was that a compliment? An opening for an introduction?

"I thought so." He reached up and fetched his hat from the branch where he'd hung it earlier. "Shall we?"

She wanted to ask who he was. She wanted to ask why he was out in the woods; he hadn't a gun that she could see, so he hadn't been shooting. And while she knew there was another estate that shared these woods, she was fairly sure this was still her father's property. "What made you think I was Miss Weston?"

"Rumor." He pointed the way out of the bracken with his cane. "Proceed, please."

"If you have a bit of cord, I could tie it around Milo's neck and take him home that way," she said in a last effort.

"I haven't." He didn't seem impatient, merely bored, as though she was preventing him from fulfilling some sort of obligation. Which, perhaps, he was; he certainly didn't look pleased about any part of it.

Abigail told herself to be grateful, and softened her tone. "Thank you. I'm sorry to put you to so much trouble."

He looked at her for a long moment. "No trouble at all, Miss Weston," he finally said, his voice a low rumble. "Shall we get out of the woods before it's too dark to see?"

Her gaze flew to the sky. "Oh! Yes." It was growing late, and she would have to change her shoes and perhaps even her dress before joining the ball. Papa would be irked, and even Mama would fuss at her to hurry. She turned and picked her way through the bracken, listening as he followed. He muttered something to his dog, who fell in step behind them, but otherwise said nothing.

For a few minutes they walked, single file, down the narrow dirt path. Abigail didn't know what to say. He walked with a quiet tread, and all she could hear was the big dog's breathing. Discreetly she brushed away some leaves caught in her hair and on her dress. She would have to steal up to her room and examine the damage in a mirror. It would have been so much worse if she'd had to crawl into that wild thicket herself, but there was no question her appearance had suffered some indignities.

As soon as the path widened, she fell back a step to walk at his side. It felt strange to walk in front of him like a princess with a retainer at her heels. He walked very easily despite the cane; if she hadn't seen it, she would have thought he had only a trace of a limp. But walking beside him she could see how he leaned, stiff-armed, on the cane.

"Did you see any sign of the rabbit when you found Milo?" she asked, trying to break the awkward silence.

"No. There was no blood on him, either, so I presume it got away."

"Thank goodness," she exclaimed. "I was *so* dreading telling my mother he'd killed a baby bunny."

He slanted her a look. "That's what terriers do. They chase vermin."

"This one isn't supposed to," she retorted. "He's a pampered little thing my father gave to my mother as an apology."

"She'd better train him and keep him indoors, then."

"Easier said than done," she said under her breath. "But you have my eternal gratitude for fetching him. What was he caught in?"

"A bramble bush." He held up the puppy again. Milo's little tongue flopped out and he panted happily as Abigail glared at him. "Cut his coat if you don't want him to get caught on every thorn he passes." He paused. "What was he in apology for?"

"Oh." She blushed and trained her eyes ahead. Mama would never forgive her for telling a complete stranger that Papa had bought Milo as an apology for the house. "Presumption."

"Ah." He tucked the puppy back under his arm. "I hope the apology was accepted."

"Obviously—accepted and taken into the bosom of her heart." Abigail rolled her eyes. "My mother will probably meet us at the door with half the constabulary behind her, ready to search the countryside for him."

"Won't she be receiving her guests by now?"

"Ah—yes, perhaps," she murmured. So he knew about the ball and when it was to start. Who was he? "I beg your pardon, sir, but I don't know your name."

For the first time a faint smile curved his lips. "Haven't you guessed by now?"

She racked her brain. What was the name of the estate that bordered theirs? Montgomery . . . Merrymont . . . Montrose Hill, she remembered in a burst of relief. "You're the owner of Montrose Hill."

There was a slight hesitation before he responded. "Indeed."

Abigail waited, but he didn't offer his name. He didn't say anything else, just strode along at the same steady pace. It was a bit rude, to be honest. "I'm very sorry you couldn't attend my mother's ball." That was also a bit rude, but she knew Mama had sent an invitation to Montrose Hill. She just couldn't remember the name of the owner.

"Didn't it work out better for you that I didn't?" he replied, seeming unperturbed. "If I'd been dressing for a ball, I would not have been in the woods to rescue your dog."

"But we might have met under more cordial circumstances."

Again he glanced at her with his unfathomable dark eyes. Abigail boldly gazed back. He was a striking figure, in a brooding sort of way. His dark, wavy hair curled above his collar, and his shoulders were broad beneath his coat. He held Milo easily in one big hand, although he wasn't a large man, but rather lean and rangy. But it was his face that held her attention.

His nose was a sharp slash, slightly crooked. His eyes were heavy-lidded, a bit sleepy looking despite the keen spark in his gaze. But no laugh lines bracketed his mouth, even though his lips looked firm and sensual. A somber man, she thought, who kept secrets.

"What would it have changed, if we met under more cordial circumstances?" he asked at last, very softly. "I don't attend balls."

"Not ever?" she blurted out in surprise.

"No." He looked away. "You'll sort out why soon enough."

"That's very mysterious," she muttered.

"My apologies. It wasn't meant to be." They had finally come in sight of the house. "Run in and fetch a maid."

She frowned at being so carelessly ordered about. "Please come in, sir. My mother will wish to thank you for saving her darling."

He sighed. "Your thanks are enough." He stopped and shifted Milo, who had begun wriggling as they drew close to home. "Shh," he said again to the puppy, who quieted a little. "He'll run off if I let him go."

"Give him to me, then." Again she put out her arms for the dog.

This time there was nothing glancing about his gaze. It ranged over her hair, pinned up with sprigs of jasmine, over her face, then slowly down her figure right to the tips of her green satin slippers. Abigail was immobilized by the intensity of it, even though he did nothing but look.

"He'll ruin your gown," he said. "I didn't carry him all the way here only to dirty you up at the end. You look too lovely to spoil."

She was saved from a reply by the appearance of her

brother, striding around the house. At the sight of them he paused for half a step, then came to join them. "Abigail! There you are. Mother was growing worried."

"Milo ran into the woods and this gentleman was kind enough to fetch him for me." She turned a challenging look on the stranger. Surely he would have to introduce himself now.

"Very kind of you, sir." James bowed. "James Weston, at your service."

The stranger's eyes slid toward her again before he returned James's bow. "Sebastian Vane of Montrose Hill."

"Thank you for bringing my sister home." James gave the puppy a black look. "I wish I could say the same for the rat."

"He's not a rat," protested Abigail, even though she'd had several unkind thoughts about Milo herself. "Mama loves him, as you know well."

"That has nothing to do with it. He's a rat catcher, and if he weren't a 'darling ball of fluff,' he'd be in the stables doing just that," James retorted, mimicking Penelope's description of the dog.

"He would probably prefer that as well." Mr. Vane held out the squirming puppy and let James take him. "Good evening, sir."

"Won't you come in? My mother will want to express her thanks." James reluctantly took Milo, holding the muddy pup away from his coat. Milo wagged his tail, his little pink tongue hanging happily out of his mouth.

"Your sister has already extended a kind invitation to do so, but I must decline." He tipped his broad-brimmed hat. "Good evening, Miss Weston. Mr. Weston." This time he barely looked at her as he turned on his heel and limped away, the big black dog still silently trotting in his wake.

"Well," said James as he disappeared back down the path. "A conquest already."

Abigail scowled at him. "You mean of Milo's? I assure you, the man could hardly stand to look at me. He wouldn't even tell me his name."

Her brother grinned. "I'm only teasing, Abby. Sebastian Vane! I gather he's a recluse. Mother was surprised when he declined the invitation to the ball, but Father assured her Vane never goes out."

"Why not?" Abigail turned to look after him. She could believe he was a recluse; he seemed unaccustomed to talking at all. But there had been something in his eyes, that last time he looked at her, something almost like longing. As if he'd wanted to accept her invitation, but couldn't. And he'd called her lovely.

James shrugged. "I think he's fallen on hard times. The limp probably doesn't help. If a man can't dance and can't afford to make a good appearance . . ."

"Oh." Abigail continued to stare toward the woods, even though Mr. Vane had long since vanished. "That needn't make one a recluse."

"Men have pride, Abby," he said. "And I know Mother will think it very bad of you to linger out here while she's greeting everyone in Richmond. Chop, chop, dear sister."

"For that, you can take care of Milo." She smiled sweetly at his expression. "Do scrub all that mud out of his ears, would you?"

She left him frowning at the little dog and went into the house, where she whisked up the back stairs to her room. A quick glance in the mirror showed she had leaves in her hair and some loose pins, but only a few

streaks of dirt on her hem. A quick brushing removed
most of it, and she sat down at her dressing table to fix
her hair.

A recluse. Why? He might have fallen on hard times,
but his house was gracious and beautiful, a handsome
brick mansion. One could easily see it, for it sat on the
ridge of the hill that rose beyond Hart House. And he
was handsome enough—even without counting his
reserve—that most girls would overlook a limp, if
they noticed it at all. When he used the cane it was
almost imperceptible. Even more, Abigail didn't sense
he wanted to be a recluse. He could have held back
when she was chasing Milo and avoided her entirely;
she hadn't noticed him at all until he spoke to her. He
hadn't needed to walk her back to the house. He hadn't
needed to give her that long, appraising look at the end,
as though he was drinking in every facet of her appearance . . .

Well. If balls were good for anything, they were
good for gossip. Surely a man as mysterious as Sebastian Vane would have inspired some whispers. She
pinned one last sprig of loose jasmine into her hair and
went down the stairs, determined to find out.

Chapter 3

Sebastian knew he was in trouble the minute the girl came crashing through the trees.

It wasn't just that she interrupted his solitary walk, where he tried yet again to force his injured leg to bear more of his weight. The doctors had told him it would always be weaker than the other, but he refused to accept that, even after seven years. Every evening he took a long walk over his property, gritting his teeth against the pain as he forced himself to walk evenly, if slowly, trying to will away the damage caused by French bullets.

It also wasn't because he'd recognized at once that he would have to help her. She was dressed for a ballroom, not a thicket choked with bracken and thorn bushes. Her pale green dress shimmered in the fading sunlight, and the ribbons at her neckline fluttered as she hurried around trees and stumbled over rocks. She was as lovely and bright as a fairy, flitting through the shady forest, and for a moment he'd been mesmerized.

But he truly knew he was doomed when she looked up at him and he saw her face. Her skin was as fine and lustrous as a pearl against the auburn curls clustered atop her head. Her pink lips had parted in surprise when she saw him, but it was her eyes that slew him: fine gray eyes, thickly lashed and wide with amazement and curiosity and no trace of alarm or censure. Sebastian had said a quiet curse then. Those eyes could enslave a man. His father had told him as much once, but then he'd gone mad, so Sebastian had suspected it was only the lunacy speaking.

Now he knew it wasn't.

He'd tried to avoid saying much of anything as he pulled her dog from the mud beneath a thorn bush, where the puppy's long fur had got snagged. It had been difficult not to look at her as they walked back to Hart House, and she tried to entice him into conversation. Sebastian had learned that conversations usually led to more gossip about him, always unflattering, and he had no idea if Miss Weston would be able to hold her tongue.

But he realized at the end that she really had no idea who he was, or what his terrible history was, and for a brief, burning moment he'd been tempted . . . before, fortunately, her brother arrived and saved him from making a fool of himself.

Still, he couldn't think of anything but her on the long, dark walk home. Usually he liked the woods. They were quiet and wild, a neglected gully of land straddling his remaining property and the grounds of Hart House. The last owner of Hart House had been an older widowed lady who rarely left the manicured lawns overlooking the river. Lady Burton had implicitly ceded these woods to him; on the rare occasions they met, she gave him a regal nod, acknowledging him without inviting any closer acquaintance. He would

have to remember that Hart House belonged to someone else now, and he must keep away. Most likely Miss
Weston's foray into the woods had been a chance thing,
inspired only by the runaway terrier, but he couldn't
risk meeting her again.

Boris snuffled at his heels, prodding him out of his
thoughts. The boar hound nudged his good knee, as if
to propel him forward.

"I know," he told the dog, lifting the cane off the
ground. He carried it in case he needed it, if his shattered
knee should ever give way. A dull ache began to burn in
his leg as he walked on without leaning on the cane, but
he let his mind drift back to the wry way Miss Weston
pursed her lips, and the pain seemed a little less present.

When he reached the top of the hill, he turned back.
From here he could see part of Hart House, ablaze with
lights. It seemed he had been one of the few to send
his regrets in response to the invitation. What was she
doing now, he wondered; dancing with all the eligible
young bucks in the neighborhood? Flirting with the
few noblemen who might have come? There were sure
to be some. And it was hard to imagine they wouldn't
all be enchanted by an auburn-haired fairy with a lu-
minous smile.

Sebastian heard the gossip, even if he didn't like to
be the gossip. Hart House had been bought by a nouveau riche man named Weston. There was some uncertainty about how he'd made his fortune—speculation,
the Exchange, or perhaps one enormous wager with the
Earl of Hastings—but there was no doubt that it was a
large one. He had two daughters and a son, all of whom
had very comfortable expectations. This was enough
to have his daughters deemed beauties, sight unseen.
Although, at least in one case, the gossips had been

absolutely right. Miss Abigail Weston was the loveliest creature he'd ever seen.

She was also young, innocent, and wealthy. Beauty and innocence had no place in his life, and while the wealth would be a welcome change, he knew that was as likely as the King coming to call on him. He would just have to avert his eyes when she passed and remind himself of the myriad reasons why she wasn't for him.

He let himself into the house, feeling around for the flint and candle on the shelf behind the door. When he'd struck a light, he went through the dark corridor into the drawing room. He shed his coat and hat before finally sinking into the old leather chair with a barely restrained groan of relief. The walk home from Hart House had been longer than his usual ramble, and his leg throbbed.

"There you are!" Mrs. Jones, his housekeeper, swept into the room. "I was beginning to worry about you, young man!"

He grinned without opening his eyes. "No, you weren't. Boris would have dragged me home."

"As if that's supposed to be some comfort. Take those boots off, and let me bring your supper." She snapped her fingers at Boris, who was sitting alertly near the door. "Food in the kitchen for you, Boris." At the word "food" the big dog leapt up as nimbly as a puppy and galloped from the room, his paws echoing on the wooden floors.

"I expect you'll need a dose of laudanum tonight," Mrs. Jones said to him in reproof.

Sebastian pictured Abigail Weston again, holding her skirts close around her hips and baring her slender legs from the knee down. "Not really, no."

"There's no need to endure a night of agony," she

told him as she collected his hat and coat. "Don't be a fool. I'll have Mr. Jones draw you a nice hot bath, and bring your dinner upstairs." She went into the hall, calling to her husband.

It was his usual routine. He would walk until he exhausted himself, and Mrs. Jones would fuss over him like a mother over a toddler. Sometimes he merely endured it; sometimes he was glad of it. Every now and then he just wanted everyone to go away and leave him in peace. Every now and then he wanted to live someone else's life and see if there really was happiness to be found in the world. If he were a different man, he could be at Hart House right now. He could see her smile, see the candlelight shine on her hair, even touch her hand and hold her in his arms for a dance. For a moment his thoughts drifted . . .

But then he gave himself a shake. He was going as mad as his father, imagining that. He was who he was, Mad Michael Vane's son, the one with the ruined leg and the bankrupt estate. The one who had nothing to offer any woman, as he'd learned only too well. The one who couldn't dance if he wanted to. He didn't even own decent evening clothes anymore. Miss Weston would be glad of her escape once she heard a bit of the gossip in town.

He pushed himself out of the chair with a grimace. He hobbled up the stairs toward his room, where Mrs. Jones was dragging the old bathing tub toward the fire while her husband heated water in the kitchen below. If he didn't have a soak in the hot bath, he'd be all but crippled on the morrow. In an hour she'd bring up some supper, cold chicken and boiled potatoes with a mug of ale. There was no money for wine anymore. He would soak in the hot water and eat his supper, alone save for

Boris snoring on the hearth, and then he'd eventually go to bed.

Alone, as always. And as he most likely always would be.

"**W**here were you?" demanded Penelope as soon as Abigail reached the drawing room.

"Chasing after Milo. That dog should be kept in a cage."

"Oh no! Not sweet Milo!" her sister protested. "He's so adorably furry."

"That fur is what got him caught in a bramble bush." Abigail wound her way through to the dining room. All the doors had been thrown open to create one giant circuit of the floor. She scanned the room for her mother, intending to reassure her Milo was safely home, being scrubbed clean in the stables by James. Mr. Vane might have refused their invitation, but not many others had; the rooms were filled with guests.

"How did you get him out of the bramble bush?" Penelope refused to go away.

Abigail wondered if she'd seen something from the window. "Our neighbor was walking in the woods, and he kindly fetched Milo out of the brambles for me. We gave the naughty dog to James to clean up, for he was covered in mud."

"Which neighbor?"

Abigail narrowed her eyes. "Mr. Vane, of Montrose Hill."

Her sister gasped in delight. "Mr. Vane! The most deliciously elusive of neighbors. What is he like?"

Of course Penelope would know about him when

Abigail hadn't even been able to remember his name. "Reserved. He refused to come in and accept Mama's thanks for saving Milo."

Penelope snorted. "That shows good sense, if you ask me. I would certainly avoid Mama if I could . . . But what is Mr. Vane really like? Why won't he come to the ball? Is he as black as a devil? Is he deformed? Is he frightening and dangerous?"

"Oh really, Penelope." She sighed. "He was very kind to forge into the woods and pull that silly dog out of the brambles. It would have ruined my gown, but he not only fetched Milo, he insisted on walking me home so I wouldn't have to carry the muddy little beast."

"So he's actually kind and amiable?" Penelope frowned. "Being moody and dangerous is so much more interesting . . ."

"What else did you hear about him?" There was no reason to hide her curiosity. Penelope would be glad to tell all she knew, and Abigail couldn't deny that she was interested.

"Not much. He's one of those reclusive sorts who rarely goes out. I can't remember more, we must ask Lady Samantha." She slipped her arm through Abigail's and began tugging her toward the front of the room. "You'll adore her. Papa was beside himself when she and her sister arrived; daughters of the Earl of Stratford, you know."

"But I wanted to tell Mama that Milo is safely home," she objected as her sister towed her along.

"I'm sure she already presumes as much," muttered Penelope. "*You* went after him, after all, and *you're* the good daughter who always makes her parents proud."

"I think you're taking this too much to heart."

"As would you, if you'd been locked away from ev-

erything interesting in life." Penelope plastered on a
wide smile as they approached a pair of very elegant
ladies, one about Abigail's own age and the other
some years older. "Lady Turley, Lady Samantha, may
I present to you my sister, Miss Abigail Weston? Abigail, here are Viscountess Turley and Lady Samantha
Lennox. Their father is the Earl of Stratford, who owns
the magnificent house across the river."

"How lovely to make your acquaintance." Abigail
curtsied, as did the other ladies.

"Welcome to Richmond." Lady Turley smiled. Tall
and slender, she looked every bit as aristocratic as one
might expect a viscountess to be. "Our parents send
their regrets, and hope to make your parents' acquaintance before long."

This was a warmer reception than Abigail had expected; in her London experience, earls and other noblemen weren't entirely eager to meet them. But it was
very welcome all the same, so she smiled. "That's very
kind of you. We're delighted you were able to attend."

Lady Samantha laughed lightly. She was a lovely
young woman, with dark blond hair and soft green
eyes. "Oh no, we must thank you! Richmond is a quiet
little town. New society is always welcome."

Abigail ignored her sister's dark look at the mention
of how quiet Richmond was. "I've always liked a little
quiet. London is so hot and dirty in the summer. We're
very pleased with Hart House, aren't we, Penelope?"

Penelope gave a brittle smile. "Of course! But I do
hope you can indulge my shameful curiosity. One of
our neighbors sent his regrets, and I confess, I'm desperate to know why. Mr. Vane of Montrose Hill. Are
you acquainted with him?"

Lady Turley hesitated, giving her sister an odd

glance before replying. "Not really. I'm sure you'll encounter him eventually, Miss Weston."

"Yes, this property borders his, doesn't it?" Penelope went on, digging without a flicker of remorse. If Abigail hadn't been burning with curiosity, she would have changed the subject, but as it was, she only tried to look polite. "I think they even share a patch of the woods. In fact, my sister met him out walking this evening."

"We met by chance," said Abigail. "He saved my mother's lapdog from a fierce bramble bush."

Astonishment flickered in Lady Samantha's face. Lady Turley stiffened, and glanced at her sister again, this time almost worriedly. "How gallant," she said after a moment's pause.

"He's a rather private man," murmured Lady Samantha. "That is . . . very gallant."

There was an awkward moment of silence. Perhaps it hadn't been a good idea to ask them. Even Penelope could tell she'd brought up something uncomfortable and didn't know what to say.

Lady Turley broke the silence. "Have you discovered the Fragrant Walk? Hart House is famous for it."

"Yes, I did discover the walk," said Abigail gratefully. "I didn't know that path had a name, but the Fragrant Walk is a perfect description."

"I hear it led to a grotto originally, but Lady Burton had that filled in many years ago."

"Indeed!" cried Lady Samantha in evident relief. "It used to be our brother Benedict's fondest wish, when he was a boy, to discover the remains of the grotto. He even begged permission of Lady Burton, Hart House's previous owner, to explore the woods in search of it."

They chatted for a few more minutes of local curiosities before Mama joined them, effectively ending any chance of gossip about Mr. Vane. Eventually they had to excuse themselves and meet other guests, but Abigail held some hope Lady Samantha in particular might become a friend. She didn't seem to have excessive pride about her, and aside from her obvious shock at Mr. Vane's name, she seemed warm and amiable.

The rest of the ball passed agreeably enough. Papa seemed as pleased as could be when the evening ended.

"I knew Richmond would be good for us," he said with relish. "Clara, my love, I'm sure there's never been a finer ball given in this town."

"I'm delighted you're pleased, my dear." She let him kiss her cheek. "But now I'm going to bed, and don't look for me before noon tomorrow. My feet!"

"I shall rub every toe with almond oil," he promised. "Good night, my beautiful girls." He stopped to give Abigail and Penelope each a smacking kiss on the forehead. "Wasn't your papa right about having a ball?"

"As ever," Abigail told him. Penelope rolled her eyes, but Abigail could tell she was pleased as well. They followed their parents up the stairs, but then Penelope trailed along right into her room.

"How do you feel now about Richmond?" Abigail sat down to remove her jewelry. "Still certain we're condemned to boredom?"

"I wonder what made Lady Samantha so tense when we asked about Mr. Vane," mused Penelope.

Abigail's fingers slowed on the clasp of her necklace. "I've no idea."

"I bet he's got some deliciously wicked secret." Penelope leaned against the bedpost, a gleam of trouble in her eye. "Why does he keep to himself, I wonder?"

"Go to bed, Penelope." Abigail was relieved when her maid, Betsy, slipped into the room. "I've no idea what to make of Mr. Vane."

But for once, she was even more interested in the answer than her sister was.

Chapter 4

"I think this is our most likely hope."

Abigail eyed the bookshop. It was large and clean, with windows that sparkled in the morning light. It looked welcoming and respectable and utterly unlike the shop in London that sold *50 Ways to Sin*. Now that they had held their ball, Mama felt they had been introduced to, and become part of, Richmond society. When Penelope asked if they might walk into town to visit the shops, Mama agreed, provided James went with them. Their brother had departed almost at once on his own errands, leaving them outside a milliner's shop. Penelope, of course, had other plans, and towed Abigail through the streets to this bookshop. "Are you certain?"

"Of course not," whispered Penelope. "That's why you have to go in and ask."

"This looks like a shop Mama might visit," replied Abigail, stubbornly resisting her sister's attempts to nudge her forward. "You're going to get us both in horrid trouble, Pen."

"I gave my word I would take the entire blame if this goes wrong. Mama would murder me, but she'd probably forgive you. And you gave me your word you would try. Please, Abby." There was a note of desperation in Penelope's voice. "I am wasting away from boredom . . ."

"We've only been in Richmond eleven days," muttered Abigail, but she relented at her sister's expression. Unlike her, Penelope wasn't happy with a good book and a cozy spot to read. Penelope craved adventure and gossip and excitement, and since getting caught reading the notorious pamphlet over a month ago, she hadn't had much of any of those things. Their mother had clamped down on Penelope's freedom like a vise. She was allowed to go to dances and parties again, but she was no longer permitted to wander freely and talk with friends; she was required to stay near their mother, and dance with the gentlemen chosen for her. She was only allowed to walk into town because her siblings had come with her.

But Abigail also knew—just as well as her sister knew—that if they were discovered on this errand, there would be hell to pay. When Penelope had been caught before, she had sworn on her very life that Abigail had nothing to do with it and hadn't even known about the pamphlet. That was a bold-faced lie, of course, but it had left Abigail free . . . free to shop where she liked. But if Mama learned she had been trying to purchase the pamphlet, she would know that Penelope had lied to her, and even worse, that Abigail had helped deceive her. Both their lives would become misery.

"Very well," she said at last. "You'd better stay far away from me. Jamie will be back for us soon, so we haven't got much time."

Wild joy and eagerness lit her sister's face. "Thank you, Abby! Thank you! I shall be utterly demure and as silent as a mouse. Just ask politely for it, and try to look mature and sophisticated when you do."

They went into the bookshop, where a little bell tinkled over the door. The shop was beautifully arranged, with bookcases lining the walls and a bench in the middle. It was calm and peaceful, just as a bookshop should be. It was also thankfully almost empty of witnesses to the impending crime. Penelope strolled to a bookcase and pretended great interest in the books there, although Abigail knew her sister's attention was focused on her.

Trying to look, as her sister had suggested, mature and sophisticated despite the thumping of her heart, she approached the counter, where a middle-aged proprietress was wrapping up a book for another lady. When that customer had left with her package, Abigail stepped up to the counter.

"May I help you, ma'am?" the shopkeeper asked pleasantly.

Abigail took out a piece of paper where she'd written two titles, one for herself and one her brother wanted. She had permission to buy those. She said a small prayer no one ever learned she'd written a third title on the list after her mother approved it. "I hope so. Do you happen to have these?"

The shopkeeper read the list, shooting her a quick, measuring look at the end. "I believe so," she said in neutral tone. "I must check in the back, especially for the last."

"Thank you." Abigail inclined her head regally and the woman disappeared into the back room of the shop. So far, so good. Over her left shoulder, she caught her sister's eyes. Penelope was holding what looked like a prayer book in front of her, but her gaze was fixed on Abigail. At Abigail's tiny nod, her eyes brightened hopefully before dropping back to the prayer book. She turned a page with exaggerated care, although Abigail noticed her eyes weren't moving across the pages.

The bell on the door tinkled again behind her. It sounded loud in the hushed bookshop. Abigail darted a wary glance around her bonnet brim, praying her brother hadn't come to fetch them early, but gasped when she saw who it was. "Mr. Vane!"

He stood half turned in the doorway, as if he'd been about to go back out. At her exclamation he seemed to flinch, but he faced her readily enough. "Miss Weston." He bowed.

Abigail curtsied. She could feel her sister's stare boring into her back, but she ignored it. "How lovely to see you again."

In daylight he was just as handsome as she'd thought before. His sleepy-lidded eyes were brown, she saw, and if he were to smile, the effect would probably be devastating. She remembered what James had said about reduced circumstances and studied him closer, but country clothing was more forgiving; she couldn't see any difference between his coat and her brother's. Why *would* such a man become a recluse?

Slowly he came toward the counter. "The pleasure is all mine."

"It certainly is not! I cannot thank you enough for helping with Milo the other night. When I returned to the house and saw how wild I looked, merely from running after him, I realized how great a service you did me." She smiled ruefully. "Going into that thicket would have left me unfit to be seen."

His gaze traveled over her. "I am delighted to see that did not occur."

A small smile touched her lips at the compliment.

"My mother begs you to call on her someday, so she can thank you herself."

"It was a trifle," he said in his quiet way.

Abigail kept smiling, even though she could see her sister from the corner of one eye, almost falling over in her attempt to get a better look at him. Penelope was keeping her word to be as quiet as a mouse, but she had made no promises to hide her rabid curiosity about elusive and mysterious gentlemen. Abigail casually turned, further blocking her sister's view. "It struck me that I don't know where my father's property ends. I would hate to trespass on your land. Can you tell me precisely where the dividing line is, so I don't intrude on you again?"

Mr. Vane's eyes flickered to the side; he had seen Penelope. Abigail said a fierce prayer that her sister, for once in her life, held her tongue and minded her own affairs. "I'm no longer entirely certain myself, Miss Weston. But you have my permission to walk in the woods at will, even if you stray onto Montrose land."

"Thank you, that's very kind." She was running out of things to say. Abigail couldn't even explain to herself why she wanted to keep talking to him, but she did. There was something appealing about him, in spite of the aloofness of his demeanor. She liked the sound of his voice, and she really longed to see him smile.

"Not kind at all," he replied. "Only fairness. When I was young, I was permitted to explore the grounds of Hart House freely and wantonly, and I did so at every opportunity. The previous owner, Lady Burton, was very gracious."

"Yes, I gather Hart House has some interesting features. I heard there was a grotto or some such thing on the grounds, but no one seems to know where it is—or was."

For the first time a spark brightened his eye. "I know about the grotto." His mouth softened—not quite into a smile, but a less grim line than usual. Abigail felt inordinately heartened by it, and her heart positively leapt when he leaned closer. "I know where it is, too."

"You do?" she gasped. "It still exists? I thought it had been filled in."

"Only by the encroaching woods. One has to forge through the brambles to get there." This time his mouth most definitely did curve, and something like triumph brought a wholly different cast to his face. He looked younger, almost rakish. "When I found it several years ago, I felt like the most intrepid explorer, as if I'd located the source of the Nile for the first time."

Abigail was having a hard time keeping her mind on the topic. Mr. Vane was the most attractive man she'd ever seen. Good heavens; she'd read about women being dazzled by a man, falling in love almost on the spot. She'd never understood how that could happen until today. Were the women of Richmond blind? Why wasn't he besieged by unmarried ladies? "You must have been very intrepid, indeed," she said, scrambling for her wits. "Lady Samantha Lennox told us her brother searched and searched for the grotto but never found it."

Like a candle being snuffed, the light went out of his face. His mouth flattened into the same flat line, and he seemed to withdraw without moving a muscle. "No."

"Will this be all, miss?" The shopkeeper's voice made Abigail jump. She turned, still reeling from his transformation—for both good and bad—and saw, with a shock of alarm, that the shopkeeper had found her books—all of them. And right on top, unwrapped and exposed for all the world to see, lay *50 Ways to Sin*.

For one horrified moment Abigail stared at it blankly. Oh heavens. She hadn't expected this sort of shop to have it. She hadn't expected the woman to hand it over so carelessly and brazenly; the London bookstore wrapped it in paper. She certainly hadn't expected to be engaged in any sort of tête-à-tête with Mr. Vane when the woman brought it out. And yet part of her was elated as well to have a new copy at last. What would Lady Constance get up to in this one?

"Yes," she burst out, shaking off her paralysis with a start. "Thank you." She plopped her reticule on top of the pamphlet to hide the title, making a show of searching inside for money and tilting her bonnet so the brim hid her blushing face.

"Can I help you, sir?" asked the shopkeeper as Abigail fumbled with her coins. There was a decided chill to the woman's voice as she turned to Mr. Vane.

"I'm looking for *The Nautical Almanac*," he replied. "The latest edition."

She sniffed. "I'll have to see."

"Thank you, Mrs. Driscoll."

Abigail peeked at him around the edge of her bonnet. Mrs. Driscoll hardly addressed him as a respectable man of property, but he didn't seem perturbed by it. She handed her money to the shopkeeper and unthinkingly picked up her reticule, only to remember a moment later and snatch up the books.

"Good day, Mr. Vane," she said, turning to him. "I hope we see each other again."

For a fraction of a second his eyes dipped to the books she held. "Perhaps we will, Miss Weston."

Oh dear Lord. He'd seen it. Abigail bobbed an awkward curtsy, her face burning. Perhaps he wouldn't know what it was. Perhaps he would think it wasn't hers. But she had never been as good a liar as Penelope, and her reaction had probably been as guilty as it could be. Head down, she hurried out of the shop, leaving him standing at the counter waiting for his book.

"What was that about?" hissed Penelope, galloping up beside her. Abigail had entirely forgotten her sister.

"I hate you, Pen," she said, keeping her eyes fixed forward. "I really, really do."

"That much?" Penelope grinned wickedly. She looked over her shoulder. "So that's the mysterious Mr. Vane! I think he fancies you, Abby."

"Be quiet," she said through clenched teeth.

"I notice you were very animated when talking to him. Do you fancy him as well?" She looked back again. "And do you know, he's watching you walk away through the window."

"Turn around," she ordered. "He might be staring because he saw *it*."

"No!" Her sister's eyes grew round in alarm. "Why did you let him see it?"

"I didn't let him, the shopkeeper just slapped it down right in front of him before I could stop her!" Abigail pulled out the troublesome pamphlet and thrust it at her sister. "We have to find a better way to get it. Presuming Mama doesn't hear of this and confine us both to our rooms, that is."

Penelope stuffed the pamphlet into her reticule. "You're right. I agree. If I'd known an eager suitor would follow you into the shop, I never would have asked you to do it today."

She shot a murderous glare at her sister and stalked away without another word. Mr. Vane was the least eager suitor she could imagine. The trouble was . . . she wished he would be. Or at least that he would show some sign that he was interested, because she found him fascinating.

On the other hand, for her own sake, she should probably hope she never saw him again. He'd seen *50 Ways to Sin*. He knew she'd bought it. All he had to do was ask Mrs. Driscoll what it was, and she'd be sunk. In fact, she probably already was. All it would take was one word about the Weston girls purchasing that wicked story, and her mother would hear it eventually. Nothing Penelope could say would save her from the consequences of that.

For now, she only hoped he wouldn't follow her.

"**W**ill that be all, Mr. Vane?" Mrs. Driscoll pushed his book across the counter as if she couldn't even bear to hand it to him.

"Yes, ma'am." Sebastian counted out the price from his purse. He no longer presumed anyone would extend him credit. It made things easier if he just carried money; he couldn't outspend his limited income if he had to pay coin for everything, and no one could complain of his custom when they were paid on the spot. Mrs. Driscoll had once been kind and cordial to him, but then his father had assaulted her in the midst of one of his fits, and ever since, Sebastian had been tarred by association. The bookshop owner always watched him warily, as if she expected him to suddenly fly at her in a rage, too.

Mr. Weston must not have established an account here yet, if his daughter also had to pay in coin. Sebastian's fingers slowed as he laid his money on the counter. He should have known he'd run into her today, the first day in weeks he'd come into town. And in spite of himself, something inside him had surged with pleasure when she turned around and said his name with every sign of delight.

He would have been content just to exchange greetings and have a chance to look at her for a few minutes. Her hair looked more reddish in the warm light of the shop, or perhaps it was the reflection of her cherry-red pelisse. Her eyes were the same clear gray, though, and he was almost mesmerized by the invitation in them. She wanted to talk to him. She smiled when he complimented her. Her eyes lit up when he said he knew where the old grotto was. Sebastian almost forgot who he was for a few minutes, dazzled by her smile and her eyes and the way her gloved hands pressed together at her bosom . . .

Then she mentioned Samantha and Benedict, and he remembered everything. He remembered everything he had lost, and every reason that he would never have more of Abigail Weston than a chance meeting in town or in the woods. He knew he ought to regret inviting her to walk anywhere she wanted, but some part of him was too selfish to do that. Just a glimpse, now and then, would do no harm. Sooner or later someone would warn her away from him, and then it wouldn't matter what he did.

Still, for some reason he lingered at the counter. He had no right to her attention. The less he knew about her, the better. But knowing wasn't the same as acting. And she'd bought something very intriguing . . .

"Have you changed your mind?" asked Mrs. Driscoll curtly. She swept his coins up as though she feared he would take them back.

"Yes." He gave her a steady look as he pulled out another coin, even though he could ill afford to spend it. "I would like a copy of that pamphlet."

Her eyes narrowed warily. "What pamphlet?"

"The one you just sold. *Fifty Ways to Sin.*"

Chapter 5

Abigail's curiosity about Mr. Vane, which had been considerable to begin with, waxed feverish after the encounter in the bookshop. That brief glimpse of animation tormented her. It made her think he wasn't a recluse by nature, but by choice, either his own or one forced upon him. Mrs. Driscoll had been almost rude to him, even though he spoke to her quite civilly. What had happened to make a respectable proprietress all but shun a local landowner? Where was that lost grotto, the one whose discovery had made him feel intrepid? And why had mention of Lady Samantha and her brother doused the light in his eyes? She was so consumed by that question she completely forgot to ask Penelope for the troublesome copy of *50 Ways to Sin*.

She paid close attention to the local gossip relayed by the ladies who came to call on Mama. She had always listened to gossip, and enjoyed some of it exceedingly, but now she gathered every word like a possible clue to the mysterious neighbor.

Sadly, no one else seemed as interested in him as she was. Even Penelope moved on to more fertile topics, like which eligible young men might retire to Richmond for the summer, a topic that was obviously

near and dear to their mother's heart as well. Eligible
young men were discussed at every opportunity, with
every lady who came to call on Mrs. Weston. At first
Abigail thought this would be sufficient; sooner or later
his name was bound to come up. It never did. No one
seemed to consider Mr. Vane eligible, which only threw
Abigail into deeper puzzlement. Why wouldn't he be?
Contrary to his vague warnings about his unsuitability,
he was a handsome gentleman of property—but no one
mentioned him.

But finally, one day while she was helping her
mother sort embroidery silks, the butler came into the
room and announced, to her astonishment, "Mr. Sebastian Vane to see you, madam."

"Ah!" Mama smiled in delight, running one hand
over Milo's fur. "At last. Do show him in, Thomson."

Abigail sat mute with shock and unexpected alarm.
He was here himself! She hadn't expected that, after
the way he refused to call. It might be a heaven-sent
opportunity to sort him out. But he also knew her little
secret, about *50 Ways to Sin*, and there was no way for
her to intercept him before he met Mama. He might
not know it was a secret. He might disapprove and be
bent on telling Mama. He might have decided she had
questionable judgment or morals. She wished there was
any way at all she could rush into the hall and have a
quick word with him, but then she realized she didn't
know what to say anyway. *Please don't tell my mother
I bought a naughty story?* Somehow that didn't seem
like a good idea.

Slowly she got to her feet as the door opened once
more. She heard a measured step, with just a hint of
tap indicating a cane, and then he stepped through the
door. His hair was brushed back, and he wore a deep

blue coat, and Abigail felt the strangest urge to run to him and stand at his side.

"Mr. Vane!" Mama went to him, her hand out-stretched. "I am so pleased to make your acquaintance at last. Thank you for coming."

"I ought to have done so sooner, Mrs. Weston, to welcome you to Richmond." He bowed over her hand.

She smiled. "Nonsense! I put little stock in trivial formalities. Come, Abigail, greet our neighbor, since you've already made his acquaintance." Mama beckoned her toward them.

"Good day, Mr. Vane." She curtsied. He bowed, his deep brown eyes never veering from her face. "How kind of you to call."

Abigail wished she could read his thoughts; his expression gave away nothing even though he studied her so intently, it seemed he must want to say something. "Good day, Miss Weston," he said after a small pause. "I trust you are well?"

Now that you've come. She blushed at the unbidden thought. "Very well, sir, thank you."

"I am glad to hear it." He hesitated again, that intense gaze seeming to caress every inch of her face. "I'm very pleased to be so welcome."

"Of course!" Mama resumed her seat on the sofa and waved one hand at the opposite chair. "Please sit down, Mr. Vane. May I offer you some tea?"

"Thank you." He lowered himself with only the slightest tensing of his jaw. Abigail realized he had propped the cane against the back of the chair and walked around it unaided. She sat on the other end of the sofa, offering Milo a piece of rope James had knotted into a toy for him. The puppy took it between his paws and settled down on the cushion, happily chewing away.

"You own Montrose Hill, do you not?" Mama prepared a cup of tea and handed it to him. "We have a fine view of the house from the lawn, and I have often admired it."

"Yes." He glanced around the room. "I might say the same about Hart House. It looked so lonely after Lady Burton's death. I'm glad to see it bright with life again."

Mama smiled. "Thank you, sir. My husband assured me it would be an ideal refuge from London, and I must confess he was entirely correct."

Mr. Vane nodded. He still hadn't smiled, and aside from that moment of almost intimate appraisal, he hadn't looked at Abigail, either. "I've lived here my entire life, ma'am, and have always found it preferable to town."

"As do I," Abigail put in, determined not to be ignored. "It's so peaceful."

He barely glanced at her. "Indeed, Miss Weston."

"I owe you a great thanks for saving my dear Milo, Mr. Vane. Abigail told me how you rescued him from the woods." Mama scratched her pet's chin, and he gave a little yap before tearing at the rope again. "I don't know what I would have done had he been lost."

"I merely pulled him from the brambles, Mrs. Weston. Your daughter deserves more credit for his rescue. She tracked him into the woods." Still unsmiling and grave, he darted a glance toward Abigail.

"And she was very pleased not to have to chase him further." Mama's tone was light as she petted her dog, but her eyes were sharp and inquisitive as she looked at Abigail, as if she could sense her daughter's tension. "It spared her favorite gown, I understand."

"Yes," she said with a smile. "I'm very grateful. We

could have found a new dog, but that dress was one of a kind."

Her mother gasped in affected outrage. "Milo, don't believe a word!" The puppy wagged his tail at the sound of his name. "I shall pretend I didn't hear that."

"I trust the pup suffered no harm from his adventure," said Mr. Vane.

"None that a brisk bath couldn't cure," Mama assured him.

"Mr. Vane suggested you cut his coat, Mama, so he wouldn't get caught in any thorn bushes." Abigail watched him as she spoke. His eyes were trained on the cursed little dog, still gnawing on a knot almost as large as his own head. She was completely perplexed. Had he really just come to pay his respects to Mama, as a neighbor? If his manners prompted him to that, why did he refuse to tell her his name the night they met? He seemed determined to ignore her, barely looking at her and replying dismissively to her conversation.

"Cut his coat! Oh, he's such a handsome dog with his fur long," Mama protested. "We'll just keep a close eye on him from now on, and not let him run through the woods."

Milo, who had been absorbed in chewing his rope toy, suddenly sprang up on the sofa. His ears stood up, his fur bristled, and a little growl rumbled in his throat. He barked a moment before the butler tapped at the door. "Mrs. Huntley, madam," Thomson announced.

"Do show her in," said Mama. "Hush, Milo." The puppy sank down on the cushion, his dark little eyes fixed on the door.

Mr. Vane was already on his feet. His cup of tea

was back on the table—untouched, Abigail realized. "It was a pleasure, Mrs. Weston," he said, reaching for his cane. "I shan't keep you."

Mama looked startled. "Why, no—do stay and finish your tea, sir."

"Thank you, no; I must be going." He bowed and turned, looking for all the world like he wanted to run out the door, but it opened before he got there, and Thomson ushered in Mrs. Huntley.

Anne Huntley was the wife of a gentleman who owned a large house near the gates of Richmond Park. It was rumored that his family was descended from a favorite retainer of King Charles II, who had granted the land himself. Since Mrs. Huntley herself had told them this rumor, Abigail supposed it was true, as well as a mark of the woman's pride. For some reason she and Mama had struck up a friendship very easily, but Milo didn't like her. Every time she called, the little dog barked until Mama had him taken away.

This time was no different—Milo erupted in a fury of yipping as soon as the woman stepped into the room— but more striking was the reaction of Mr. Vane and Mrs. Huntley to the sight of each other.

Mrs. Huntley gasped and clapped one hand to her bosom, stopping in her tracks.

Mr. Vane, his face more stony than ever, bowed very formally. Without another word he left.

Mama, still trying to calm Milo, didn't notice. But Abigail could have sworn Mrs. Huntley drew away from his approach as if he had the plague. She was now the second person who had looked at Mr. Vane as though she smelled brimstone in his presence.

Impulsively, she scooped up Milo from the sofa. "I'll take him outside so you can enjoy Mrs. Huntley's visit," she told her mother, and without waiting for permission, she rushed out. "Hush, dog," she muttered to Milo as she hurried toward the hall. How could Mr. Vane have made it so far, so quickly? He walked with a cane, while she was practically running. By the time she had snatched a lead from the hook behind the door, Mr. Vane was already striding down the drive.

"Mr. Vane," she called. His stride hesitated only a moment, and he didn't look back. Cursing under her breath, Abigail slipped the lead over Milo's head and put him down. Now that he was away from Mrs. Huntley, he had stopped barking, and trotted along eagerly enough as she hurried after the mysterious man. "Mr. Vane!"

He only stopped when she caught up to him. "Yes, Miss Weston?"

"You left so suddenly," she said, trying to catch her breath. "I hope Milo didn't cause it." The little pest was sniffing around his boots, with no sign of the frenzy that had gripped him just a few minutes ago. Now that she thought about it, Milo barked at most everyone except Mr. Vane.

He looked down at Milo. "No."

"I hope you didn't leave because of me," she dared to say.

"Why would you think that?" He glanced at her, then back at the dog. "Nothing of the sort."

"You seem determined to avoid looking at me," she said softly. "If I've done something to offend—"

"You haven't." He stepped over Milo and continued walking. Abigail realized he had come on foot from Montrose Hill. Excellent; that gave her more time to draw him out.

"But you *are* avoiding me." She kept pace with him, Milo at her heels.

"No," he said, staring straight ahead. "I never intended to stay long; your other visitor barely hastened my departure."

"Yes, and I'm *so* anxious to hear all about Mr. Huntley's illustrious roots," she muttered. "For once I agree with Milo."

Her companion made a noise like a faint snort.

"I think you agree with him, too," she said, encouraged. "I gather Mrs. Huntley was the reason you left so quickly."

He sighed. "If I didn't go, she would have, and that would have been uncomfortable for your mother. I had expressed my niceties, so I took my leave."

"Why on earth would she have left?" Abigail thought it was better to pretend she hadn't noticed the antipathy between them. "You aren't so fearsome as all that, sir."

He slanted a look at her. "How would you know?"

Abigail tilted her head and met his gaze thoughtfully. "You just aren't. Not in my opinion."

He stopped walking. "And your opinion is infallible?"

"Of course not!" She laughed. "I never said so. But I expect I'm more fearsome than you, as you look like you want to run the other way every time we meet."

And again his mouth softened. It was the only change in his face, but it had a remarkable effect. "How do you know what I want?"

"You wouldn't tell me your name the first night we met," she pointed out. "You started to duck back out the door when you saw me in the bookshop. Today you barely glanced my way, even when I spoke directly to you. What conclusion would you draw, if you were in my place?"

For a long moment he just regarded her in silence. Abigail met his gaze without flinching, ignoring the little jerks on the lead as Milo tried to wander away. "Yes," he said at last. "You are correct. I do want to run the other way when I see you."

"Why?" She hurried to keep up as he walked on, more briskly than before. "What have I done?"

"Absolutely nothing," he said, adding under his breath, "and I pray it stays that way."

"Then what ought I to do?" They were making good progress down the road. She had run out without a shawl or a bonnet, and had to squint against the sun when she looked up at him.

"Absolutely nothing," he repeated. "For your own sake."

"But if I've been doing nothing and it disgusts you, it makes no sense that I continue doing nothing."

He paused. "You don't disgust me." He pointed past her with his cane. "There is the path to my home. Pardon me, Miss Weston."

She let him pass, but kept dogging his heels, dragging poor Milo in her wake. "If I don't disgust you, why won't you speak to me? There was only that one moment, when you told me about the lost grotto, when I felt we were cordial."

He heaved a soundless sigh. "I'm speaking to you now, aren't I?"

"Without saying anything," she grumbled. "We are neighbors, sir. Surely we can have an amiable relationship."

With unexpected speed and grace he whirled on her. Abigail nearly tripped as she leapt back once, then again until her back hit a tree as he stalked toward her. He loomed over her, so close she could see the lines around his eyes, but not so close he was touching her. "Amiable," he whispered. "We will never be amiable."

"Why n-not?" she stammered. Her heart was beating a tattoo inside her chest.

He smiled, but there was nothing light about it. It was a black and bitter expression, and the sight made her eyes grow wide. "Because I am a wicked man, Miss Weston. Don't you listen to the gossip? Madness runs in my family. My estate is utterly ruined. People call me a thief. They even say I killed my father. Ask anyone in town, and they'll warn you to stay far, far away from me. To a beautiful, innocent young woman, I might as well be the devil incarnate."

"*Did* you kill your father?" As soon as the words left her mouth, Abigail wished them back.

"What do you think?" he asked in the same soft, dangerous tone.

She frowned. "I doubt it."

"But you don't *know*. That should warn you to run away."

She stared at him. "You intrigue me."

He leaned closer. In confusion she closed her eyes. "And you intrigue me," he replied, his breath stirring the hair at her temple. "That's why I avoid you."

"Isn't that all the more reason not to avoid someone?" she asked unsteadily. She could smell his shaving soap and a fresh scent that put her in mind of a sun-drenched field. This was attraction, potent and primitive and reckless.

He shuddered. "Not in this case." She forced her eyes open. His face was still taut and tense, but his eyes were dark with longing. Slowly he reached up one hand, as if he would touch her cheek, but at the last moment he let it fall.

"Why did you come today, if you mean to avoid me?" She had no idea what she was doing, arguing with a man who baldly admitted he wanted to run the other way when he saw her . . . even though she intrigued him.

He stepped back. "Foolishness."

She didn't move. "Will you show me the grotto, before you begin ignoring me forever?"

"No."

"Then I shall have to find it on my own." She eased away from the tree. "You did give me permission to walk in the woods. Do you mean to rescind that?"

He looked like he very much wanted to say yes. "No."

"Very well then." She stepped closer to him, thrilling at the way his eyes darkened even more and his breathing hitched. He did find her intriguing. Abigail had heard enough rumor and innuendo in her life to discount at least half of anything the gossips said. She hadn't heard enough about Sebastian Vane—yet—to decide what she thought of it in his case, but the edge in his voice when he threw the rumors in her face hinted at a man more wronged than wicked. She'd get to the bottom of that later, but for now . . . "I intend to search every inch of these woods until I find it."

"As you wish, Miss Weston."

She glanced at him from under her lashes. "If you don't want to see me again, you had better avoid the woods at all times."

"I will bear it in mind."

"Then I suppose this is good-bye, Mr. Vane." She tugged Milo out of the bushes where he'd been happily snuffling, and walked past him, very near. When her shoulder almost would have brushed his, she paused and looked up at him. The grim distance was gone from his face; he watched her with a mixture of wariness and fascination. She chose to focus on the fascination, hoping he was as helpless against it as she was. "But I hope it's not."

She turned and walked away without looking back, her pulse pounding in her ears.

Chapter 6

Abigail decided it was time to cast off subtlety. When she got back to the house, she sent Milo away with a footman and went in search of her sister, who turned out to be in the bright conservatory at the southern side of the house. "You should have seen the way Mrs. Huntley reacted when she saw Mr. Vane was here this afternoon."

Penelope put down her book without a second glance. Abigail thought she saw the edge of a pamphlet sticking out from between the pages. At least Pen was being more cautious about reading *50 Ways to Sin* this time; Mama never went into the conservatory, claiming it made her sneeze. "Why did no one tell me he was here?"

"He barely was here." Abigail dropped onto the chair opposite Penelope. "I was astonished to see him at all—"

"Were you?" murmured her sister with a sly look.

"He only came to receive Mama's thanks for rescuing Milo." She made a bored face. "He hardly spoke a word to me. But then Mrs. Huntley arrived, and I vow, if he could have bolted out the window, I think he would have."

"That's somewhat understandable," Penelope said. "I don't know what Mama sees in her. I cannot endure one more telling of her husband's illustrious connection to a king's hawker two hundred years ago."

"Yes, it's odd how a royal connection makes such humble roots vastly more appealing." Abigail grinned, and her sister snickered. "I had the same thought as Mr. Vane about escaping the room, although I hope I hid it better than he did. But the strangest thing was, when Mrs. Huntley came into the room a moment later, I thought she'd faint at the sight of him."

Penelope sat a little straighter. "Oh?"

"Pen, she looked as though he made her stomach turn."

"Did he say anything to her?"

Abigail shook her head. "A polite nod, nothing more. Then he rushed out the door!"

Penelope was entranced. "Goodness! Why? He seems perfectly ordinary—a bit reclusive, and desperately smitten with you, but otherwise unexceptional."

"He is decidedly not smitten with me," Abigail returned. "He admitted he's avoiding me."

"Because he wants to throw you to the ground and ravish you into unconsciousness."

Abigail felt her face grow warm. "Well—probably not . . . unfortunately . . ."

Penelope shot upright with a jerk. "You do fancy him! I knew it! Oh, Abby—"

"If you tell anyone, I shall lead Mama straight to your hidden copy of *50 Ways to Sin*," Abigail interrupted. Her sister just grinned, a lively, devilish expression. "Speaking of which, I believe I was entitled to read it first."

"Here. It's a delicious one." Penelope drew out the

illicit pamphlet and tossed it to her. "What sort of wicked thoughts are you having about the mysterious Sebastian Vane?"

Abigail shoved the story into her pocket. "More curious than wicked. He's so intriguing, Pen . . ."

"The dark, brooding sort always are," agreed her sister.

"But he told me he's unsuitable, and he said I would soon sort out why. So far I haven't, though. None of Mama's visitors gossip about him. All I have are Mrs. Huntley's shocked reaction and Mrs. Driscoll's barely civil treatment in the bookshop, and for the life of me I cannot make sense of either." She didn't mention what he had said to her on the path just today; any mention of madness or murder was inflammatory.

"And you want me to help you find out more," guessed Penelope.

Abigail nodded. "Will you?"

"Of course!" her sister exclaimed. It was amazing how one prurient story had restored her to good humor. "We should ask Lady Samantha. She's not some stuffy matron who would insist nothing smelled wrong even if she'd just trod on a rotten egg."

"When are we to see her again?"

"Day after next, if the weather holds. Remember the picnic?"

"Oh yes." Abigail's mouth curved. Her mother had planned a picnic down by the river, to include Lady Samantha Lennox. Papa was so eager for them to become friends with the earl's daughters, he had given Mama carte blanche to entertain whenever and wherever she liked, as long as the Lennox sisters came. Fortunately, Abigail genuinely liked Lady Samantha. "That should serve nicely."

The next evening when he went out for his walk, Sebastian took Abigail Weston's warning to heart. Avoid the woods at all times, she'd said, so he did. As usual, he walked toward the woods, but then only skirted the edges. Boris, who was accustomed to romping through the thickets and chasing small animals, whined and barked at him before loping into the woods on his own. Sebastian forced himself not to watch the dog disappear down the winding path that led toward Hart House. The chances that he would run into her again were remote, but the odds seemed to be against him lately.

He sighed and walked on. Once he would have taken her words as an invitation. He would have found reason after reason to lurk about the edge of Hart House land, doing his best to "happen" across her path. He would have responded to her smiles and sunny laugh with teasing and laughter of his own. He would have invited her to walk down the Fragrant Walk, which seemed specially designed for the purpose of stealing kisses. He probably would have shown her the grotto as well, where one might steal more than a chaste kiss from a willing girl.

That had certainly been his and Benedict Lennox's intent, when they'd gone hunting for the grotto as boys. Well, not originally; when they'd first heard tales of an old grotto, females of any sort hadn't figured in their plans. They'd been all of nine and ten years old, convinced it would be a grand hideout from thrashings and tutors and other outrages. Old Lady Burton had been amused by their earnest request to search for it, but she'd given her permission, and for ten years they'd climbed and crawled through damned near the entire woods. Over the years their plans for the grotto had changed from hiding out of sight of tutors, to storing various contraband they coveted, to seducing local wenches there. Since they'd never found it, all the plans were only castles in the air.

But then Sebastian had uncovered it—literally, by falling through the bracken that had grown over the steps. He would have told Benedict about it immediately if they hadn't had a furious argument the day before. Sebastian was never quite sure why they argued so hotly. At the time, all he'd been able to think about was his newly purchased commission. Of course he'd known Benedict envied him—who wouldn't have?—but Benedict was heir to an earl, forbidden from doing anything dangerous. But that last night Benedict had been in a fury, and all but provoked a fight. They had nearly come to blows before Ben stormed off.

In hindsight Sebastian thought it must have been Benedict's own burning desire to buy a commission, too, that set him off. He could sympathize; Lord Stratford was a harsh and demanding father, and Benedict had long yearned to escape. Sebastian had assumed that last quarrel would be forgotten by the time he returned, but that had been the last time they were friends. When he came home from the army, everything had changed, and those days of boyhood friendship were distant memories.

He reached the dip in the hill, a little hollow before the ground swelled and rolled gently down to the river. He stopped and gazed down the slope. From here he could see across the river to Stratford Court, the massive Tudor mansion where Benedict had grown up. Its red brick looked black now as the shadows grew long, the windows gleaming like quicksilver where they caught the fading light. From here, one could raise a lantern that could be seen from the second floor bed-chambers on the north end of the house. He'd done it often enough as a boy, signaling to Benedict.

His jaw hardened. That was another lifetime ago. That was before a Frenchman shot out his knee. Before his father lost his wits. Before he came home from war to find that his father, sinking deeper into lunacy every day, had sold two-thirds of Montrose Hill lands at a mere pittance—mainly to the Earl of Stratford, Bene-dict's father. Before Sebastian had forced himself out of bed, against doctor's orders, and tried to mend the damage, only to have doors around town shut in his face. People whispered that Michael Vane was pos-sessed by demons. They demanded his debts be paid immediately. They watched his son through wary eyes, as though they expected him to tear off his clothes and run naked through the town assaulting people, too. People he had known all his life suddenly began cross-ing the road when they saw him. People he had trusted and respected refused to receive him.

Then his father disappeared, which only made things worse. There were whispers that he'd dispatched his father to his grave, an unforgivable sin no matter how deranged the father had become.

That one was the cruelest irony. His father had dis-appeared, not turned up dead. A missing man couldn't be judged incompetent, which meant Sebastian had no grounds to contest the sale of the land in court. A miss-ing man wasn't the same as a dead man, which meant Sebastian couldn't even inherit the remaining property and begin to rebuild his estate. With his father missing, he was effectively bankrupt, unable to sell Montrose Hill but barely able to maintain it. In his darker moods, he thought that if he *had* decided to kill his father, he damned sure wouldn't have done it in a way that made things worse for him. At least the rumor that he was a thief made some sense, even if it was equally untrue.

Sometimes, Sebastian thought he might have preferred to go mad. Perhaps then he wouldn't feel his losses so sharply.

He turned to go back up the hill. He couldn't go farther down it; that land, which had once been part of his estate, belonged to Lord Stratford now. According to the records, his father had sold that prime piece of land, some eighty acres situated along a graceful sweep of well-drained riverfront, for fifty pounds. The attorney who handled the gift—it could hardly be called a sale—had been apologetic when Sebastian confronted him, but consistent: Michael Vane had insisted on selling it, and he'd been pleased with the price. No one had known he was mad then. There was nothing that could be done about it. Sebastian was lucky he had anything left.

As he climbed, Hart House came into view off to his right below. The white stone glowed softly in the twilight, a fine jewel nestled in the verdant woods and lawns around it. Unlike Montrose Hill, there was no shortage of funds at Hart House. It had struck him quite forcibly during his ill-conceived visit the previous day. The Westons had plenty of money. They weren't scraping by, trying to hold on to the last shreds of respectability. Abigail Weston had no idea what she was doing, circling around him like a bee over a flower, not realizing the flower was poisonous. He supposed she had wild romantic notions about him; nothing else could explain her interest. He had tried to warn her off. The only trouble was . . .

His gaze strayed toward the woods. She said she intended to search every inch of them for the grotto. Perhaps she meant it, perhaps she didn't. The grotto wasn't far from the Fragrant Walk, although it was well hidden. He pictured her crawling through the hedge and wild bracken that had overrun the entrance. He pictured her tumbling down the steps, cracking her head and twisting her ankle. He'd have to check the damned grotto every day to make sure she wasn't lying hurt at the bottom, her fair skin bruised and cut, her stunning eyes bleak with pain. And if he meant to do that . . .

Boris wandered out of the woods, his tail wagging happily. He trotted over to Sebastian, tongue hanging out, and butted his hand. Sebastian scratched his dog's ears, wondering if Boris had met her in the woods. That would also be just his luck, that his dog would get to see her when he couldn't.

"I'm a bloody idiot," he told Boris, still scratching. The dog just leaned against his good leg and moaned as Sebastian dug his fingertips into that one spot behind the left ear that left Boris weak with bliss. With his other hand Sebastian reached into his coat pocket and pulled out a somewhat crumpled pamphlet. *Fifty Ways to Sin*, read the title in plain type. It might have been a political treatise, it looked so drab. If Miss Weston hadn't blushed so beautifully when Mrs. Driscoll brought it out, Sebastian wouldn't have given the little booklet a second glance. If she hadn't tried to conceal the title, he wouldn't have been driven to buy his own copy. He'd told himself it would likely prove to be some morality tale, or perhaps a guide for young ladies on how to avoid lecherous gentlemen. What else would a respectable, proper young lady buy?

Instead it had been an erotic story, an explicit account of an encounter entirely in the dark between two people who were strangers to each other. With unfortunate vividness, the scene had played across his mind's eye—and it was Abigail Weston he imagined, giving herself to him with wanton abandon. He had to take himself in hand and satisfy the fierce craving of his body, the images were so real. Just the thought of her reading the same story was enough to make him hard again. He was tormented by the question of how she would react to the arousing tale. Horror? Alarm? Shame? Or maybe . . . curiosity. Interest. Even desire. She'd bought it, after all—and she sought out his company.

The real trouble was that while he knew he should avoid her, he wasn't sure he had the will to do so for long.

Chapter 7

Abigail had thought no one could be more brazen than Penelope, but she was proven wrong at her mother's picnic. Among the guests was a young lady named Lucy Walgrave, who quickly proved herself a gossip extraordinaire. She seemed almost as fascinated by Sebastian Vane as Abigail herself was—although in a much more macabre way.

"Do you know your neighbor Sebastian Vane?" Miss Walgrave asked, her eyes sparkling. The young ladies had a table to themselves, a little removed from Mama and the older guests. "Have you heard much of him?"

"Lucy," said Lady Samantha in quiet reproof.

Her friend patted her arm. "I know, but they live so near to him! They're bound to hear everything eventually." Lady Samantha looked away with a troubled expression, and Lucy turned expectantly to Penelope.

"Er—slightly," said Penelope with a fleeting glance at Abigail. "My sister met him, as have my mother and brother."

"Only briefly," Abigail added.

Lucy leaned forward eagerly. "That's more than many can say! I've lived here six years and only crossed his path twice. People call him the Misanthrope of Montrose Hill. He hardly speaks to anyone, just walks his grounds with that enormous black dog. No one ever saw that dog before his father disappeared; some people wonder if it might be a familiar."

"A witch's spirit?" asked Penelope, shocked. "Ridiculous!"

Lucy flipped one hand. "Oh, I don't believe it! It's just a coincidence, most likely. Still, he's a very fearsome-looking man, don't you think? He might be handsome if he smiled, but he never smiles, at least not that anyone's seen."

"I've seen him smile," said Lady Samantha softly.

"Oh yes." Lucy made a pious face. "I always forget you knew him *before*."

"Before what?" Penelope asked what Abigail was thinking.

"Before the war." Lady Samantha was rather pale, but her voice was even and clear. "He was once a very dashing and eligible young man, but he was wounded at Waterloo, and—and things went rather badly for him after that."

"His father went mad," said Lucy with an air of confiding some horrible secret. "Barking, raving mad. He ran naked through the streets of Richmond, screaming curses and ranting about the devil pursuing him. He assaulted people and had to be restrained before he could kill them."

Abigail exchanged a look with her sister; Penelope looked as surprised as she felt. So that hadn't been exaggeration. "Is that why some people in town seem to shun Mr. Vane the son?"

"Partly," said Lucy. "When he first came back from the war, he appeared to go a bit mad, too. He threatened several people, and then when his father disappeared . . ." She shook her head, although not with any apparent sorrow. "Well, it just seemed he was following in his father's footsteps. Mrs. Fairfax swears she felt a chill when he passed her once!"

"Mrs. Fairfax fancies she feels a chill every hour," said Lady Samantha. "Lucy, you're being unfair."

"Everything I said is true," her friend protested. "I haven't repeated the most salacious rumors."

"But only because I'm sitting here," replied Lady Samantha wryly. She turned to Abigail and Penelope. "Mr. Vane was once my brother's friend, and was often at Stratford Court. It was a very long time ago—nearly ten years by now—but I still hate to hear people speak ill of him."

"Then what is the truth?" Abigail knew this was her chance to ask. "I heard all manner of things: madness, ruin, thievery . . ." She hesitated, but Penelope gave her an encouraging nod. "Even that he killed his father."

"See?" murmured Lucy. "You knew they'd hear it all anyway."

Lady Samantha's eyes flashed. "It's a lie that he killed his father. Old Mr. Vane wasn't well at the end, but his son would never have done anything to harm him. He took such devoted care of his father, once he came home. The worst happened while he was away in the army." She mustered a smile. "I'm sure you have nothing to fear from him."

"I don't," said Abigail. "It was just a shock to see a reserved man of property almost given the cut direct in Richmond."

Lucy leaned forward. "You saw him in town?"

"At the bookshop," Penelope answered. "He seemed mysterious and intriguing to me, but his behavior was ordinary."

"And yet Mrs. Driscoll was almost rude to him," added Abigail. "It was striking, for he was very civil to her."

Lucy nodded in a knowing way. "When Mad Michael—that's what they called old Mr. Vane—when he was in one of his fits, he tore off his clothes, right in the middle of Richmond, and attacked Mrs. Driscoll, shouting that she was the devil's own handmaiden and was trying to lure him into hell. It took three men to drag him away from her, and she was quite bruised as a result. I don't wonder that she avoids the son as well."

This time the look Penelope gave her wasn't merely startled, but a little alarmed. Abigail ignored it. "That would be quite frightening," she allowed, "but surely the younger Mr. Vane wasn't party to it?"

"Oh, it was before he'd returned from the war."

Penelope frowned. "Then why avoid him and treat him so coldly?"

Lucy darted a glance at Lady Samantha. "He wasn't so reserved when he first came home. He threatened to beat Sir Richard Arnold, and nearly did come to blows with other gentlemen."

"Over what?"

Again Lucy hesitated. It was Lady Samantha who answered. "Old Mr. Vane sold off a great deal of his land. His son was rudely surprised when he came home." She seemed about to say something else, but instead paused, and when she went on, seemed to choose her words with care. "I daresay any man would have felt the same, let alone a man who'd been gravely wounded and come home to find his father so unwell."

That fit with the picture forming in Abigail's head. He'd been gone, unable to keep his father from hurting anyone or selling his land. Coming home wounded, only to be confronted by a parent sinking into madness and an estate suddenly gone . . . Surely it would make anyone lose his temper.

Lady Samantha pushed back her chair. "You must excuse me, I need to stretch my legs a bit after that excellent picnic."

"Shall I walk with you?" Abigail started to rise, but Lady Samantha shook her head.

"No, I'll be back in a few minutes. I never miss the dessert course." She headed up the lawn toward the house.

As soon as she was out of earshot, Lucy leaned forward. "Now that she's gone, I can tell you the rest of what I know about Sebastian Vane." Abigail's stomach clenched in apprehension. "She doesn't like to hear an ill word about him, but she's the only one in her family. Mr. Vane used to be quite welcome at Stratford Court, but now his name is never spoken there. It's true that old Mr. Vane sold off all his property; he positively beggared the estate. People suspect his son did away with him to put a stop to it before everything was gone."

"What really happened to Mr. Vane the elder?" Abigail asked.

"No one knows!" Lucy nodded somberly at Abigail's surprise. "He disappeared. No body was ever found, but the only people in the house were the housekeeper and her husband, and Mr. Vane the son. The son tried to have him declared dead, but since there was no body . . ." She shrugged. "All too easy to push a man into the river."

"But why?"

"To get rid of a lunatic, of course, and to inherit." She grimaced. "It must be so horrifying to have a madman in the family."

"If the father can't be proven dead, the son wouldn't be able to inherit," Abigail pointed out.

Lucy paused. "I suppose that's true. Perhaps that's why Mr. Vane turned to thievery."

"What?" exclaimed Penelope.

Their guest nodded. "Soon after the father disappeared, a large sum of money went missing from Stratford Court. Well, Sebastian Vane had been heard having a loud argument with Lord Stratford just a few weeks earlier, during which he threatened to 'make the earl pay.' Those were his words. And then, when the money vanished . . ."

Abigail frowned. "Was Mr. Vane arrested?"

Lucy craned her neck, peering in the direction Lady Samantha had gone, then lowered her voice even more. "He was never arrested, and it was because of Samantha. You heard her say Mr. Vane used to be her brother's friend. What she won't tell is that he was also mad in love with her, before the war and all the trouble with his family. And she loved him, although it was a great secret because she was so young and he was only a gentleman while her father is an earl. Well, when he came home, I heard he went to Stratford Court and asked—demanded!—to marry her. Her dowry would have solved all his problems, don't you see? But Lord Stratford refused, for obvious reasons, and that was why they quarreled so bitterly. It left Vane in desperate need of money, so he stole several thousand guineas from the earl. And he wasn't arrested," she added as Penelope opened her mouth to speak, "only because her brother Lord Atherton, who was once Vane's friend, persuaded his father not to, for her sake."

Abigail regarded her doubtfully. "It seems very difficult to break into a house, steal a large sum of money, and escape without being caught, all with a shot-up knee."

Lucy waved this aside. "But because he was so often there, he would have known exactly how to get in and find what he wanted. I think it's very likely he did it."

"If he stole a lot of money," asked Penelope, "why is he still bankrupt?"

"I don't know," exclaimed Lucy. "Maybe he's not, but just told people he is. It would add proof to the rumor, wouldn't it, if he suddenly had plenty of money? Or maybe he was just too wily to spend it all at once. He might have it buried in his garden for all we know, and only digs up a few guineas when he needs them."

Penelope still looked unconvinced. "The Earl of Stratford must be a very devoted father, to overlook such a loss and allow the thief to freely walk the same streets as his daughter."

"Well, everyone believes he stole it," said Lucy, almost defensively. "No one will extend him credit. I daresay no one thinks he's likely to kill anyone else, but a thief will keep stealing. And I know this for a fact: Lord Atherton hasn't spoken to Sebastian Vane since then. I heard they had a bitter falling out over Vane's romance with Lady Samantha. Lord Stratford is an important man around here, and his favor matters. None of his family will even say Vane's name."

Abigail cleared her throat. "Lady Samantha just did, and she was rather kind to him."

The other girl gave her a faintly pitying look. "Isn't it obvious? She's still in love with him. I daresay he's still in love with her, too, and that's why he never goes out. Could you imagine how cruel it would be to live so near your heart's desire and know you were doomed never to have it? And she, of course, is forbidden to see him or speak to him, which must be why she's never married even though she's at least a year older than I am."

There was a moment of shocked silence. "Well," said Penelope at last. "How melodramatic."

Lucy shook her head with a sad sigh. "Isn't it? And she's such a lovely girl and so sweet. It's so dreadful to hear such tragic scandals connected to her name."

"But not too dreadful to repeat them," said Penelope under her breath as she jumped to her feet. Fortunately their guest didn't appear to hear. "Enough of that gloomy topic. Miss Walgrave, would you care to see the Fragrant Walk?"

Lucy looked a little disappointed that the gossip was over. "I don't want to trouble you . . ."

"It would be no trouble at all." Penelope summoned a gracious smile. "Come, you'll adore it. My brother declares he's never seen a more romantic spot in his life."

Miss Walgrave brightened. "Does he? Why, I must see it, then."

Abigail shot a grateful look at her sister as their guest gathered her shawl. She knew very well Penelope was luring the other girl away to give her time to digest that last shocking tidbit in peace. Her sister merely smiled and linked arms with Miss Walgrave, baldly lying about Jamie's interest in the Fragrant Walk, which Abigail had never once heard him mention. It would serve him right if Penelope set every young lady in town on him; Jamie had refused to attend any of Mama's entertainments, which had somehow only made him more appealing in the eyes of the local unmarried ladies.

But it seemed Mr. Vane might have a different reason for avoiding social occasions. Good heavens; murder and thieving and a broken heart. Could he really be so in love with Lady Samantha after so many years that he couldn't bear to see her? Abigail tried to consider it analytically and suppress any sort of unpleasant feeling. It was possible, she decided, although not very likely. If Mr. Vane really couldn't bear the thought of seeing Lady Samantha even in passing on the street, he would do much better to sell his house and live somewhere else. It didn't seem as though he had many friends in Richmond to exert any hold on him. And seven years was a long time to shut one's self away from all society. Abigail allowed that she might be more passionate in her feelings than some, but she couldn't imagine any unrequited infatuation being enough nourishment for her soul over the course of one year, let alone seven.

The rest was much more serious, of course. Could he have killed his father? She didn't want to believe that. Perhaps it had been an accident . . . She didn't know what to make of the stolen money, but she had noticed that Miss Walgrave's telling of that portion was couched more as supposition than fact. There must be more to the story, and she hated to convict a man based on gossip, especially from such an enthusiast as Miss Walgrave. She thought of the way Mr. Vane threw the charges in her face the other day. Surely only a man of ice-cold blood and iron nerve could bring up his crimes in that way.

She stood and headed toward the house, taking her time. Even if Miss Walgrave had been exaggerating, there was something in Lady Samantha's demeanor that made Abigail think part of the story might have a germ of truth. Lady Samantha did grow pale every time Mr. Vane was mentioned. She defended him when everyone else seemed quite happy to malign him or ignore him. And there had been that look her sister,

Lady Turley, gave her when Penelope first mentioned Mr. Vane at the Westons' ball. It had been concern, as if Lady Turley feared for Lady Samantha's well-being. For a moment Abigail wished she could see Lady Samantha and Mr. Vane together, to judge any attachment, and then she decided she didn't actually want to see that.

She was so deep in her thoughts, she almost missed Lady Samantha. The earl's daughter stood on the very edge of the terrace, her back to the river. Above the roof of Hart House, over the trees, Montrose Hill House was clearly visible in the distance. In the warm sunlight, the faded brick was a soft pink, the regular rows of windows gleaming like silver among the vines that climbed one side. From here it looked gracious and comfortable, the quintessential English house.

Almost as soon as Abigail spied her, Lady Samantha abandoned her study and resumed walking toward the picnic. She caught sight of Abigail and stopped, a faintly rueful smile on her face. "Miss Weston. I didn't realize Montrose Hill was so near to Hart House."

"It's not, really. My father paid a call and said it must be nearly two miles. The hill makes it look closer."

"Ah. I'm glad your father called on Mr. Vane." Lady Samantha bit her lip. "You must have noticed that Lucy's chatter was . . ."

"A bit gleeful in its scandalousness?"

"Yes." The other girl's eyes darkened. "I wish she wouldn't repeat every shocking little thing she hears."

"It smacks of unfairness," Abigail agreed. "Whatever Mr. Vane's family troubles, it's horrible to whisper of murder about him."

"He used to be a very eligible young man. He still would be, most likely, if only . . ." Lady Samantha stopped and forced a smile. "If only idle neighbors like us would stop talking about him! I'm no better than Lucy, am I?"

"You are far kinder to Mr. Vane," said Abigail quietly. "And since you were acquainted with him at one time, I credit your words much more than Miss Walgrave's."

Lady Samantha hesitated. "I knew Mr. Vane a very long time ago," she said at last. "Even I wouldn't suppose I know what sort of man he is today, and I shouldn't talk of him as if I do. Perhaps you'll form an entirely different opinion."

"Perhaps," Abigail agreed.

She certainly intended to try.

Chapter 8

On the next fine day, Abigail went to the kitchen and asked for a luncheon packed in a basket. She wore her favorite walking dress, the one that made her eyes look a little blue, and a plain straw bonnet. She carried the book she'd bought the other day in town. When her mother stopped her on the terrace and asked where she was going, Abigail replied, innocently, "I'm going for a walk, and if I find a convenient spot to read, I have a new novel."

Her mother wasn't suspicious. "Very well. Don't go too far, dear, and be back in time for supper."

"Yes, Mama." Abigail smiled and headed for the woods.

Unfortunately, she didn't make it far. "Where are you going?" Penelope asked, passing her in the garden.

"For a walk."

"Oh, I fancy a walk," said her sister.

"It's going to be long and quiet."

"There's nothing else to do," replied Penelope. "Let me get my pelisse."

"I plan to walk until I find a cozy spot to read." Abigail pulled the book out of the basket and held it up. "You'll be bored."

Penelope flipped one hand. "I'm already bored. You can read anytime. Don't be so dull, Abby! I'll just be a moment." She hurried into the house.

Abigail huffed. She glanced around. All was quiet and peaceful at Hart House, with a gentle breeze from the river and a sunny sky overhead. Penelope was probably bored out of her mind, but her company was the last thing Abigail wanted right now. She intended to walk through the woods in search of the grotto, and if she happened across Mr. Vane's path, she wouldn't be disappointed. She was wildly curious to know if he truly meant to avoid her, or if he felt the same inexplicable pull she did. Even though she told herself there was only a slim chance he would happen to be walking in the woods at the same time she was, on the same paths—especially after saying he would avoid the woods—there was no denying the anticipation that quickened her step.

Or rather, *had* quickened her step until her sister interrupted. Really, why should she suffer because her sister couldn't find someone else to torment? If Penelope would adopt an interest in something like needlework or practicing the pianoforte, she wouldn't be bored at all. It would also restore her to their mother's good graces, something Penelope ought to consider more important. Abigail pursed her lips, and started walking again—not quickly, but not slowly, either.

"You didn't wait for me," complained her sister breathlessly when she caught up several minutes later.

"You took too long."

Penelope snorted. "You're walking out to look for him, aren't you? I cannot believe you would scheme to slip off and meet a mysterious and possibly dangerous gentleman without me."

"I have no expectation of meeting anyone," said Abigail, keeping her eyes on the path ahead of her. "I told you I intend to read."

"And you just happened to be wearing a bonnet that flatters your face and your favorite dress." Penelope smirked.

"Yes, I plead guilty to wearing my favorite dress," said Abigail dryly. "That must be a sign of ill intent!"

"I don't blame you," her sister remarked. "I'd like to meet the smoldering Mr. Vane as well."

Abigail just sighed and shook her head. There was no deterring her sister sometimes.

"You're not worried he might kill you in the woods?"

"No!"

Penelope laughed. "Or steal from you?"

"He'd only get a book and a basket of food." She glanced at her sister. "You don't believe those rumors?"

Penelope snorted. "If you'd walked to the Fragrant Walk with Lucy Walgrave, you'd doubt every word that came from her lips, too. I like a good gossip myself, but only if it seems plausible."

Abigail grinned. "I suppose some of it was plausible . . ."

"Do you think he really is dying of love for Lady Samantha?"

Her grin disappeared. "Seven years seems a long time to pine for someone."

"True," conceded Penelope. "Any lover worth his salt would have kidnapped her to Gretna Green by now."

"Or perhaps Miss Walgrave's report is outlandish in every respect," Abigail retorted. "Lady Samantha seems old enough to have done something by now if she loved him and knew he loved her. I certainly would have, at any rate."

"Really," murmured her sister with a speculative glance. "Is that why we're walking about the woods?"

"No." Abigail kicked a loose stone from the path. "I am walking in the woods because I like them; they are cool and quiet and free of chattering busybodies—usually. You are walking in the woods because you are a pest."

Penelope was immune to such criticism. "There are much better places to read on the lawn or the terrace, and you know it. If you're not walking out in hopes of meeting Mr. Vane, there must be something else you want to see." She narrowed her eyes and studied Abigail closely for a few minutes. "The grotto," she said at last.

"I'm surprised it took you that long to guess. But Pen"—she stopped and turned to her sister in all seriousness—"don't tell Mama. She wouldn't think it ladylike to go in search of a cave."

"A grotto is no ordinary cave." Penelope grinned. "I can't believe you didn't invite me."

Abigail sighed. Penelope would want to search as if they needed to find the grotto to save their family from ruination. Abigail preferred to wander, keeping her eyes open for a grotto, of course, but not supremely focused on the search. She did want to read her book, and if Mr. Vane happened to cross her path . . . "It might not even exist. Lady Turley said it had been filled in."

"Then why are you searching for it?"

She didn't look at her sister as she replied, "Mr. Vane said he found it once, so I thought I'd have a look."

For a few minutes Penelope didn't say anything,

which was unusual. "You know, Abby," she began at last, "I don't think badly of you for being intrigued by him."

"Yes, I know; dark and reclusive and mysterious, how alluring!" She made a face.

"Well, yes," conceded her sister. "But we've gossiped about enough gentlemen that I can see this one is different for you."

Abigail swatted a trailing vine out of her way as she framed her reply. Too little admission would only prompt her sister to pester her more; too much admission . . . would be even worse. "It's one thing to presume about a gentleman we've never met, based on reports in the gossip rags. Mr. Vane is our neighbor, and he was kind to me. I think it's unfair of people to shun him because of his father's illness and call him a murderer and a thief without proof, just as I think it's unfair for some people to believe you and I are ambitious schemers bent on buying titled husbands. I want to give him the benefit of the doubt, that's all—and so far he's done nothing to warrant being avoided."

"That's all true, but I think there's even more to it." Penelope cursed as a bramble bush caught on her skirt. "Am I wrong?"

Abigail hesitated. "Perhaps. Perhaps not, but . . . I would like to find out."

For once her sister said nothing. She gave Abigail a long, searching look, and finally nodded.

They walked in silence for a little while. Abigail tried to keep a mental map of their location to avoid getting lost, but gave it up after a while. Hart House was behind them, to the east. Montrose Hill, on the other hand, would be ahead and to the right, up the slope of the hill she could feel rising beneath her feet.

She had no idea where the grotto might be, but if Mr. Vane had discovered it, it only stood to reason that it might be near his home. She tried to subtly steer them up the hill, and for once her sister didn't complain about the climb.

"You know, Lucy Walgrave is a chatterbox of the worst kind," said Penelope all of a sudden. "I don't think even *she* believes half of what she says. I certainly don't."

Abigail grinned at her sister gratefully. "Nor I."

"That's why I set her on Jamie."

"You didn't!" Penelope just smiled her evil little smile at Abigail's horrified, amused exclamation. "What did you do?"

"I might have mentioned that he's ready to settle down. I might have told her he likes the pianoforte, and poetry, and ladies who paint."

Abigail choked on a laugh as her sister named everything that would send their brother running. "What did Jamie do to you?"

Penelope gave a gusty sigh. "Nothing. Nothing! Not a bloody thing. He let Papa buy this house and drag us out to a summer of exile, and then he fled the premises. Have you seen him once except at dinner? He avoided the ball, he never pays calls with us, he won't even take a boat out on the river with me. He deserves to be pursued by a chatterbox and made to suffer for his unpardonable dullness."

"When has Jamie ever paid calls?" Abigail pointed out. "He attends balls in London only when Mama insists. And having ladies like Miss Walgrave pursue him isn't likely to make him change his behavior, if that was your intent."

"He still deserves it, for being so maddeningly

absent most of the time," growled Penelope. "I swear he's sneaking back to London, and if he can do so, why can't I?"

"He's not. He just finds ways to amuse himself without forcing his company on other people."

Penelope stuck out her tongue. "Admit it, Abby. You'd be as bored as I am if not for the mysterious Mr. Vane."

"Hardly mysterious," said a familiar voice.

Penelope shrieked, seizing Abigail's arm so hard they both almost fell to the ground. "Good Lord, did you want to frighten us to death?" she demanded, whirling around. "Where are you, sir?"

He stepped from behind a wild flowering shrub. "On my own property."

Penelope folded her arms and looked him up and down. So did Abigail, although—she hoped—without her sister's brazen staring. He was just as she remembered, tall and handsome and somber. His long brown coat hid the cane, but now she could see by his posture how he leaned on it, his left shoulder a little higher than the right.

"Are you?" said Penelope tartly. "I don't see a fence."

"But I've lived here all my life and know where my land ends and your father's begins," he replied. "I daresay after you've lived here thirty years or more, you'll be able to locate the boundary as plainly as any fence."

"Do not, under any circumstances, suggest I will live here for thirty more years," said Penelope under her breath. "Do you plan to shoot us as trespassers?"

"Penelope," said Abigail sternly, wishing she could shake her sister. "This is our neighbor, Mr. Sebastian Vane. Mr. Vane, may I present my rude and impertinent sister, Miss Penelope Weston?"

"I thought as much." Penelope grinned, her smile returning as bright and good-natured as ever. "It's a pleasure to meet you, Mr. Vane."

"And you, Miss Penelope." His gaze moved to Abigail at last, and something seemed to light up inside her. "How do you do, Miss Weston?"

"Very well, sir." She tried to keep the smile off her face. So he hadn't been able to avoid the woods at all times, as he'd threatened. "What a surprise to encounter you here."

He acknowledged the hit with a slight tightening of his lips. "Boris went out, and hasn't come back. He is why I'm in the woods at the moment. My housekeeper coddles Boris like a child, and she grew worried when he didn't come back for his midday meal."

"Who is Boris?" Penelope wanted to know.

"My dog." He hesitated, then touched the brim of his hat. "I apologize for interrupting your walk. Good day, Miss Weston. Miss Penelope."

"Wait!" Abigail called as he turned away. "We'll help you look," she blurted out. "Since you were so kind to help me rescue Milo. We owe it to you."

"I'm sure he's fine," he said, watching her with those dark, somber eyes. "But thank you very kindly for the offer."

"What if he's fallen into the grotto? Or become trapped under a bramble bush? He might be hurt." Abigail forged through the tangle of vines and bracken toward him. "Now I shall be worried about him, too."

Mr. Vane hesitated. His gaze darted toward Penelope, and Abigail turned a fearsome glare upon her sister, who owed her a tremendous favor.

Penelope blinked, then burst out, "Oh yes! We'll help look for him. Is he small and adorable like Milo?"

"He's a large boar hound, so high," said Mr. Vane evenly. He held his hand at the level of his waist. "Black. Drools a good bit."

Penelope blinked again. "That big, is he?"

"When he barks, it tends to frighten ladies half to death," Mr. Vane went on. "It's a very deep, fierce bark."

"And yet he's well trained and won't hurt anyone." Abigail gave him a reproving look. "Isn't he?"

He sighed as he gazed down at her. As usual, his expression was neutral, but now that she stood at his side, Abigail thought she could see something like amused frustration in his eyes. "Yes, Miss Weston," he said, almost reluctantly.

"Have you any idea where he's likely to be?" She shaded her eyes as she put her head back to see him better.

"No." He didn't seem very concerned about it, either, his gaze still fixed on her as if in unwilling fascination.

Abigail smiled. "Then we'll just walk through the woods until we find him."

"Yes," said Penelope with notably less enthusiasm.

Abigail turned back to Mr. Vane. "If he's hungry, isn't he likely to be nearer home?" She started in the direction of Montrose Hill. "Perhaps he's already started back."

"Perhaps," allowed Mr. Vane as she walked away from him, "but the house is that way." He pointed to her left.

Without a word she switched directions. "Does he like bread or cheese? I have some in my basket, along with an apple."

For a moment he said nothing. Abigail kept walking, listening hard, until she heard a muffled curse and the quick sound of his steps as he hurried after her. Penelope, she assumed, was somewhere behind him. "He likes cheese."

"Excellent! We'll tempt him out of hiding with some." She raised her voice. "Boris! Come, Boris! I have cheese!"

He glanced at her. "He'll want to follow you home if you feed him cheese."

Abigail laughed. "Ridiculous! He'd run right back to you once Milo begins yipping at him for hours and hours every day."

He gave a quiet snort of disbelief. "Hours and hours?"

"Sometimes without end. You can see I've fled the house entirely to escape it."

"That's what sent you into the woods," he murmured. "I see."

"Milo?" Penelope had caught up again, by ducking under a low tree branch and skirting a large puddle. "Milo is the sweetest little creature in the world. He does not bark all day." She darted a sly glance at Mr. Vane. "My sister is determined to discover the lost grotto in these woods."

His gaze lingered on Abigail. "Indeed. I doubt it's in any condition to be explored by ladies."

"So you've seen it?" asked Penelope brightly, as if Abigail hadn't told her he had. "What's it like?"

"Dark," he said. "Cold. It's a cave."

"It's a grotto," Abigail corrected him. "Not a natural cave but one deliberately cut. Often they have lovely touches or some clever use. I read about one in Italy that served as a bathing chamber."

"It sounds scandalous," said Penelope with relish.

"It isn't." Mr. Vane's voice was tight.

"Then we could make it so. It can be our refuge from Mama. I'll smuggle down a bottle of sherry."

"First we need to find Boris," Abigail reminded her. She could just imagine what else her sister would smuggle to the grotto, if they ever found it.

Penelope met her eyes for a moment, then grinned. "Right. Boris," she called in the high, singsong voice she used with Milo. "Where are you, Boris?"

Mr. Vane made a sound like a strangled laugh.

"Boris!" Penelope wandered a little farther away. "Where are you, big, naughty, drooling dog? Abby has some cheese for you!" She kept calling and walking, keeping her back directly to them. Abigail said a silent thanks to her sister, even though Penelope sounded sillier and sillier, adding all manner of ridiculous endearments to her calls.

"Would Boris come if he heard her?" she asked.

Mr. Vane was watching Penelope disappear into the trees. "I have no idea."

"How do you summon him?"

"With a whistle." He pushed up a low-hanging branch so she could walk beneath it. "He'll come home eventually."

"You must be worried, or you wouldn't have come to look for him." She tilted her head to steal a glance at his face. "I'm surprised to meet you today. You did vow to avoid the woods at all times."

His mouth quirked. "Did I? I don't recall that. Part of it lies on my property, you know."

A faint frown touched her brow as she tried to remember his exact words. Perhaps he hadn't actually said he would avoid the woods, but he had certainly implied it. The frown lifted. She had warned him to avoid the woods if he didn't want to see her. If he hadn't done that, he didn't really want to avoid her.

"Do you share your sister's nefarious plans for the grotto, if you should find it?" he asked.

Abigail laughed. "I don't think she's truly interested in the grotto. Penelope is bored in Richmond. Her plans for diversion grow more shocking and more fantastical with each day she doesn't have a more intriguing scandal to discuss."

She could feel his measuring gaze on her for a long minute. "I'm sure she'll find some scandal in Richmond if she listens hard enough."

"Oh! She's already heard one about you," said Abigail airily.

"No doubt," he muttered grimly. "There are plenty to choose from."

"Indeed."

"Now you see why I warned you."

She stopped and waited until he also stopped walking and faced her. "I prefer to form my own opinion of a man's character, thank you, not swallow others' ridiculous notions whole. As does my sister, and the rest of my family," she added as he looked unimpressed. "You're not the only one people talk about, you know. If one believes the scandalmongers in London, my father is a jumped-up parvenu who made his fortune through illicit business dealings. My sister and I are nouveau riche heiresses out for the blood—and marriage proposals—of highborn gentlemen, through any means necessary." She raised her brows at his expression. "I will understand if you want to disavow our acquaintance."

Slowly, almost imperceptibly, his mouth softened. The cool distance in his gaze faded, and he regarded her with grudging amusement. "You're a difficult woman to dissuade, Miss Weston."

"On the contrary," she protested. "I'm entirely susceptible to reason and logic. I have a great weakness for appeals to justice and fairness, and I daresay I could pardon almost any act committed by a parent in defense of his child. It's merely wild rumor and gossip that I treat with suspicion."

He stared at her with narrowed eyes. Abigail's heart thumped hard against her ribs. In the distance, she could still hear Penelope calling for Boris, but otherwise it was just the two of them, she and Mr. Vane, alone in the woods. "I've never met your like, Miss Weston."

"I hope that doesn't make you want to flee in terror." She put her head to one side with a little smile.

His gaze drifted downward, slowly, tracing every inch of her figure until Abigail blushed. "No."

"Oh. Well . . . good," she said, having trouble remembering exactly what she'd said.

His eyes seemed to grow darker. "You might not say that if you knew what it does make me want."

This time her breath did stop in her chest, even as her heart seemed to have been jolted to thump at twice its normal pace. "Why? What do you want?"

His mouth curved. Not in a sweet, lighthearted way, but in a way that could only be called seductive. His eyes had grown as dark as a moonless midnight sky, and even though he hadn't moved an inch, Abigail could swear he was somehow much closer to her. "Many things I cannot have."

"Don't we all!" She managed a shaky laugh. "I wish my hair was blond, like my sister's. I wish my eyes were any color at all—green, blue, brown, even black."

"You're wrong to wish for those things. Never wish your hair was blond; such a pale insipid shade would never do you justice. You glow with passion and joy, as rich and warm as your hair." He reached out, and with one sharp tug, loosened her bonnet ribbons and pushed the hat to hang down her back so he could touch her hair. "Never wish your eyes were blue or brown." His thumb brushed over her cheekbone as he studied her face. "They are as fresh and clear as a new dawn, filled with promise and hope. You're perfect as you are." Abigail tilted forward, expecting a kiss—yearning for a kiss—but he stepped backward instead, giving her an almost physical start. She had been so focused on him, held so immobile by his burning gaze, she felt unsteady and disoriented without it. "We're not making very good progress looking for Boris."

"You said you weren't worried about him!" She scrambled to catch up as he strode onward without another glance at her.

"I'm not, but you were."

"Oh—well—I don't want him to be lost or hurt . . ."

"Boris is more than capable of finding his way home," he said. "He knows these woods as well as any creature who dwells in them."

"If you're not worried at all, then why were you in the woods looking for him?" She could barely keep up, he was moving so briskly. Did he regret what he'd said? If he didn't, how he could practically sprint away from her?

"You make an excellent point, Miss Weston. I should return home at once and leave you and your sister to an uninterrupted stroll. Forgive me." His eyes flashed her way as he touched the brim of his hat.

"Well, that's a fine thanks, after we both offered to help find your dog." She stopped, clutching one hand to her side as her lungs heaved. "Good day, Mr. Vane."

He continued a few more steps before he, too, stopped. For a moment he stood motionless, then he turned and walked back toward her, not quickly as before, but a deliberate prowl. Abigail held her ground and waited, keeping her chin up. She didn't shy away from his gaze, even though he looked almost angry.

"You ask what I want," he said, his voice low and even. "Very well. I want to walk normally again. I'd give anything for two good legs." He shifted his weight to prop the heel of his left boot on a nearby stump. "Instead I've got a shattered knee that aches in every heavy rain and betrays me at odd moments, sending me to the ground like a true cripple. I will never be able to walk without a cane again, nor dance with a woman, nor climb a tree, nor ride a horse comfortably."

She stared at his wounded knee, her lips parted in dismay. "Oh . . ."

He put one finger on her lips. "I also want my land back. My father sold it for a pittance and everyone agrees the sale was legal, even though he was mad as a hatter at the time. I want my mother's grave to be on my property."

Abigail gasped. "You cannot repurchase even that part?"

His smile was bitter. "Even if the buyer would sell it back to me, I haven't got the funds."

She bit her lip. That was terrible. What comfort could one offer in the face of that?

He put his foot back on the ground and took a step toward her. Abigail had to tip back her head to meet his eyes. "And the last thing I want is something I can never have."

She wet her lips nervously. His eyes tracked the motion. "What is that?"

He just smiled that twisted smile again. "It doesn't matter. I've accepted my lot. You should believe some of what they say about me in town; I'm no noble hero."

"Really?" She arched one brow. "Your father went mad and ran naked through the streets of Richmond? You killed your father? Your dog is a witch's familiar?"

"A witch's—?" He broke off and shook his head. "I hadn't heard that one. Boris is an ordinary dog."

"Of course he is! Rumor is so ridiculous. I never believe half of what I hear." She hurried after him as he started walking again, but at a normal speed this time.

"You should believe more. My father really did run mad," he told her. "He regularly ran through these woods, and even into town, wearing only his nightshirt—if he wore anything at all. He refused to bathe or eat for weeks at a time, he refused to have his hair or nails cut, he looked like a wild beast. I didn't kill him, even though he begged me to." He slanted a challenging glance at her. "I'm sure they also told you I'm going as mad as he was. You can add my good name to the list of my hopeless desires."

"You're not mad at all." She rolled her eyes. "Aggravating, perhaps."

"Then why are you still speaking to me?"

Abigail bit back the tart reply that leapt to her lips. He was trying to chase her away, but the way he'd looked at her a few minutes ago, when she asked what he wanted, tormented her. The way he'd touched her face resonated deep inside her. "Because I like you," she said softly. "I like talking to you, even when you're telling me to run away from you. You look at me as if—"

This time he stopped so suddenly, she ran into him.

Instinctively she clutched at his shoulder, and his arm went around her waist to catch her. Abigail's eyes grew wide as she stared up at him. His eyes were no longer hard and angry, but dark with raw longing. "As if I want you?" he asked, not making any effort to release her. "I do. I came into the woods today because I wanted to see you, even though I said I wouldn't—even though I know I shouldn't. I want you in every wicked way a man can want a woman. And if I had you, I could show you many, many more than fifty ways to sin."

Her eyes had grown wide at his first words, but she froze in shock at the last bit. "What?" she squeaked.

"You know what I mean," he murmured. His hand moved up her back, his fingers spread wide to hold her to him. "The pamphlet you bought in Mrs. Driscoll's shop."

"You *read* it?"

He nodded.

Abigail made a silent vow to murder her sister for this. She'd known it would land her in trouble somehow. "But—but—why did *you* buy it?" She really wished she could look away, but her wits—and her will—seemed to have gone missing.

"Because you bewitched me, and I wanted to know you, even if just what you read." He wound a stray wisp of hair around his finger before smoothing it back from her temple. "Why did *you* buy it?"

Abigail's heart was beating a tocsin against her breastbone. It was tempting to blame it on her sister, but she'd found that issue so arousing . . . "Curiosity," she finally whispered.

Something flared in his eyes. "Indeed. You torment me, Miss Weston. Was your curiosity . . . sated?"

A tide of heat rolled through her, igniting her skin from her toes to the top of her head. Abigail swayed, lowering her eyes to hide her thoughts as much as to avoid his searing gaze. "It—it was illuminating," she stammered. "Educational."

"Sufficient to quench your hunger . . . for knowledge?"

He knew. She could hear the thread of amusement in his tone. He knew she'd read it and reread it for the sheer wickedness it portrayed. Lady Constance's lover had come to her in the darkness, blindfolded her, and instructed her how to touch her own body for her pleasure while he watched. Abigail was sure her thoughts were written on her face as she recalled every sinful way Constance had caressed herself—and how she had done the same, in the privacy of her bed. She prayed he never knew that she had thought of him while she did it. "Partly," she whispered.

He only held her tighter. "Read it again," he whispered, his lips against her ear. "Tonight in your bed. Put your hands on yourself and see if Lady Constance had the right of it."

A screech echoed through the woods.

"Penelope!" she gasped as Mr. Vane bolted past her. She took off running after him, grabbing up her skirts in one hand as her basket swung wildly on her other arm and her bonnet bounced on her back. For a moment real panic seized her; she'd completely forgotten about her sister, who was far more at home in a modern city than in the woods. Penelope could be injured or trapped. But as she crashed through the bracken toward the sounds of her sister's voice, she realized it was cursing and not real cries for help. She slowed her pace a little as Mr. Vane tore on ahead. For a man who called himself a cripple, he could move astonishingly fast. He vaulted over a dead tree and disappeared around a thicket, running with only a slight limp. By the time Abigail caught up to him, nearly down a slope thick with dead leaves, she was just in time to see him help Penelope out of a thick swamp of mud. From the looks of her skirts, Penelope had fallen on her knees in it, and she gave Abigail a scalding look as she staggered up the hillock that must have tripped her.

"The dog is probably better able to survive in the woods than I am," she said through her teeth.

Relieved that her sister wasn't trapped or injured, Abigail nodded.

Mr. Vane tramped up the slope, his boots covered in mud to the ankle. "Are you hurt, Miss Penelope?"

Penelope grimly surveyed her skirt. "Yes, I believe I am. Grievously. Abby will have to bring me tea and cake for several days while I recover. And something to read, as I may be confined to my bed."

"Of course," Abigail murmured, knowing what her sister meant.

Penelope glanced between them. "I'm going home now." Without waiting for a reply from either, she started off, holding her muddy skirts wide. Her slippers squished with every step.

Abigail hesitated. She wished Penelope hadn't screamed when she had, before he could have said just what he did want, but now the moment had passed. Perhaps he would have said that he didn't really want her, that he was in love with Lady Samantha. Perhaps he wanted her, but only the way Lady Constance's lovers did: wanton and willing but only for one night. Surely if he felt anything else, he would say so—and he hadn't. Perhaps she was just a fool. "Thank you for helping my sister, Mr. Vane. I'm sorry we interrupted your search for Boris. I hope you find him soon." She ducked her head and started to go.

"Miss Weston." His voice was low, but she stopped at once. "Forgive me." Cautiously Abigail turned around. His expression was still unreadable, but the heat was gone from his voice. "I shouldn't have said those things to you."

She blushed. "Oh. I-I've been impertinent to you, too."

One corner of his mouth crooked. "Why do you think I like you?" She blinked in hopeful confusion. He hesitated, his gaze dark and probing. "Do you truly want to see the old grotto?"

She nodded.

This time it was a real, though slight, smile that curved his mouth, the same expression that had so entranced her in the bookshop. "Meet me at the end of the Fragrant Walk tomorrow at two o'clock."

Abigail gasped. "You'll show me?"

"You shouldn't endanger the rest of your family hunting for it."

She was startled into a laugh, and his reluctant smile grew a little bit. Oh, he was definitely handsome when he smiled. "Until tomorrow, Miss Weston." He touched the brim of his hat, and was still smiling when she finally tore her eyes away and hurried after her sister.

Sebastian watched until she vanished into the trees and he could no longer hear her footsteps. God above. He wasn't sure if he'd just been offered a new chance at happiness, or an insidious opportunity to ruin himself for good.

Either way, he was going to see Abigail Weston again tomorrow, and he couldn't bring himself to regret it.

He limped back through the woods to where he'd dropped his cane. He stooped to pick it up and could swear her perfume still lingered in the air. He set the cane against his injured leg and headed for home, hardly aware of the ache in his knee after the mad dash into the mud. It had felt good to drop the cane and just run, not tensing with each step in anticipation of pain. He'd pay for it later, but for now he felt almost like his old self, able to help a woman in distress the way a gentleman should.

And it had made Abigail look at him with gratitude and respect, which was almost as appealing as when she stared up at him with that arousing combination of desire and embarrassment. He wondered if she would do as he dared her to do, and reread *50 Ways to Sin*. He wondered who she would imagine watching her as she pleasured herself . . .

He took an uneven breath. God damn him for a fool. As if he didn't have enough torment already.

He headed toward home. At the edge of the trees, just before he emerged onto the grassy slope leading up to Montrose Hill, he put his fingers in his mouth and gave a piercing whistle. Boris had been a convenient excuse; the moment Mrs. Jones remarked that the dog was still out, Sebastian had put on his hat and headed for the woods. Avoiding Abigail Weston hadn't put an end to his fascination—no, it had made it stronger. In the few days since he'd seen her last, he'd been driven half mad by wondering about her. If her interest would fade when she heard confirmation of the rumors about him. If her professed desire to find the grotto was just a taunt. If he could possibly keep himself away from her for long.

The answer to all those questions was obviously no.

A few minutes later Boris trotted up to meet him. Sebastian gave the dog a good scratch behind the ears. Boris was wet and covered in mud, and Mrs. Jones would lock him in the stables until he dried, but for now his long tongue flopped happily out of his mouth. He must have had a grand time, and best of all, he hadn't shown himself too soon and interrupted anything.

"Good boy," Sebastian told the dog. "Well done."

Chapter 9

Penelope insisted on hearing details on the walk home. Abigail put her off—how much could have happened in the few minutes they walked alone?—but she was forced into admitting that Mr. Vane had offered to show her the grotto.

"Good," declared her sister. "I didn't want to go out there again."

"And you won't tell anyone," ordered Abigail.

Penelope scoffed. "As if I would ruin your *amour*! One of us should have something exciting happen. I'm rather disappointed it isn't to be me, but I shall endure . . . somehow . . ."

Abigail made a face and swatted her sister's arm. "Try to suffer in silence, please."

"Heartless creature," Penelope returned. "I sacrificed my dress to give you a moment alone with him! Look at this—it's ruined!"

"And now you will tell Mama you need another dress, so I shan't waste any tears over it."

Penelope huffed and grumbled all the way home, which gave Abigail time to think. And by the time they reached home, she had decided on a course of action.

She liked Sebastian Vane. Nothing about him made

her think he was dangerous or unhinged, rude or nefarious. The gossip about him was bad, it was true; but the very depths of depravity described made her doubt. If people would repeat that nonsense about a dog being a figment of witchcraft, they would repeat anything. There had to be more to the story about old Mr. Vane's disappearance, and thieves were everywhere. So far she knew with certainty only that Sebastian Vane was the son of a man who went mad, which seemed beyond his control and hardly something he would have chosen. He was wounded, but not crippled, in honorable military service. As for his financial state, he still owned a very lovely property in Richmond, which counted for something.

And he wanted her. Just remembering the scorching look in his eyes made her feel hot and restless. She wasn't ready to be as debauched as Lady Constance, but she was more than eager for Mr. Vane to show her some things. He could start with kissing, for one.

The next day Abigail took care not to meet anyone on her way out of the house. She was safe from Penelope—her sister was still pretending to favor her ankle—but she wasn't taking any chances. And meeting Papa or James would be even worse, so she watched and waited and chose her moment to escape, leaving only a vague word with her maid that she was going for a stroll and would be back by dinner.

She reached the Fragrant Walk but saw no sign of Mr. Vane. Her steps sped up as she went, expecting to see his tall, rangy figure around every bit of shrubbery. By the time she got to the end of the gravel, where the path diverged into a walk that led back toward the lawn and a narrower track that disappeared into the woods, her heart was pounding.

He wasn't there.

Perhaps she was early. Perhaps he was late. Perhaps he had changed his mind. She hitched her shawl more securely over her shoulders and headed down the path that wound through the trees, although a little more cautiously.

The woods grew thick very soon after leaving the well-raked walk. After ten yards she could barely see the sunlit lawn behind her. After twenty she bit her lip; she would feel like a great fool if she got lost in the woods. He had specifically said to meet him on the Fragrant Walk. If he arrived there ten minutes from now and she was nowhere to be seen, he might think she hadn't come. And if he didn't intend to arrive there at all today, well, wandering through the trees wouldn't make her feel any better.

She was about to turn around when a familiar dog came trotting easily through the thicket. It was Mr. Vane's dog, looking even larger and more fearsome than he had the other night. She stopped in her tracks as he came right up to her and sniffed the hem of her skirt. For all that she'd defended him yesterday, seeing the animal himself today was somewhat intimidating. He seemed calm and unthreatening, though, so she gingerly held out one hand.

"Have you brought cheese again?" Mr. Vane stepped out of the trees behind his beast. Abigail snatched back her hand. "I told you, Boris adores cheese."

"Does he?" She looked doubtfully at the big dog, who looked as though he could eat a whole leg of ham in one meal. Boris instantly sat, his tail thumping the ground, and gazed at her with attentive black eyes.

"Cheese is his favorite thing in the world. He'll be your willing slave for a morsel of it."

"He's a very fierce animal to be controlled by cheese."

Mr. Vane shrugged. "Every male has his weakness, I suppose."

"I hope so," she murmured, thinking more of the man than the dog. She extended her hand to Boris once more. With surprisingly gentleness, he sniffed her fingers and butted his head into her palm. Abigail patted him, and the dog panted and closed his eyes a little.

"You have made a friend," said Mr. Vane dryly.

She smiled, now scratching Boris's ears. He gave a whimper like a puppy and scooted closer to her, stretching his neck. His head came up almost to her bosom, and she scratched his ears a little nervously. His tongue flopped out of his mouth until it looked like he was grinning at her. "You're not as fierce as you look," she told him, relaxing a little.

"Certainly not when he senses the chance of getting some cheese."

"Well." She slanted a look at the dog's master. "I have got some in my pocket." She'd brought it on a whim.

He raised a brow. "Do you normally bring food when setting off to explore a grotto?"

She flipped one hand. "I've never seen one before, but it seemed best to be prepared. And, as you see, it's already paid off." Boris was now nearly lying across her feet, openly begging for more affection.

"Boris," said Mr. Vane, and in the blink of an eye the big dog scrambled to his feet and trotted back to his master. "Let's go," he said, sounding grim.

Abigail raised her chin. "Not if you don't want to show me. I've no interest in being a thorn in your side."

He gave her a searing glance, so intense the air seemed to shimmer for a moment between them. "A thorn you are not." He hesitated, his expression softening. "Forgive my lack of manners. I've not been much in company lately, and have quite forgotten how to speak to a lady." He put out one hand. "Will you still come?"

Her heart leapt. Holding up her skirt, she put her hand in his, and stepped off the dirt path into the bracken with him.

"Have you always known about the grotto?" she asked as they walked.

He brushed a thick fern out of the way with his cane. "Since I was a boy. Hart House was built for a royal mistress—one of Charles II's, I think—and as such was filled with all manner of follies and whimsies. The grotto was only one of them, but one of the few to survive the intervening decades."

"I understood Lady Burton had filled it in years ago."

"The woods did it for her." He turned his head from side to side, frowning at the trees. "Over there, I think. It's been a while since I visited it."

They pushed through a stand of beeches and skirted a muddy pond like the one Penelope had tumbled into. Squinting at the sky and trees from time to time, Mr. Vane led her around a patch of bramble bushes and down a gentle slope. Abigail couldn't see anything that looked remotely like a grotto. She had imagined a clearing, with an archway or a gate and stone steps leading into a cleft in the ground, perhaps with a stream running down the middle: something dramatic and worthy of its mystical name. Instead they were in a thick spot of forest, shaded by the canopy of trees overhead and surrounded by overgrown shrubbery running rampant over a small rise. Wild harebells grew all around them. It was quiet and shady, but there was no sign of a cave when Mr. Vane finally stopped.

As if he could read her thoughts, he cocked one brow. "Disappointed?"

"Not at all!" She turned around, searching for any glimpse of the grotto. "I just—I just don't see it yet . . ."

"And yet you're less than ten feet from it." She peered at the ground as if it might erupt at her feet, and he shook his head. "It took me nearly ten years to discover it."

"I don't doubt it," she murmured. "But why did you let it disappear into the forest again?"

His expression turned wry as he unsheathed a large knife that had been strapped against his good leg. "Once I found it, my curiosity was satisfied; its elusiveness made it fascinating, and once it was no longer elusive, I was content to leave it as it was." He strode forward and began cutting at the vines and plants that covered a large boulder.

Abigail seated herself on a nearby fallen tree and watched as he worked. "Perhaps it will so move me, I'll be drawn back. Perhaps I'll restore it and care for it and come often, if it proves a refuge."

"Oh?" He took off his hat and tossed it onto a nearby bush. "Why would you need a refuge?"

His hair was brown, falling to his collar with a gentle wave. Abigail watched the few stray beams of sunlight dapple his head and shoulders as he bent down to rip out some sprawling plant. She followed his example and shed her own bonnet, placing it on the trunk beside her. "Why wouldn't I need a refuge?" she parried his question. "Who can say they never have need of a quiet, private place?"

"Who, indeed?" he muttered, lifting a fallen sapling and shoving it aside. "The grounds of Hart House offer no quiet place?"

"Not enough of one. No sooner do I find one than my sister is sure to invade it and pester me with some mad scheme or diversion; she's utterly bored in Richmond." While his back was turned, she took out the hunk of cheese, wrapped in cloth, from her pocket and broke off a small chunk for Boris, who lapped it from her fingertips gently and eagerly.

"Your sister was with you in the bookshop the other day. I presume she enjoys that better than the woods?"

Abigail pressed her lips together, remembering what Penelope had made her buy in the bookshop. "Yes."

"Is it a refuge from her you seek?"

"Sometimes." She felt bad impugning her sister, and fed Boris another morsel of cheese in atonement. "Not often. Penelope is the best sister in the world. But when she's bored, she can be a trifle . . ."

"Tiresome?" he suggested when she hesitated.

"Demanding."

He grunted, slashing a trailing vine from the path he was clearing. "So demanding she compels you to dig up a long-buried grotto?"

"I never demanded that. You offered," Abigail pointed out.

His dark eyes turned toward her. She tensed for him to argue, but he only slid his knife back into the sheath strapped at his hip. "So I did." He swept one arm to the side. "Your grotto, my lady."

She jumped to her feet and scanned the ground. "Where?"

"Come." He retrieved his cane—again she realized he'd set it aside without her noticing—and waved her to come closer. "The steps become visible only a moment before you fall headfirst down them."

She edged closer, finally spying the rough stone stair disappearing into the earth. Vines still rambled over the opening, but he had cleared away just enough to expose the top few steps. They must have been completely covered. "How did you ever discover it?"

"By falling headfirst down it one day. The vines appear solid, but if you walk on them . . ." He grimaced.

She took a cautious step down, and then another. "It seems as though the earth will swallow us up."

He stepped down behind her and put his hand at her back. "Don't worry. I'll make sure it doesn't." Together they went down, slowly and carefully. Mr. Vane pushed back the encroaching vines just enough to allow them to squeeze under, and when they reached the bottom, there was enough space to stand comfortably upright.

It was cool and dark, but remarkably dry. As her eyes adjusted, Abigail could make out the stone walls cutting down into the earth. Dry leaves crunched underfoot as she went forward one step, then another. Ahead of her was only darkness, thick and impenetrable. "We should have brought a torch," she said, starting as her voice echoed back at her. "We can hardly explore if we're blind."

"You didn't bring a candle?"

She glanced at him, but as it often was, his expression was neutral. "I didn't think of it," she confessed. She didn't add that she'd thought mostly of seeing him, and had presumed that if they found the grotto at all, it would only be after some considerable searching.

Mr. Vane gave a small shake of his head as he rummaged in his pocket. "You must think through all the consequences of your actions, Miss Weston." He drew out a short candle and a flint. "Grottos are dark places."

"I knew that."

When he had lit the candle, he handed it to her. The light of a single flame didn't illuminate very far, but against the absolute blackness of the grotto, it seemed brilliant. "Lead the way."

"How far does it go?" She took the candle carefully, avoiding a stream of wax that ran down the side. "Will we come out by the river if we just keep going?"

"I don't know. I never just kept going."

"Why not? I thought it was your childhood dream to discover it. How could you not explore every inch of it, once you found it?" she asked teasingly.

He ran one hand over his head. "I only found it the night before I left to join my regiment, bound for Spain in '11. I hadn't time that night to explore every inch, and later . . ." He shrugged.

Abigail hastily turned away. Later he had been wounded, occupied with an infirm parent, and then dogged by rumors of madness, murder, and theft. "Then we shall explore it now together," she said firmly, holding the light aloft and starting forward. "And if we locate any buried treasure, we will share it evenly."

"I would be content not to locate any wild animals."

She laughed, the sound ringing around them. "Won't Boris defend us?"

"Boris won't come down here. He prefers to remain above ground." He turned and looked up. "See?"

Abigail peered past him to see Boris watching from the top of the stairs. He showed no sign of following them, but sat with his head cocked to one side as if wondering what made them do something so foolish as descend into the earth. "I hope we won't need him."

She fancied Mr. Vane almost smiled for a moment. "I hope not, too."

Slowly they proceeded down the passage. After about ten feet it turned sharply to the left, and once around the turn the dim light from the opening vanished. With the light seemed to go the last trace of warmth as well, and Abigail shivered as she hiked her shawl over her shoulders.

"Are you cold?" murmured Mr. Vane, very close behind her.

"Not much. I think it was just the sunlight disappearing."

His eyes reflected the candle's flame. In the flickering light his face was imposing and forbidding, and Abigail's stomach twisted in on itself. She didn't really know him, but here she was exploring a cave with him in secret. "Don't be nervous," he said softly, as if he could read her thoughts. "I have a good sense of direction. I shan't let us get lost."

"I feel as though we should be unspooling a string behind us, to follow back."

The corner of his mouth crooked upward. "Have you brought a string?"

"No."

"Neither have I." He looked at her. "Shall we go back?"

With a deep breath, she shook her head and moved forward. Slowly they followed the passage as it turned and curved deeper into the ground—or so Abigail imagined. Her fears of getting lost faded, though, as there were no other passages branching to the sides, just the one they followed. The air grew cooler, scented with moist earth and moss. Every now and then a wisp of air rushed past them, making the flame dance, and once Abigail thought she heard the distant scurrying of tiny feet, although she never saw the creature.

"Why do you think you never found it when you were a boy?" she asked. His footsteps echoed louder than hers, as his boots scuffed the stone floor and his cane gave a soft tap with every step.

"Lack of focus, most likely. It didn't take much to distract us once we were deep in the woods."

"Us?"

He hesitated. "I wasn't the only boy in Richmond keen to discover the grotto. It was the object of many grandiose plans."

"Such as?" She wondered what he'd been like as a boy, before terrible things had happened to him.

"The usual pursuits of boys," he said vaguely. "Hiding from tutors, escaping punishment, and so on. Much like your sister mentioned yesterday, it seemed an ideal refuge, hidden in the woods and thought by most people to be long lost."

"But ten years! It must have seemed ridiculous that you would find it by accident, after spending all those years searching for it."

"We spent more of our time close to the river," he said. "The trees were better for climbing there."

"Of course." She laughed, until the candle flickered wildly. She stopped dead in her tracks.

"What's wrong?" He put his hand on her back and stepped in front of her, as if he could see better than she could what lay ahead.

"I thought the candle would go out," she whispered, staring at the dancing flame and willing it to stay lit.

For a moment they both remained motionless, mesmerized by the flame. "We should turn back," said Mr. Vane.

The flame steadied, and so did Abigail's nerve. She looked up at him. "Not yet. See? It's fine." The flame burned as brightly as ever. It was reflected in his dark eyes as he looked down at her, his hand still on her back, his arm still around her.

"As you wish." He let her go and swept out his arm, beckoning her to take the lead again. "Let us continue, then."

It seemed they had been walking forever, although Abigail thought that if their path were laid out above-ground and well lit, it would probably fit inside the dining room at Hart House. And still the darkness stretched ahead of them without end. She would never have admitted it aloud, but the grotto was proving a little disappointing. It was just a narrow passage under ground, as dark as sin and as cold as winter. She hadn't really expected it to hold a magnificent pool lined with mosaics and statues, as she'd seen in one illustration, but she had expected there to be something of interest. Who would simply dig a tunnel in the middle of a forest? Finally, just as she was beginning to wonder how deep it was—or if they ought to turn back—the grotto opened up. The ceiling rose above them, the walls expanded, and she realized they had come to a chamber. And there was something about the walls . . .

"Look," she gasped. "The walls are sparkling!"

Mr. Vane put out his hand. "Cut glass, embedded in the walls."

"Oh, if only we'd brought more candles!" Abigail held the lone light up, watching the flame dance and flicker in the thousands of shards of glass covering the walls. "What a marvel! Who would have guessed it from the surface?"

"Someone went to some trouble," he agreed.

"Well." She grinned. "It's a sort of buried treasure, I suppose."

He turned and looked at her. Again the candlelight caught his eyes. "Cut glass isn't a treasure."

"But the beauty it can present is." She moved the candle in an arc, smiling at the sparks that seemed to leap from the walls. It would be magnificent in the light of a dozen candles.

"Yes," he admitted.

"It's quite the most marvelous thing I've ever seen." She roamed around the chamber, holding the candle close to the walls to see the glass. "Goodness! How much effort must have gone into creating this room!"

"I agree." He didn't follow her, and when she turned around she could hardly see him. Outside the limited range of her candle, he was cloaked in shadow, his neck cloth and face ghostly in the dark.

She studied the sparkling glass. Each shard seemed to be set just so into the walls, creating a mosaic of color. "It makes one wonder why the grotto was allowed to fall into such disuse. Although I suppose it isn't very convenient to the house."

"I've noticed that when people want something enough, there is no inconvenience that cannot be overcome," he said after a moment.

She smiled. "True. I certainly shan't be put off visiting again." She continued walking around the room, following the wall and watching the flame's reflection leap from shard to shard. Every now and then she noticed some bits of silvered glass, mirroring the light of her candle better than the rest.

"So you've seen the mysterious grotto; are you ready to go home now?" he asked after she had gone all the way around the chamber.

It was so quiet and still, she could hear her own breath. She wasn't ready at all to leave. "So soon?"

He didn't move. "What else is there to do?"

She wanted to sit and study the walls. She wanted to spread a blanket on the floor and spend an hour here, teasing more of those elusive smiles from him. But there was no blanket, they had only one candle, and she suddenly felt unsure of herself.

"Miss Weston," he said when she didn't answer his question, "we should go. Before anything regrettable happens."

She wet her lips. "What do you plan to do that you might regret, Mr. Vane?"

The question seemed to check him. He turned away, tipping back his head to survey the ceiling, which seemed to be just as encrusted as the walls. "I never plan to do anything regarding you, and yet somehow something happens every time we meet."

"Surely you cannot regret this." She raised the candle high again. "Wouldn't you have explored the grotto earlier if you had known this might be here?"

Slowly he turned to face her again. "No."

"No?" she exclaimed in astonishment.

"It wouldn't have been the same."

"Yes, it would have," she protested. "I don't think anyone's touched it in decades—"

"It wouldn't have been the same," he repeated, "without you."

Abigail's heart leapt into her throat. She drew an unsteady breath, and the flame flickered as her fingers clenched around the candle.

"It's not safe to explore a cave alone," he went on, his voice still low. "Promise me you won't come again on your own."

"I want to see this room again, with more light . . ."

He hesitated, and seemed to retreat into reserve again. "I only asked that you promise not to come alone. Bring your sister, if you want, and a supply of lanterns." His words echoed as he headed back the way they had come, out of the chamber.

Abigail felt another pang of disappointment, but started after him. Even with the candle, she didn't want to be alone in the grotto. "Mr. Vane, wait," she called, just as another stray puff of air caught the candle flame and snuffed it out before she could shelter it. She froze, paralyzed by the swift plunge into absolute darkness. "Mr. Vane?" she said, her voice rising a little.

"I'm here." This time she heard his cane, tapping firmly on the floor. "Keep talking and don't move."

"I'm not very frightened of the dark, but this came on a little suddenly." Her eyes felt like they were turning inside out, she was staring so intently into the void. "And now it does seem as though we walked a very long way to get to this chamber, and how shall we find our way out without the candle?"

"We'll find our way out." His voice was as steady and matter-of-fact as ever, which calmed her nerves somewhat. She could hear his steps still, but because of the echo she had no idea if he was getting closer to her or farther away. Her own feet felt glued to the floor, as if to move would be to become irretrievably lost.

"Do you still have your flint? I hope we can relight the candle. Next time I shall bring a lantern, I swear!" She gave a shaky laugh.

"I still have the flint, right in my pocket."

"Thank goodness!" She tried to laugh, but it sounded more like a gasp of terror. "I knew we ought to have brought Boris. He could have led us out . . ."

He gave a soft tsk. "Boris would be useless. He would eat your cheese and run off to follow some scent."

"Truly?" Her skin was beginning to crawl. She imagined the ceiling of the chamber collapsing and entombing them both. Her parents would never know what had happened to her.

"Truly. He's also a little afraid of the dark." The soft tap of his cane sounded nearer, to Abigail's straining ears.

"Is he?" She gulped. "I couldn't blame him for being frightened of this darkness."

"Everything is exactly the same as it was when you could see," he said. "Close your eyes and you won't know it's dark."

"I don't see how I could forget." Her voice wavered.

"Close your eyes," he commanded softly. "Trust me."

She closed her eyes. "Where are you?"

"Getting nearer."

"How do you know?"

"Because I can hear your breathing. Put out your hands."

Reluctantly Abigail reached out in front of her, keeping her eyes tightly closed. She felt dizzy and off-balance, and when something hit her elbow, she would have staggered and fallen if he hadn't seized her arm and yanked her to him. Gasping in relief, she clutched at his coat and burrowed into his side, desperately happy not to be alone, even if they were still entombed in the pitch-black grotto.

Sebastian wrapped his arms around her and tried not to think how perfectly she fit against him. She was shaking like a leaf in a windstorm, and for a minute he just held her, letting his own pulse calm down. When the light had gone out, he'd cursed—and then he heard the panic in her voice, and cursed himself. What an idiot, bringing a young lady down into a cave without any forethought at all, not even a lantern that would remain lit. If he'd had an ounce of sense, they would be strolling along as before, the air between them humming with awareness but still separating them.

Now, though . . . nothing separated them. The hum had become a crackle of desire, at least in his head. He raised one hand to touch her hair and inhaled deeply of roses, the same scent of roses that drifted in his windows all summer from the overgrown flowers his mother had planted decades ago. Abigail Weston smelled dangerously of home.

Gradually her trembling lessened and then stopped. Sebastian made no effort to release her, and she didn't move. Against his will, the images from *50 Ways to Sin* drifted across his mind. Lady Constance had called the darkness very freeing, and she was right—it freed his imagination from all restraint and sense. He imagined kissing Abigail Weston until she forgot all about the darkness. He imagined letting his hands roam over every soft, silky inch of her skin until she begged for more. He imagined laying her down and making love to her, driving her wild with passion so that he wouldn't be the only one dying of desire . . .

"Mr. Vane," she whispered against his chest.

A tremor went through him; his whole body was taut and hard. "Sebastian," he said before he could think better of it. "No one calls me by name," he said in lame explanation. He couldn't possibly say that he just wanted to hear her say it.

He felt her indrawn breath. It pressed her bosom against his ribs. "Sebastian," she breathed, and he ground his teeth together. Not only bewitching eyes and perfect legs, but a soft, seductive voice. He wasn't going to hell for lusting after her; he was already in hell. "What should we do now?"

Almost unconsciously, his arm tightened around her. She didn't protest—in fact, she leaned a little more of her weight on him. He held her in his right arm, which was putting more burden on his wounded knee, but he didn't give a damn. He turned his head so his lips brushed her temple. "What do you want to do, Abigail?"

If she said she wanted to find the way out as quickly as possible, he would do it. He would let her go and get them out of this benighted grotto, and then go home and burn that wicked pamphlet that was making him think of so many other things they could do in the dark. In fact, he hoped she would say it, and save him from the temptation before him.

"The other day," she whispered. "In the woods. When you held me and told me to read that story again . . . I wondered . . . I thought for a moment that you might have been about to . . ."

"To kiss you?" he finished when she didn't. He felt the slight tremor that went through her. "Were you relieved or sorry that I didn't?"

For a long moment she was utterly still and silent. He let out his breath, slowly, telling himself he was glad she was relieved, even though his body didn't agree.

"Sorry," she said, the word barely audible.

That did it. He lifted her chin, brushing his thumb over her lips to assure his aim was true. "So was I," he murmured, and kissed her.

Despite being an outcast in Richmond, he hadn't quite been a monk, and before the war he'd been considered eligible. Still, it had been a long time since he'd kissed a woman in a meaningful way. And Abigail . . . suddenly it seemed as though he'd been waiting his entire life to kiss her.

She made a startled sound when he tipped her head, but she parted her lips and let him taste her, so sweet and hot he told himself he should stop at once. But it was as though his restraint and command of himself, once breached, began to crumble like dust. His cane clattered to the floor as he wrapped his other arm around her. She stretched up on her toes, holding tight to his coat, and slid her tongue over his. He shuddered at the invitation, innocent but bold. His hands drifted down her back, molding her to him, and instead of starting in shock, she sighed and arched her back. She was still kissing him, making the most arousing little moans a woman could make. Her fingers tugged at his hair. Rapidly losing his grip on conscious thought, Sebastian finally gave in to the screaming urges of his body. He cupped his hands around her hips and pulled her, hard, against his erection.

She gasped, clinging to his neck. His brain felt fevered; some devil was whispering in his ear of all the ways he could please both of them without actually taking her virginity. His hands burned to touch her skin. He flexed his spine, thrusting his hips against hers.

"Oh my," she gasped, her voice raspy against his throat. "This—this is what Lady Constance wrote of, isn't it?"

It shattered the spell. He jerked backward, keeping his hold on her elbows but now at arm's length. Every inch of him throbbed in frustration. Sebastian closed his eyes and struggled to regain his control.

"Sebastian?"

He flinched at his name, spoken so invitingly. He was probably leaving bruises on her arm, but he could barely move. "Partly," he said through clenched teeth.

"No," she whispered. "There's more, isn't there?"

Sebastian didn't say anything. The answer seemed obvious to him.

"Is it the same?" she asked in the same hushed, hesitant voice. "In the light?"

Christ above. He imagined making love to her in full daylight, her dark auburn hair streaming over her bare breasts. He imagined kissing his way up her legs, able to admire every bit of her. He imagined her eyes dark and smoky with passion as he brought her to climax, holding himself deep inside her the way Lady Constance described her lover's actions. How could a man blindfold her and miss that sight? "No," he managed to reply. "It's better when a man can see his lover, and feel her gaze upon him." His body spasmed at the thought. "I expect it is the same for a woman."

The silence seemed to echo more loudly than his words. "Oh," she said at last, her voice husky with desire. "Better than that . . . ?"

One hundred times better, he silently answered her. And one thousand times worse for him, if he couldn't rein in this craving. With one boot he felt around for his cane, stooping to collect it when it rattled on the stone floor. "Let's find our way out," he said, taking a firm grip on her hand and beginning a slow, steady search for the passage that would lead them out of this cursed cave.

"Are you angry?" she asked, a thread of bewilderment in her question.

"Only at myself."

"Why?" When he didn't answer, she pressed his hand. "I—I wanted you to kiss me," she murmured, as if he hadn't known that.

"That was more than a mere kiss."

"I know." This time he could hear the little smile, the subtle satisfaction of a woman who recognized a man's hunger for her. Instead of dashing cold water on his desire, it only made him want her more.

"Perhaps I ought not to say that, but I've read Lady Constance's stories, and I always wondered if they could possibly be true . . ." She fell silent for a moment. "Do you think I'm wicked for reading them?"

Good God in heaven, no. "Why would I think that?"

"Because . . . Well, because they're shameless and wicked."

"Passion? Pleasure?" He stopped and faced her, even though the darkness around them was still absolute. "I assure you, those are neither shameless nor wicked, so long as both parties are willing."

Her breath was quick and shallow. "Even if the lovers are not married?"

He closed his eyes. Of course he couldn't tell her marriage made no difference, that it was possible to have both passion and pleasure without ever coming in sight of a vicar. She was an heiress, destined to marry some fortunate fellow, and he hoped she was very happy in that marriage. "I wouldn't know. I've never been married."

"Neither have I," she said—unnecessarily. "But perhaps the shameless, wicked aspect makes it even more pleasurable."

He missed a step and almost fell over his own cane. "I'm sure it can be just as pleasurable in marriage."

"How can one assure that?"

He could hardly think. They were probably walking in circles in this glass-covered chamber, trapped by his inability to stop thinking about pleasure and wickedness and the fact that she was far more willing than she ought to be. Probably not as willing as Lady Constance, who really did seem to be shameless in her amours, but too willing for his weakened restraint. He told himself that if he ever did make love to Abigail Weston, he wanted it to be in a better spot than a cold, dark cave, because he wanted to see every little flicker of ecstasy cross her face. If only he hadn't read that damned story . . .

Of course, he would never make love to Abigail Weston.

"I take it that was but one of Lady Constance's adventures," he said to divert her. "*Fifty Ways to Sin* implies there are fifty stories."

"Oh—I suppose. I never thought of that. It first appeared this spring. You—you won't tell anyone I bought it, will you?"

He almost smiled. "Never."

"I was very surprised you bought it. I didn't think gentlemen much cared for the stories."

"I didn't know what it was when I bought it."

"Right," she said quickly, and cleared her throat. "Gentlemen in London think it's horrible. Constance's lovers all bear striking resemblances to men of town. Any man whose name is connected with them usually gets up in arms and issues a public denial."

The story he'd read had been lavishly complimentary of the man's ability and physical attributes. Sebastian thought most men would fancy being thought such masterful lovers. "What a brilliant bit of publicity that must be."

Her laugh sounded surprised. "I suppose it must be!"

His heart leapt. He'd made her laugh, and it filled him with unexpected exuberance. He almost turned and kissed her again, not strictly from desire this time but simply to share his delight in her happiness. In the nick of time he stopped himself; the effects of the first kiss still sizzled through his veins. If he kissed her again, he couldn't guarantee it would be brief or chaste. He tightened his grip on her hand and swept his cane in a wider arc, searching for the doorway. For both their sakes, he needed to get them out of here.

The cane caught. He prodded around, and realized they had reached the wall. Another few steps, and the wall turned a corner. He heaved a great sigh of relief. "Good news, Miss Weston: I have found the way out." He tugged on her hand and began walking with more purpose. "Mind the doorway."

Abigail's smile faded. As much as she wanted to get out of the pitch-black grotto, she also felt a perverse longing to stay. Now she knew what Constance had described in her last story. There was an intimacy and freedom in the darkness that one never had in the light. She doubted Sebastian would have kissed her if the candle hadn't gone out, and she knew she wouldn't have been able to ask him about passion and pleasure if she'd been able to see his face, and he hers. She'd admitted to her fondness for *50 Ways to Sin*, her craving for passion, her desperate curiosity about taking a lover, even outside of marriage, and he had been neither shocked nor horrified. What's more, as long as he held her, she wasn't afraid of the dark. Her fear had gone away almost as soon as he pulled her into his arms, comforting and protective.

And then there was the way he'd kissed her. That, Abigail sensed, was passion—not the flowery, extravagant sort that Lady Constance described, but real, raw passion.

Even though it felt they had walked an eternity to get to the glass chamber, now the passage seemed short and direct, and before long the blackness ahead of them lightened to gray. As the light grew stronger, so did Abigail's worry about what would happen aboveground. He hadn't said a word since telling her he'd discovered the way out of the grotto, and she didn't know how to prolong the intimacy of the darkness in the bright light of day—although she really wanted to.

He released her hand when the steps came into sight. He didn't look at her as he held the vines out of the way for her to climb out of the grotto. Boris raised his head as they emerged, and scrambled up from his nap to come lick Abigail's hand. She petted the big dog and covertly watched his master scrape the moss and cobwebs from his cane.

"Thank you," she said quietly.

He stabbed the cane into the dirt and reached up to retrieve his hat from the bush where he'd left it. "Don't visit the grotto alone, Miss Weston. I hope you see it's not entirely safe." The softer side of him was gone, it seemed. His voice was once more flat and cool, and the hat hid his face from view.

"I think it might be safer for my peace of mind, alone," she murmured. She picked up her bonnet and slipped Boris the last bite of cheese from her pocket. He wagged his tail and gave a playful woof before bounding away down a path. "Will you tell me the truth about something?"

"Yes."

"Do you want me to leave you in peace?"

He turned, watching his dog run away. "I don't see how you can."

"I won't walk in the woods anymore, if you don't want to see me again."

She could just see the corner of his mouth turn upward, but when he spoke, his voice was even and controlled. "That would hardly leave me any peace. You know I want to see you again."

"Then why—" she began, but he had not finished.

"I've already admitted I want you. I've already told you I want to show you every manner of sin Lady Constance writes of, and then some." He finally faced her, and the dark hunger in his eyes made her skin heat. "But I'm trying to exercise some honor where you are concerned. Try not to make it more difficult than it already is."

All she could think about was his lips on hers, the way he held her, the feel of his body, thrumming with tightly-leashed strength, hard and taut against hers. She was as wicked as Constance. "Then why won't you call on me?"

"And say what?" He arched one brow. "Shall we sit in your mother's drawing room and discuss the latest escapades of the notorious Constance?"

She flushed. "Obviously not . . ."

"Would we pick up where we left off in the grotto?" His eyes drifted down, and Abigail felt it like a physical caress on her bosom. It made her want to fling herself at him, and it made her angry.

She shook her head, yanking on her bonnet and

tying the ribbons with jerky motions. "I see. You don't mind kissing me in the grotto, but you can't be bothered to call on me like a gentleman. You don't want to marry me, just to have a little fun."

"Your father would never consent."

"Did you ask him already?" she asked in exaggerated surprise. "He didn't say a word to me!"

A muscle twitched in his jaw. "Don't be ridiculous."

"Why is it ridiculous?"

For a moment she thought he would reply with just as much anger and feeling. His eyes flashed, and his fingers flexed around the head of his cane. But then, like a lamp being turned down, the heat and hunger drained from his face. "Because you're not for me," he said gently. "No matter how much I want you, I know I can't have you—just like a sound knee or a restored estate. You deserve better. And so I ought not to have kissed you, or even said anything."

"So you regret kissing me?" She could barely form the words, choking on dismay.

He hesitated. "No."

She nodded, mortified and furious at once. Part of her wanted to beg him to kiss her again, the future be damned, but the rest of her wanted more—not just a brief, forbidden taste of passion, but love, true and lasting. "Thank you, Mr. Vane. I understand now. You wanted those other things, and tried to get them even though you knew you might fail. I suppose that tells me something."

"It's not the same," he retorted.

"No, not at all." She glared at him. "You don't get to decide what I deserve. I *would* like you to show me passion—and I know you could. But I want more than that."

She turned on her heel and stormed away, waiting—hoping—for him to call after her, to stop her, to apologize, to snatch her into his arms for another scorching kiss. And she heard . . . nothing.

When she finally whirled around, seething with frustration and ready to ring a peal over his head, he was gone.

Chapter 10

It rained the next day, which perfectly suited Sebastian's mood. He would have snarled at the sun if it had risen as usual, tempting him to take his usual walk into the woods. As the rain beat down upon the roof and streaked the windows, he could at least comfort himself that she wouldn't be in the woods, either. But then, after her last furious words to him at the grotto, perhaps she would never walk there again.

He glared at the crackling fire and brooded over it. On one hand, he knew he was right to scare Abigail Weston away. There were numerous reasons, and he knew each and every one was sound. She was an heiress; he was deep in debt. She had loving and attentive parents who would want to see her well matched in marriage; he was rumored to be as mad as his lunatic father had been, a murderer and a thief. She was a beauty; he was a cripple. She had a tender heart and a warm spirit that would make her attractive to any man; he was too far gone in his lonely ways to make any woman happy. He told himself that even if he tried to get her, he would fail, and yet . . .

There was that spark that seemed to leap between them. It seemed to have caught something long-forgotten inside him and set it smoldering, and he wasn't even sure he wanted to put it out again.

He shifted in his seat with a sigh, causing Boris to raise his head from the floor and thump his tail hopefully. Boris wasn't put off by the rain. Boris would love a good run through the trees, and if by some chance he met Miss Weston, he'd greet her like his long-lost love and be petted and scratched until he fell on the ground in an exaltation of puppy love. Sebastian's mouth thinned. His dog knew how to treat a lady and win her favor better than he did. "We're not going out today," he said sternly. Boris scrambled to his feet and gave a low woof, butting his head against Sebastian's hand. He trotted to the door and back, then again when Sebastian didn't get up, making the low whine that was apparently a dog's way of pleading. Boris was restless and unhappy inside.

Just the way his master felt.

"Fine." He lurched out of his chair and limped through the house, throwing the door open. Boris bounded out eagerly, then turned to wait for him. "Go on," he told the dog with a wave of his hand. "She won't be there."

The dog's tail drooped, but he turned and headed across the lawn, heedless of the rain.

For a moment he hovered on the brink of following. Abigail wouldn't be in the woods, of course, but he could walk off some of the simmering discontent that had plagued him all day. He knew he'd been harsh to her, no matter that he told himself it had been for a good reason. If only the damned candle hadn't gone out . . .

He shut the door and went up the stairs to his bedchamber. Tucked between the pages of *The Nautical*

Almanac was the troublesome pamphlet. *Fifty Ways to Sin*, it promised; a quick look at the front indicated this was issue number twenty-five. What else had Lady Constance of the exceedingly loose morals got up to? Were her other adventures as risqué as this one? Whatever they were, Abigail found them enthralling—and that, unfortunately, made him enthralled as well.

The wisest course would be to burn the pamphlet at once, but after a moment he slowly flipped the front page open. This time one sentence leapt out at him—not a sentence describing the lascivious acts her mystery lover urged upon her, but one that simply illuminated her feelings: "I had overlooked one source of variety, and that was surprise," she wrote. "It would be impossible to convey the depths of my fascination . . ."

He stared at the window. Hart House was hidden by the trees, down the hill to the east. Abigail had asked him to call on her. If he wanted to see her again, that was the easiest way to do it. But after the way he had behaved yesterday, he couldn't just present himself on the doorstep. He had to make it up to her . . . somehow.

"**I** vow it rains more in Richmond than it does in London."

Normally Abigail would have laughed at her sister's grumbling. Today she found herself annoyed. "It does not."

"How many days since we came here has it rained?" Penelope flung herself onto the chaise and sulked.

"Two or three." Abigail trailed the newest toy for

Milo, a ball of rags tied to a string, which was in turn tied to a stick, around the settee. The puppy lowered his chin, wiggled his tail, and pounced on the clump of rags. Abigail let him tear at it with his teeth for a minute before twitching it away. Milo jumped to his feet and watched it roll away before pouncing again. He showed no signs of growing tired of the game, and as there was nothing else to do, Abigail kept flicking the toy around.

Even so, she didn't resent the rain. If it hadn't rained, she would have been forced to decide if she wanted to walk to the grotto again. When she had returned home after the infuriating parting from Sebastian—Mr. Vane—she'd been all but resolved to make daily visits to the grotto, equipped with lanterns and blankets and picnic lunches. She would invite her sister. She would clear a path to its entrance. She would tell people she had found it herself, and conduct tours of the glass chamber for everyone in Richmond until her memory of what happened there had been completely obliterated.

Fortunately the rain gave her temper time to cool. It didn't enlighten her about the motives or desires of their neighbor, but it allowed her to decide against revealing the grotto. Even if she never laid eyes on Sebastian   Mr. Vane, she reminded herself in aggravation—ever again, she could still keep the grotto as her own secret refuge. One never knew when a secret might be useful, and it was doubtful he would go near it again, if he could be believed. And this time she wanted to believe him; if he could still refuse to call on her after what had happened yesterday, he wasn't the sort of man she wanted. If he could kiss her—her stomach tightened—as passionately as that, but not exert any effort to court her or

even to see her again, he was a rake and a devil and she
wanted no part of him.

Even if it made her want to cry.

Milo, who had been stalking the ball of rags from
beneath the furniture, gave a sharp bark and pounced.
This time Abigail let him drag the toy under the sofa,
where he began ripping at the cloth with little growls
of delight.

She walked to the tall French windows and gazed
out at the lawn. The rain wasn't torrential, but it had
been coming down since before dawn, and the garden
was thoroughly drenched. No one would be out walking today.

Unwillingly her eyes strayed toward the wood. He
admitted he wanted to see her. She wondered if he
would regret his harsh words, and then she wondered
why she was making herself sad and angry over a man.
Abigail thought of herself as a very sensible girl. Unlike
Penelope, who loved drama and passion of all kinds,
Abigail had secretly prided herself on being more sane
than her sister. She would never pine for a man who
didn't treat her properly, she'd told herself—and now
she was doing just that.

"Idiot," she whispered, closing her eyes tightly to
keep any trace of moisture from leaking out. She must
feel this way because Sebastian—Mr. Vane, curse
him—had given her her first real kiss, the first kiss that
made her burn and ache for more. No doubt she would
have been more shocked than aroused by that kiss if
she hadn't spent so much time reading those wicked,
fanciful stories by Lady Constance, who was surely
the greatest liar in the world. They had weakened her
mind until his mysterious manner and history couldn't
fail to provoke her curiosity. Being unbearably attractive also helped him, she granted, and the fact that she

had first met him when he saved her from being torn to shreds by the bramble bushes must have influenced her perception of him. Really, it was all just a lot of coincidence and happenstance that made her think she was attracted to him. She simply needed to meet more gentlemen, and she would forget about the lonely, wounded man who had shown her the grotto and held her when the candle went out. Oh yes—the candle was also to blame, because none of this would have happened if it had just stayed lit.

That final thought brought a reluctant smile to her lips. She truly was an idiot, blaming everything in sight for her dark mood. So she'd let herself become infatuated with the wrong man; it had happened to other young ladies, and Abigail was sure they had all survived it. So would she, and in a few days or weeks, this would all seem like the height of self-indulgence.

She turned away from the window. "It will make the day pleasanter if we do something."

Penelope glared at her. "What is there to do? I can't even walk around the house." Penelope had made the mistake of saying her ankle hurt after her tumble into the mud the other day. Her intention had probably been to make Abigail feel profusely sorry for her, but Mama had overheard and made her wrap it up, and promise not to walk on it for a few days.

"I could read to you," Abigail offered. She had barely read a page of her new novel, thanks to the disturbing influence of a certain neighbor.

Penelope rolled her eyes. "How sad that neither of us can think of anything more interesting to do than read—without having anything delicious to read."

Abigail lifted one shoulder. "I like to read, and not just naughty stories. I shall take myself away to do it without disturbing you."

"Wait," growled her sister. "Very well, you may read to me." She leaned back on the sofa with a martyred expression, propping her wrapped foot on a cushion.

Milo scrambled from beneath the sofa and stood at attention in the middle of the room. His head cocked to one side as he listened. Then he gave a sharp yip and ran to the door, tail wagging. Abigail expected someone to come in, but the door remained closed, and Milo continued barking, dancing expectantly in circles.

"Milo, be quiet, silly dog!" Penelope leaned over and fished his toy out from under the sofa. She swished the stick from side to side, making the bundle of rags leap about. "Come chase it, puppy."

He ignored her, continuing his anxious prancing before the door. Abigail went to let the dog out. He'd left a wet spot on the dining room carpet the other day, and now everyone was under strict orders to let him outside the moment he gave any sign of distress. From the way Papa glared at Milo, Abigail thought he might be regretting his gift. The little dog was adorable and very sweet, but far more work than anyone had expected.

Before she got to the door, though, it opened to reveal the butler. Milo bolted between his feet toward the hall, yipping shrilly. Thomson merely watched him go, then turned to Abigail. "This was just delivered for you, Miss Weston."

Surprised, she took the small package he held out. It was wrapped in paper and tied with a string, but bore no clue to the sender or the contents, only her name written on the front. "Thank you, Thomson. Would you make certain Milo doesn't escape into the rain? I don't think anyone wants to chase after him today."

"Indeed not, ma'am," he said with a commiserating glance. He closed the door, and Abigail heard him calling to a footman to catch the dog, whose barks echoed through the hall.

"What is it?" Penelope asked.

"I've no idea." She picked at the string until it came loose, and unwrapped the paper. The outer layer came off, revealing a note atop yet another paper-wrapped item. From the weight and feel of it, Abigail guessed it was a book. Mystified, she unfolded the note.

"Well?" demanded her sister. "Tell me, or I shall rip it from your hands and read it myself!"

"It's from Mr. Vane," she said softly, reading the note aloud. " 'My dear Miss Weston, Allow me to express my deepest apologies for what transpired in the woods the other day. I have worried for your sister's health ever since her fall, and I hope she suffered no lasting harm.' "

"Well, that's very kind of him," exclaimed Penelope, gratified that someone appreciated her suffering. "What a gentleman!"

" 'In the event that she may be confined to bed, as she feared, I hope you will accept the enclosed as a way to pass the time until she is well again,' " she read on. " 'And I hope the additional enclosure may offer—' " She stopped abruptly at the next words.

"What?" Penelope vaulted off the sofa and stumped over to her side.

"The rest is just for me," she mumbled, shoving the note into her pocket. Her heart slammed into her ribs as she tore off the last layer of paper. It was a book, an old but well-kept one. *The Children of the Abbey* was printed on the front in old-fashioned lettering.

"He knows you well," said Penelope, distinctly unimpressed. "A book."

Abigail ignored her. After a swift glance at the door

to make certain it was securely closed, she let the book fall open to the spot where something had been hidden between the pages. Penelope sucked in her breath, and for a moment they just stared.

"It's a new one," whispered Penelope in hushed excitement. "Look: issue twenty-six."

Abigail snapped the book closed and clutched it to her chest. "No one must know. Promise me, Pen!"

"What sort of idiot do you take me for?" Penelope demanded. "Why did he send it to you?"

Her face felt hot. "To *us*. Because he saw me buy it in town, most likely. He might not even know what it is . . ."

Penelope gave her such an incredulous look, Abigail had to turn away for fear her guilt would be obvious. But all Penelope said was, "If it's to *us*, I should get to read it, too."

"Of course." Abigail was so distracted she pulled out the pamphlet and handed it over. "You must give it back later," she added.

"Naturally!" In a flash, Penelope hid it under her shawl. "I'll go hide it right now." She opened the door and peered out, then slipped into the corridor.

Abigail pushed the door shut and retreated to the window. Her hands trembled as she took out the crumpled note and smoothed it, angling her back to the door for additional privacy.

"I hope the additional enclosure may offer some pleasure to you as well, more so than you found in the grotto," Sebastian wrote. "Your parting words were bitter to me, all the more so for being true. You were right to disdain me, and I hope this may supply some small atonement.

"I cannot pretend to be the gentleman you think I

am, nor can I regret what occurred in the glass chamber. However, I have ever since regretted everything I said to provoke your anger, along with my command that you avoid the grotto. I had no right to do that, and hope you will find it more to your liking the next time you visit. Your servant, S. Vane."

Her heart was pounding by the time she reached the ending. He was sorry! Well, not entirely—not for kissing her—but for what he'd said at the end. And he invited her to visit the grotto again, although with no mention of whether he would meet her there.

She considered it a moment. He admitted he wanted to see her. He made no secret of the fact that he wasn't going to call on her. Therefore, logically, he would meet her at the grotto. Of course, he hadn't said when . . .

She traced one finger over his swooping signature, then opened the book. Why had he sent her this? It was old, at least thirty years, with a faint scent of dust about it, but the pages were still smooth and whole. It was a Gothic romance from Minerva Press, rife with sighs and swoons and lamentations of all the ills endured by the characters. Abigail's lips curved softly as she read snippets from a few pages. It was the perfect sort of book for a day like this, neither serious nor deep.

She started to close the book, and noticed something written on the flyleaf. The ink was faded, but by raising the book to her face she was able to make it out: Eleanor Vane, it read in a light, delicate handwriting.

For a moment she didn't move. It must have been his mother's book. She had heard a dozen rumors about his father, but not one word of a mother. And yet here was her book, obviously well-preserved and saved for many years . . . until he gave it to her.

Something else occurred to her then. She hid the

note inside the book and rushed into the hall. A footman was just coming back into the house, grim-faced and holding a dripping Milo under one arm. Apparently their attempts to catch him before he got out had been unsuccessful. The butler was waiting with a lead in hand, eyeing the dog with resignation even as the puppy wriggled to get down.

"Thomson," Abigail asked, "who delivered the package you just brought in?"

"Mr. Vane did, Miss Weston."

"Himself?" she exclaimed. "You should have bade him come in and get dry!"

"I did, ma'am, but he refused. Merely tipped his hat and walked away."

She flew to the window and peered down the lane that led toward Montrose Hill. It was deserted, the tree branches bowed low, their leaves sodden clumps. She pressed the book to her chest. To get *50 Ways to Sin*, he must have gone into town. Then he had walked two miles to Hart House, in the rain, to bring it to her, with a note apologizing for what he'd said.

She smiled at the rain, and went upstairs to read. Not just *The Children of the Abbey*—although she intended to read that, too—but everything else he had sent her.

Chapter 11

Two days later the rain blew away, leaving the day fresh and bright. At breakfast, Mama declared that she simply had to get out of the house, and meant to go to London to visit her favorite shops. Penelope perked up at that news, but Abigail shook her head at her mother's inquiring glance.

"I'd rather stay home. It's too nice to spend the day in the carriage driving to town and back."

Her mother's sharp gaze lingered on her a moment, but she only nodded. Penelope, however, gave her a wicked smirk. Abigail ignored it and buttered another piece of toast. Her sister could think what she liked. Frankly, she still considered Penelope to be in her debt, after sharing the unexpected delivery the other day.

When her mother and sister had gone, she collected her things and set out for the grotto. It was much easier this time, with the house essentially empty. Milo yipped and circled her feet hopefully when she reached the door, but she patted his head and told the footman to keep him inside. The last thing she needed to do was lose her mother's puppy in the woods.

At the end of the Fragrant Walk, she hesitated. She thought she remembered the way to the grotto, but wasn't entirely confident. Still, she'd found her way home without trouble, and it hadn't been very far at all. At one time the path must have led right to it. Holding her skirts out of the mud, she set off through the trees.

It was surprisingly simple to find. She'd remembered a large boulder as a landmark, and when she went around it, she saw the clearing. Now it really was a clearing, with much of the brush stripped away. To her surprise, there was a rustic stone wall at the grotto's entrance; it had been completely obscured by plants before. Most of the stone had crumbled away, but without the concealing growth, she could make out the arched shape of it. The stone steps were visible as well, slicing down into the earth and disappearing beneath the stone wall.

She approached the stone steps, searching for Sebastian. He had definitely been here, and done a great deal of work exposing the grotto. She remembered how he'd had to hack away at the vines and plants and even drag a fallen tree out of the way before. Today there was no evidence of any of that. Of course, there was also no evidence of his presence at the moment. Perhaps he'd only wanted her to see it, and that had been behind his comment in the letter. She felt a little deflated at that possibility. She wanted to see the grotto again, but that wasn't why she was here today.

On that thought, the man she'd actually wanted to see stepped out of the trees on the opposite side of the clearing, a large bundle in one arm and a lantern in his other hand. For a moment they stared at each other.

"I didn't know if you would come," he said at last.

She nibbled her lower lip. "Didn't you want me to?"

"Very much," he said with a searing look. "But after

the way we parted . . ." He shrugged. "It seemed long odds you would."

Abigail walked toward the grotto. "You cleared the steps. No one could miss it now."

He limped forward. "You were right. It shouldn't remain lost."

She looked around the clearing again; it was much more than a morning's work, she realized. It must have taken a full day or more, and given the weather lately . . . "You came out in the rain to expose it."

He didn't deny it. "I needed something to occupy my mind."

She hesitated. "Thank you for the book."

"Thank you for accepting it."

That made Abigail laugh a little. "I could hardly give it back!"

A ghost of a smile crossed his face. "If you had truly wanted to, you would have found a way."

Her own lips twitched with a smile. "Perhaps I brought it with me today to do that."

She'd meant to tease him, to make him laugh and ask in pretend alarm if she had in fact come only to return his gift. But instead he took it as an invitation to examine her from head to toe, with such bold, unabashed interest, it left her flushed and breathless.

"I don't think so," he said in a low voice, looking her in the face again.

Flustered, she blurted out the first thing to cross her mind. "Perhaps I brought the other gift."

This time he did smile, a slow, dangerous look that made her knees weaken. "Now why would you do that?" He moved a step closer and leaned down until she thought he meant to kiss her on the cheek. "Unless you meant to read it to me?" he whispered in her ear.

She forgot to breathe. "No . . ."

He lifted his head and gave her another simmering look. "Perhaps you'll change your mind." He shifted his burden and held out the lantern. "I did bring a light this time."

Abigail stared at it blankly. The thought of reading that story to him—! It was shocking and alarming and she was horrified to realize she wanted to try it. She imagined how he would watch her as she read Constance's most recent adventure, in the shadowy quiet confines of the grotto. She imagined what he would do, when he saw how arousing she found it . . .

She gave herself a shake to banish that wicked image. "How sensible to bring a lantern! Now we'll be able to find our way out."

"Yes," he said, "if that's what you desire." He gestured to the steps. "Will you light the way?"

Last time, she hadn't planned to go into the grotto. She could pretend that everything between them had been unexpected and spontaneous. This time, if she went with him, she couldn't pretend innocence. This time, if she went, it would mean she was willing to take what he offered, whatever that was.

Although . . .

He had once said they would never be amiable. He had once agreed that he must avoid walking in the woods if he didn't want to meet her. He had once refused to show her where the grotto was . . . and yet here they were today. If he could change his mind about all that, perhaps he could change his mind about more. He'd said he was no noble hero, but he was still a gentleman, one who claimed he was trying to be honorable toward her.

Besides, she wanted to see the grotto with more light than a candle.

She took the lantern and led the way down the narrow stone steps. As before, the cold air wrapped around her, but she barely felt it this time. With the extra light, he didn't follow as closely behind her, but she still heard every rustle of his coat, every scrape of his boot as he limped along, much more noticeably than ever.

"Have you left your cane behind?" she asked, finally realizing he didn't have it.

"Yes. It's a nuisance when I have to carry something."

"Shall I fetch it?" she offered.

"By all means. I left it in the glass chamber."

A shiver rushed over her skin. She told herself it was because of the cold, and not because of what had happened between them in the glass chamber, but the cold didn't explain the way her heart skipped a beat and the way her lungs seemed too tight to take a full breath. "So you've already been there."

"Can't you tell?" he asked.

She frowned, and opened her mouth to ask what he meant, but instead she gasped. There was light ahead. She held her lantern a little higher, peering around the gently turning corridor, and then stopped in the doorway of the glass chamber, struck dumb.

Four other lanterns sat around the chamber, shutters wide open. Their light filled the chamber with a bright glow that made the glass on the walls and ceiling sparkle like jewels. "It's amazing," she whispered.

He took the lantern from her, reaching up to hang it on a rusty iron hook that protruded from the ceiling above her head. "You didn't get a chance to see it properly the last time." He lowered his arm slowly, tugging loose the ribbon on her bonnet as he did so. His raised hand caught the crown of her bonnet and lifted it away. "That is why you came, isn't it?" He dropped the bonnet behind him.

"Well—partly." She didn't know what to say. His eyes were burning dark, almost scorching her skin. It flustered her and entranced her and made her vividly remember what had happened the last time they were here.

"Only partly?" He tucked a loose wisp of hair behind her ear. "Why else?"

"To thank you for the book," she whispered.

He gave her his dark, faint smile again. "You already said that. Come." His fingers trailed down her arm to clasp her hand. "It's even more spectacular from the center of the room." He led her to the center of the chamber, where Abigail was finally able to wrench her eyes away from him and take in the view.

The domed ceiling wasn't high—she thought Sebastian would be able to touch it if he raised his arm—but somehow the room felt spacious. This time she could see more than a small patch of wall at once, and as she slowly turned on the spot, she noticed something.

"There's a pattern," she whispered. Somehow, hushed voices seemed appropriate in such a setting.

"More than just a pattern." Sebastian tossed down his bundle, which turned out to be two large cushions, onto a rug that had been spread on the floor. He held out a hand to her. "Lie down." She gaped at him. He wiggled his fingers. "Trust me. This is the best way to see it."

She gave him her hand, and let him lead her to one of the cushions. He helped her sit and then lowered himself onto the other cushion with only a slight grimace. "Lie back, and look up," he told her.

Abigail's mouth fell open again in wonder as she

obeyed, tucking her skirts around her feet. He was right—it wasn't a pattern. It was a portrait, a swirling glass mosaic of sea creatures, swimming and leaping and writhing around the walls. The little mirrored bits of glass she had noticed on her first visit were the eyes of fish, octopods, whales, and sea monsters. "There's a mermaid!" She pointed in excitement at one side of the ceiling. A blue-skinned maiden with a long green tail and yellow hair had one arm extended as if in entreaty.

"And her beloved," said Sebastian. "Look . . ." Abigail followed his finger across the dark ceiling to another long-tailed creature, his hand reaching toward the mermaid's. More little flecks of silvered glass winked like stars between them.

"Amazing," she breathed again. For several minutes she just gazed upward, trying to take in every detail. The expressionless figures were rather crude in depiction, for all that their creation must have taken hours and hours of painstaking work, but something about their posture struck Abigail as sad. "I wonder why they're so far apart," she murmured. "It seems they should be together."

"Mythological creatures rarely found happy endings."

"In stories where a man fell in love with a goddess," she agreed, "or a god with a human girl. But these are two of a kind. Why couldn't they be together?"

"Sometimes it's not as simple as that."

"No?" She turned her head to look at him. He was lying on his back, but with his head on the side to face her. "What do you think it means?"

He raised his eyes to the merman again, above her. "This house and grotto were built for a king's mistress. I suppose it was a nod to the fact that she couldn't merely swim around to his part of the ocean. Too much divided them for their union to be anything other than fleeting."

Abigail looked at the merman, too. Somehow his face seemed blank and expressionless, as if he knew they would never meet. He was reaching toward her, true, but his hand was flat, and could have been in demand for fealty more than in affection. But the mermaid . . . Her figure had an element of yearning. It was a silly thing to think about a creature who was made only of cut glass. But the hand that wasn't reaching for the merman was clutched to her heart, and her extended hand was palm up, beseeching.

"Do you think the King saw this?"

"I've no idea."

"But what do you think?" she persisted. "Can you picture a King of England, lying where we are now?"

He was quiet for a moment. "If he loved her, I expect he did. But I daresay love was uncommon between kings and their mistresses."

"I think she really loved him," said Abigail softly. "Why else would she have had this built?"

"From what I understand, mistresses aren't always the most practical creatures," he said wryly. "It may have amused her, nothing more."

"No!" she protested. "Surely not!"

"It's far enough from Hart House, who's to say she ever saw it herself?"

"She must have seen it—how could anyone know this was here and not come to see it?"

He gave a quiet chuckle. "Not everyone is like you, my dear."

She closed her eyes and smiled. "Silly and romantic? You have found me out."

"Not silly," he said, still sounding amused. "Romantic, I already knew."

She laughed, and for a moment they were both quiet. "Did you know it was this beautiful when you hinted I should come back?"

"Before yesterday, I hadn't been here since you marched away from me the first time." He hesitated. "I deserved that."

She happened to agree, so said nothing.

"It has been a very long time since a lady looked at me with anything less than disdain or fear," he went on in the same low voice. "Even though I knew you were different, I was still certain you would learn the same distaste for my company. In truth, you would be wise to do so."

"Now why—?" she began indignantly, but he held up one hand. He had turned his face back to the ceiling, and she could only see his profile.

"You admit you've heard the rumors about me in town. While Boris is nothing but an ordinary boar hound, the rest isn't as fanciful. My father did run mad, and everyone expects me to go mad as well."

"But you're not!" she interrupted.

His jaw tightened. "If you'd come to Richmond seven years ago, you might well have thought differently. When I returned from the army, I discovered my father had sold nearly all our land, for hardly anything at all. A few shillings an acre, and one of the largest estates in London was nearly gone. I . . . did not take it well." A black and bitter smile twisted his mouth. "I raged a good bit, to tell the truth. I called on the men who'd bought the land—*my* land—and demanded they reverse the sales. Some of them laughed at me, some of them took offense. More than one visit degenerated into both parties hurling curses at each other, and ended with me slamming the door behind me. Word spread that I was just as mad as my father, and dangerous to boot. Within a few weeks everyone regarded me with the same alarm as my father."

"But surely your anger was understandable."

"I thought so," he said in a flat tone. "Others . . . did not. I threatened some of them."

That also seemed understandable to her, but it would only have fueled suspicions about him. Abigail tried to imagine her own father losing his grip on reason, frittering away his fortune. Her brother would put a quick stop to it, one way or another, she thought—but of course Sebastian hadn't been there to stop his father. The trouble had happened while he was away. And from the grim set of his face, he didn't like talking about it.

"What was he like?" she asked instead. "Before."

He raised his eyebrows. "Before?" He thought a moment, then a faint smile curved his mouth. "Very clever. Whenever there was a problem, he would set about righting it, often in the most ingenious manner. He was a scholarly man. He would visit Mrs. Driscoll's bookshop every week with an order for a new scientific tome or pamphlet. She admired him. When I was a boy, there were always experiments going on around the house. He made his own candles, in search of ones that burned longer and brighter. He was fascinated by fire and light, and once constructed a series of glass tubes which he intended to use to heat the drawing room more evenly, so one wouldn't have to sit in front of the fire to be warm."

"Did it work?"

"No," he said, his smile growing. "The tubes shattered. He had connected them to a large kettle of water over the fire, to fill the tubes with steam. His plan was for the steam to circulate through the tubes and bring heat to every corner of the room, but instead they exploded, one after the other. I'll never forget the astonished expression on his face . . ." The smile faded. "Later, when he lost his mind, he almost burned the house down, trying something similar."

Without thinking she groped for his hand. He started, but then his fingers closed gently around hers.

"What happened to him?" she finally asked. She knew what gossip said: that Mr. Vane would fly into violent rages and attack people as if he meant to kill them, and had to be restrained. And that finally Sebastian had taken him into the woods and killed him, burying him in some secluded spot no one had located. Or perhaps drowned him in the river. Or even perhaps taken him to London and committed him to an asylum, where he might still linger for all anyone knew.

None of that made sense to Abigail, though. If he'd committed his father to an asylum, it would be easy to prove the man wasn't dead. And she just didn't believe he was a killer.

"There's no way to know. I've always wondered if he concocted something that poisoned him unintentionally, or if he suffered some injury he never bothered telling anyone about that damaged his brain. He was always a bit eccentric. When he went mad, it happened rather subtly. He could seem quite lucid, from what I hear, only to erupt in a fit of delusion and fury that alarmed and shocked everyone around him. The lucidity fooled everyone for a while. His attorney swore he seemed in full possession of his wits even as he was selling off his land for pennies an acre." He rolled his head to look at her. "Or do you mean that night?"

"Never mind," she said hastily, but he squeezed her hand.

"No, I'll tell you. It won't change anything. My father was confined to his room—for his own safety. I woke after midnight to find his door unlocked and him escaped. I searched the woods, we dragged the pond, and Mr. Jones combed the meadow, but no trace of him was ever found."

"None? How is that possible?"

Slowly he shook his head. "These woods are thick, and they go on for miles. I daresay the grotto isn't the only place one could fall into a hole in the ground and disappear forever. And then there's the river, which could sweep a man miles away in an hour's time."

Abigail frowned. "Why do people say you killed him, then?"

"Because there's no proof I didn't. Because it's what they would have done, perhaps. But most likely . . . because it's my fault he got loose."

Her eyes grew wide and she forgot to breathe. His dark gaze held hers as he went on. "I was the one who locked his door every night, but that night it was unlocked. I forgot to do it. I . . . I still needed laudanum to sleep then, from time to time, and because of it I didn't hear him slip out. And it cost him his life."

"That is not the same as killing someone," she said in a very low voice.

His mouth quirked bitterly again. "But the result is the same, isn't it? The madman vanished. No one needed to live in fear anymore." He shrugged. "I only hope his end came without much suffering."

She was too stunned to move, but her horror must

have shown on her face. "Is that terribly callous and cold to admit?" He rolled onto his side, facing her, and propped one hand under his head. "Have I ruined your good opinion of me yet? Because you might as well know: I'm not sorry he's dead."

"Are you certain he's dead?" she asked falteringly.

"Yes," he said without hesitation. "His mind was so far gone by then, he couldn't have survived long. For a few days I thought he might wander home, but of course he didn't. No, I'm absolutely certain he's dead." He paused, watching her closely. "And even more . . . I'm glad."

Abigail was too shocked to speak.

"He begged me to kill him," he said, his voice grown so quiet she barely breathed in order to hear him. "He knew he was losing his wits; he fought against it but the madness would swallow him whole for days at a time. One night he turned to me, tears running down his face, and begged me to put an end to it. "You've got a sword," he cried. "Put it through me." There was a long pause as he clenched his jaw and stared into the shadows beyond the lanterns, and Abigail bit her lip until it almost bled, imagining the anguish that request must have caused. "I couldn't do it. There was nothing anyone could do to save him, he wanted to die, and shamefully, secretly, I knew it was the only way out of his hell. But I couldn't do it."

"Of course not," she cried softly.

Sebastian shook his head. "Sometimes I think I should have. Sometimes I think I failed him as a son, for not doing what he asked. Instead I hid every sharp instrument in the house and set myself to watching him day and night. Not that it made any difference. Everyone who knew how deranged he had become only heard that he disappeared one night, and decided I must have put an end to him." Again that bitter smile. "It fit with the mad, enraged image they had of me, I suppose."

"They're wrong," she said in a low, passionate voice. "Wrong, both now and then."

His fingers tightened around hers. He tipped his head to face her. "You're a rare woman, Abigail Weston. You deserve so much better than a wreck of a man."

"You're not a wreck."

"I don't feel like one when I'm with you." He leaned closer, looming over her.

Abigail could see the mermaid over his shoulder, reaching for her love and doomed never to have him. For decades—centuries—she'd been alone in the dark, unseen and unrequited, helpless to change her fate. Poor mermaid. "I already told you, you don't get to decide what I deserve."

His mouth curved. "I remember." His lips brushed against hers before he lifted his head again. For a moment he studied her, his hair hanging loose and casting his face in dark shadow. Abigail waited, breathless and yearning but unsure of what to do. She'd made a mistake last time, too curious to know the truth of Lady Constance's stories. This time she tried to shut the notorious stories out of her mind; they were fiction, bits of fancy. Sebastian was real and alive and she wanted him to be her true experience of love and passion.

And then he kissed her, in truth this time. His mouth settled over hers, hot and wicked. His hand cupped her nape, raising her neck to a subtle arch. His thumb stroked her cheek before tugging at the corner of her lips. Nervously she obeyed, softening her lips under his until his tongue parted them. She shivered as he tasted her mouth, then tentatively she slid her tongue along his.

His breath hitched, and he moved, lowering himself more on top of her. One arm slipped beneath her, his fingers splayed over the back of her head. With his other hand he lifted her free arm and laid it gently on the cushion, curving gracefully around her head. His fingers swirled over the pulse in her wrist, then drifted down the underside of her forearm.

She was gripping his coat, her hand trapped between them. His kiss went on and on, now light and tantalizing, now plunging deep in blatant possession. His fingers played up and down her raised arm until she quivered from the maddeningly light touch.

"Is this why you came today?" he breathed, barely raising his lips from hers.

She blushed so hard, he could surely see it even in the dim light. "Not specifically . . ."

"Shall I stop, then?" His fingers brushed the delicate skin under her collarbone, and Abigail trembled, unable to do more than make a small negative motion with her head. His voice grew even softer. "Did you think of me when you read the story I sent you?"

A riot of images streamed across her mind's eye. Lady Constance had taken a musical man to her bed, where he played her body like his instrument, wringing a symphony of sighs from the wicked woman.

There was no point trying to deny she had thought of Sebastian, just as it was foolish to deny that she'd come today hoping he might kiss her again. Abigail felt restless and alive, her skin craving his touch. She had felt this pull toward him from the beginning, and *50 Ways to Sin* only made it worse, giving her imagination fuel—wicked, delicious ideas that inspired both amazement and desperate longing. Especially the last two issues.

"Yes," she whispered.

She felt the fine shudder that ran through his frame. "I have no blindfold," he murmured, "nor oil of roses." His head dipped, and his lips brushed against the hammering pulse at the base of her throat. "But like Constance, you have only to say the word 'stop' . . ."

"What should I do?" Her heart was pounding so hard, she could hardly hear her own voice.

"Raise your arms above your head," he whispered. She closed her eyes as she obeyed. "It would be beyond my endurance to watch you pleasure yourself," he went on. "I pictured it, though. Just the thought of touching you nearly drove me to distraction. You're a temptress, Abigail. So ethereally beautiful, I'm stricken dumb in your presence. Abigail with the starry eyes that stole a piece of my soul the first time you looked at me. Abigail with the bright smile and the kind heart and the curious nature. Abigail who haunts my dreams . . ."

She gasped at the feathery light touch on her throat. "Abigail who makes me burn," he murmured. His hair brushed her bosom as he kissed lower, his lips as soft as velvet against her skin.

"Every night I imagine what I would do, if I had you in my bed." She made an inarticulate noise as he stroked the sensitive underside of her arm, his fingers drifting all the way down her ribs to tease her waist. "Every night I dream of bringing you to the point of ecstasy." His fingers swirled over her belly, from hipbone to hipbone. "I imagine how soft and pale your skin must be, here . . ." He traced swooping circles over her hips. "And how exquisite you would taste."

"You—you would put your mouth there?" she managed to choke out. Even through layers of dress, petticoats, and pantalets, she could feel every touch of his hand.

"Everywhere," he confirmed. "When a man is patient and attentive, he can bring a woman great pleasure with his mouth. Like so . . ."

She started as he pressed a kiss to her navel. Something inside her clenched as he repeated the kiss, over and over across her belly, up her ribs. He wasn't touching her skin at all, but she could almost believe he was.

"Constance's lovers have one thing right," he said, against the bottom of her breast. "A woman's passion is paramount; her pleasure is their pleasure." He cupped her other breast in his hand, his long fingers first gentle, then firm. "Bringing her to climax is his soul's only purpose, in the act of love."

Abigail was shaking. His thumb teased her nipple until it grew rigid and sensitive, straining toward his touch. She ached for him to caress her other breast, rather than just nuzzling it, but as if he knew, he moved his mouth to that other nipple and closed his lips around it.

She arched. She twisted. She gasped and blushed as he suckled her through the cloth. She squeezed her eyes closed until tears leaked from her lids. Oh God . . .

He shifted again, and laid one hand on her knees, which she had drawn up in her writhing. He slid his hand down the inside of her thigh. Abigail let her knees fall apart; her clothing was a barrier between them that was both frustrating and comforting. She felt the same riot of feeling Lady Constance had described, but without the licentiousness. They were both still fully clothed, after all. More than one of Constance's lovers had brought her to climax without removing a stitch of clothing. Sebastian seemed to know she wasn't quite as daring as Constance and he made no effort to seduce her into deeper wickedness. It affirmed her trust in him, and also allowed her to let him settle his hand between her thighs, resting on the throbbing spot hidden there.

"You slay me," he said, his breathing fast and ragged. Slowly his fingers stroked her through her skirt. "How your face reflects your passion . . ." He pressed another kiss on her bosom, on her bare flesh this time above the neckline of her dress. Abigail threw one arm around his neck to keep him there; she tilted her hips, straining toward his touch. His lips on her skin seemed to double the fire burning inside her. It spread through her limbs, fevered her brain, and yet burned hottest where his hand pressed toward her most female place.

Sebastian almost lost his grip on his control when she twined herself around him. God almighty, her skin tasted sweeter than he'd dreamed. The little moans of pleasure and encouragement she made were like kindling on the blazing desire inside him. He'd very carefully not disarranged an inch of her clothing—even a single step down that path could prove too dangerous—but her response, fully clothed, only made him wild to know what it would be like if his hands touched her bare skin, if she writhed beneath him completely willing and eager for him.

And now she was clinging to him, straining toward him. He could barely breathe as he continued the soft, slow stroke. He could barely think beyond the sound of her wanton gasps and the ever-more-strident demands of his own body, hard and erect and ready to burst. He was desperate to move and yet as rigid as stone, not trusting himself. He could do this—only this—he could bring her to completion, he could hold himself back . . .

She arched her neck, her fingers digging into his

neck. She sucked in a short breath, then another. Her legs jerked. He pressed a little harder, circling tightly over the spot that made her jump, and she gave a startled cry that turned into a long gasping sigh of release.

His heart hammered in his ears. He left his hand cupped over her mound, fighting off the urge to throw up her skirts and feel how wet she must be, how soft and ready she would be, how tight and hot and . . . virginal she was.

Sebastian squeezed his eyes shut. He was half sprawled on top of her, her arm still around his neck, her legs tangled with his and trapping his hand between her thighs. He could swear he still felt her climax pulsing beneath his fingertips. If he turned his head even an inch to the side, his lips would be on her breast. Just the rise and fall of her chest was dangerous to his wavering sense of honor. With a great deal of regret, he gingerly eased away from her.

"What made you change your mind?" she whispered, her voice low and husky. "About me?"

He gritted his teeth as he sat up. He was still so hard for her, it hurt to move. "I have never changed my mind about you."

"About seeing me," she amended. "You swore you would avoid the woods to avoid me. You wished me luck finding the grotto on my own. You refused to call on me because we hadn't a thing to talk about. But you sent me a book and met me here today."

He studied her, feeling an unexpected lurch in his chest. She lay in sensual abandon on the threadbare rug and cushions he'd dragged down from Montrose Hill. "I wanted to know if my peace offering had been acceptable."

A shadow fell over her face. "Oh."

He repented the evasive answer. He caught her hand and raised it to his lips. "I wanted to see you again, even though I don't deserve it. You should have refused to see me after I spoke so crudely, but here you are. I meant what I said: you are a rare woman, and I cannot stay away from you."

She smiled, and the room seemed to glow brighter. "I knew you didn't mean it."

His lips quirked. He had meant it. He'd been alone so long, avoided and reviled for so long, he'd forgotten what it felt like to have a friend. But Abigail, he was realizing, was just that: a friend. Someone he could be at ease with. Someone who cared about his feelings and thoughts. Someone who leapt to his defense instead of shrinking from his presence.

Of course, she was also far more. The pulsing desire to make love to her was only held at bay, unabated in the slightest. He turned her hand over, stroking his thumb over her palm. "No one else in Richmond would have forgiven my abominable behavior."

"Do you ever wish to change people's minds?"

He turned toward her, bracing his arm behind him. "No. People who believe I killed my father . . . I don't give a bloody damn what they think." He circled one finger around her hand, hooking it under her wrist and raising it to press a kiss to her palm. "I care what you think."

She raised her eyes again. "I think this grotto is the most delightful place in Richmond."

He smiled. Anyplace where she was would be every bit as delightful as this cave, in his opinion. "I quite agree."

Chapter 12

The afternoon in the grotto eliminated the last shred of doubt in Abigail's mind: she was utterly fascinated with Sebastian Vane.

All her anger over his early behavior was washed away, not only by the way he gave her his mother's book but by the way he cleared the grotto for her, not even knowing if she would return. When he spoke of his father, going slowly mad before disappearing one night while Sebastian was unable to stop him, she'd wanted to put her fingers in her ears. How awful people were, to call him a murderer when he'd been a gravely wounded young man facing the loss of his father, the ruin of his expectations, and the pain of his injury. Who would not turn away from the neighbors who thought he was evil?

But she knew differently. She refused to be cowed by other people's wrong assumptions, and she was outraged enough by the extremity of them to want to prove them wrong.

"Why haven't we invited any neighbors to dine with us?" she asked the next day as she sat with her mother and sister.

"What do you mean, Abby? We had a ball barely a

month ago, and a picnic," Mama replied in surprise. "Of course, it's always lovely to have guests . . ."

"Precisely. And we've barely become acquainted with one neighbor." Abigail ignored the way her sister's eyebrows shot up. "Shouldn't we invite Mr. Vane? Without him, Milo might still be lost in the woods, wild and savage by now."

"Wild and savage!" Mama smiled. "What a way you have with words, dear. I'm sure James would have found him if Mr. Vane hadn't been there."

"But Mr. Vane was there, and he did save Milo," she argued.

"And I thanked him, when he called," Mama replied, gently but firmly. "I don't think he'll come to dinner. Your papa says he's a very reserved fellow who prefers to be left alone."

"If he won't come, there's even less harm in issuing an invitation," Penelope remarked. "You'll get the credit for inviting him, without having to entertain him. Besides, he might think us rude if we don't, as such close neighbors. Everyone in Richmond was invited to the ball, but a dinner invitation shows more solicitude."

"Exactly," said Abigail immediately, feeling very grateful to her sister. "What's the harm in issuing an invitation?"

Mama leaned back on the sofa and fixed a sharp gaze on her, idly stroking Milo with one hand. "What's your interest in inviting him, Abigail?"

"Neighborly gratitude, Mama."

Mama said nothing, but her expression remained suspicious. Abigail fought to keep from squirming, but feared she'd failed when her mother said, "Penelope, would you please go upstairs and fetch my embroidery case?"

"Oh, it's right here, Mama, on the table," said Penelope.

"Then go upstairs and find the length of blue silk."

"I'll ring for Maria to fetch it."

"Penelope," said Mama, a faint ring of steel in her voice, "go find it yourself."

Her sister's face creased in frustration. She knew she was being ordered from the room, and she wasn't happy about it. She rose, slowly, and threw down the ladies' magazine she'd been reading. "Where is it, Mama?"

"I don't know, you must look for it." This time Mama looked away from Abigail and pinned that sharp gaze on her youngest child. "Go, Penelope."

Dragging her feet, Penelope went.

Mama set Milo aside and crooked her finger. "Come here, dear."

Abigail's heart sank. Feeling every bit as reluctant as her sister had been, she moved to sit beside her mother on the sofa.

"What is your interest in Mr. Vane?" her mother asked bluntly.

She prayed she wasn't blushing. "Neighborly, Mama." Her mother's eyes narrowed. "And perhaps a little more," she added, knowing confession was better if made willingly and quickly.

"How much more?"

Now she knew she was blushing. Still, she didn't look away, and she clenched her hands together in her lap to keep from fidgeting. "What do you mean?"

"I know you've gone for several walks in the woods. I know you're very fond of finding a peaceful spot to read, and I am not calling you deceitful," Mama said. "But I can't help wondering if perhaps you've met him on your strolls and formed an attachment."

Abigail cleared her throat. She hadn't planned on making *this* much confession, but lying about it now would be a crucial error. "Well, yes, when Penelope and I went walking the other day, we did meet him. He was looking for his dog, who'd got lost in the woods, and since he was so kind when Milo ran off, we offered to help him look."

"And did you find the dog?"

"No, Penelope fell in the mud, so we came home."

Mama just sat watching her, saying nothing, for a long, long moment. Abigail tried to tell herself she wasn't really lying—everything she'd said was true, after all—and that there was nothing to be gained by saying more.

"I have long trusted you, Abigail," said Mama at last. "You're a girl of such good sense. But even sensible girls can lose their heads over men, particularly handsome, mysterious men like Mr. Vane." She nodded at Abigail's slight start. "He's a very handsome fellow; did you think I hadn't noticed? I know those woods straddle Hart House and Montrose Hill lands, and he has every right to walk in them, too. I merely want to assure myself that you're still being sensible."

Abigail thought about it for a moment. She didn't *think* she was being foolish and rash. She had asked other people about him; Lady Samantha called him a decent gentleman. Many of the rumors about him didn't even make sense, so she felt sensible in regarding them with doubt. And for the rest . . . Was it possible for love and attraction to make sense? She didn't know that answer.

"Yes, Mama," she said. "I believe so."

"I hope so." Mama watched her another minute. "Is

he more charming in the woods than he is indoors?"

She blushed. "I—I think I would say he is less reserved."

"How much less reserved?"

To Abigail's intense relief, she was spared having to reply by a tap on the door. Her relief was short-lived, though, as the butler stepped into the room and announced, "Mr. Sebastian Vane to see you, ma'am."

Mama's face didn't change, but she slowly turned to look at Abigail. "Indeed? Show him in, Thomson." And as the butler bowed and left, she murmured, "How very timely."

Abigail's eyes widened. "I had no idea, Mama! You mustn't think I mentioned him earlier because I thought he might call!"

"No?" Mama rose. "I wonder."

Abigail flushed in misery. What luck, that Sebastian would choose to call—after repeatedly refusing to do so—right as she was trying to persuade her mother to think better of him. Of course it smacked of planning. Still, that discomfort was nearly blotted out by the burst of delight his arrival caused. Tense with anticipation, she stood beside her mother as the door opened again.

Penelope came in first, her hands conspicuously empty. "See whom I met in the hall!" she said happily. And then he was there. Milo gave a shrill bark, and leapt off the sofa to run and sniff his feet. Sebastian wore a dark blue coat and gray trousers, a little plain but more refined than what he wore into the woods. His boots shone, and the white of his cravat showed how tanned his face was. This time his gaze landed on her first. Abigail bit her cheek to stop herself from beaming like a lovesick girl, and ducked her head in a curtsy.

"Mrs. Weston," he said, bowing. "Miss Weston."

"A pleasure to see you again, Mr. Vane." Mama smiled. "Won't you sit down?"

"Thank you." He glanced down at Milo, whose nose was practically stuck to his boot. "This is the fondest welcome I've received in some time."

"Do pardon Milo." Mama reached for the bell. "I'll have him taken upstairs."

"No need. A dog learns through his nose." He stooped down and held out his hand. Milo sniffed each and every finger, and then began licking them.

"He likes you," said Abigail warmly. "If a sniff means 'How do you do, sir,' a lick on the hand means, 'Stay for tea.'" Penelope laughed, and Mama smiled.

Sebastian glanced up at her. "I think you're correct, Miss Weston. Dogs are much simpler than people. All it takes is a thorough sniffing to tell if someone is a friend."

"That's not as clever as it sounds," remarked Penelope. "I can tell just by looking at some people whether or not we're meant to be friends."

"Penelope," said her mother in a low, warning tone.

"Milo approves of Mr. Vane," said Abigail quickly, motioning to the puppy's continued licking. "This is quite the most entranced I've ever seen him."

"It is indeed," Mama conceded. "You have a way with him, Mr. Vane."

Sebastian rose. "I'm delighted to have won his favor." He pulled out his handkerchief to dry his fingers where Milo had licked. When he went to replace the handkerchief in his coat pocket, though, his cane slipped from where it had been propped against his leg, and in catching it, he dropped the handkerchief. With a joyful yip, Milo seized it in his teeth.

"Milo, no!" Mama reached for her dog. He scampered out of her grasp, his stubby tail wagging furiously; being chased was one of his favorite games. "He's such a naughty creature sometimes," she said apologetically to Sebastian.

"He's not naughty, he's just a puppy who doesn't know better." Abigail was astonished to see a faint smile light his face. "Is he your first dog?"

"Clearly," said Mama, adding with a sigh, "and likely the last!"

Sebastian cleared his throat. "May I try to teach him something?"

There was a moment of silent astonishment in the room. Mama recovered quickly. "Of course!"

"Please do," added Penelope.

"Have you any sort of food he particularly likes?"

Mama blinked. "He likes everything, Mr. Vane; bits of cheese and ham, bacon, cake . . ."

He smiled again. "I wouldn't feed him cake; dogs need something to chew. If you have a bit of cheese . . ." He glanced at Abigail, who remembered Boris. "My dog is excessively fond of cheese," he explained. "Nothing makes him obey like a small lump of it."

"Penelope, ring for some cheese at once," Mama exclaimed. "I simply must see this!"

Cheese was fetched in just a few minutes. Milo had retreated under the sofa with his prize while attention was diverted from him. Sebastian cut a small lump from the block of cheese the maid brought, then went down on his good knee and snapped his fingers. "Milo," he said in a voice of unmistakable command.

The dog gave a little yip; he knew his name. But he stayed under the sofa.

"Come," said Sebastian firmly. He didn't move except to tap the floor in front of him. "Milo, come."

And he set the cheese on the floor where he had tapped.

Nose quivering, Milo emerged. He still held the handkerchief in his mouth and his tail still wagged, but he glanced at Mr. Vane curiously. Mama watched with hope.

Milo tossed his head, shaking the handkerchief, then trotted across the room. He stopped short of Sebastian, but when Sebastian still didn't try to grab him, the dog sidled closer. His nose twitched at the cheese. Finally he dropped the handkerchief and came right up to the cheese and ate it.

Mama let out a breath of relief and made a motion to get her pet, but Sebastian stayed her with one upraised hand. Never taking his eyes off the puppy, he held out another lump of cheese with his fingertips. When Milo tried to nip it from him, Sebastian raised it just above his head. As Milo craned his neck back to follow the treat, his hindquarters sank, until he was sitting, seemingly mesmerized by the bite of cheese.

"Good dog," said Sebastian in the same firm voice. "Sit." After a moment of waiting, he gave the puppy the cheese, patted his head, and got to his feet. Milo jumped up at once and began sniffing the floor, but Sebastian ignored it.

Abigail hurried to retrieve the handkerchief, spotting a rip in one edge. "I'm so sorry, Milo's bitten a hole . . ."

"Mr. Vane, I shall send you a large box of new handkerchiefs," said Mama, gazing in delight at Milo, who was still sniffing attentively at his feet. "If you can teach Milo how to behave—"

He shook his head. "You can teach Milo, Mrs. Weston—and you should. It does you no good if he only obeys me. You must all of you take turns teaching him to obey, so he will learn it's a general rule, not something particular to one person." He cut another tiny bite of cheese and walked across the room. "Milo, come."

The puppy barked and ran after him. "Sit, Milo." Again Sebastian lowered the cheese until the dog had no choice but to sit if he wanted to keep his mouth near it. "Good boy." Milo nipped the cheese from his fingers, and got another pat on the head. Sebastian came back to stand near Abigail. "Milo, come." Again the dog ran after him, and this time sat without being prompted. "Good boy." This time he only petted the dog's head.

"You forgot to feed him cheese," pointed out Penelope as Milo continued to sit in expectation, his little tongue hanging out.

"I did not forget," Sebastian told her. "Affection is the real reward. He must learn to come just for that. If you only train him to come when you have cheese, he won't listen when you don't. If he only gets the cheese some of the times you command him, he will obey even better, for he never knows if this is to be the time he gets the reward or not, and he won't want to miss that chance."

The door opened to reveal Papa, who stopped short. "Mr. Vane," he said in surprise.

"Sir." Sebastian returned Papa's bow. His smile, however faint, had vanished, and he looked as formal and proper as Abigail had ever seen him.

"Mr. Weston, you'll never guess what Mr. Vane has just done," exclaimed Mama. "He has taught Milo to come when called!"

Papa raised his brows. "How fortunate you visited, Vane. An invaluable service!"

"I only showed Mrs. Weston how I trained my dog when he was a pup," Sebastian explained. "I hope it will help her train Milo."

"Is your dog a terrier?"

"No, a large black boar hound."

Papa nodded approvingly. "Ah, a proper dog."

"Mr. Weston," scolded Mama. "How could you?"

"What?" Papa spread his hands innocently. "I only meant one couldn't mistake a boar hound for an over-fed cat." He grimaced as his wife and younger daughter cried in protest. "Yes, I know he is adorable and sweet and all that anyone could want in a pet."

"Let us have some tea," said Mama firmly. "We shall teach Milo more tricks later." She carried her puppy back to the sofa just as the maid brought a tray. By careful maneuvering, Abigail managed to take the chair opposite Sebastian, but away from her mother. She reminded herself to be her usual self, not betraying any interest, but her father, of all people, saved her. He had come to speak to Mama about a barge, and like the house, it came out that he'd already bought it.

"Mr. Weston, you're too indulgent," said Mama with a smile. Apparently the barge was more pleasing than the house had been.

He winked at her. "I'm still in search of the Egyptians to sail it for you, my dear." He turned to their visitor. "Vane, there must be some good boating to be had on the river. Where would you advise Mrs. Weston to plan her first barge outing?"

For a moment Sebastian seemed frozen, as if the sudden focus of attention on him was uncomfortable. Then his face eased into the half smile that so teased Abigail. "I daresay merely sailing up the river would be delightful. The countryside is magnificent, once you get past the turn at Hampton Court."

"A capital idea," declared Papa. "Shall we plan it, Mrs. Weston?"

She smiled. "Far be it from me to deny it! Mr. Vane, will you join us on the expedition?"

His gaze darted to Abigail. "I would be delighted, ma'am."

By the time he rose to take his leave a short time later, all the details for the barge outing had been fixed. Papa had, of course, suggested they invite the Lennox ladies. Abigail, still mildly curious about the rumored attachment between Lady Samantha and Sebastian, glanced at him, but he showed no sign of distress. It set her mind more at ease. Lady Samantha might have some lingering regret or affection, but so long as Sebastian didn't grow melancholy and tense at the sound of her name, Abigail didn't see the need to wonder.

When he had gone, she picked up her embroidery again, trying to act as though it had been a very ordinary call. But it hadn't been, not to her—her heart almost sang with delight that he had come. It hadn't been to be polite this time; he had come for *her*. She stabbed her needle through her cloth and drew the bright blue floss through, feeling as bright and happy as the bird she was stitching.

"Well, well. I never thought I'd see Sebastian Vane in this drawing room," remarked her father.

Her face warmed. She tried to guess, without looking up from her sewing, if he meant that comment for her.

"I suspect we'll see him again," said her mother.

"Will we, now?"

This time she could feel Papa's sharp gaze on her. Abigail glanced up, affecting surprise. "At the barge expedition, of course. Mama invited him and he accepted."

Papa raised one brow. "Yes, and from what I've heard, he never accepts invitations. Or pays calls."

"Perhaps he'll take a fancy to one of us," Penelope piped up. "You should be pleased, Papa; isn't that why you bought this house in the first place?"

He snorted. "That is not why I bought this house."

Penelope rolled her eyes. "We heard you telling Mama exactly that! 'Just think of all the eager gentlemen who will line up to court our daughters in this hall,'" she said, lowering her voice and pulling a wily expression that made her mother raise one hand to her mouth to hide a smile. "'We have to buy this house for our grandchildren's sake! In fact, we may not *have* grandchildren if we don't buy this house!'"

"That's enough out of you," said Papa, but with a twinkle in his eye. "I understand why ladies wear those curls around their temples; it's to hide the size of their very keen ears."

Penelope shrugged, petting Milo, who had crawled into her lap. "I didn't think it was a secret. But if you want us to get married, you ought to welcome any potential suitors, don't you think? Who knows; this might be Abby's only chance."

"Thank you very much," exclaimed Abigail in pretend outrage. "I will try not to get in the way of all your suitors, who number . . . wait a moment, let me count . . . Oh yes, there are none."

Her sister snorted. "There aren't enough interesting gentlemen in this entire village to fill a barouche. I'm glad they aren't pestering me."

Papa shook his finger at her. "I ought to marry you to the first country curate who asks."

"Only if he's dark and mysterious and gives very short sermons."

"Enough," said Mama firmly. "No man will be called a suitor before he's asked permission of your father. Penelope, where is my blue silk? I specifically asked you to fetch it."

"I couldn't find it."

"Then let us go look together." Mama rose and waited until Penelope, reluctantly, did the same, and they left. Abigail could hear her sister trying to beg off the errand as soon as the door closed behind them.

"Well." Papa slapped his knee. "Let's have a stroll outdoors, shall we, Abby?"

Her mother must have said something to him, either earlier today or perhaps in that secret communication her parents seem to share, when volumes could be spoken with a single glance. Abigail put aside her embroidery and went with him.

They went outside and paused for a moment to take in the view. It was a beautiful day, the sky clear and the light soft. The lawns looked as lush as velvet, rolling down to the river. It was quiet and peaceful out here, and Abigail took a deep breath, letting her shoulders ease.

"Do you like Richmond, Abby?"

"Oh yes. It's not as entertaining as London, but I like the quiet."

He chuckled. "I'm glad someone does. Your mother will always prefer town, I suspect."

"Do you prefer it out here, Papa?"

"It's a pleasant change. I'll be glad to go to London in the winter, and glad to return to Richmond again next summer." He cast her a sideways look. "And is it only the quiet that appeals to you?"

She widened her eyes. "What do you mean?"

Her father snorted. "Mr. Vane, the so-called Misanthrope of Montrose Hill House, in my drawing room. I don't think he was here to see me or your mother."

Abigail thought about how to reply. Her father was no fool, and he'd see through any evasions she tried. Finally she decided it was best not to deny, but not to confirm. "Do you not like him, Papa?"

He sighed, and nudged her forward. They walked across the terrace and over the gravel path, onto the grass. "When I bought Hart House, more than one person warned me about him; he's mad, they said, dead broke and a cripple. Build a tall wall around your property if you don't fancy a deranged leech making off with one of your daughters." Abigail scowled, but her father went on in the same affable tone. "I've met the man a few times now, and didn't see any sign of madness. I can't say whether he's bankrupt or not, but he's still in possession of an unentailed house and property, which is not insignificant." He paused. "But that pales to the other reports I heard."

"You mean that he killed his father and turned to thieving?"

"Something like that," agreed her father.

Abigail knew that tone. It sounded unconcerned, but it wasn't; he was trying to draw out her thoughts without rousing her temper. He'd got her to confess to all manner of childhood mischief with that tone. She tried to turn it back on him. "He told me all those rumors, too."

Her father glanced at her, startled. "*He* told you?"

She nodded. "He came to call on Mama once before, and I spoke to him. He took his leave rather abruptly when Mrs. Huntley arrived."

"That's hardly a sign of madness—more like sanity," muttered her father.

"Exactly what I thought." She wrinkled her nose and laughed as he grinned. "So I had a word with him, to make certain there had been no offense taken, and he told me what everyone says about him—what Mrs. Huntley would say about him, I suppose."

"Hmm." He stopped and turned to face her. "They're serious charges, Abby."

"But there doesn't seem to be evidence," she pointed out. "Otherwise he'd have been arrested, don't you think?"

Papa didn't look pleased by her response. "Lack of proof doesn't mean he's innocent."

"It can hardly mean he's guilty, either."

That seemed to please him even less. For a long moment he said nothing, but appeared to be thinking hard, judging from the furrows on his brow. "It's one thing to suffer some disdain over your origins," he said at last, "and another to suffer it because of your own actions. Have you thought what it would mean for your standing, if you encourage this man? Your sister's teasing aside, I did hope to raise my family up by purchasing Hart House. I know you and Penelope are snubbed by some merely for the circumstances of my birth, but I have very high hopes for both of you."

"I don't care about the opinion of those people," she tried to say, but he shook his head.

"You don't care because you've been insulated from most consequences. It's crass to speak of it, but the truth is that money has made the difference. Even people who shudder at the thought of their sons dancing with an attorney's daughter will grit their teeth and smile when that attorney's daughter is an heiress. I know you are much, much more than that," he added at her expression. "But not everyone does. Have you any idea what they will say if you attach yourself to a man of even worse reputation and no fortune?"

It took her a moment to master her voice. "Anyone who would condemn a man—or a woman—simply because of his fortune, or misfortune, is a fool!"

"Abigail." He put his hand on her arm. "You're not chasing after this man, are you?"

She blushed. "No!" Not really. Was she?

His close scrutiny didn't let up. "You've got a sensible head on your shoulders, and I find it hard to believe you'd do something like that. If any of my children gave me trouble in that way, I always thought it would be Penelope," he said, making her smile a little uncomfortably. "Your mother would box my ears if I didn't listen to your preference in choosing a husband, but she'd also be horror-struck if you threw yourself away on a scoundrel. I'm willing to reserve judgment of Vane where rumor and gossip are concerned, but you know as well as I that there's no smoke without some fire. If I come to believe he's capable of anything remotely like what people say—"

"They say his dog is a witch's familiar, Papa." She raised her brows. "I've met that dog, and it's as much a witch's pet as Milo is."

His lips twitched. "He did teach that damned rat a useful trick."

"Mr. Vane's reputation is not, I believe, based on his character or his actions," she said softly. "I hope you trust me more than to think I would discount that."

"And what, precisely, have his actions been toward you?" He folded his arms and cocked his head.

Abigail swallowed. "Measured, Papa. Polite but wary. He wouldn't tell me his name the night he saved Milo, and he warned me himself about his reputation.

If he's a fortune hunter, he's doing a very poor job of it, at least with regard to me. Lady Samantha told me he was once an eligible young man in Richmond, before he came home wounded from the war to find his father gone mad. I saw Mrs. Driscoll treat him with near-contempt and impatience, and he endured it without a flicker of anger. I think he's accustomed to being treated with apprehension and disapproval, and has simply withdrawn to avoid it. Wouldn't you, if people said such awful things about you? I—I think he is a decent gentleman acting to preserve his dignity."

"Perhaps so." Papa shook his head. "I hope so. I admit he doesn't seem like a villain. But Abigail—" He put his hands on her shoulders. "I said I would reserve judgment, not acquit him entirely. Take care your feelings and wishes don't blind you to his faults."

"I won't," she promised. No man was without fault. She was sensible enough to remember that.

She just couldn't believe Sebastian's faults included murder and robbery.

Chapter 13

Sebastian wasn't entirely sure what his visit to Hart House had gained him, but he was glad he'd gone—and that astonished him.

The last seven years had been about endurance, as everything he'd once counted on had been stripped away. He'd learned to cope with a lame leg, a meager income, the solitude of being a pariah. The whispered charges of patricide and thieving stung, though there was nothing he could do about them, and eventually he grew a hard shell of indifference. It was lonely, but it enabled him to survive.

But now there was Abigail. Not only was she undaunted by his attempts to warn her away, she persisted in trying to know him. She asked what his father had been like, before, rather than focusing on the scandal surrounding his disappearance. Sebastian hadn't thought of those long-ago happy days with his brilliant, eccentric, exciting father in years. She felt the same irresistible attraction he felt. She was kind and patient enough to forgive his cruel parting the first time at the grotto. And Sebastian began to feel that he would be a very great idiot if he ignored this chance.

But he had treated her badly, and there was only so

much he could do to atone. A book wasn't enough, even though there was no one to whom he'd rather give one of his few remaining mementos of his mother, and he thought—hoped—Abigail would appreciate it. *Fifty Ways to Sin* had been a last-minute addition, and one he worried about, but that, too, had pleased her. Clearing the grotto had yielded greater benefits than he'd expected, thanks to the mural. She'd likened it to buried treasure, but to his mind, the real treasure had been the way she held his hand and professed her faith in him.

Abigail had split a crack right through the hard shell around his heart. Just seeing her made his heart lurch, and touching her set his blood roaring through his veins. But kissing her . . . Kissing her stripped away every notion that he should—or could—avoid her, and left him only with the insatiable desire to see her again.

And that meant he had to force himself out of his hermetical ways and call on her. London ladies expected gentlemen to call on them. Abigail had invited him herself, more than once. Calling on her would be another chance to see her—and another chance to please her. Although his first visit to Hart House hadn't gone well, he acknowledged with some reluctance that it might have been his fault. He'd acted on instinct when Anne Huntley, a notorious gossip, arrived, but perhaps his abrupt departure had only served to make him look as reclusive and guilty as the townspeople called him.

So he went to Hart House, not entirely certain that he would be welcome. It would have been far easier to remain as he was and not risk exposing himself to further disdain. But if he wanted any chance at all of more than a few furtive kisses in the grotto, he would have to win Abigail's father's approval. And although the visit was cordial and pleasant, he sensed Thomas

Weston would demand more of him than drinking tea and teaching a lapdog a few tricks.

Unfortunately he had no idea what he could do. Sebastian was well aware of his disadvantages. If he'd had any idea how he could repair his reputation and his fortune, he would have already done it.

And then a letter arrived, almost like a gift from God. Mrs. Jones brought it into the kitchen one morning, where Sebastian was working on the broken mechanism of the spit jack. "This just arrived by messenger," she said.

"Oh?" Sebastian put down his tools and took it. Letters were rare, with the most frequent missives coming from his maternal grandmother. Those came only once a year, though, so this must be something else. He broke the seal and unfolded it.

"Is it bad news, sir?" Mrs. Jones asked a few minutes later, as he was still sitting in stunned silence.

"Yes," he murmured. "No." He looked up at her. "My uncle's dead."

"I'm very sorry to hear it," she exclaimed. "Mr. Henry Vane?"

"Yes." Sebastian didn't know what to say. He'd barely known Uncle Henry, who was several years younger than his father. Henry had been ambitious and freethinking, determined to seek his fortune and see the world; no estate in England would hold him, he'd declared more than once, and he proved it, joining the navy and sailing as a ship's purser. Every other year or so he would come to Montrose Hill to regale them with his tales from the seas, and then his plans for making his fortune in trade in the East Indies. Sebastian remembered watching his uncle ride away at the end of his last visit, some ten years ago, feeling a bit envious.

Part of his desire to join the army had sprung from that envy; he would have joined the navy but for his father pleading with him to remain on dry ground.

After the war, Sebastian had tried to contact his uncle, desperate for any guidance on how to address his father's deepening madness. Henry's reply had been kind but distant, saying that his affairs in India had taken a turn for the worse and he was unable to offer any help. The last Sebastian had heard from his uncle had been a brief letter of condolence in response to word of Michael Vane's disappearance and presumed death.

But now his uncle was dead, too, and Sebastian could hardly comprehend what the letter conveyed. Due to the great distance involved, it had taken some time for word of Henry's death to reach his solicitor in England. And when the solicitor executed Uncle Henry's will . . .

"I am writing to inform you that under the terms of your uncle's will, the entirety of his estate has descended to you, as his closest living relative," wrote Mr. Black, the Bristol solicitor. "If you will reply by post at your convenience, we may arrange a transfer of the funds and some few items of property, primarily family mementos, which Mr. Vane left in my care."

He didn't list the amount, but he didn't need to. Anything would be a godsend at this point. Sebastian's mind whirled. He doubted it was a great fortune, but it might be enough to ease his debts. It probably wouldn't allow him to repurchase any of his lost lands, but if he were no longer scraping for every farthing . . .

He wouldn't be a penniless suitor.

"I have to go to Bristol," he said abruptly, climbing to his feet.

Mrs. Jones's eyebrows went up, and then comprehension dawned in her face. "Oh, indeed? Is there some good news as well?"

"Yes." He smiled morosely. "Even the good news comes on the heels of sad tidings."

"Well, if anyone's been due a little good news, it's you, sir," she replied loyally. "No matter what heels it comes on. I'll have Mr. Jones fetch a valise and see to hiring a chaise."

Sebastian went up the stairs toward his bedchamber to pack, then paused in the corridor. He had moved into the room closest to the top of the stairs after the war, when his injured leg ached so badly, every step saved was priceless. He had stayed there after his leg healed because it let him keep closer track of his father, who once tried to sneak out of the house after midnight with some gunpowder and a hammer, rambling about a brilliant plan to create lightning in the stable.

But now he looked down the corridor, toward the large master chamber and the adjoining bedroom that had been his mother's so long ago. It was dim down that way; all the doors had been closed for years, and the windows were no doubt coated in dust.

Slowly he walked down the corridor, his cane seeming to echo more loudly than usual. At his father's door he paused again, then gently opened it.

The finer furnishings had been sold, and what remained had been stripped of any fabrics. The rug was gone, taken out so no rodents would ruin it. The bare windows were hazy with dirt but allowed the blaze of the afternoon sun into the room through the bars that still covered them. Sebastian took a deep breath, catching the faintest whiff of camphor. His father had suffered from an inflammation of the lungs before he disappeared, and Mrs. Jones had used the camphor liberally to ease Michael Vane's breathing. For a moment he felt again the grief of watching his father waste away, the alarm of having to restrain him, and the shame of thinking, in weaker moments, that it would be a mercy when his father died.

He walked through the room and opened the door into the adjoining bedroom, where his mother had slept. She'd died when he was only a child, and his father had used her room as his private study after that. Eleanor Vane's room was as barren as Sebastian's memory was of her, devoid even of furniture. Only the wall coverings offered any clue to the woman who had once lived here. Wreaths of delicately painted vines and flowers ornamented the light blue paper, and when Sebastian looked closely, he could see tiny figures on swings beneath some wreaths, whimsical little creatures forever caught in a moment of artless joy. It was a small sign that there had once been love and happiness at Montrose Hill, and somehow the fact that they had survived seemed to hint that there would be again, someday.

For the first time he thought about bringing a bride to Montrose Hill.

Abigail looked up at the sound of footsteps approaching, and smiled in surprise. "Boris!" She put aside her book and scratched the dog's ears, glancing hopefully down the path behind him. "You're not out by yourself, are you, boy?"

"No." Sebastian came around the bend in the path. "Although if he were, I'd look for him right here."

"Here?" She grinned, reaching into her basket for a treat for the dog, who instantly sat and regarded her expectantly. "Have I discovered his favorite spot in the woods?"

"His favorite spot is at your feet," said Sebastian dryly. "He is your devoted servant."

"I'm always ready with a bribe." She fed Boris a piece of cheese. "I wonder how you'd like a bit of sausage."

"Don't," said his master at once. He came to a stop in front of her and looked down at his dog, who completely ignored him. Boris's eyes were trained on Abigail as he licked his chops for every last trace of cheese. "He'd never go home with me again if you fed him sausage."

"Well, he wouldn't be allowed inside Hart House, where Milo rules over all. You wouldn't like that at all," she told Boris. "He's a terrible pest, that Milo."

Sebastian just grinned, and Abigail's heart skipped a beat. "You seem happy today," she said on impulse. "It suits you."

He tilted his head and looked at her without any of the reserve that usually filled his face. That reserve had fascinated her and intrigued her, but Abigail realized she liked this side of him even better. "I might be," he said.

"Oh?" She arched one brow. "I hope you decide you are."

"I've had some news."

"Good news, I hope," she prompted when he said no more.

"I'm not sure, but it requires me to go away for a few days."

"I see," she murmured. "I hope it turns out well . . ."

He lifted one shoulder. "It involves someone I hardly knew. But I wanted to see you before I left, and lo, Boris did, too." He nudged the dog with one boot, but the animal stayed put, lying at Abigail's feet.

"Is he going with you?"

"No. I'll tell Mrs. Jones to let him out. Perhaps he'll find you in the woods."

"Will you be back in time to attend my mother's barge excursion?" Abigail knew from the look on his face what the answer would be. She tried not to feel disappointed; a man couldn't help it when something required him to go away.

"Unfortunately not. I shall send her a note with my regrets." He sat on the log beside her, just far enough away to keep from touching her.

"I'm sure she'll be very sorry to hear it." Abigail broke off another bite of cheese for Boris, who nipped it delicately from her fingers and rested his big head on her knee, gazing up at her in soulful adoration. "Is it a long journey?"

"To Bristol."

Abigail nodded. At least two days' journey. "When do you leave?"

"Tomorrow. It's been a while since I traveled." He stretched out his left leg and frowned at it. "Not since I came back from the war in a miller's cart, now that I think about it."

Abigail gasped, thinking of being jolted about like a sack of flour, let alone with a severely injured leg. "A miller's cart!"

He shrugged. "The army's got little use for a man with a shattered leg. And the longer one remains under an army doctor's eye, the more likely they are to want to cut off a bad limb. I scraped together some funds and took myself off as soon as I reached English soil." He paused. "I'd just learned of my father's condition as well, and needed to go home. A miller's cart served my purpose."

She bit her lip. "I hope you're able to make a more comfortable journey this time."

He grimaced. "I expect so! At least there's a happier prospect at the end of this one."

"Oh?" She glanced at him from beneath lowered eyelashes. He was being very coy about it, but there was a subtle hum of excitement about him that she wasn't used to seeing. What news was taking him away? Had he found some way to reclaim his property? Had he inherited a fortune? She was dying to know but held her tongue.

He grinned, sending her heart soaring. It must be good news—even if he wouldn't tell her, she felt a happy thrill that something had pleased him so much. "You must forgive me for being vague," he said, as if he could read her thoughts. "I don't entirely know what it betides for me, but I have hopes it might be happy."

"I hope so, too!" She beamed at him.

His own smile lingered as his gaze dropped to her mouth. "I have *very* high hopes," he murmured, shifting his weight toward her. "Will you kiss me for luck?"

"Of course," she whispered as he tipped up her chin and brushed his mouth over hers. "I wish you more good luck than that . . ."

"You should." He cupped her jaw in his hand, his thumb stroking her cheek. "I could use some luck." He kissed her again, this time the lingering, deep kiss that made her burn. She inched closer, remembering how it had felt to be in his arms when he kissed her, and in a sudden movement he twisted off the log, falling to his knees in front of her and gathering her close. Oh yes—that was it. Abigail slid her arms around his neck and kissed him. She shivered as his fingers drew down her cheek, along her throat, toward her bosom. She pressed her toes into the ground and arched her back, whimpering in pleasure as his hand curved around her breast and his fingers circled her nipple. Even through the cloth of her dress she felt his touch like a shock of electricity. He groaned deep in his throat, and tore his mouth away from hers.

"I want to kiss you everywhere," he breathed, pressing a hot kiss to the skin below her ear. His fingers still played over her nipple, teasing the sensitive nub into erect attention.

Abigail's heart thundered. Her skin felt taut, eager to be touched. She clutched his shoulders and tried to pull him back to her in mute acquiescence.

He resisted. He held her at arm's length as his gaze slid over her, every bit as arousing as a touch could be. "If I wasn't mad before, I am now." His eyes seemed to darken as he unbuttoned her spencer. Abigail shivered as he eased it off her shoulders, but she was the one who pulled it completely off.

Sebastian's face grew still and yet somehow fierce; he lowered his head and brushed a reverent kiss at the base of her throat. Abigail dug her fingers into the rough bark of the log. She closed her eyes as his hands moved lightly over her shoulders, brushing the sides of her breasts before sliding behind her and working at the lacing of her dress.

His kisses drifted along her collarbone as her bodice came loose. He darted a wary, yearning glance at her. Abigail could only nod and whisper, "Yes." A shadow of a smile touched his lips before he tugged at her sleeves, pulling the bodice down to expose her shift and stays.

Her bosom felt shockingly bare and exposed, even before he untied the ribbon of her chemise. Her heart seemed to be beating a thousand times a minute as she waited, eager, anxious, desperate, for him to do . . . something. Another hard shudder racked her when the cool air hit her bared breasts; her nipples, already tight, seemed to draw up so hard they ached.

"Abigail," Sebastian breathed. "My darling." And then his mouth was on her skin, on the swell of her bosom. He kissed her, soft little kisses as though he was murmuring against her skin. She strained toward him, and his arm went around her waist, anchoring her to him. Abigail flung her head back, reveling in the sensuous caress. This only exposed her further, and she shamelessly thrust her chest forward, begging for more. Lower, lower his mouth moved until finally he kissed her where he had originally said.

She shuddered as his lips moved over her nipple, teasing and tormenting as his fingers had done. He flicked his tongue and she jerked. He darted a single gleaming glance at her before he parted her knees and moved between her legs, pressing forward until his hips met hers. For a moment he held her tight against him, his eyes closed, and Abigail realized with a shock that she could feel him, hard and erect.

She could hardly breathe.

He groaned and closed his lips around her aching flesh.

Her face burned. Her heart hammered. Sebastian Vane was on his knees before her, making love to her. She felt wild and wanton with her dress falling down and his mouth on her breast, her blood racing and coursing so hotly through her veins, she felt the reckless desire to tear off her clothes to cool her skin. It was shocking and scandalous, but when he lifted his mouth from her breast, giving one last teasing swirl of his tongue, she only turned so he could do the same to the other side. And all the while she was exquisitely conscious that he was aroused, too.

Abigail said a silent word of apology to Lady Constance. She'd suspected that *50 Ways to Sin* was unrealistic and exaggerated. She'd had no idea at all.

And then—then— She almost choked on her own breath. He was drawing up the hem of her skirt. His palm was smoothing up the side of her calf—now over her knee—now higher— "Sebastian," she whispered uncertainly, still clinging to him.

"I know," he murmured, his lips on her breast. "Trust me . . ." And then he parted the gap in her pantalets and touched her.

Abigail started so violently she almost fell over backward. Sebastian's grip around her waist tightened as he stroked her again.

"Trust me," he repeated in a ragged whisper. "I won't make love to you, but let me give you this . . ."

He had touched her before, in the grotto. Abigail remembered it well. But this . . . This was more vivid, more intense, more personal. She could feel the warmth of his hand cupping her bare flesh, the shock of his fingers parting her, and then—she gasped so hard her head swam—the intrusion of his finger sliding inside her.

Sebastian exhaled slowly, as if he couldn't let his breath out at once. "I want you." His voice was a thread of sound. "So desperately . . ." His finger withdrew, only to return, this time with a soft touch on that knot of exquisite sensation. Abigail clutched at him, stripped of speech. His gentle but inexorable touch continued;

he had angled himself so now his erection was against her inner thigh, and as she moved, her body reacting on instinct to his caresses, he rocked his hips.

Now she understood why Lady Constance called lovemaking an intimate dance. Their bodies moved together in concert, she straining and writhing against him, he holding her tight and driving her ever wilder. When the storm building inside her finally crested and broke, Abigail almost wept on his shoulder as it shuddered through her. Sebastian's arm felt like iron around her, although his hand was still deft and gentle between her legs. When his fingers finally slipped out of her, Abigail quivered, feeling drained and bereft.

She held tight to his neck when he made a slight motion to withdraw. She thought she'd fall on the ground if he let go of her now. She didn't want him to leave, not today, not ever; he'd woken some deep, restless urge inside her that wanted more. It was a little terrifying how eager she was to test the rest of Lady Constance's descriptions. Just the hard, heavy shape of Sebastian's erection, surging against her hip, made her want to see it and touch him and know what other mysterious pleasures he could show her. She hadn't really thought she was *that* wanton, and it alarmed her that she'd almost forgotten why.

"Well," she whispered, "I hope that brings you luck."

His shoulders tensed, then eased as he gave a short laugh. "It most decidedly has. I feel quite the luckiest bloke alive right now."

Abigail smiled, unconsciously arching her back. He pressed another kiss against her bosom. "I'm feeling quite lucky myself. I'll miss you," she added on impulse.

He tipped up his face to look at her, his expression

open and almost vulnerable. "And I you." He tugged her skirt back down and then took her hands in his. "You are . . ." He hesitated. "Very dear to me, Abigail."

She blinked. It was a fine sentiment, but not quite as passionate as she had hoped for.

"I . . ." He seemed to be struggling for words. "I wish . . . You—you will still be at Hart House when I return, won't you? Your family has no plans to return to London?"

"None I am aware of," she said slowly. "How long will you be gone?"

"A fortnight." His gaze dropped to her breasts, still bared. "Perhaps a little less."

She wet her lips, beginning to feel awkward. "My mother has planned a musical evening in eight days' time, so I expect we'll be here." She waited, but he didn't say why he wanted to know so urgently. She pulled loose from his restraining hand and tugged her chemise back into place. "Would—would you—?" Blushing, she turned her back, trying not to flinch at the feel of his fingers smoothing her bodice back into place and drawing the lacing tight. It seemed a very mundane ending to such an encounter, and she didn't face him as she got to her feet.

"Abigail." He caught her hand as she reached for her basket. She looked up, uncertain. He brought her hand to his lips, then pressed it against his heart. "If I were to call on your father . . . would you be pleased?"

Her heart gave a leap, and a cautiously hopeful smile broke out on her face. "I suppose that would depend on what you said to him."

"I hope to ask him a question of the utmost importance."

Something fluttered in her stomach. "I'm sure he will give you a thoughtful and honest answer."

Slowly he nodded, looking at her with . . . with . . . Abigail blushed at the word that was filling her mind. She thought it was love. She almost held her breath, waiting.

"And if I were to ask you a very important question, would you also answer me honestly and thoughtfully?"

Tense with anticipation, she managed to nod.

He pressed her hand. "That is all I can ask." He cupped her cheek and kissed her. "Good-bye for now," he murmured.

She made herself smile. "Good luck."

"I will see you in a few days, my darling," he promised, just a glimmer of a smile lighting his eyes. "Boris! Let's go, boy." And without another word, he turned and walked away, the black dog loping after him.

Abigail watched him go, reluctant to lose sight of him. When he had vanished down the path she exhaled, wilting a little. She'd been sure he was about to propose marriage, or tell her he loved her. But surely he wouldn't have asked about Papa if he didn't intend to do it when he returned. After all . . . he wanted her— probably as much as she wanted him. She laid one hand on her bosom, and her skin seemed to hum with the memory of his fingers and mouth doing such wicked, wonderful things to her. It might be possible to feel something similar with any attractive man, but Abigail was sure that what she felt for Sebastian wasn't ordinary. What had happened between them just now had definitely been extraordinary.

She wondered what news was taking him away. It must be something good, it *must* be. She had never seen him so lighthearted and pleased. Her heart gave a great bound at the thought that he had learned something, received something, gained something that altered his feelings about marriage.

In a much brighter mood, she collected her book, which had fallen on the ground, and her basket, which Boris had stealthily emptied of both cheese and sausage while his master made love to her. As she was brushing the dirt off the cover of her book, she noticed Sebastian's cane. It was still leaning against the tree trunk, right where he had left it when he sat down next to her . . . and asked her to kiss him for luck . . . and ended up lavishing kisses all over her. Where he had implied that he loved her and would propose when he returned. Abigail knew she ought to leave it, in case he returned for it, but then on impulse she snatched it up as she left. With an irrepressible grin stuck on her face, she headed for home.

Sebastian was halfway home before he realized he'd left his cane behind. Somehow kissing Abigail Weston had driven his hurt knee right out of his mind, and the taste of her skin had dulled any pain from walking without the cane. He thought about going back to get it, then shrugged and continued on the path to Montrose Hill. He had another cane at home, and now he was more impatient than ever to go to Bristol.

He prayed to God there were some funds in his uncle's estate. Ten thousand pounds would make him a gentleman of means again; not a wealthy man, but independent and secure. Eight thousand pounds would clear him of debt and restore him to financial security. Four or five thousand would enable him to support a wife, especially if that wife had money of her own. Even two thousand pounds would be enormously helpful, paying some of his debts and freeing him from the heaviest interest payments.

Of course, simply marrying Abigail would restore him to financial comfort. Rumor in town was that each Weston daughter had a dowry of forty thousand pounds or more. She was right: it *was* pride that held him back. He was not a fortune hunter and he refused to give people the opening to call him one. If only he could clear his debts. That would be enough to allow him to stand before Mr. Weston with a clear conscience and an untroubled spirit. He couldn't change his crippled leg, and even with forty thousand pounds he could probably never regain his full estate, but he wouldn't be a parasite.

With just a bit of good fortune, he could bring everything around. He never wanted her to look at him and wonder if her money had influenced him. He had lost every other bit of dignity. It was one thing if other people whispered that he'd married her because of her money—given the disparity in their fortunes, it was probably inevitable—but he couldn't bear it if Abigail thought that. She, at least, should know without a doubt that he married her because he loved her.

For a moment his steps slowed. He could have told her that today. The news about his uncle could have waited until he returned from Bristol, when he would know exactly what the news was and what it meant for him. He'd almost said it, when she gazed at him with those starry eyes and waited. And yet somehow . . . he hadn't said it.

He shook himself and quickened his pace again. It would be better to tell her he loved her when he could follow it up with a proper marriage proposal. There would be time for all that when he returned, with—God willing—his respectability and pride restored. And then he would have all the time in the world to make love to her.

Chapter 14

Sebastian's departure dimmed Abigail's interest in walking. She still went out, but only met Boris once. Since the dog was pursuing something small and quick through the bracken, she didn't even get a friendly lick on the hand. The grotto held no real allure anymore, either. Even though Sebastian had left the rug and cushions there and told her it was hers, she knew it wouldn't be the same without him. And then the weather turned cloudy and cool, putting an end to her rambles entirely.

Confined to the house, she had plenty of time to relive every moment of their last encounter. She contemplated every word he spoke, searching for any definite sign of his intentions. It was impossible that he meant nothing, she decided. Sebastian was scrupulously honest. Any man who would tell her that he was likely to run mad was hardly the sort who would tease her and lead her to believe he intended to propose if he had no thought of doing so. She wished he had told her what took him to Bristol, but his manner made her think he wasn't very sure of it. Perhaps one of his investments had become more profitable. Perhaps he'd been offered a promising opportunity. He might be reticent in either of those circumstances.

And yet, if he really had no idea how beneficial it might be—as when he said he had high hopes and asked for a kiss for luck—would he have mentioned speaking to her father? Abigail could think of only one reason he would want to speak to Papa. Surely if Sebastian really doubted the outcome of his trip, he wouldn't have mentioned Papa. But if the trip wasn't the deciding factor, why hadn't he simply said he loved her then, when she was in his arms as willing as any wanton?

A fortnight seemed a very long time in the face of so many questions.

Penelope interrupted her ruminations one day as she sat with a book on her lap, watching the clouds scud across the sky through the windows of the conservatory. "Something to cheer you, Abby!" she announced.

"Where did you get it?" Abigail gasped as Penelope flourished a copy of *50 Ways to Sin*, instinctively glancing about for any eavesdropping servants or parents.

"Don't worry, I made certain the door was closed before I revealed it." Penelope wrinkled her nose. "I've learned my lesson on that score."

"Where did you get it?" Abigail repeated, reassured enough to take it out and open to the first page. "Is it good?"

Her sister snorted. "As if there's been a bad one! I didn't like it as well as the last, but it's still quite thoroughly naughty. Never mind how I got it. Look at page two."

Abigail read for a moment, then gasped in shock. "Two lovers at once?"

"Indeed." Penelope lowered her voice even more. "Brothers."

"Oh my." Abigail choked on a disbelieving laugh. "As if finding one gentleman to love isn't difficult enough!"

"I daresay Constance has lower standards than you, Abby." Penelope put her head to one side. "Has the esteemed Mr. Vane written to you?"

She carefully folded the pamphlet cover closed. "No, nor do I expect him to. He didn't ask."

"Well, he must not plan to be gone very long, then," said Penelope. "The man is mad in love with you."

"How would you know?"

"From the way his eyes follow your every move. Because he came to call even though the rest of Richmond thinks he's a misanthrope, and because he won Mama's heart by making Milo obey. And I think you're in love with him because you've been sad and quiet ever since he left." She tapped one finger against her lips. "Now that I think of it, you were like that even before Mama mentioned his note begging off the barge party. Did you meet him on one of your solitary walks in the woods?"

Abigail bit her lip, debating what to say. Her unanswerable questions were weighing heavily on her mind, but Penelope wasn't always the most thoughtful confidante. "Yes. He told me he was going away."

"Aha!" Her sister's eyes gleamed. "Where did he go?"

"To Bristol, and I do not know why," she said before her sister could ask. "He estimated he would be gone no more than a fortnight."

"That's not so long," Penelope said, almost consolingly. "I'm sure it will pass before you know it."

There was a tap at the door and a maid peeked in. "Pardon, Miss Weston, Miss Penelope, but your mother asks you to come to the drawing room to receive callers."

"Of course, Jane," said Penelope brightly. She had lunged out of her chair to stand in front of Abigail, who was frantically trying to conceal *50 Ways to Sin*. "We'll be right there." Jane nodded and ducked back out of the room. Penelope wilted. "That was close!"

"I think the orange trees concealed it." The pamphlet was now safely hidden between the pages of Abigail's book. "I'd better run upstairs and hide this. Tell Mama I've gone to fix my hair."

Penelope nodded and hurried off to the drawing room. Abigail went to her bedchamber, heart still thumping from almost being caught. She couldn't resist taking a peek at the story, and ended up reading it all. It was even more shocking than the previous tales; Lady Constance met two friendly gentlemen, and—unable to decide which suited her more—took them both to her bed. Abigail had already accepted that the stories were the most improbable fiction, but this surely went too far. Constance seemed to regard her lovers with warmth and respect, if not love, but at least she gave each of them her full attention. How could she embrace two men, figuratively and literally, at once? Abigail reread one page, to be certain. Yes, Constance most definitely managed new ways of finding pleasure and giving it.

The blush still lingered on her cheeks as she went to the drawing room, having hidden the story in the bottom of her sewing basket. She took a moment to compose herself, and opened the door.

Sitting beside Penelope on the settee was Lady Samantha Lennox. She had called before with her sister, Lady Turley, but this time she was accompanied by someone else. He sat with his back to the door, but leapt to his feet at once and turned as Abigail came in.

"Here is my eldest daughter, Abigail," said Mama

warmly. "Abigail, come meet our guest, Viscount Atherton. He is Lady Samantha's brother."

"How do you do, sir?" She curtsied.

"Very well, Miss Weston." Benedict Lennox, Lord Atherton was tall and handsome, with black hair that lay in thick waves at his temples. He wore the crisp uniform of the King's Guard, which beautifully displayed his athletic figure. His bright blue eyes brightened in frank appreciation as he bowed to her. "It's a pleasure to make your acquaintance."

For no good reason, Abigail blushed again. She murmured something polite and went to take a seat, only realizing a moment later that the only seat left was next to Lord Atherton. She greeted Lady Samantha and accepted a cup of tea from her mother, all the while vividly conscious of the gentleman beside her.

"It's so very kind of you to call with Lady Samantha, sir." Mama hardly needed to express her pleasure aloud; Abigail could almost see it radiating off her mother. She stole a glance at Penelope, who was sipping her tea without taking her eyes off Lord Atherton. Well. Perhaps her sister would find Richmond more interesting now that there was an inarguably splendid viscount sitting in their drawing room. She wondered if her father would be lying in wait outside the door to encourage the man to start courting one of them.

"The kindness was yours, in receiving me," replied Lord Atherton. "My sister has told me so much about the new tenants of Hart House, I implored her to bring me to call. She's had no peace from me."

"It's true," said Lady Samantha with a fond smile. "It's impossible to resist him once he begins imploring."

"But our door is always open," declared Mama, stroking Milo's fur. The puppy was curled up next to her on the sofa. He must have made friends with the visitors, to have ceased his yapping already. "Particularly to any friend of Lady Samantha's."

"I'd like that very much. I'm on leave from my regiment for a month, and would be honored to help show you the delights of Richmond while I'm here."

Penelope made a noise like a muffled snort.

He turned to her. "I sense doubt, Miss Penelope. On which score, I wonder: my desires, or the delights of Richmond?" From the gleam in his eye, Abigail thought he knew which one it was.

Penelope smiled brightly, avoiding her mother's gaze. "Who could doubt either?"

"Which is no sort of answer at all!" He turned to Abigail. "Have I intimidated your sister? Please tell me I haven't, Miss Weston. I would hate to have begun so badly with my new neighbors."

She had to laugh. "When you know my sister better, my lord, you'll know how impossible that is! I believe she meant to say,, we would be pleased to learn the delights of Richmond; thank you very much for offering to show us."

"It will be my pleasure." His eyes were so very blue, and the little lines at the corners suggested his good humor was perpetual. Even his voice was attractive, rich and well pitched. "What have you seen so far?"

It took Abigail a moment to register the question as he gazed at her with such interest. "Oh!" She blushed, unaccountably flustered. "Not much, I'm afraid."

"Have you been to the crest of Richmond Hill? The botanical gardens at Kew? The palace at Hampton Court?" His voice grew more anguished with each shake of her head. After the third, he laid one hand on his breast and turned to Penelope in mock humility. "Miss Penelope, I humbly beg your pardon. Who would not be bored, with only the village for amusement?"

Now that she had been publicly supported in her disdain for all of Richmond, Penelope smiled modestly. "I've greatly enjoyed the shops in the village."

"And you, Miss Weston?" Lord Atherton turned to her again, his eyes shining with mirth.

"The village is charming," she agreed. "But I enjoy simpler pleasures: a jaunt in the boat, a walk in the woods."

"Ah, the woods." Now real feeling warmed his voice. "I remember these woods well. They are almost more familiar than Stratford Court to me. When I was a boy, Lady Burton was gracious enough to grant me leave to explore at will. I spent hours there." He shook his head ruefully. "My sister would summon me home with a light in a particular window, lest I be punished for being out too late."

"Can you see Stratford Court from our woods?" Penelope raised her eyebrows. "I didn't realize that."

He cleared his throat. "You must go a little higher on the hill."

"Oh, you mean Montrose Hill?" Penelope nodded, not noticing the way both guests seemed to freeze in place for a moment. "Did you ever discover the grotto in the woods?"

Abigail almost choked. How could Penelope—and in front of Mama, too? She would never forgive her sister if Mama banned her from walking in the woods.

"No," said Lord Atherton after an almost imperceptible hesitation. "I don't believe it still exists. It was filled in years ago."

"Right," said Penelope, finally catching Abigail's

eye for a moment. "Such a pity. It would have been fascinating to see."

"Where was there a grotto?" asked Mama. She was idly stroking Milo, but Abigail knew her ease was an illusion. She had the attention of a hawk.

"It was rumored to be somewhere in the woods, Mrs. Weston," answered Lord Atherton. "A bygone curiosity from the days of the Stuarts. But like all rumor, it was founded on nothing reliable. No one's seen it in living memory."

Except me, thought Abigail, thinking of a cut-glass mermaid pining for her love, and the secluded intimacy of the chamber. And Sebastian.

"I never heard of it." Mama's keen gaze touched Abigail for just a moment. "Abigail, you must be careful when you walk in the woods. I wouldn't want you to fall down an old grotto."

"I am," she quickly assured her mother.

"There's little cause for worry, Mrs. Weston. Lady Burton always believed it had been filled in even before she owned Hart House." Atherton gave a penitent grin. "If it were still in existence, I would surely know, for I scoured those woods for years. She indulged an eager boy in allowing me to hunt for it, but alas; it must have been buried decades ago. I never found any trace of it—and I really *looked*. I longed to prove everyone wrong by discovering it."

"I suspect that was the grotto's greatest allure," Lady Samantha added.

Her brother laughed. "So it was! Not even pirate treasure would have been more appealing—although I must confess, when I was a boy I hoped to find the grotto filled with pirate treasure!"

Everyone laughed. Abigail caught her sister watching her, though, and she tried to deliver a stern message with only her eyes. Penelope gave her a tiny nod and sipped her tea.

The conversation took a more mundane turn, and after a while the guests took their leave. Mama invited Lord Atherton to join them on the barge party in a few days' time, which he promptly accepted. Everyone rising to their feet roused Milo from his puppy nap, and he leapt off the sofa and began racing around the room, yipping excitedly. When someone opened the door, the dog took advantage and ran into the hall, then right out of the house.

"Oh dear," sighed Mama. "Not again." By now Milo's escapes had taken their toll even on her. Her attempts to train him to come when called hadn't been as successful as Sebastian's had been.

"We'll catch him," Lord Atherton promised immediately, his eyes dancing. "Come, Samantha! A chase!" Briskly he strode off after the dog.

"I can't run in these shoes!" his sister protested, looking at Penelope in chagrin.

"I wouldn't bother," muttered Penelope. As usual, she made no effort to chase Milo.

From outside came the whinny of a horse. Mama gasped, jolted out of her resignation. "Oh my! He'll be trampled." She rushed out of the room, and Abigail went with her.

Outside, the dog really was tempting death this time. A tall black stallion was tossing his head and dancing skittishly from side to side while Milo ran laps around the gravel, darting under his hooves, then under the carriage, then circling in front of the carriage horses as he evaded Lord Atherton's and the groom's attempts to catch him. The more Milo barked, the more restive the horses grew, snorting and stamping their feet. Any one of their hooves could crush the puppy.

Mama gave Abigail a worried look. "I will never forgive your father," she said in despair.

"I'll get him," Abigail promised. She watched the chase for a moment, waiting for a good opportunity. Lord Atherton was obviously enjoying himself, waving at the harried groom to go around the carriage while he stalked the dog on the near side. But Milo was too wriggly; just as the viscount was about to grab him, Milo twisted and turned and went right under the carriage, between the groom's boots, and toward the trees along the drive . . .

Where Abigail had run to wait for him. "Milo," she called, crouching on her knees. "Come, Milo, I have cheese for you." She held out her hand as if she had a something in it. It worked on Boris, who was admittedly far better trained. She held her breath, hoping against hope it would fool Milo.

The puppy stopped a few feet away from her, his tail wagging. "Milo, come," Abigail repeated firmly. She waited, not moving. After a moment, the little dog gave himself a shake, then trotted forward. As he licked her fingers in search of the cheese, Abigail seized him by the scruff of his neck. "You don't deserve a treat, wicked creature," she told him. The puppy barked at her, then accepted disappointment philosophically, and began thumping his short tail against her arm.

"Well done, Miss Weston!" Lord Atherton strode up, regarding her with respect. "He's a wily creature."

She laughed. "And slippery! We're all well versed in chasing Milo by now." The puppy licked her chin at the sound of his name. Abigail grimaced. It was just her luck to be chasing the dog every time she met a gentleman.

"At least he's an appreciative captive." Atherton grinned, scratching Milo's head. The puppy struggled to lick his hand, too.

"He made it into the woods once and got caught in a bramble bush. If he's so appreciative, he could stop running away at all."

He laughed. "Perhaps it's not in the nature of puppies." He fell in step beside her as she walked back toward her mother, now joined by Lady Samantha and Penelope. "May I ask a very presumptuous question?"

"I suppose," she said in surprise.

He glanced toward the woods. "Talking of these woods and the grotto has made me long for one more walk. Might I have permission?"

"Of course!" Properly he ought to ask Papa or Mama, but there was no chance that either of her parents would deny the request. Papa would probably invite Lord Atherton to walk anywhere on Hart House grounds he liked, including inside the house.

"Thank you." He tilted his head to see her better. Her face felt warm. There was no mistaking the admiration in his eyes. Gentlemen had admired her before, but she wasn't used to seeing it so unabashed and overt. "Would tomorrow be acceptable? I don't wish to intrude on any plans your family might have made."

"Oh no," she assured him. "We haven't any engagements tomorrow."

His smile grew wider. "Excellent."

They had reached the others. Lady Samantha expressed her relief that Milo wasn't hurt, and patted his head. Lord Atherton helped his sister into the carriage, and swung into the tall black stallion's saddle;

the horse had calmed down now that Milo no longer yipped at him. Mama waited until they were halfway down the drive before turning to her daughters.

"What a charming gentleman!"

"Which of us do you think he'll marry?" asked Penelope gravely. "Oh, how happy Papa will be that he was proven right about buying this house!"

Mama raised her eyes to the heavens. "If Lord Atherton—or anyone!—asked for you, miss, I'd force your father to agree! Good riddance, I'd say!"

"I don't think you'd have to push Papa very hard."

Mama just gave her a dark look as she took the puppy from Abigail. "Thank you for saving him yet again, Abby." She snuggled her pet into her arms. "Are you hurt, little Milo? You must stop running outside like that. Let's make sure you haven't got anything caught in your fur." She went back inside the house, still cooing over the dog.

"Thank you for saving my precious darling, Abby," Penelope mimicked their mother's voice. "I adore him more than either of you!"

Abigail choked on a laugh. "Not true! Although he doesn't have your impertinence."

Her sister's eyes gleamed. "Speaking of that . . . You were very deep in conversation with Lord Atherton when I came out with Lady Samantha. What were you speaking of?"

"The dog." Abigail kept her smile fixed on her face as she watched the guests depart. "And you thought Richmond would be dull."

"Lord Atherton will have to provide a great deal more excitement to cancel out the rest of Richmond," her sister retorted. "Still, he's a far more attractive diversion than I expected to find here."

At the end of the drive, Lord Atherton looked back, right at her, and tipped his hat. Lord, Penelope was right, Abigail thought in a bit of a daze. He was blindingly handsome.

"He asked to come walk in the woods tomorrow," she confided in a low voice. "I said he could, of course; won't Papa be so pleased?"

Penelope raised one eyebrow. "Did he really? Well, well."

"What?" She frowned at her sister's expression.

"Perhaps he won't want to walk alone." Penelope assumed a very prim and proper expression. "If you don't feel like making the sacrifice, I might find it in my heart to escort him—safely away from your grotto, of course."

Abigail snorted with laughter. "A truly loving sister!"

Penelope just continued looking pleased. "I trust we shall see much, much more of the handsome Lord Atherton."

Chapter 15

True to his word, Lord Atherton came the next morning.

Mama's eyebrows rose when he was announced. Penelope shot Abigail a look of delight. The man himself gave them all a blinding smile when the butler showed him in. Warm greetings were exchanged, and then he turned to Mama. "If it's not an imposition, I hoped to take a stroll in your woods, ma'am."

"Of course, sir!" She smiled at Abigail. "My daughter mentioned you might. You're very welcome to walk there anytime you like."

"Thank you. Miss Weston told me much the same thing, but I didn't want to presume upon your kindness by just roaming all over your property," he explained with an apologetic air.

"Nonsense! Papa would be perfectly content if you did so," Abigail said with a smile. Her father had been as pleased as punch when she told him of Lord Atherton's request. "He said you may walk in these woods as often as you like, since they're so familiar to you."

"That's very kind of him." He grinned, his eyes twinkling. Today he wore regular clothing, and his gray coat made his eyes seem even bluer. "Although I fear he's too generous; it's been at least a decade since I roamed these woods. I may become hopelessly lost!"

Mama smiled. "Abigail could direct you to the best paths. She's very fond of walking in the woods, and knows them quite well."

"Indeed?" He turned to Abigail. "Miss Weston, would you walk with me?"

There was a moment of ringing silence. Penelope's face was blank with surprise; Mama's was bright with delight. Abigail felt her cheeks grow warm. "Penelope has walked with me many times," she tried to say.

"But her ankle is still tender from the injury she received the last time she walked out," said her mother. "She was favoring it just this morning."

Penelope gave a faint shrug and pretended absorption in her embroidery floss. Abigail took a deep breath. "Of course. I'd be happy to walk with you, my lord."

Lord Atherton's smile deepened. "How wonderfully kind of you. I worried it would be too great an imposition."

"Not at all," she said, blushing harder.

"No, Abigail never turns down a chance of a walk in the woods." Penelope's smile was a little barbed. "She knows every path, my lord; you couldn't become lost if you wanted to."

Their guest laughed. "The ideal guide! I couldn't ask for better."

Abigail, wishing her sister had never invented a twisted ankle—and betting that Penelope regretted it as well now—went to get her bonnet.

"Are you truly fond of the woods?" Lord Atherton asked as they strolled across the grass. Contrary to his claim that he didn't remember anything, he was leading the way toward the river, away from her usual haunts nearer Montrose Hill. Abigail resisted the urge to glance back up the hill; Sebastian was in Bristol.

"Yes. I like the quiet among the trees."

He nodded. "I do, too. Well—I should say I appreciate it now. When I was a boy, I most liked their distance from my tutors and lessons."

"No!" she protested in mock disbelief.

" 'Tis true," he admitted with a deep sigh as they reached the shade of the trees. "Many times I slipped out and crossed the river in my small punt, knowing no one would find me here. These trees became, in my imagination, deepest Africa, the wilderness of the Americas, the remotest reaches of the Orient. And since my tutors couldn't cross the river once I'd taken the punt, I might as well have been there."

She laughed. "That must have frustrated them to no end!"

"I hope so!" He grinned. "It was worth any punishment."

"Did you explore alone?"

He hesitated. "Sometimes. Do you usually walk alone?"

"Whenever my sister doesn't come, which is most of the time." There was a tree lying across the path, at least two feet in diameter. The bracken was too thick to go around it. Abigail gathered up her skirt to climb over it.

"Do you prefer solitude?" Lord Atherton vaulted over the trunk and held out one hand to her. "Or company, Miss Weston?"

She gave him her hand and stepped up on top of the trunk. "There are benefits to both."

He held up his other hand and helped her jump down. "There definitely are," he murmured, not retreating when she landed quite close to him. "But I prefer company, at the moment." Abigail tipped her head back and almost forgot to breathe at his expression. Was he flirting with her?

"Do you?" Her voice sounded as breathless as she felt.

"Very much so." His gaze didn't waver from hers. Abigail felt a little dazed, unable to look away. It was hard to believe he had once been Sebastian's dearest friend; they were as alike as oil and water, as far as she'd seen. But perhaps she was being too hasty. Lord Atherton was charming and glib and handsome, but he might be more like Sebastian than not, once one got to know him. Sebastian was the very model of a man whose exterior hid more than it revealed about his true self.

She realized he was still holding her hands. At that, she jerked her eyes away and racked her brain for something to say.

"You must have explored Montrose Hill grounds as well," she blurted out. "When you were acquainted with Mr. Vane."

Lord Atherton's arm flexed, but his face didn't change. "Vane? Oh yes. That was a great many years ago, though. How . . . how did you know we were acquainted?"

"Your sister told me you were once good friends with him," she rushed on. "As boys. I suppose your search for the grotto must have ranged across his property, too."

He gave her an odd look. "Yes, I suppose it did. Er . . . Have you met Vane, Miss Weston?"

"Yes." She tried to keep the memory of their last rendezvous out of mind, but her body remembered. Her nipples grew taut and hard inside her bodice and her heart thumped a little harder. "He's our neighbor; of course we've met him."

That seemed to surprise him. "He's grown very reclusive, I was told."

Instinctively her ire rose. How cruel it was to shun a man, then blame him for being a recluse. "He's been very cordial to us," she declared. "The first time I met him was in these woods; he saved my mother's dog from a bramble bush, and carried Milo home for me because the silly animal was covered in mud and would have ruined my gown."

"Who would not rescue a damsel in distress?" exclaimed Lord Atherton with a laugh, seeming to relax. "I meant no condemnation of him! I've not spent much time in Richmond for several years, and have only the reports of others. Perhaps I was misinformed."

"Oh." She smiled a little sheepishly. "Many people aren't so kind, but I've found him perfectly civil. I cannot abide it when people believe every wild rumor and story that flies around."

"You're a very wise lady," he replied. "I once knew him as a brother. We did spend hours in these woods, searching for the lost grotto and generally avoiding our tutors." He paused again, as if searching for words. "But he's had a difficult run of luck these last several years. We had a falling out some time ago and haven't spoken since. I fear he's no longer the person I once knew."

"I daresay we all change as we grow," she said, trying to be diplomatic. "Do you regret the rupture?" She really wanted to ask what had caused it, but was certain he wouldn't tell her if Lady Samantha had been the reason. On the other hand, he might know more of the truth behind the gossip. He admitted they had once been like brothers, and Abigail longed to know exactly why such a friend would have abandoned Sebastian.

Lord Atherton didn't answer for a long minute. "It was his wish," he finally said in a markedly lighter tone. "I respect that. Not all friendships are meant to endure forever." He raised one hand and pointed at a double oak, the trunks joined into one twisted mass before they split some ten feet off the ground. "I was convinced that tree was planted to mark the grotto. I once dug all around the roots, to no avail."

Abigail made herself smile. It was nowhere near the grotto, and he wasn't going to tell her anything she didn't know. She murmured something vague, and they talked of other things.

And the whole while she walked with Lord Atherton, she wondered what Sebastian was doing in Bristol.

Lord Atherton soon became a regular—and very popular—visitor at Hart House. During Mama's barge excursion, he jumped into knee-deep water to rescue Penelope's hat, which the wind had carried away. He kept his promise to take them to Richmond Hill, complete with picnic, and to Hampton Court, always with a gathering of young people. For the visit to Hampton Court, they were joined by a number of his fellow Guardsmen, out from London for the day, which made for a very merry party that ended with a race to the center of the maze. There was much shrieking, some shouting, and one challenge to a duel—with forks in place of swords—over the last strawberry tart in the hamper. Abigail thought she hadn't laughed so much in years as she had at the sight of Lord Atherton, eyes narrowed in ferocious concentration beneath his tousled black hair, clashing his fork with that of Lieutenant Cabot. And when Lord Atherton was declared the winner, by virtue of having poked Lieutenant Cabot on the cuff first, he sliced his prize into pieces and shared it among the ladies.

He was handsome, charming, witty, and gallant. His entertainments were always a delight, with interesting people invited; even the weather was perfect whenever he planned something. There seemed to be absolutely nothing wrong with him . . . except that his attentions were becoming noticeably focused.

At the beginning, Abigail thought her sister had taken a liking to him. When he saved her hat during the barge party, Penelope acted as if it had been her most treasured possession, while Abigail knew very well it was an old hat in need of new trimmings. At Hampton Court, after he regaled them with ghost stories, Penelope dared him to prove them true, and the two of them investigated a few shadowy corridors while everyone else walked out into the sunshine. Abigail, who had seen her sister shred gentlemen in London with a single word, suspected Lord Atherton would have had a far easier time winning Penelope's favor.

But for some reason, he didn't seize any opportunity she offered him. Instead, he turned to Abigail. It was small things at first—waiting to help her out of the carriage, or maneuvering to sit near her when he called. Abigail noticed them only because they were the opposite of what he would do if he returned Penelope's potential interest. Still, she told herself none of those actions meant much, and her sister's feelings seemed unperturbed by any of it; she never expressed any affection for him, or even any particular wish for his attention. If anything, Penelope's opinion of him seemed to diminish over time, although not for any reason Abigail could see.

It was too much to hope, however, that no one would notice his preference, especially as it grew more marked.

"You're the belle of Richmond," said Penelope after he left one day.

"Don't be silly," Abigail protested.

"He brought you flowers."

"He also brought you flowers, and Mama," said Abigail swiftly.

"Yours were bigger, and he gave them to you himself," Penelope pointed out with maddening truth. "No one thinks he's courting Mama or me."

"You're ridiculous." But Abigail's eyes strayed to the lovely arrangement Lord Atherton had brought. It was beautiful yet simple, exactly suited to her taste. Who but a suitor would go to such trouble and expense? Deep down, she knew her sister was right about the other bouquets. He'd brought her mother irises and her sister daisies, but Abigail's bouquet was fresh rosebuds, pale pink-violet, dewy soft and so sweetly scented she wanted to keep them next to her all day. It also mocked all her protestations that he was just being a kind neighbor.

"Hmph." Penelope tilted her head. "Have you heard from Mr. Vane?"

She gave a tiny shake of her head, her gaze lingering on the roses. "I didn't expect to. He didn't ask if he could write to me, and he isn't going to be away very long."

"Right," said Penelope after a moment. "It hasn't even been a fortnight."

It had been a week and five days. Abigail knew precisely how long he'd been gone. And even if she didn't expect to hear from Sebastian, she would have been glad to receive a letter. Very glad, actually; she missed his wry humor and slow smiles and the way he looked at her. None of that could be conveyed in a letter, of course, but it would warm her heart to know he was thinking of her. Lord Atherton was pleasantly distracting, but once he was gone, she thought of Sebastian.

Unfortunately, without any sort of declaration or promise, she didn't know what to say to the inevitable reaction of her family. Penelope was not the only one who was convinced that Lord Atherton was courting her.

"There's my girl," said Papa fondly when they met in the drawing room before dinner that night. He kissed her cheek. "A future earl on the lead!"

She pressed her lips together. "Papa, really."

"No?" His eyebrows went up without dimming his wide smile. "Is he trying to make off with your mother, then? I declare he's been in this house more than I have been of late."

Abigail gave him an aggravated look. "It was one bouquet! May a gentleman not give a simple bouquet without being convicted of aspiring to marry a girl?"

"Convicted!" Papa laughed. "Don't mistake me, Abby—I didn't mean to tease you! On the contrary, my dear, I couldn't be happier. A viscount, son and heir to an earl. And quite a handsome fellow, too. I knew Richmond would be good to us."

"Well, he hasn't said anything to me," she replied.

"Did he ask you for permission to pay his addresses, and you forgot to mention it?"

"Not yet," said her father equably. "But I won't be surprised." He must have finally noticed her aggrieved look. "Wouldn't you be pleased, Abby?"

It was hard to know what to say. It would be wrong to say Lord Atherton's presence offended her, or made her unhappy. He was charming and handsome, and she was genuinely glad to see him when he called. He told amusing stories and appeared as interested in her thoughts as in his own. The fact that he brought flowers was also hard to dislike. If only . . .

If only it were Sebastian showing such devotion. Or any devotion at all.

"We've only just met him," she finally answered, unable to give a direct answer. "Don't you think it's a bit soon to leap to such a conclusion about his intentions?"

"Perhaps," allowed her father. "But mark my words, Abby; gentlemen of Atherton's rank don't pay such particular attention lightly. He's very struck by you, and it may come to naught"—he put up one hand as she turned to him anxiously—"but I wouldn't be surprised if it led to more." He paused and studied her expression. "Is this about Vane?"

Abigail opened her mouth, realized she *really* didn't know how to answer that, and closed her mouth.

"Well," said Papa at her silence. "It will work itself out. If his feelings are engaged, he won't slink quietly from the stage, and nothing holds a man's feet to the fire like a rival. Time will tell, eh?" He pinched her cheek and heaved a mock sigh. "I can't believe I'm discussing this with you! I used to bounce you on my knee—just last month, it seems. And now my girl is a lovely young woman, looking to run the poor fellows ragged like her mother did to me."

"Mama did not run you ragged," she protested. "If anything, she says you ran her to ground and wore her down with protestations of undying love until she agreed to marry you just to have a little peace!"

"So I did. And I was right, too." He winked. "I know what I speak of when I tell you to keep the young bucks at bay. Make him chase you."

Abigail huffed. "Everyone is leaping to conclusions, assigning me suitors from all over Richmond. Are you that eager to see me married off? Nothing of the sort has happened! I hope you tease Jamie this way, too."

"If your brother ever pays any attention to a woman, I assure you he'll hear of it," he promised. "Penelope will see to it. Speaking of whom . . ." He turned. "Penelope! Come here, minx. I have a bone to pick with you. How, pray, did that dog get into my study the other day?"

"It was raining, Papa, and I couldn't let Milo outside," his younger daughter said with a straight face. "He needed new territory to explore."

"And a new table leg to chew!" He shook his finger at her. "I ought to make you scrub the stains out of the carpet, miss . . ."

Abigail trailed behind them into the dining room as they continued their good-natured argument. What did she think? She would like to see Sebastian again. She wanted to know what he had been hinting at when he asked about speaking to her father. She wanted to walk in the woods with him again, and she wouldn't mind at all if he kissed her again the way he'd done that last time, as if he had all the time in the world and meant to spend it making love to her.

On the other hand, she truly did enjoy Lord Atherton's company. It was flattering to be the object of his attention, whatever he intended by it, and it made her parents so pleased. Perhaps too pleased, she thought with a trace of alarm; Papa was in exceptionally high spirits tonight, and the frequent smiles he gave her left no doubt of the cause. He'd hardly been coy about his desire to see both his daughters well married. Lord Atherton fit the bill from head to toe: wealthy and handsome, charming and noble. Papa hadn't prohibited her interest in getting to know Sebastian, but he would jump for joy if she encouraged Lord Atherton.

Abigail closed her eyes for a moment, telling herself she was being silly. Wouldn't it be a grand joke on her if Lord Atherton merely turned out to be a flirt? He might be sending bouquets to five other young ladies. He might not call on her again. There was certainly more than one rake in London who would tease a woman with his attention, then abruptly turn to another lady without a word of pardon or explanation. In another week or so he might lose interest in her and she would have made herself fret over nothing.

And it didn't matter anyway, because she was sure Papa would listen to her. If she told him another man had won her heart and wanted to marry her . . . someone like Sebastian . . . she believed her father would give his consent. Whomever he might prefer for a son-in-law, he would honor her choice.

She almost laughed out loud at how silly she was. No one had proposed to her—or even asked to court her—and she was making herself anxious over how she would choose. Rivals! When neither one had declared himself a true suitor. What a goose she was. With a slight shake of her head, she picked up her glass and joined in the teasing toast her sister was making to their brother, who had just returned from a brief trip into London and was late to dinner.

But Lord Atherton's attention did not wander. And there was still no word from Sebastian.

Chapter 16

***

"At last, a free day!"

Abigail had to laugh at Penelope's declaration. They had come into the village with James, but with no special purpose in mind. For once they'd had no callers that morning, and by midday even she had felt restless enough to want to get out of Hart House. It was alarming how easily she'd got used to the stream of company. "Free of what—visitors and entertainment?"

"Just free," said her sister airily. "Isn't it pleasant to have some peace?"

"I thought Richmond was too peaceful for your taste."

Penelope snorted. "Not of late! We've been everywhere, it seems, with hardly a moment to ourselves."

Abigail narrowed her eyes. "Are you impugning Lord Atherton?"

"No," said her sister too quickly. "How could I possibly? So handsome, so tall, so titled!" She laid one wrist on her forehead and pretended to swoon.

Abigail swatted her. "Unlike that Penelope Weston: so cross, so fickle, so rude!"

"Rude! He's not here—for a change—and I called

him handsome, tall, and titled, not overbearing, oblivious, and arrogant."

"Miss Weston! What a pleasure to find you here."

Abigail cringed and gave her sister a warning look as they turned toward the speaker. Lord Atherton was striding toward them, sunlight flashing on the golden head of his walking stick. He swept off his hat and gave a courtly bow, a broad smile on his face.

"How do you do, sir?" Abigail curtsied, and then nudged her sister into doing the same.

"Very well, now that I've met you." He set his hat back on his head. "May I walk with you?"

"Oh dear. We were just about to turn for home," said Penelope. "Perhaps another day!"

He glanced at her. "That is a terrible shame. I was hoping to ask a favor of you."

"We were in no hurry to go home." Abigail wanted to smack the simpering expression off Penelope's face. It wasn't like her to show such dislike of anyone, let alone a handsome man. "If there's any way we could help, we would be delighted to do so."

Lord Atherton grinned again. "Thank you, Miss Weston, I knew I could count on you." Penelope gave a quiet snort. Abigail could tell he heard it by the twitch in his jaw. "I'm in need of advice regarding my sister Samantha. It's her birthday soon, and I've been away so long I haven't the slightest idea what to give her."

"We can try," said Abigail with a laugh. "But I would hate to be responsible for leading you astray. Perhaps we could ask some delicate questions the next time we see her—"

"No, I wouldn't want to put you to such trouble," he said with a charmingly abashed air. "As a brother,

I shan't be held to the highest standard. I merely need some inkling of the right sort of gift."

"It doesn't sound as if you're in much need of help, then," pointed out Penelope. "If our brother were even to remember the date of our birthdays, it would be such a shock we would fall senseless to the floor."

"Hush, Pen," Abigail scolded her. "James isn't that bad."

"He is," she retorted. "He wished me a happy birthday just three months ago. On *your* birthday."

"I think he was teasing you."

Penelope scoffed. "That's what he would like us to believe."

"Well, I'm quite sure it's Samantha's birthday and not Elizabeth's," said Lord Atherton. "Heaven save me if ever I confused them! Will you help me, Miss Weston? I assure you, I'm utterly desperate and promise not to hold any suggestion against you. Anything you say will surely be far better than my own inadequate ideas— particularly since I have absolutely none."

"I'll do my best."

"Brilliant. I shall be forever grateful." He offered his arm, still regarding her warmly. "Where can we begin our search?"

Abigail hesitated a moment before taking his arm. There was a gleam in Penelope's eye that made her wary. For some reason, her sister seemed to have taken a militant dislike to Lord Atherton. "I don't suppose she's expressed a desire for anything?"

"A new hunter." He made a face. "I don't love my sister *that* much."

"Desperation has its limits, I see," said Penelope sotto voce.

Lord Atherton's arm flexed, but his charming smile

didn't waver. "What would you buy *your* sister for a gift?"

"How about a book?" suggested Penelope, belying her innocent tone with a sly glance at Abigail. "Every girl likes to have something good to read. Abigail certainly does."

Lord Atherton gave Penelope a measured look for a moment before turning back to her. "Is that true, Miss Weston? Do you appreciate having a good book to read?"

"Yes," she replied, glaring at Penelope. "I do. As does my sister."

"I do indeed," exclaimed Penelope fervently. "I pine away without a steady supply of new stories to occupy my mind."

Abigail shot her sister a deadly look. "I, however, would buy Penelope a scarf." To tie over her mouth, before she mentioned precisely what sort of "new stories" she meant. "A thick, woolen scarf."

Penelope widened her eyes. "I'd much rather have a book, Abby. What was that fascinating book you were reading the other day? The one you simply couldn't put down?"

She blushed. Penelope meant Eleanor Vane's book, which she had begun reading while Sebastian was away. "Do you want to purchase a book for your sister, Lord Atherton? The bookshop is right across the street."

"Let's have a look," he said at once, steering her that way. Penelope skipped along beside her, ignoring all Abigail's attempts to catch her eye and issue a warning. If Penelope said one word about *50 Ways to Sin*, she would regret it to her dying day. "Are you a great reader, Miss Weston?"

"I love a good book," she replied. If she turned her

head toward him, her bonnet brim blocked the sight of her sister, so she did so. "Does Lady Samantha as well?"

"Er." He had a very endearing look of penitent humor. "I don't really know. But if you choose one *you* would like, I would be very pleased to give it to her and hope for the best."

Penelope laughed brightly. "Oh, you might want to reconsider, my lord! Abigail won't choose a proper, noble work like Fordyce's Sermons. She has more adventurous taste."

"I'm relieved to hear that," he said, reaching for the door of Mrs. Driscoll's shop. "Samantha would fling a book of sermons straight at my head. After she recovered from the shock of receiving such from me, of course."

"What sort of books *do* you prefer?" Penelope batted her eyelashes.

"Why don't you go look for a book of your own, Penelope, while Lord Atherton and I try to find one that might suit Lady Samantha?" Abigail suggested pointedly. "Since your mind requires so much occupation."

Penelope looked from her to Lord Atherton. "Very well." She walked away and took a book from the shelf.

Abigail breathed a sigh of relief. Her sister was in a very odd mood today. "I'm sorry if she seems impertinent," she whispered as Lord Atherton led her to a bookshelf far from Penelope. "Sisters do tease each other something fierce at times . . ."

"Was she teasing you?" He propped one shoulder against the bookcase and crossed his arms. "Or me?"

Abigail raised her brows. "Why on earth would she want to tease you, sir?"

He grinned. "Miss Weston. It cannot have escaped

your notice that your sister questions my intelligence every chance she gets."

"And you are the very noblest of gentlemen for not holding it against me," she assured him, making him laugh.

"Indeed not." His voice softened as he studied her face. "I rather delight in hearing you defend me."

She made a face and shook her head. "You don't look in much need of a defender. You're taller than Penelope, and could beat her handily at cards or foot racing."

"It is so rare a gentleman has an opportunity to challenge a young lady to cards or foot racing, though," he said in mock regret.

"Penelope wouldn't hesitate to challenge anyone, if she thought she could win," muttered Abigail.

He laughed quietly. "I, too, enjoy winning—some things more than others." His smile faded a little, but his deep blue gaze remained fixed on her. "Your good opinion would be a priceless prize to me."

She blushed. "You already have that, my lord!"

"Do I?" He shifted, leaning a little closer. "Then I shall strive to win your *very* good opinion."

Abigail's lips parted in amazement. He was flirting with her—out in public. It was hard not to be a little flattered, even if she wasn't sure how she felt about it. She wet her lips, trying to think how to respond, when Mrs. Driscoll saved her.

"May I help you find something, my lord?" The shopkeeper curtsied, her pleased smile encompassing both of them. "Or you, Miss Weston?"

"I don't know, Mrs. Driscoll," he said with a bow. "I've already begged Miss Weston's aid, but then I distracted her. Have we found anything?" he asked Abigail.

"No," she said, hoping her face wasn't bright pink. "I was looking for a copy of *Ivanhoe*. I don't know if Lady Samantha will enjoy it, but it's one of my favorites."

"Ah, yes!" Mrs. Driscoll all but clapped her hands together. "A very popular book, that one. All the Waverley novels are. I'm sure we have a copy. No, my dear Miss Weston"—she put out a hand as Abigail turned toward the shelf again—"let me check in the back. These books might be a bit dusty, and I keep the finer editions on my own shelves."

"That sounds ideal," said Lord Atherton in delight. "Mrs. Driscoll, you're a treasure."

"I do my best, my lord," she said modestly, but her smile was proud. "I'll be back in a trice."

Abigail watched her bustle off. "I hope she has it. It was very popular when it was published; I had to borrow it from the lending library because all the booksellers were sold out. Perhaps we should hunt for another book in case she hasn't got it . . ."

"If you wish." He turned to survey the shelves with her, although only a few moments went by before the shopkeeper was back, a handsome edition with dark green leather spines in her hand.

"Here it is, in three volumes," she said, presenting it to Lord Atherton.

He slipped one volume out of the case and examined it before handing it to her. "Would you be pleased to receive such a gift, Miss Weston?"

"Oh—yes," Abigail managed to stammer, holding it gently before laying open the cover to admire the type, clear and crisp. It was a beautiful edition, with the title stamped in gilt on the spine. "Very much so."

"Excellent." He handed the case with the remaining two volumes to the shopkeeper. "I'll take it, Mrs. Driscoll."

"Is it a gift for this young lady?" Mrs. Driscoll had dimples, Abigail noticed. And her eyes could twinkle. It was such a surprise, she didn't quite take in the woman's words for a moment.

Lord Atherton tilted his head and looked at her. A faint, mischievous smile curled his lips. "Perhaps it should be. After all, she chose it . . ."

"What?" She flushed, coming back to herself with a start. "Oh no, it's a gift for Lady Samantha!"

"I doubt she would gaze at it with the reverence you just showed." He cast a meaningful glance at her hands, still unconsciously smoothing the cover. "I would like you to have it, as thanks for helping me."

"Oh—oh no, sir." She held out the volume with an apologetic laugh. "If you buy the book for me, I haven't helped you at all! You asked for help finding a gift for your sister, not for me."

"You have." He resisted her efforts to return the book, but cupped her hand in his and guided it toward Mrs. Driscoll, who took the book and added it to the case. "Have you any other books similar to this one to recommend, madam?"

"Indeed, sir, I do!" With another twinkle of her eye, Mrs. Driscoll hurried off.

Abigail bit her lip. That edition of *Ivanhoe* would cost a pretty penny. And while it was just a book, it was a deeply emotional and stirring book. "It's too kind of you."

He was still holding her hand, his fingers tracing hers. She could feel every bit of it through her gloves. "On the contrary," he said in a low voice. "It is not nearly how kind I wish to be to you."

"Have you found something?" Penelope's voice made her start.

"No," she said, flustered and grateful for her sister's interruption.

"Yes," countered Lord Atherton, his voice once more light and teasing. "Just not for Samantha."

Penelope's sharp gaze narrowed. "For whom, then?"

"For your sister." He squeezed her hand lightly. Belatedly realizing he still held it, Abigail pulled free, blushing fiercely.

"Really!" Penelope looked at her in surprise. "How perceptive, my lord. A new book is the way to my sister's heart."

"And she said it was one of her favorites," added Lord Atherton. "*Ivanhoe.*"

"My mother won't allow me to accept it," she protested. "It's much too generous."

He only grinned. "Not by half, Miss Weston. Pardon me; I must go fetch my purchases from Mrs. Driscoll." He tipped his head and walked away.

Penelope stepped up beside her. "It's more serious than I thought, Abby," she murmured, watching him move through the shop, drawing the eye and attention of everyone. "He's buying you *books* now."

"Hush!"

"You're fooling yourself if you think Mama won't allow you to accept it," went on her sister. "Mama will be over the moon, although not as much as Papa will be. Your wedding will be planned by the end of the day."

"It's only a book," she whispered repressively.

"He meant to buy a gift for his sister, and now he's buying one for you." Penelope craned her neck to watch him banter with Mrs. Driscoll, making the older woman smile and laugh as she wrapped up his selections. "Although maybe one for her as well. I wonder if it's another novel, or a handbook on pig breeding. He certainly didn't spend much time choosing it . . ."

Abigail averted her gaze. Lord Atherton was just as handsome from the rear as he was from the front, not that she should be noticing. "What is your point, Penelope?"

Her sister looked her in the eye. "What about Mr. Vane?"

She tensed. "What about him?"

Penelope gave her such a disbelieving look, she flushed. Darting a wary glance at Lord Atherton, still busy with Mrs. Driscoll, she took her sister's arm and towed her out of sight behind another bookcase. "I don't know, Pen. He left and I've not heard a word from him. And he made me no promises before he left, either. Am I supposed to close myself in my room and refuse all callers until he returns?"

"No, but you're enjoying Lord Atherton's company!" charged Penelope in a furious whisper.

Abigail closed her eyes for a moment. "As would you, if you ever stopped baiting him. And if you say my manner is too friendly toward him, you should know it's partly to make up for your snide treatment," she added as her sister opened her mouth. "Why don't you like him?"

Penelope scowled. "He's too eager for our approval."

Abigail snorted. "Heaven preserve us from a gentleman who isn't looking down his nose at us as 'those Weston upstarts.' You're impossible to please; you know that, don't you?"

"Perhaps you're too easy to please!"

"Penelope, I'm sorry he's not a rude, brooding

scoundrel with a giant scar covering half his face. Should I snub him because he's handsome? Should I give him the cut because he's amusing and considerate?" She paused. Her sister glowered at the books in front of her. "I never noticed you being so particular in London. If a handsome, charming viscount asked you to dance there—"

"But he didn't!" Her sister whirled on her. "And I just wonder which man you're leading on, Abby."

"Which—?" She caught herself and lowered her voice before giving full vent to her shock and indignation. "You're being a widgeon. And I'm not talking to you about it anymore."

A throat clearing behind her made her jump. Lord Atherton stood there, packages in hand. "Am I intruding?"

"No more than usual," said Penelope under her breath.

"Not at all!" Abigail pushed past her sister and pinned a bright smile on her face. "Did you find a gift for Lady Samantha?"

"I did indeed." He looked away from Penelope's grim expression to her, and his face eased into a smile. "An older novel called *Sense and Sensibility*. Mrs. Driscoll said it was a favorite with ladies. Have you read it?"

"I have," exclaimed Abigail in delight. "A wonderful book." She darted a fleeting glance at Penelope. "It's about two sisters of very different temperaments."

His mouth curved. "Perhaps it will prove enlightening, then." He held out one package, tied up with brown string. "This is for you, with my deepest gratitude."

"Thank you, sir." She accepted it with a gracious smile. She had protested enough already; it was only a book; and Penelope was still glaring at him as if he'd burned her entire cache of *50 Ways to Sin.*

"Since you were on your way home when I waylaid you"—he winked at her—"may I walk you to your door?"

"You're very kind to offer, but our brother is in Richmond as well," demurred Abigail. She wasn't leading anyone on; she would say the same thing to anyone.

"He's probably very annoyed at us for not meeting him already," added Penelope. That was a lie—James had probably forgotten all about them by now—but Abigail didn't protest. The weight of the novel in her arm felt like a weight on her conscience. Was it misleading to accept Lord Atherton's gift? She was uncomfortably aware that her sister was right: her parents would be very pleased when they heard of it, and would think it meant far more than it really did—or at least more than it meant to her.

For a moment she hovered on the brink of returning it. As much as she hated her sister for suggesting that Lord Atherton was courting her and that she was leading him on, even more she hated to think that Lord Atherton might feel the same way. Because, of course, when Sebastian returned . . .

She paused on that thought. What would happen when Sebastian returned? She had no idea. He might begin courting her in earnest, as he'd hinted, but he might not. She still felt a helpless attraction and fascination for him, buried inside her like an ember waiting to ignite at the first touch of his mouth on hers, but he might not feel the same—or rather, he might not feel anything more. She wasn't reckless enough to throw herself into an affair like Lady Constance; Abigail wanted more. She wanted him to want her in every way. She wanted him to go out of his way to meet her, to call on her—perhaps with flowers in hand—and to look at her as if he couldn't tear himself away. Just as Lord Atherton was doing.

She sighed quietly. She had no idea what she'd do when Sebastian returned. If he slipped back into his cool, aloof personality and rebuffed her, she might be glad to have the company of someone who could distract her. Surely it would be easy to fall in love with the attentive Lord Atherton, if she knew Sebastian would never love her. If only Sebastian would return; the longer he stayed away without sending her any word, the more she began to doubt everything that had happened between them.

"Then let me see you safely into his company."

Abigail blinked, then realized he meant her brother's company. "Thank you, Lord Atherton." She took his arm. It was too late to return the novel without being graceless and rude. She would keep it, but as a reminder to keep her head about her.

Mrs. Driscoll was waiting to hold the door for them. "Good day, Miss Weston," she said, bobbing her head. "Good day, my lord."

"And a very good day to you, Mrs. Driscoll." Lord Atherton gave her a brilliant smile. "I am relying on your advice about this." He held up the wrapped package of his own.

The woman put up her hands. "If Lady Samantha has any objection, send it back, sir, and we'll find something to tempt her," she assured him. "I've never yet failed to find just the book my customers want."

"I knew I could count on you," he said humbly. "Between you and Miss Weston, I shall be lauded as the best of all brothers this year."

Mrs. Driscoll tittered—actually giggled like a girl. Penelope shot a look of pure disbelief at Abigail, whose face surely mirrored it. Lord Atherton, though, merely set his hat back on his head and led them outside.

"Where shall we find Mr. Weston?" he asked, drawing Abigail to his side as a large wagon rumbled past.

"At the coffee house, most likely," murmured Abigail, unsettled to realized that her arm was securely linked through his. When had that happened?

"Ah, Grenville's! An excellent place to while away the time." They started off, although in no great hurry. More than one person greeted Lord Atherton. That wasn't very surprising; Abigail had seen men all but fall to their knees in London when they met a nobleman. But Lord Atherton was welcomed home as a favorite son, with everything from reverence to smiles and teasing comments. Even more surprising was that she and Penelope were included in these greetings, in a way they never had been before. It was hard not to think that just appearing on Lord Atherton's arm had raised their social status in Richmond more than anything they did on their own could have. Again, the thought crossed her mind that Papa would be beside himself with delight.

But it was also hard not to compare this reception to the one Sebastian got. Mrs. Driscoll had treated him coldly, but she was abundantly cordial to Lord Atherton. Abigail's smile felt a bit wan as Mrs. Huntley herself made a point of greeting her and Penelope very warmly, with a deep curtsy to Lord Atherton. Mrs. Huntley, who had looked at Sebastian as though he were the devil himself.

"I suppose this is how it feels to have an earl for a father," Penelope whispered in her ear.

Abigail bit her lip. "Do you think that's it?"

"If you say it's due to how handsome and charming he is, I shall be sick."

She gave her sister a black look and didn't deign to reply.

"No one greets Jamie that way," Penelope pointed out. "He's handsome enough, and I daresay he could be charming if he put his mind to it. And he's got money, too."

"He hasn't lived here all his life," replied Abigail, realizing too late what she had invited her sister to mention.

"Mr. Vane," exclaimed Penelope in full voice. Leaning close in expectation of a whisper, Abigail reared back, almost colliding with Lord Atherton.

"Miss Weston, are you all right?" Lord Atherton caught her and steadied her, but Abigail ignored him as she raised her head and searched . . .

"Mr. Vane," called Penelope again before she picked up her skirt and hurried across the dusty street.

Abigail's eyes frantically roamed the crowd. Lord Atherton's arm, still around her waist, went hard and stiff as her fingers curled into his jacket. Where was he?

Diagonally across from them, motionless in the busy thoroughfare, stood Sebastian Vane, his gaze fixed on her.

Chapter 17

Sebastian returned to Richmond in some mental disquiet.

On the one hand, he had cause for optimism. According to the Bristol solicitor, Uncle Henry had left nearly four thousand pounds. While not as much as Sebastian had wished for, it was still a good sum. It would take some time for all the money to be extracted from Henry's investments, but Sebastian didn't want to waste a moment. From Bristol he'd gone directly to London and visited his own solicitor, to begin making plans to pay off his most onerous debts. He would still be a far sight from prosperous, but it was a step in the right direction.

But his optimism was tempered by the knowledge that it was only a modest step. Four thousand pounds wouldn't cover half the debt his father had left him, and as soon as one creditor was paid, the others might catch wind of it and begin clamoring for their own repayment, with interest. They'd mostly given up asking, since he'd been unable to pay for so long. Still, he wanted them dealt with before any hint of him marrying an heiress got out and brought them all to his door in pursuit of Abigail's dowry. It struck him that he could stretch his windfall, if he was canny about it, so he'd told his solicitor to make overtures to every creditor and try to bargain on the amount owed by intimating that this was likely the creditor's only chance to see any of his funds returned.

He was well aware that it might not work, but he'd worry about that when the time came. For now, he wanted to see Abigail. He'd been away from her for sixteen days, every one of them long and lonely. Pride be damned; he wanted her, and if she would have him, he was a fool to wait until he was respectable and well-off—especially since that might never happen. The morning after he arrived home, on the last coach from London, he put on his best coat and hat, tucked his gift for her into his pocket, and set out for Hart House, barely noticing the pronounced limp he'd acquired after so many long journeys in public coaches.

He was quickly disappointed, however. "Miss Weston is not at home," the butler told him.

"I see. Is she expected back today?"

Thomson just looked at him in the stony-faced way butlers so often had.

Sebastian amended his question. "I meant to inquire if the family is still in residence, and hasn't returned to London."

"No, sir," said the butler at once. "They are still in residence."

That was a relief, tempering the disappointment. He took a deep breath and nodded. "Thank you." He turned and started toward Montrose Hill.

"Sir." Thomson cleared his throat. "I believe they have only gone to town for the afternoon. If you would care to leave your card . . ."

He didn't have cards anymore, but Sebastian's

heart jumped. "No need," he replied. "Thank you."
He touched his hat and walked away, this time toward
Richmond village.

It was less than a mile, but by the time he reached
the village his knee ached. He'd got out of the habit of
nightly rambles while he was away, and felt it. Still, it
would be worth it to see her again, and his eyes seemed
unable to fix on any point as he searched for her. Without thinking he headed for the bookshop, wondering if
she'd read the book he sent her . . . or if she'd read the
pamphlets again.

He was a little distracted by that last thought, and
failed to keep his attention on the people around him.
It was the sound of his name that brought his head up,
halting his steps. "Mr. Vane," cried the voice again as
he scanned the crowd. It took him a moment to realize it was Penelope Weston's voice, and that she was
hurrying across the street toward him, and that Abigail
was behind her, as beautiful as ever with her eyes wide
and her lips parted in surprise, and that holding her in
his arm, gazing down at her in tender concern . . . was
Benedict Lennox.

"Mr. Vane!" Beaming, Penelope Weston bobbed a
quick curtsy in front of him. "How brilliant to meet
you here again!"

With a jerk, he tore his eyes off Abigail and Benedict. "Is it?"

"Yes! We'd been wondering when you would
return—my sister and I were just discussing it, in
fact—and here you are! Rather like fate, don't you
think?"

It did feel like fate—his fate, anyway, which was apparently to lose everything that meant anything to him.
He could feel his face hardening as Abigail tipped up

her face to Benedict and said something. Ben raised his head and looked right at Sebastian without a trace of expression before dropping his gaze back to Abigail and replying to her. Sebastian's fingers shook, they gripped his cane so hard. He was dimly aware that Penelope was still waiting for a response, but he couldn't make one. When had Benedict come home? When the devil had he become so cozy with Abigail? He was practically embracing her on a public street. And the way she was looking at him . . .

"I beg your pardon, Miss Weston," he said, groping for his wits. "What did you say?"

"I said welcome home," she said, her voice gone soft. "I hope your trip was pleasant."

"Yes." From the corner of his eye he could see Abigail crossing the street, Benedict close behind her. "I hope all was well with you?"

Penelope Weston made a face. She glanced over her shoulder at her sister and her companion, drawing nearer. "It could have been better, if you ask me."

Somehow he guessed she meant Benedict. The thought that at least one Weston sister preferred him was comforting, even if it wasn't the Weston sister *he* preferred. "I'm sorry to hear that," he murmured, and then Abigail reached them.

"Mr. Vane," she said, her voice a little out of breath. And for a moment Sebastian was lost again, caught in her shining gray gaze. "How lovely to see you again."

He bowed. "And you, Miss Weston."

"Well, well," said Benedict in a hearty tone. "Vane! It's been years."

Sebastian straightened to his full height and stared his former friend in the face. He'd always been a couple of inches taller, and even with the cane he still had a slight advantage. "Indeed."

"Are you already acquainted?" asked Penelope, who seemed to be the only one of them who retained full possession of her powers of speech. "Oh, but of course—you've known each other for years."

Sebastian clenched his jaw for a second. "We've not seen each other much of late, Miss Weston."

"No," agreed Benedict at once, his smile growing harder and more fixed. "How surprising you know Mr. Vane, Miss Penelope."

"We're neighbors." Sebastian held tight to his temper. He wished Abigail would say something, but then, he couldn't think of anything that would soothe the shock of seeing her on Benedict's arm—no, not politely holding his arm, but clutching his jacket and letting him put his arm around her waist. Sebastian's own arm flexed and tightened, remembering how it felt to hold Abigail. And remembering how and why he had held her only a few weeks ago. "Perhaps you've forgotten how near Montrose Hill and Hart House are to each other."

Benedict's eyes narrowed. "Happily I've had the chance to rediscover it." He glanced down at Abigail. "Miss Weston was kind enough to walk with me through the woods, indulging me as I revisited childhood haunts."

He looked at Abigail, whose cheeks were a dull scarlet. "That was very kind of her."

"Half those woods are Mr. Vane's, you know," put in Penelope. "I hope you weren't trespassing, Lord Atherton."

Sebastian was mean enough to take some enjoyment from the irked look Benedict shot Penelope, who merely gave him a sunny smile. But Benedict's words ruined his pleasure immediately. "Oh, not half, Miss Weston. A good portion of it actually belongs to my father." He turned to Sebastian, brows raised. "All the riverfront acreage, isn't it?"

"Yes." Sebastian had to force the word past his lips. All that land did belong to Benedict's father, the Earl of Stratford, because Michael Vane had sold it to him for fifty pounds. And when Sebastian had tried to speak to the earl about it, Stratford laughed in his face—which was almost as bad as Benedict's reaction. Benedict had been indifferent and dismissive and said it was just as well, for his father would manage the land far better than a madman could.

That had been his last lengthy conversation with Benedict, come to think of it. And it wasn't one Sebastian wished to renew, now or ever.

He bowed slightly. "I don't want to keep you from your shopping. Good day, Miss Weston, Miss Penelope." He looked right at Benedict. "My lord."

"Oh no!" exclaimed Abigail, putting out her hand.

He stopped at once. She had let go of Benedict's arm to reach toward him, and part of him yearned to take that hand and pull her to his side. He wrapped his fingers more firmly around the cane's head and waited. Everyone waited, in fact, all watching her.

Her cheeks flushed darker and she cleared her throat. "You're not interrupting, Mr. Vane. We—my sister and I"—she paused, then went on without looking at Benedict—"are very glad you've come home. I'm sure Boris was beside himself!" She smiled, but no one else did, and so it withered on her lips. "I hope your trip was as rewarding as you'd hoped," she added, a little uncertainly.

Sebastian looked at her. She was as beautiful as he'd remembered; even the slightly flustered air and pink cheeks reminded him of their last meeting, when he'd brought her to climax in his arms. The memory made him excruciatingly aware of the box in his pocket, tried up with a bit of red ribbon. His uncle had left him a cameo pendant that had once belonged to his great-grandmother, a small but delicate piece. Sebastian had bought a new chain for it and imagined fastening it around Abigail's neck, the cameo nestled between her lovely breasts. He'd imagined bestowing a kiss on the spot where it would rest.

But it seemed he might have lost more than he gained in the fortnight he'd been away. "Thank you," he said in reply to her remark. "It was unremarkable."

Penelope clapped her hands together. "Well! The four of us can't just stand here all day; we're blocking half the street. Do visit Hart House soon, Mr. Vane. I've never been to Bristol and look forward to being regaled with exciting stories."

"I doubt it could live up to your expectations," he told her. "If Richmond bores you, Bristol would numb you."

"Bored in Richmond!" Benedict laughed. "Ah yes, I remember your lament, Miss Penelope. Surely it's grown on you since we visited Kew and Hampton Court?"

"My opinion of those places improved," she replied. "Although you promised to show us a ghost at Hampton Court and I didn't see even a floating veil. And then we came back to dull little Richmond."

"I can't have you think that of my home." Benedict gave her a teasing smile. "How about a dinner party, to breathe some life into the place? My mother would be delighted to have one; she's been talking of it since I returned home. What say you, Miss Penelope?"

The Weston girls exchanged a glance Sebastian couldn't quite interpret. Surprise, but also something else. So they hadn't been invited to Stratford Court yet. "That's very kind, sir," said Abigail with a forced smile. "I'm sure it would be delightful."

"Excellent. We'll send out cards at once." This time when he faced Sebastian, there was a definite challenge in Benedict's eye. "How about it, Vane? Will you join us as well?"

He burned to say no. He never wanted to see Lord Stratford again, let alone dine at his table. But on the other hand . . . He glanced at Abigail. It was hard to blame her for wanting a man with two good legs and a respectable fortune. It was, unfortunately, harder to see her choose Benedict Lennox, of all people. She had stepped away from Benedict now, though, closer to her sister, and that alone made him take a deep breath and say, "Of course."

Benedict's smile faded a little. "Excellent." He turned back toward the Weston ladies. "Shall we continue in search of your brother? I believe you said he was waiting for you at the coffee shop."

"No, he isn't!" Penelope sounded almost gleeful. She raised one arm. "James!"

Mr. Weston nodded in greeting as he joined them. "Atherton, Vane; how do you do?" He surveyed his sisters. "I see I'm just in time to rescue you."

"That's a fine apology for being late meeting us," Penelope accused him.

James Weston gave her an amused look. "You seem to be in good hands, but I know my duty. Gentlemen, thank you for entertaining my sisters. I shall return them to the safety of Hart House now."

"Not a duty, but a pleasure." Benedict laid one hand on his heart as he bowed. "Thank you again for your invaluable assistance, Miss Weston."

"You're very welcome, sir," murmured Abigail.

"Good day, my lord!" chirped Penelope. "I do hope Lady Samantha appreciates the immense effort you expended on her behalf!"

With one last sharp glance at Sebastian, Benedict touched the brim of his hat and strode away, swinging his walking stick at his side. One might even think he did it to excess, as if to demonstrate how his cane was merely for show, and that he was very agile without it.

"I left the carriage down the street." Mr. Weston looked at Penelope. "I hope you didn't stir up trouble with Atherton."

She made a face. "Why do you always suspect me of something dreadful?"

Her brother snorted. "Experience! Tell me what you did, he looked a bit out of humor . . ." They began walking.

Abigail, though, lingered. "Have you been home long?"

"Since last night, on the late coach from London."

"Welcome home," she said softly.

He bowed his head. "Thank you." The image of her in Benedict's arms had scoured away all the things he meant to say to her.

There was a long moment of silence.

"I see you've met Lord Atherton," he said. He had to know. "He seems quite taken with you." All he wanted was one word, one indication that she didn't return Benedict's obvious attraction to her. He could excuse Benedict's interest in her—that was perfectly understandable—but did she welcome it?

She shifted the package in her arm uncomfortably, as if it was too heavy. "We met him only recently. He was in town, seeking a gift for his sister, and asked me—and Penelope," she hastily added, "to advise him."

That was no reply at all to his remark that Benedict was taken with her. It had been as clear as day to Sebastian, but if she didn't even pretend not to have noticed . . . He told himself he couldn't blame her, but at the same time he could already feel the armor re-forming around his heart. He tilted his head in the direction her siblings had gone. "I don't want to keep you. Shall we?"

Abigail nodded, too disconcerted to say anything. This was not the reunion she had imagined. He didn't seem at all pleased to see her, with not one word of delight at running into them. Sebastian fell in step beside her, without offering his arm. Now the weight of *Ivanhoe* felt like a small boulder in her arm. Even if he had no idea what it was, she did—but from the hard set of his shoulders and his remote expression, she imagined he suspected.

"I'm glad your trip was a success," she said to break the oppressive silence. Penelope seemed to be inciting James to a race, for they had already made much quicker progress.

Sebastian glanced fleetingly at her. "I suppose."

"Wasn't it?"

His mouth was a firm line and his eyes were fixed straight ahead. "I'm not certain."

She began to be annoyed. He was acting as if she had offended him when all she had done was be cordial to a neighbor. She hiked *Ivanhoe* a little higher into the crook of her elbow. If Sebastian Vane felt such an interest in her actions, he could have done something about it—as Lord Atherton had done. He could have declared himself that day he kissed her so scandalously. He could have written to her while he was away. He could have asked her if she had formed an attachment to Lord Atherton instead of being tight-lipped and taciturn. "Lord Atherton has been very kind," she said to provoke him.

"And attentive, I see."

Again she felt the weight of *Ivanhoe*, but she merely smiled. "Yes, indeed! It would have been very quiet around Hart House otherwise."

This time his glance lingered. "He's been to call often, then."

She flipped one hand. "Often? A few times."

"And you walked through the woods with him."

"Once," she agreed.

"And met him in town today."

"By chance," she said in the same light, pleasant tone, to contrast with his flat one. "Just as we met you." She waited a few more steps before adding, "What is Bristol like? I've never seen a port city."

"Crowded," he said. "Dirty."

She nodded. "It sounds very different than Richmond. My brother went to Portsmouth once, and wrote the most amusing descriptions of the people there."

Her companion said nothing for a long moment. They had almost reached the carriage, where Penelope and James were already seated. The groom stood at the step waiting to help her in. "There was nothing of interest in Bristol to write about."

"Perhaps not, but a letter would have showed you thought of me." She raised her brows. "But perhaps you didn't. I shouldn't presume."

He caught her hand and pulled, yanking her around to face him when she would have turned toward the carriage. "I thought of you," he said in a low, taut voice. "Every day."

"And I thought of you," she replied quietly. "The only trouble was, I didn't know what to think."

His grip tightened around her wrist. "After the way we parted—"

"What?" she pressed when he stopped. "Nothing was promised between us."

"No," he said grimly. "Clearly not."

Abigail flushed painfully red. He had undone her dress and kissed her all over, making love to her skin with his mouth. He had put his hands beneath her skirt and made her feel like the wickedest, most wanton woman alive. And not only had she let him, she'd reveled in it. She had wanted more.

But now all her hopes of what might happen on his return seemed foolish and naïve. He appeared to have no memory of any desire to speak to her father now; today he looked cold and withdrawn again. "Well," she said before she could stop herself, "perhaps that's my fault. You asked a great deal, and I gave it without exacting any promise."

He released her hand as if it scalded him.

"But before you charge me with—with *anything*," she went on in a growing fury, "ask what right you had to expect devotion. You know what I want, sir; I have never been coy about it. And if you cannot or will not give it, why shouldn't I look elsewhere? *You* told me to do so!"

"Abigail," he said softly.

She slashed one hand through the air. "I'm tired of being deemed a heartless flirt. I am willing to follow my heart, yes, but not to certain disappointment. If that's all you have to offer, then perhaps I should encourage another gentleman to pay attention to me." She raised her chin. "If you've decided you feel differently, you know where to call on me." And she turned her back on him and marched to the carriage, flinging her-

self up the step without help from the groom and into
the seat next to her sister. "I'm ready to go home," she
announced.

James's eyebrows shot up, but he signaled the driver.

Penelope leaned in close. "Abby, did you just have
an argument with Mr. Vane?" she whispered incredu-
lously. "In the middle of Richmond?"

"I did not." She kept her gaze fixed ahead and refused to look at Sebastian as the carriage started forward.

Penelope craned her neck. "He looks thunderstruck!
What did you say to him?"

"Nothing I didn't fully believe." She glared at her
brother, who promptly turned to gaze in apparent fascination at the passing scenery.

Penelope finally settled back in her seat, eyes wide
with approval. "Then I'm sure he needed to hear it."

Abigail said nothing. Her heart beat so hard, her
hands still trembled as she clutched the gift from Lord
Atherton. Sebastian Vane did need to hear it, just as
much as she needed to say it. If he wanted her, it was
time for him to prove it.

Chapter 18

Sebastian walked home in a very dark mood.

Everything Abigail said was correct. He had promised her nothing. He had told her to run away from him. He had also taken advantage of her sensual curiosity and trusting nature to satisfy his own craving for her. He did know what she wanted: not just passion, but love and marriage. The irony that he had been on the brink of offering both didn't escape him, but of course Abigail didn't know that—because he had let his visceral reaction to Benedict Lennox override his every thought and intention.

Goddamn it. Benedict Lennox, of all people. There was a twisted sort of humor in it, he supposed; once Ben had envied him everything. Sebastian had been taller and stronger, more adept on a horse, and a far better shot. His father's lack of title had meant Sebastian was permitted to do things like join the army, while Benedict, the heir to the Earl of Stratford, was flatly refused any chance at military glory.

The memory of their rash youthful views of the army brought a bitter smile to his face. Military glory had faded quickly into a lifetime of disability for him, while Benedict, confined safely if unhappily at home, was still whole and healthy.

Even worse, of course, was that Sebastian's estate had been even more crippled, with the primary beneficiary being—indirectly—Benedict. Sebastian didn't think it would make him feel better if his father had sold the land to someone other than Lord Stratford, but the fact that Benedict would inherit what should have been his . . . He had to breathe deeply to keep from cursing again over that quirk of fate.

So Benedict was able-bodied and had a larger inheritance. None of that was in Sebastian's control. It wasn't as if Benedict had shot his knee, or even snatched up his property for a pittance. Fate was often unkind.

But Abigail . . . He didn't know if he could take losing Abigail as philosophically. Not that he had ever truly had her to begin with. No promises.

The box with the cameo struck his thigh with every step, like a constant little prod to his temper. What did he want? He had promised her nothing, but only, he'd told himself, because he had nothing to promise her. His damned pride had kept him from telling her he was falling in love with her, and now she had decided to look elsewhere. Who could blame her?

He veered off the road into the woods, feeling like he could beat something. He thrashed a fern from his way with his cane. He ground his heel into the dirt as if to punish his knee for being weak and painful. It cost him his footing; when he lurched to adjust, his right foot landed on what looked like dry earth, but what was in reality a thick mat of leaves, dried on top but wet beneath. In the blink of an eye he had skidded down the gentle slope of the trail to land on his arse in the exposed muck of the forest floor.

For a moment he just sat, heart thudding. It certainly wasn't the first time he'd fallen, but it was the first in a while. Normally he paid more attention to where he stepped. If he hadn't let emotion blot out his usual caution . . .

His usual caution had warned him to stay away from Abigail. He'd managed to ignore it somewhat, for the chance to kiss her. But he'd held back from declaring himself in any way before he left. If only he'd ignored that little voice a bit more, he might not be here. He could be walking arm-in-arm with her, telling her about Bristol and his uncle, perhaps even making his proposal.

Gently he tested his knee. It felt sound. With a grunt, he pushed himself off the ground, groping for his cane before resting any weight on his left leg. A few wary steps, and he decided the knee wasn't much worse than before. Aside from a wet backside, he was unscathed.

A sudden thought made him reach for the pocket in his coattail. The box was dented on one side, but when he pulled off the ribbon and opened it, the cameo inside was just as before: a delicate profile of a lovely lady, carved from ivory and set on a light blue background. He ran one fingertip over the golden frame.

No, it wasn't his usual caution that had kept him from Abigail. It was fear. He hadn't called on her when invited because he was afraid she would find him lacking. He hadn't told her about his trip to Bristol before he left because he feared the news wouldn't be as good as he hoped. He hadn't told her he loved her because he didn't want to expose his heart in a way he hadn't done in years—even though she was the least likely person in the world to throw it back in his face. Everything he had done, and not done, had been because of fear.

Sebastian knew about fear. He remembered lying in a makeshift army surgery, afraid to fall asleep in case he never woke up. He remembered forcing his father into his room at night, cringing at each raspy raving his father uttered, afraid that he would die, afraid that he would recover. He remembered wondering how on earth he would pay his bills and mortgages, driven by fear he would lose everything. All those fears he had survived and overcome.

A lesser inheritance wouldn't have rendered him less eligible in her eyes; any bettering of his situation could only help. She already knew about his crippled knee. She already knew *him*. And somehow, she'd accepted him.

His mouth firmed and he closed his hand around the cameo. He was an idiot. If he wanted the girl, he would have to win her. Every lady deserved to be courted, pursued, made to feel wanted. Through his own stubbornness and pride, he had made his task harder, but that didn't change the one settled fact in his mind and heart: he wanted her. He needed her. He loved her.

And if he had to fight to win her, he would fight to his last breath.

Abigail had decided two things by the next morning. If Lord Atherton called, she would refuse to receive him and plead that she had a headache. That was a little bit true, as she still hadn't sorted out what to do about his attentions. Her parents were so pleased, and he was so charming; if she'd only met him, and never Sebastian, who could say what might have happened?

But she *had* met Sebastian, and she even thought

she'd fallen in love with him. That was her second decision. If he called, she would see him, although with the excuse of a headache ready to use at a moment's notice. If he came to explain why he'd been so grim, she wanted to hear it. Since he'd shown a marked aversion to calling on her, though, she thought she would have some time to ponder this.

She put *Ivanhoe* on the shelf beside her bed, next to *The Children of the Abbey*. For a long time she contemplated the pair of them. *Ivanhoe* was a favorite of hers, a rich, breathtaking tale of love and gallantry, and this was a very handsome new edition, leather bound with gilt titles. *The Children of the Abbey* was an old book, smelling of dust, and the story itself was more than a little silly.

But the difference . . . She traced one finger down the spine of the older book. *Ivanhoe* had been a moment's lark to Lord Atherton. He heard her say she liked it, so he bought it for her. It had no meaning to him except as a way to impress her and please her. *The Children of the Abbey*, though, had belonged to Sebastian's mother. Even if—as she suspected—he gave it to her in part because he couldn't afford any other book, let alone one like *Ivanhoe*, it had some meaning to him. Surely he wouldn't have kept it pristine all these years for no reason. It was a Minerva Press novel, cheaply bound and no great triumph of prose or sentiment. Surely that betokened some depth of feeling, the way his care for the glass chamber in the grotto had. She refused to believe he had cleared all the brush from the entrance, swept the passage, and carried a rug, cushions, and lanterns all the way into the forest for any other reason— all without even knowing if she would meet him there.

She hadn't been to the grotto since that day, when

she'd lain on the rug with Sebastian to see the mermaid. She rolled over onto her back and stared up at her plain plaster ceiling. Her parents would probably be very startled if she asked permission to create a mosaic on it . . .

A tap at the door sounded. "You've a caller," said Thomson when she opened it. "Mr. Vane."

Well. That was a surprise. "Show him to the drawing room," she said. "I'll be down in a few minutes."

She took a minute to compose her thoughts and went downstairs. Sebastian stood by the window, looking out, his back to her. Something about his posture struck her as chastened. "Mr. Vane." She curtsied in the doorway.

He spun around. For a moment his expression was surprised, unguarded. For a moment he looked at her with a world of wonder and yearning in his eyes, and Abigail's heart gave an unsteady thump.

He bowed, and when he rose his face was once more composed and inscrutable. "Miss Weston."

"Won't you sit down?" She waved one hand at the sofa.

He hesitated. "Could we perhaps stroll in the garden? As pleasant as it would be to converse with your mother and sister, what I have to say today is for your ears only."

Abigail did a quick calculation. If Mama knew he was here—and she was willing to bet Thomson was telling her right now—she would come join them. But the garden was entirely visible from the house. If they walked on the paths nearest the terrace, there was a good chance Mama would only keep an eye on her from inside. "Very well. Let me fetch my shawl."

She led the way outside, wondering what he had to

tell her. They crossed the terrace and descended to the gravel path through the neat knot garden.

"Once again I must apologize," Sebastian said in a subdued tone. "I didn't behave well yesterday."

"No," she agreed.

He seemed to be struggling to decide what to say. "Perhaps I should begin with some old history. You must have noticed that Lord Atherton and I were somewhat acquainted."

She heard the slight hesitation before the last word. "I knew that. Lady Samantha told us you and he were once friends, and he himself told me the two of you explored the woods as brothers together in search of the grotto."

The look he shot her was quick and sharp. "We did." He seemed to be limping more than usual today. "We were the best of friends at one time. His father was strict and demanding, mine was distracted and often swept up in his latest scientific scheme. We both escaped into the woods. Searching for the long-lost grotto was only one of our missions. In the hours we spent exploring, we were ideal companions. No adventure was too daring for us; we were equals in every way, in those woods.

"But of course our stations were very different. He was the heir to an earl, while my father was a mere gentleman. When we finished university, the war was raging and we were both keen to join the fight. I dreamed of adventure and he dreamed of glory; I suppose he'd always wanted to be a soldier, even when we were lads. My father agreed, however reluctantly, but Lord Stratford absolutely forbade Ben—Lord Atherton, that is—to do the same. I bought a commission and we had a bitter row."

"He was envious," she murmured.

"He was," Sebastian agreed. "When my head had cooled, I realized that he must have been desperate to go, not just for adventure and glory, but to escape his father. Stratford was . . . not a kind or loving father, as mine was. I know he beat Ben, sometimes harshly, and he was never satisfied, let alone pleased, by anything Benedict did. But I was headstrong and young, bent on doing what I wanted and less considerate of his feelings than I ought to have been. I went off to war and he had no choice but to stay home."

Abigail thought of Lord Atherton's crisp uniform the day he had first visited. The King's Guard, an elite but essentially ornamental brigade. An earl's heir wouldn't be permitted to go to war, but he had found a way into the army.

"Everything had changed when I came home, of course," said Sebastian in his wry, understated way. "Including our friendship. I suppose my father's madness had something to do with it. Everyone in Richmond knew he was growing deranged far before anyone thought to write to me about it. But even worse was that my father . . ." He made a slight stumble before catching himself with the cane. "I told you my father sold most of his land at ludicrous prices. He sold most of the choicest pieces to Lord Stratford.

"I already admitted that I went a bit mad over this. The worst confrontation was with Lord Stratford." His mouth twisted. "It struck me as particularly cruel that my closest mate's father would take such advantage of my father's decline. I thought my friendship with Atherton would carry some weight with Stratford. I thought that if he would just agree to reverse that sale, I could bear the loss of the rest. The land was nothing to him; to this day, he's hardly done a thing to it. And if I could just regain those acres near the river, including the family crypt—"

She snapped around in astonishment. "*He* bought your mother's grave?"

Sebastian nodded. "For a few shillings an acre." He blew out a breath, hinting at residual frustration. "But Stratford's a hard man; he refused. We argued, rather heatedly. He asked if my wits had gone begging as well, and offered to sell the land back, for a mere five thousand pounds. I stormed out, slamming the door in his face. On my way out of Stratford Court, I met Lord Atherton, who took his father's side. He pointed out that at least his father wasn't a madman, and would take better care of the property than my father could. The sale was legal, he told me, and I should show some dignity and accept it."

She had nothing to say. Could Lord Atherton, who was always charming and laughing, truly be so heartless?

"You might think it was callous of him to say that," Sebastian went on. "I suspect . . . I suspect it was because of his sister. Samantha was a child when I left for the army, but it was clear she had some girlish fancies about me. Of course they were merely fancies—we would have been more star-crossed than Romeo and Juliet, given our fathers—but to her they must have seemed possible. Benedict was always very protective of her, and he would sometimes bring her on our forest explorations when we were young. Before I left for the army, she told me she loved me and would wait for me to return so we could be married."

Abigail, who had been listening first in interest, then in growing astonishment, stopped in her tracks. "Samantha?" she exclaimed, thinking of the composed young woman doing such a bold and brazen thing. "How forward—and how unlike her!"

He grimaced. "She was only thirteen then. No one is in their right mind at that age. Certainly not I, who dreamt of nothing but making off with a bottle of my father's brandy."

"Someone once told me you had withdrawn from society because of Lady Samantha," Abigail said slowly. "That you were so in love with her, you couldn't bear to see her after her father denied you her hand."

"If I'd asked, I would have been denied," he agreed. "Contemptuously and swiftly. But I was never in love with her, and I never asked. She was a very sweet girl and I was fond of her. We'd known each other nearly all our lives, and perhaps if my knee hadn't been ruined and my father hadn't run mad . . . if I'd had a fortune and a respectable reputation . . ." He shrugged. "But I didn't, so it hardly mattered.

"She was the reason Benedict turned on me for good, though. I told you about the night my father disappeared." Abigail nodded once at his faintly questioning glance. "Benedict came to Montrose Hill that night. He accused me of hiding Samantha in the house, of luring her away—on a desperate elopement to repair my fortunes, I suppose. It was while he was searching the house for her that I discovered my father was missing."

"Could she have been there?"

He gave her a weary look. "Could a sixteen-year-old girl have gone from Stratford Court across the river to Montrose Hill and back, alone at night? I never saw her. The housekeeper and her husband never saw her. Benedict had no proof she'd ever left home. She was in her bed when he returned." His voice hardened. "That was the last time his lordship and I had spoken before yesterday. He accused me of seducing an innocent girl, a girl I had once thought of as a sister. He said nothing when rumors began swirling that I had murdered my father, even though he was there and saw the empty room. He said nothing when his father accused me of stealing from him in vengeance for the lost land. He was not as I remembered him from our boyhood, and I find it hard to think cordially of him."

There was no doubt of that. His voice had grown fierce and harsh as he spoke, and his face showed how cruel his disillusionment had been. Abigail, who was by nature a very loyal soul, felt her own indignation gather. Even allowing that Sebastian might have been a more rakish sort as a young man, he didn't have it in him to toy with a girl's affections, especially a girl so young. She could make some allowance—some—for Lord Atherton wanting to protect his sister, but not to the point of standing by while the gossip hounds devoured his friend without cause. Without thinking she put her hand on Sebastian's arm. "I'm sorry."

Her touch seemed to rouse him from his moment of anger. His face relaxed as he glanced down at her hand. "You have nothing to be sorry for. I'm the one apologizing. I was at fault for being unable to hide my disdain when we met yesterday."

When she had been holding Lord Atherton's arm, with his expensive gift in the crook of her elbow. Abigail began to feel a little sorry for upbraiding Sebastian. It must have been a bit of a shock to him, since the last time he saw her she'd let him undo the front of her gown and do wicked things to her breasts. The memory of his lips on her bare skin made her heart skip a beat. He hadn't promised her anything directly . . . but it dawned on her that his actions had all pointed toward more attachment than he'd declared. He wanted to make love to her, but restrained himself. He said he was trying to behave honorably. He sent her his mother's book in apology. He made the grotto presentable and made sure she saw the treasure hidden within. He came to call on her family, to widespread astonishment. He hinted that he would speak to her father, when he returned from Bristol. And he'd gone looking for her as soon as he arrived home.

"Before you left," she said hesitantly, "you said you had a question for my father."

His eyes were hooded, wary. "I'm no longer certain I should ask it."

"Why not? Did something happen in Bristol to change your mind?"

"Not in Bristol, no," he said. "My uncle died. I went to Bristol to see his solicitor because he left me his estate—some four thousand pounds."

So it had been good news, in a way. She tamped down the spark of relief and delight. "I'm very sorry he died."

He nodded. "Thank you." There was a long pause. "You said yesterday that you have never hidden what you want. If your desires have changed since I left—"

"No," she said. It was true. Now that he was standing in front of her again, tall and serious and so close she could touch him, her heart was clear.

"I wouldn't blame you if you preferred Atherton."

"But I don't," she whispered.

Something leapt in his eyes. "Is every part of this garden visible from the house?"

She gulped. Her skin tingled. "All but the section

there by the wall, where the roses climb over. There is an arbor . . ."

"Will you show me?"

Without a word she turned onto the path that led to it. The wall screened the kitchen garden from the formal garden. If one followed the path around the side of the house, it led to the Fragrant Walk. She kept her steps slow and deliberate, even though she wanted to race out of sight of any prying eyes. She said a fervent prayer that Milo had caused some trouble inside to keep Mama away from the window; ten minutes was all she asked.

The instant they rounded the side of the wall, Sebastian dropped his cane. She whirled at the sound, thinking he had stumbled again, but he caught her face in his hands and kissed her. It was the kiss of a starving man, and Abigail melted under the intensity of it. She slid her hands up his chest, under his jacket, feeling the hard, quick beat of his heart. He snaked one arm around her waist and hiked her against him, almost roughly. She sighed in pleasure. Oh yes; she knew what she wanted, and it was right here in his arms.

"I missed you," he breathed. "More than words can say."

"And I you." She pressed her lips to his jaw.

"Even with Lord Atherton's attentions to divert you?"

She laughed, tugging lightly on his cravat. "What was I supposed to do, throw him out? What if Penelope wanted him?"

His lips quirked in that slow smile. "She may have him, for all I care."

"And for all I care," she whispered, drawing his mouth back to hers for another kiss. They only had another moment or two. Anyone walking from the woods—or the stable, for that matter—would see them clinging to each other as though it would pain them to separate. Perhaps it would; when Sebastian raised his head and rested his cheek against her temple, Abigail only tightened her grip. Another minute, another second . . . She was greedy, wanting to snatch as many seconds as she could, in case it was another fortnight before another embrace.

Reluctantly he stepped back from her. "I brought a gift for you." He took a small box from his coat pocket.

Abigail pulled off the ribbon, opened the box, and gazed at a small Wedgwood cameo pendant on a gold chain. "It's lovely," she sighed. "Oh, thank you."

He smiled—a wide, honest smile, perhaps the first one she'd ever seen on his face. "I've never been happier to give a gift," he said before he kissed her again, softly and sweetly this time. This was the kiss of a man in love, she thought in dizzy joy.

"Ahem."

Abigail started, and Sebastian turned. Mama stood on the walk behind them, Milo nestled in the crook of her arm. She wore a pleasant but stern smile, an expression Abigail had never seen any other person achieve. "How lovely to see you again, Mr. Vane," Mama said. "I wondered if you'd got lost in the garden."

"No, Mrs. Weston. I was admiring your roses."

Mama glanced at the roses climbing the wall beside them. Abigail took advantage of the momentary distraction to slip the cameo in its box into her pocket. She suspected the visit was over, and was proven right when Mama stayed with them, answering all Sebastian's polite questions about the plants and design of the garden and leaving Abigail to trail behind. This time, though, she didn't mind. The box in her pocket was tangible proof that she was right, about Sebastian and about her heart.

And that meant everything was going to work out perfectly, she just knew it.

Chapter 19

The invitation from Stratford Court caused a commotion when it arrived at Hart House. Mama was beside herself; she dashed off a note to Papa, who had gone to London on business, that he must return as speedily as possible to dine with the earl and countess. She told James he would accompany them, no matter what other plans he had made. Penelope, the sly opportunist, asked for a new gown and shoes, and was immediately granted permission to go into Richmond and order them. Abigail, too wrapped up in her own happy daydreams, barely acknowledged the invitation.

"You don't seem surprised, Abby," said her smiling mother.

"No, Lord Atherton mentioned it when we saw him in town the other day."

Mama's eyes narrowed thoughtfully. "Nor do you seem especially pleased."

"Oh, I'm sure it will be delightful."

Mama studied her a moment longer, then went to shut the door. She came back and sat beside Abigail on the sofa, taking the embroidery hoop from her hands. "What happened between you and Mr. Vane yesterday?"

"We strolled in the garden and talked."

"You were in buoyant spirits when he left."

She smiled. She couldn't help it. "I'm in love, Mama."

A thin line creased her mother's brow. "What of Lord Atherton?"

"He's charming and very handsome," she replied, "but he's not the man I love."

Her mother sighed. "Vane hasn't spoken to your father."

"No, but Papa said he would respect my choice."

"He will take your desires into account," Mama corrected her. "There are some strong arguments against Mr. Vane."

"But there are equally strong explanations."

Mama pressed her fingertips to her brow. "I'm afraid to ask."

"Don't you want me to be happy?" She scooted closer to her mother. "Mama, he's a good man. He's a war hero! His father went mad, it's true, but that has nothing to do with the son. And madness is what led old Mr. Vane to wander off one night."

"But then what happened to him, dear?"

"No one knows. No one," she repeated forcefully. "Sebastian looked for him—why wouldn't he?" Her mother raised one brow, and Abigail slashed one hand through the air. "Does it serve him at all to be thought a murderer? To have his estate tied up because his father can't be proven dead? It doesn't even make sense, Mama."

"But it is a black mark, and a very alarming one," replied her mother. "We want you to be safe as well as happy, Abby. And unfortunately the rumors, to say nothing of his motives in pursuing a girl with a large dowry, are not to his credit."

She set her jaw. "When you married Papa, he was just an ambitious young man, reading law in his father's office. He had very little. What made you risk yourself on him?"

"Do not start, young lady."

That was the warning tone. Abigail subsided; she wanted her mother's support, not an argument. "You've always called me very sensible. I've met handsome men before, fortune hunters and rogues, and not been swayed by their flattery. Why don't you trust me now?"

Her mother didn't answer for a long moment. "I suppose it's easier to trust when you refuse them. There's much less at risk then." She sighed. "Oh, Abby. I do want you to be happy. But Mr. Vane must prove himself worthy of you. If he cannot . . . Better a broken heart now than a lifetime of regret." She rose. "There's no reason to rush into anything. I must go send our acceptance to Lady Stratford."

Abigail nodded as her mother left. That was better than an outright refusal, but less than she'd hoped for.

At least Sebastian had agreed to attend the Stratford dinner. She didn't want to think how awkward that would be without him.

Sebastian walked up the once-familiar drive to Stratford Court with very mixed feelings.

On one hand, he would see Abigail. Since their parting and informal betrothal, he'd been counting the hours until they would meet again. He hadn't seen her since that glorious day in the Hart House garden, despite daily walks along her favorite paths in the woods.

For that alone he could thank Benedict for this invitation.

But on the other hand, he had little doubt that Lord Stratford would be no more cordial than he'd been the last time Sebastian was here seven years ago, hobbling on crutches and seething with resentment over the riverfront acres. Just the thought of the earl's response made his spine stiffen and his jaw clench. If Stratford provoked him . . .

If Stratford provoked him, he would do nothing. He was not that angry young man anymore. Nothing Stratford might say or do could spoil this evening. He forced his shoulders to relax as he shed his coat and handed it to the butler. He barely saw where the footman led him, straining his ears for the sound of her voice. And just as he went into the grand drawing room, he heard it. She turned at his entrance and smiled, so beautifully he thought he could face down a hundred Stratfords, just for the sight of her.

Still, it was odd meeting the family after all these years. Lady Stratford, still as slender and chilly as he remembered, treated him as a complete stranger. Lady Turley—once Lady Elizabeth Lennox—was reserved but gracious, making only a small acknowledgment that they had ever met; her husband, Viscount Turley, he didn't know. Lady Samantha smiled at him, but with a flicker of awkwardness. Sebastian, his memories of her freshened by confiding in Abigail, spoke politely to her before moving on. Benedict was at his most charming, even condescending to shake his hand. And Lord Stratford . . .

The earl looked down his prominent, hooked nose. Sebastian bowed, ignoring the scorn in his glittering eyes, and after a moment Stratford made a motion that might be called a nod. Then he turned his back and walked away, which suited Sebastian perfectly. He joined James Weston, who was entertaining the younger ladies with a story from his recent visit to London involving an opera singer and a dog who got loose on the stage during her aria.

At dinner he was seated at the middle of the table, between Lady Turley and Mrs. Weston. Abigail was at the end, near Lady Stratford and Benedict, where he couldn't see her around the enormous epergne in the center of the table. He refused to be ruffled by anything, and spent his time making conversation with Mrs. Weston, who told him all about Milo's training. All in all, it was a better evening than he had expected.

It was after dinner that things began to deteriorate.

"What shall we do?" asked Benedict when they had all retired to the drawing room. To Sebastian's immense relief, the gentlemen had not remained in the dining room over brandy for more than a quarter hour. Aside from a few subtly malicious comments from the earl, that had passed quickly enough.

"Cards," suggested Lord Turley.

"Riddles," countered his wife.

"Perhaps a bit of dancing," said Benedict jovially.

"That would be lovely," said his mother with a regal smile. She turned to Mrs. Weston. "Have you any objection to the young people dancing, Mrs. Weston?"

"Not at all!"

"Brilliant." Benedict rubbed his hands together. "Elizabeth, would you play for us?"

"Am I not invited to dance, too?" She laughed even as she laid one hand on her belly. It had come out during dinner that she was expecting her first child.

He grinned. "If you won't play, I shall have to, and that would be a great tragedy for everyone."

She tapped her brother on the arm. "Very well. For you—and to spare our ears."

Benedict turned, but Sebastian had already foreseen what was coming. There were three young ladies: Abigail, Penelope, and Samantha. There were four gentlemen who might dance: Benedict, James Weston, Lord Turley, and Sebastian himself. Perhaps it hadn't been deliberate that Benedict suggested dancing, but Sebastian didn't think it was beneath him to name an activity that would put Sebastian at a disadvantage. And the last thing he intended to do was watch Benedict take Abigail by the hand and dance with her while he sat lamely by. If it ruined his knee for all time, he was going to dance with her tonight. He bowed to Abigail. "May I have the first set, Miss Weston?"

There was a shocked hush in the room. Sebastian ignored it, keeping his gaze fixed on Abigail. Her eyes widened, but then a bright, delighted smile split her face. "Of course, sir." She put her hand in his, and he smiled back.

"Lady Samantha, will you do me the honor?" James Weston bowed to that lady, who looked startled. She murmured an agreement, although not without a quick glance at her mother.

Benedict recovered quickly. "Miss Penelope." He made a flourishing bow. "Will you?"

"With great pleasure, sir."

Sebastian thought he'd never heard Penelope speak so kindly to Benedict, but he forgot about that as he led Abigail to join the figure. Her brother and Lady Samantha lined up next to them, separating them from Benedict and Penelope—not that it mattered to Sebastian. Once upon a time, he'd been very fond of dancing, and tonight he was going to dance with Abigail. Napoleon himself could line up next to them, and Sebastian wouldn't have cared. Barely three feet away, Abigail smiled at him, her gray eyes as bright as stars.

The first few steps were a bit uncertain; it had been a long time since he'd danced. But Abigail subtly motioned which direction, and his feet began to remember. Every time he took her hand or caught her in his arm, he remembered: this was how it felt to be normal. This was how it felt to forget about his wounded leg and give himself over to the joy of dancing with a woman.

All too soon it was over. Abigail curtsied, beautifully flushed from the dancing. He bowed, and they shared a smile. He could swear he knew what she was thinking—*You dance far too well to be the cripple you name yourself*—and he had to admit she was right. His left knee ached, but no more than usual after a long walk through the woods. It was nothing to the thrill of pleasing her. He even danced another set, this time with Penelope as Benedict claimed Abigail. He still got to dance with Abigail again when the partners changed, and that was all he cared about.

After the dancing, Mrs. Weston summoned her daughters for a quiet word. Sebastian took the opportunity to discreetly stretch his leg. He had learned that it stiffened up after exercise if bent, so he took a turn around the room.

Benedict intercepted him. "I'd like a word," he said in a low voice.

"Another time, my lord." Sebastian kept his eyes on Abigail. God above, he felt alive and vital in a way he hadn't in years. Holding her in his arms, proving he could dance like a normal man, had sent his spirits soaring. But it was the look in her eyes that made his heart leap. He almost wanted to thank Benedict: this dinner had been a bloody brilliant idea, and the dancing an even better one.

"Miss Weston," said Lady Stratford in her cool, clear voice. "Perhaps you would favor us with a song? Your mother tells me you're quite accomplished on the pianoforte."

"I'm sure no one could surpass Lady Turley's beautiful playing," said Abigail with a smile at the lady. "But I would be delighted to play for you." She got up and made her way toward the instrument.

"Now, Vane," Benedict growled.

He glanced at his one-time friend. "Can't it wait, my lord?"

Benedict lifted his chin, his eyes blazing with challenge. "No."

He took another glance at Abigail, seating herself at the pianoforte. Lady Samantha had gone with her, and was spreading out a selection of music. He would rather hear her play than listen to anything Benedict had to say, but he didn't want to cause a scene. That wouldn't achieve his other goal tonight, to set the elder Westons at ease about his fitness as a husband. "Very well."

Benedict led the way to a small green salon, where Sebastian dimly remembered being once before. "Old Samwell scolded us here," he said without thinking, naming the earl's steward from nearly twenty years ago. "For stealing oranges from the orangery." He'd endured it facing a portrait of some long-dead Stratford ancestor from the time of the Stuarts, with a long curling mustache and a faintly amused air, as if he found the steward's tirade as annoying as Sebastian had. And once Samwell was done, Sebastian and Benedict had collapsed into a fit of snickering about it.

"What?" Benedict frowned at him before recognition flickered in his eyes. "Oh yes. A long time ago."

Sebastian glanced around the room. The same Stuart ancestor smirked down at him from the wall. "It's not changed a bit." He faced Benedict, who most certainly had changed. "What did you wish to discuss, my lord?"

"There's nothing to discuss." Benedict's expression grew smooth and hard. "I merely wanted to let you know that I intend to marry Abigail Weston."

He almost smiled. "Did I miss an announcement at dinner?"

"I haven't proposed yet, but I will."

Once he would have laughed. Now he thought about doing the same thing, although not in any spirit of goodwill. "You seem very certain she'll accept."

"I have reason to be." Benedict's smile was edged with gloating.

"Oh?" He leaned on his cane and raised his brows. "What is that?" He felt fearless tonight, brimming with confidence. Abigail wouldn't accept Benedict; she was in love with him. And he was in love with her. Recklessly he discounted any and every obstacle, every argument he himself had once made against marriage. He knew her, in a way Benedict never would or could. He knew what made her heart beat faster and what made her laugh. He knew what moved her and what aroused her. He was an idiot to let pride cost him a chance at real, lasting happiness. He knew—he *knew*—that if Abigail had to choose between them, she would choose him. Part of him almost itched to propose to her tonight, just so Benedict could get his comeuppance.

Benedict scoffed. "Do you even need to ask? Don't you think she looks very much at home here?"

"She's not something your father can buy for you," said Sebastian.

The other man's face darkened. "How dare you suggest that."

"No? You were the one who invited her here. No doubt seeing how fine a home you can offer her, at some point in the future, bears some influence."

"Envy doesn't become you." Benedict heaved a sigh and looked bored.

Sebastian shrugged. "No. It's not envy. I know I have nothing much to offer her but myself. Only she can decide if that's enough."

"Be damned if she will!"

He raised his eyebrows. "Someone else will decide for her?"

Benedict flushed. "I meant she won't choose you, Bastian."

Somehow the childhood nickname cut deeper than anything else Benedict could have said. Sebastian inhaled a long breath to keep his composure. Benedict seemed to realize a moment too late what he'd said; he turned his back and walked toward the door. Before he had gone more than a few steps, though, the door opened and the Earl of Stratford stepped inside.

"Well, Vane, that was a pretty display."

Sebastian didn't know what the earl meant, so he made no reply. He couldn't stop the instinctive tensing of his muscles, though. The Earl of Stratford had been a fearsome figure seven years ago, and his aura of menace hadn't dissipated much since then. Even Benedict stopped and stood a little straighter.

Stratford folded his arms and cocked his head. "A

cripple dancing! That might win the ladies' pity, but not much else."

"I've never wanted anyone's pity."

"Not even when you came to beg me to return what your father legally sold?" Stratford's eyes gleamed in contempt.

Sebastian would regret that visit to the end of his days. He'd been distraught, barely twenty-three, with a shattered knee and a father raving about demons trying to kill him. He *had* begged the earl to reconsider the sale, thinking that if he could somehow restore that one part of his life, it would make the rest better, too. "He wasn't in his right mind when he signed that document, and you knew it."

Stratford affected a look of exaggerated surprise. "How could I have known?"

"Fifty pounds for eighty acres of good land."

The earl had a cruel smile. "I offered him one hundred pounds. He insisted more than fifty was too generous."

Sebastian felt as taut as a bowstring. His hand tightened on the handle of his cane. "How sporting of you to acquiesce so easily."

Stratford shrugged. "Why let an opportunity go to waste?"

Sebastian looked from father to son. How many times had he sympathized with Ben over his father's cold and calculating demeanor? Even now Benedict gave no sign of disagreement; he just stood listening, his mouth flat and his expression distant. "I expected nothing more of you, sir."

"I suggest you make your final farewell of Miss Weston tonight. Benedict brought her here for approval, and I have decided to give it." He looked at his son. "Her dowry is acceptable, and I grant you she's pretty enough. If you want her, have her. I expect you to conclude the business within a week."

"Father," said Benedict in a low voice. Something about it touched distant memories: Ben, complaining that his father was impossible to please. Ben, worrying over the unavoidable punishments for falling short. Ben, bruised and quiet after it was administered. Sebastian had hated the earl all those years ago—still did—but now he looked at Benedict and wondered why he put up with this abuse still. But perhaps Benedict was more like his father than he realized. After all, when Sebastian had told him what Stratford had done, Benedict had taken his father's side so staunchly, he hadn't spoken to Sebastian again for seven years.

Not for the first time, it made Sebastian angry. Benedict had no choice but to submit to his father as a boy, but he was a man now. Sebastian wanted to punch Benedict's face for speaking so callously about marrying Abigail, but the earl's careless presumption that if his son wanted her, he would have her, enraged him. She was far more than a pretty heiress, and she wasn't Stratford's to award.

"Well done, Ben. Now all you have to do is get her approval." Sebastian glanced fleetingly at the earl. "I expect it will be easier to obtain than your father's ever was."

"You impudent rat. Don't you speak to my son that way." Stratford glared at Benedict. "Are you going to take that, from a mad cripple? What sort of man are you?"

"He's going now," said Benedict through white lips.

Sebastian nodded. "I'll reserve my felicitations until I see the notice in the papers." He turned toward the door.

"Good riddance," growled Stratford. As Sebastian made to pass him, Stratford turned and stood blocking his path. Intent on escaping the noxious presence of the earl without giving way entirely to his temper, Sebastian didn't pay enough attention to where he was. His cane caught on the side of Stratford's shoe just as he put his weight on his bad leg—and just as Stratford twitched his foot to the side, sending the tip of the cane sliding over the polished floor. He tried to catch his balance but it was too late; he crashed down onto his injured knee, barely throwing out his hands in time to keep from landing full flat on his face.

For a moment he thought he would pass out. Pain seared up his leg, even worse than when he'd first been shot, and his stomach heaved on instinct. He nearly bit through his tongue to keep the howl of agony at bay. It was all he could do to stay on his hands and knees, shaking as his every nerve tightened in anguish.

But then, dimly, he heard the earl speak. "Clumsy, too," said Stratford in mild contempt. "You're barking mad already if you thought any woman would want you over my son, Vane." He walked away, sending the cane rattling across the floor with a flick of his toe.

Christ. He had to get out of here. It had been a mistake to come after all. Everything he'd gained by holding his own and facing his tormentor—and dancing with Abigail—was wiped away by the prospect of lying retching on the floor. Sebastian gritted his teeth and raised his head, praying he could get back on his feet unaided. If he had to crawl out of Stratford Court . . . he would, but it would be bitter. Slowly, carefully, he brought his good leg forward. Nausea roiled his stomach again as he had to rest his full weight on the hurt knee. He paused to take a deep breath, bracing himself . . .

A hand appeared in front of his face. Benedict, white-faced and grim, bent down.

"He doesn't need your help, Benedict," said Stratford from the other side of the room, where he was pouring himself a drink. "He doesn't need anyone's help. The Misanthrope of Montrose Hill!"

Sebastian looked up at Benedict. Neither said anything. Slowly Sebastian raised his hand, and took Benedict's proffered one. With a firm pull, Benedict helped him rise, then handed him the cane. Sebastian gave him only a curt nod, setting the cane alongside his wounded leg. The knee throbbed as though a red-hot knife had been driven into it, but he refused to make a sound of discomfort. Slowly, gingerly, he turned, making sure the cane was firmly settled every second.

"You look a bit ill, Vane." The earl sipped his drink. "Leaving early, I daresay; what a pity."

And now he was being thrown out. There was no mistaking the meaning in Stratford's words. For a moment he wondered if he could endure returning to the drawing room and taking his leave of Abigail, and then he decided against it, on the very real chance he would humiliate himself by blacking out.

"Thank you, Lord Stratford," he said, still fighting waves of nausea, "for a magnificent dinner. Please convey my compliments to Lady Stratford." Again he turned. "My Lord Atherton." And he bowed, clenching his teeth against the renewed anguish.

Every careful step toward the door was agony, but he preferred to hobble like a cripple than go too fast and fall again. He left the green salon and felt a burst of relief, followed closely by dread at the prospect of getting home in this state. Oh God; he'd never make it. Montrose Hill might as well be on the moon. It was a long walk to the river, where he'd have to row himself across, then walk three miles or more uphill. He paused in the grand hall, trying to gather his thoughts. Was there any alternative?

"Mr. Vane?" Penelope Weston's curious tone vanished when she saw his face. "Oh my goodness," she gasped. "You look dreadful!"

He gritted his teeth and tried to smile. "Thank you."

"No, I mean you look ill." She touched his arm. "Come sit down."

He raised one hand. "No, I—I was just going home. It's time for me to take my leave."

She gave him a searching look. "Let me get Abigail. You're as white as a ghost—"

"No!" He closed his upraised hand into a fist and forced his voice back down. "Please don't. As you said, I—I fell ill. Don't get her."

Penelope's gaze dropped to his white-knuckled grip on his cane. Then she looked up, past his shoulder, and Sebastian heard the murmur of the earl's voice. He couldn't resist glancing back, too—the last thing he wanted the earl to have was the satisfaction of seeing him whipped and beaten—pushing himself a little more erect as he did. Stratford's scathing eyes raked him once more before he turned and walked away, back toward the drawing room, but Benedict still stood there watching. For a moment their eyes met. Benedict hesitated, looking torn, then followed his father.

"That low-mannered wretch," breathed Penelope beside him. She was glaring at Benedict's retreating back with pure venom. She glanced back at Sebastian. "You didn't fall ill, did you, Mr. Vane. You just *fell*. And he—" She stopped. "Let me help you, if you won't let me fetch Abby."

He managed to nod. He might not make it without her help. "Just outside."

Somehow they made it down the stairs. Penelope hurried ahead and had the footman holding the door open when he got there. He had crossed the graveled drive by the time she caught him again, this time with her father's servant in tow. "Adam is going to help you home," she announced. "And if you protest, I will run inside and tell my sister you are severely wounded."

Sebastian almost refused, until he remembered again how far it was from the dock to his home. He nodded once. "Thank you, Miss Weston."

"I don't know why you won't let me tell Abby anyway," she added softly. "She's a good nurse, very patient and sympathetic. And it's not your fault—"

"Please don't," he interrupted. "Not tonight." Not tonight, when he had danced with her like an able-bodied man. Not while she was still at Stratford Court, where the earl could blacken his name even further. He needed to gather himself and regain his composure before he saw her again. "My health isn't really your concern."

"No, but lying to my sister is," she pointed out.

Adam had brought the punt up. Sebastian forced himself to move, limping down the dock and managing to lower himself into the boat without casting up his dinner over the side. Sweating and panting again, he looked up at Penelope, watching him with concern. "Good night, Miss Weston. Thank you."

She waited until the boat was several yards from the dock before calling after him, "You can hardly keep it from her for long, you know. I'm the very worst person in the world at keeping secrets."

He knew. No doubt she'd tell Abigail before the night

was over, especially if Benedict made his proposal. The loathing in Penelope's face when she watched Benedict walk away had been potent and plain. But the last thing Sebastian wanted was for Abigail to see him as he was now, on the verge of being sick all over himself. He clutched his knee with both hands so hard his fingers cramped, as if he could somehow squeeze the pain out of it. He couldn't do more than nod in response to Penelope's last warning. Abigail would learn about it, but she—and her parents—wouldn't see him like this.

"Shall I fetch a doctor, sir?" asked Adam as he rowed.

Sebastian shook his head.

"My older brother was at Waterloo," said the servant after a moment of silence. "Came home without his arm. He never wanted a doctor, neither. He barely got the priest in time." He rowed a few more strokes. "My mum swore she'd beat me if I ever refused to see a doctor when one was called for."

"I hope you won't send her after me," he said, trying to breathe through his nose.

"O' course not. I was only thinking how Miss Abigail Weston reminds me of my mum sometimes. Kind and thoughtful but not afraid to speak her mind and impose her will."

The thought of Abigail taking a whip to him almost made Sebastian smile. Then the boat scraped over the bottom as they came into the opposite shore, knocking his knee against the side and causing him to catch his breath. Adam climbed out and tugged the boat farther ashore, then gave him a hand. Sebastian took it gratefully, managing to stagger out of the boat without falling.

"I'll have to run up to the house to fetch the gig,"

Adam told him. "The family wasn't expected back for another hour or more." He paused. "Miss Weston's direction was that I'm to take you right to your door, sir."

Sebastian nodded, too exhausted to protest. It would take him an eternity to walk home, and he wasn't fool enough to argue with the man. He sank down on a stone bench near the landing and listened to the servant's footsteps hurry up the lawn.

He glanced across the river. Stratford Court was like a castle tonight, the windows aglow. Abigail had looked so beautiful, his fairy princess again in her pale green gown.

Well. Not quite his. Perhaps never to be his.

Perhaps it had all been for naught. Stratford Court was an awesome sight, and Benedict would make her mistress of it. Perhaps it would sway her. Perhaps her parents would persuade her to accept Benedict. Perhaps he'd been too long a misanthrope, too long alone. There was a raw, passionate attraction between them, but it might not be enough. Perhaps he'd been a fool to let his original perception waver, that she was meant for someone better. Just because she made him feel like a whole man again didn't mean she wouldn't be able to appreciate a suitor who really was a whole man. Perhaps he couldn't compete with Benedict even if he tried.

Sebastian clenched his fist and pressed his knuckles into his forehead. No. He wasn't thinking clearly now—the pain was warping his mood and thoughts. The girl he knew and loved wouldn't be so quickly or so thoroughly dazzled by Ben's title and fortune that she forgot everything else. She loved him; he knew it. She said she didn't want Benedict.

Her parents, though . . . might not feel the same.

He shifted his leg gingerly. The thought of Mr. Weston's sharp eye and even sharper ambition made him doubly glad he'd left Stratford Court. Mrs. Jones would wrap up his knee, and in a day or so he'd be back to normal; still limping, but no worse than before. It had been a bit of hubris, thinking he was well again, but his trust remained unshaken. He would go back to Hart House and take his chances. If Abigail didn't want him, he had to hear it from her, not from Benedict.

Chapter 20

Abigail knew something was wrong when Sebastian left the room with Lord Atherton, but only the latter returned. Her worry increased when Penelope, who'd excused herself to freshen up after dinner, returned to the drawing room after an even longer absence. Her sister's antipathy toward Lord Atherton, which seemed to have abated this evening, was back in full force. Abigail couldn't guess what, but she was sure something had happened involving the three of them. Penelope managed never to speak another word to their host, and Lord Atherton's cheer seemed a bit subdued. Between her growing bad feeling about Sebastian's disappearance and her raging curiosity about Penelope's grim mood, she could hardly wait for the party to be over, and breathed a sigh of relief when her parents finally took their leave.

As he walked them out to the carriage waiting to take them back to the ferry crossing the river, Atherton drew her slightly aside. "May I call on you tomorrow, Miss Weston?"

"Hmm? Oh—certainly, my lord."

He grinned. "Splendid. I hope you enjoyed Stratford Court."

"Very much, sir," she said with a distracted smile. "I do hope Mr. Vane wasn't terribly ill." Lord Stratford had said he'd felt unwell and been forced to leave early. Abigail had a sinking feeling the dancing had wounded his leg more than he'd let on, if he'd departed so abruptly and unceremoniously.

Atherton had taken her hand to help her into the waiting carriage; at her words his fingers twitched around hers. "I'm sure he'll be fine."

"But what a sad thing to happen at a party." She shook herself. "Good night, my lord."

"Good night, my dear Miss Weston." He stood back and watched them drive away.

"What a glorious evening!" Papa was in high spirits. "That's living, I tell you. My love, what did you think of the chimneypiece in the dining room? Shall we replace the one in town with pink marble?"

Mama smiled. "Too grand for my taste, Mr. Weston! I'm very content with the one we have, thank you."

He grinned. "As you say, madam. But what a dinner—and what hosts! Abby, my dear, did you enjoy it?"

"Yes, Papa," she murmured.

"Very good," he said with a wink. "I'm very glad to hear that, indeed."

She forced another smile, trying to catch her sister's eye. Penelope had thrown herself into a corner of the carriage and was glaring out the window. When they reached the ferry, where the earl's man was waiting to take them across, Penelope climbed into the prow and crossed her arms, exuding a forbidding air during the short trip across the river to the deserted landing at Hart House. She only turned around when Papa exclaimed in irritation, "Where's Adam? I told the fellow to be waiting for us."

"I sent him on an errand, Papa. And look, here he comes."

Papa sighed, but let it go. Abigail, though, caught the way her sister hurried to exchange a quick word with Adam, who had just driven up in the carriage. She saw Penelope's face ease at whatever he said to her.

What in the world had happened?

Thankfully, Penelope didn't make her wait much longer. The maid had barely left after helping her prepare for bed before Penelope slipped into her room. "I have something to tell you," she said without preamble.

"I hope so!" Abigail beckoned her to the window seat and grabbed a shawl. "Where did you go this evening? You were gone an age. And what did Adam tell you?"

Her sister held up one hand, grimmer than Abigail had ever seen her. "Bother that. I just went to freshen up, but as I was returning to the drawing room, I saw Mr. Vane in the corridor. Abby, he could hardly walk. He was doubled over his cane, his face was as white as a sheet, and I thought he would be ill. I—I think he fell on his wounded knee."

"What!"

Penelope made a shushing noise at her exclamation. "He swore to me he was fine, but I didn't believe it. Conveniently, Lord Stratford and Lord Atherton both came out of the room behind him at that moment. Naturally I presumed they would leap to help a stricken guest, but neither of them did a thing. They both looked right at him, clutching the balustrade for support and inching along, and they both walked away."

"But Sebastian?" Abigail exclaimed. "How did he leave?"

"I sent Adam to help him. He refused to let me fetch

you," she added as Abigail opened her mouth in outrage. "I don't think he wanted you to see him."

"But why?" She covered her mouth with one hand, feeling sick. It was bad enough to think he became ill and left without saying good-bye. But he'd been hurt, and he allowed Penelope—not her—to help him.

"If I had to guess, I'd say Lord Atherton or his father had something to do with it." Penelope's eyes flashed. "Not only did they see him struggling to walk, Lord Stratford looked almost pleased. You must have noticed he's a cold man—I didn't like him one bit—but I don't think he spoke a word to Mr. Vane all night. Doesn't that seem odd to you?"

Abigail said nothing. This was all her fault. If not for her, Sebastian would never have gone to Stratford Court and dined at the table of a man who called him a thief and a murderer. He must have dreaded it—she could still hear the echo of fury in his voice as he described Lord Stratford's reply to his request to regain his property—but he'd gone. And then he'd risked his knee to dance with her. What if the dancing had weakened his knee and led to his fall? She could picture Lord Stratford mocking any sign of weakness or infirmity. Her eyes prickled with tears to think she had been so selfishly happy to dance with him when it hadn't been good for him at all.

"And if I were you, I would refuse to receive Lord Atherton again," Penelope went on. "He also saw how unwell Mr. Vane was before he walked away. Surely even you can't excuse that."

"What?" She shook her head. "He's coming to call tomorrow. But Pen, what did Sebastian say?"

Her sister's eyes narrowed. "He's coming tomorrow? Why? Did you hear what I said? He saw how injured your Mr. Vane was, and he did nothing to help him. A guest he'd invited!"

"He asked if he could call, and since you hadn't told me any reason not to see him, I agreed." Abigail jumped up and began pacing. "I wish you'd come to get me, no matter what Sebastian said. He's so stubborn . . ."

Penelope tucked her knees under her chin and stared out the window for a moment. "Are you in love with him, Abby?"

The word brought a warm, happy smile to her face. "I am." She went to her desk and took out the cameo, safe in the box. "He gave me this."

"Oh, it's lovely!" Penelope gave her a wry smile. "Better than a book, even."

She blushed as she stroked one finger over the delicate carving. "Yes." She remembered the kiss he'd given her along with the jewelry, and her heart skipped a beat. She was in love, and unless she was very much mistaken, he was in love with her, too.

"I'm going to Montrose Hill tomorrow," she murmured, still fingering the cameo. She should have worn it tonight. "I have to know he's well."

Penelope seized her hand. "Excellent thought! I'll tell Mama you're reading in the conservatory—"

She shook her head. "You're a dear to lie for me, but I think I'll tell Mama where I'm going."

"What? Abby, she'll never let you go . . ."

"I shall go anyway." It was time to take a stand. If Sebastian could face down Lord Stratford, she could face down her parents.

Unfortunately, her plans went awry from the first, next morning. With one task after another, her mother kept her busy. Normally she was free to do as she liked, but this day her mother seemed bent on keeping her close, filling every vase in the house with fresh flowers, sorting linens, writing letters, even getting her hair trimmed. At first she went along with good grace; surely by the afternoon she would have done everything, and gained some favor from her mother. She thought her errand to Montrose Hill House was a very reasonable one, and she was perfectly willing to take her sister and a maid as chaperone.

But the hours ticked by and Mama showed no sign of letting up. Abigail began to feel aggrieved as she helped organize her mother's jewel chest. There was no reason Marie, her mother's maid, couldn't do this just as well. "May I be excused now?" she asked as she put away another bracelet.

"Not yet, dear." Mama smiled. "I believe this chest is too full. I've had some of these pieces for many years, and I don't think they all suit me." She held up a strand of pearls. "Try this one." Abigail obediently held it up in front of her neck. "No, no, put it on," urged her mother.

"I've already got a necklace, Mama."

Her mother's sharp gaze touched the cameo pendant. "So I see. But take it off for a moment and try the pearls."

Abigail sighed but took off the pendant. "Mama, I would like to go for a walk."

"Not today. I would like you to remain at home." Her mother studied her as she put the string of pearls around her neck. "Yes, it looks better on you than it does on me. You may have it, Abby."

"Thank you, Mama." She reached for the clasp.

"Oh, leave it on, dear," exclaimed her mother. "Jewelry isn't meant to be left in a box."

Abigail's fingers tightened around the cameo. "Why must I stay home?" She'd never been denied before. Outside the window, the sky was a flat blue, with towering mounds of clouds. It might rain later, which would spoil her plan to walk to Montrose Hill.

"Because I want you to," said her mother absently, still sorting through her jewels. "These would look so lovely with your eyes." Mama held out a pair of amethyst earrings in gold filigree. "And the opals might do for Penelope . . ."

She pressed her lips together. "I want to call at Montrose Hill. Mr. Vane left early last night, and I want to be sure he's not unwell."

"Not today."

"Penelope would go with me if I asked her, and I would take Jane," Abigail persisted. "It would be only neighborly, Mama."

"If Mr. Vane is unwell, he won't want company. But I shall send a kettle of soup and some oranges, with our good wishes."

Abigail bit her lip in frustration. Perhaps she should approach her father. Yes, that would be ideal; he would have another chance to see how decent Sebastian was. She was just about to excuse herself to go find him when the butler tapped at the door.

"Lord Atherton and Lady Samantha Lennox to see you, madam," Thomson announced.

Mama rose at once, looking pleased. "How delightful! Marie, finish putting these away. Thomson, I hope you showed our guests to the drawing room."

"Yes, ma'am."

"Very good. Come, Abigail, let's not keep them waiting." She headed for the door.

And just like that her chance was gone. Mama didn't even give her time to change necklaces, and she was forced to slip the cameo pendant into her pocket.

In the drawing room, Abigail made the polite greetings and sat beside her mother on the sofa. She didn't really feel like having visitors today, partly because of her desire to go to Sebastian and partly because of Penelope's story from last night. As Lord Atherton talked and laughed with his usual good humor, she studied him through newly critical eyes. Could a man so charming and thoughtful really turn his back on a friend, on a guest? If he could stoop to treat Sebastian that way, there must be a core of coldness in him. She allowed that his side of the story might be different, and it would be hard to condemn him for choosing to defend his sister instead of his friend. But her heart and her allegiance lay with Sebastian, and she couldn't help the instinctive disapproval of Lord Atherton for being less than she'd thought him.

"You're very quiet today, Miss Weston," he said to her after a while. "I hope you're well?"

She made herself smile. "Yes, very well. Forgive me, I'm a little tired."

"As am I," said Lady Samantha. "Last night was so delightful, I couldn't fall asleep for hours. I'm so glad you came to dine."

"Perhaps a turn in the garden will revive us," suggested Atherton. "Mrs. Weston?"

"Of course." Mama's eyes flickered Abigail's way. "Fresh air will do you some good."

Abigail had no choice but to smile and fetch her bonnet. On the terrace they met Penelope, with Milo on a lead. "There you are," remarked Mama. "Milo must be exhausted! Let me take him, Penelope. You may walk in the garden with our guests and your sister."

Penelope handed over the lead with reluctance. Abigail wondered if she'd taken the dog out explicitly to avoid Mama or their callers, but now she was as caught as Abigail was. Her sister flashed her a glance, then maneuvered to walk beside Lady Samantha as they reached the garden, leaving Abigail no choice but to walk with Lord Atherton.

"Miss Weston," he murmured. "I'd hoped to have a private word with you."

"We're virtually alone now, sir."

He glanced at their sisters, some distance ahead. "Would you show me the Fragrant Walk? I remember it was very beautiful."

Abigail's heart squeezed in apprehension. "There's so much beauty in the world. I constantly find new things that enchant me right here in the garden."

"Will you humor me this time?" He gave her a charming smile.

Inwardly she groaned, but she put her hand on his offered arm. "Of course."

She tried to talk of inconsequential things as they strolled, but it was hard. Mention of the climbing roses brought back memories of her stolen embrace with Sebastian, right by the pink tea roses. Any comment about the looming woods made her think of the grotto, and the sensual pleasure Sebastian had shown her there. When she commented on the gathering clouds and found her eyes caught on Montrose Hill, visible from this side of the house, she gave up.

Lord Atherton noticed her disquiet. He slowed to a

stop as they reached the edge of the Fragrant Walk. "Perhaps we shouldn't walk on."

"Yes, it's grown quite threatening. I think it may rain soon." She made to turn back, but he stopped her.

"Stay a moment. I have something to say to you." He came a step nearer. "You're a very lovely girl, Abigail."

Oh dear. This couldn't be what she thought it was, could it . . . ? She smiled as lightly as she could. "Why, thank you, sir! I'm flattered you think me so."

"I'm not the only one who thinks so." He took her hand. Abigail's smile faltered. "But I do believe I'm the most appreciative."

"I can hardly comment on that." She wondered if it would be rude to pull her hand away. As if he sensed the thought, he clasped his other hand around hers.

"Has no one else told you so?" He arched one brow as he toyed with the buttons at her wrist, holding her glove closed.

Sebastian had. He'd called her ethereal, so beautiful she struck him dumb. She cleared her throat at the thought of Sebastian. "Yes."

Lord Atherton's eyes narrowed a tiny bit before he dropped his gaze to her hand. "I suppose I can guess who." He undid a button. "Did you believe him more than you believe me?"

Her mouth was dry. She wanted to run away before he could say anything more. "It's not—not a matter of belief," she began awkwardly. "Calling someone beautiful is a compliment, an expression of the speaker's belief, and whether the recipient of the compliment believes it or not has no affect on the speaker's feelings. I suppose it only matters if the recipient trusts that the person paying the compliment believes it."

He smiled. "How astute you are. Do you believe me when I say it?"

She wished her sister would come interrupt them. She wished Milo would come streaking down the path with a squealing rabbit in his teeth. She wished for something, anything to disrupt this increasingly uncomfortable conversation. "I would never question your integrity, my lord."

"So very proper, Miss Weston." He'd got all three buttons undone, despite a few efforts on her part to slide her hand free, and now he began inching her glove off her hand with a slow tug on each finger in turn. "I beg you, call me Benedict."

"I think that would be too familiar, Lord Atherton."

"But I'm giving you permission." He took a step closer. "I would like us to be more . . . familiar."

She said nothing. Somehow when Sebastian had asked her to call him by name, it had seemed heartfelt; no one ever called him by name, he'd said. But Lord Atherton had invited her to call him Benedict, and she knew quite well his family called him Ben. It was an invitation to familiarity, but only a partial one.

Not that she wanted to be completely familiar with him. She had to put a stop to this. She drew a deep breath and tried to tug her hand loose, but only suc-ceeded in pulling her hand out of her glove entirely. "My lord," she began, but he put one finger on her lips.

"Let me finish, my dear; please." His eyes gleaming, he raised the limp glove to his lips. "Your parents have been very kind to me."

"What did you expect? They're kind people."

"It's no secret in town that your father is ambitious for his children."

Her temper began to stir. "Is yours not the same?"

He laughed. "He's exactly the same."

Abigail had a feeling the Earl of Stratford was much worse than her father in every way. There was something very cold and hard about His Lordship. "My sister will wonder what's become of us!" She forced a laugh. "And my mother. She'll ring a peal over me for straying this far from the house."

"Not today she won't." He stayed her motion toward the garden by catching her bare hand. "I spoke to your father last night, my dearest Abigail."

Oh dear. She cast a longing look over her shoulder, but her sister and Lady Samantha were nowhere to be seen. "Indeed? I'm sure he was very pleased to speak to you, sir."

"Benedict. And yes, he was delighted by our conversation."

She thought about yanking loose and running for it. She knew what he was going to say—what had pleased her father so much—and she didn't want to hear it. Benedict Lennox was a charming, handsome fellow, everything her parents wanted for her, and she had absolutely no desire to marry him. She didn't even want him to ask, for then there would be no awkward scene where she had to refuse. "He's at home today," she tried once more. "If we return to the house, I'm sure he'd be delighted to see you . . ."

He held tighter to her hand. "Abigail. I am trying to ask you a very serious question."

"Now? Surely it's too early in the day for serious conversation."

Her attempts at delay seemed to have annoyed him at last. His jaw hardened. "Why not?"

There was no escaping it. She stiffened her spine

and looked him in the eye. "Very well. What is your question, my lord?"

For a moment he didn't move. There was a crease of frustration between his brilliant blue eyes. For a moment Abigail had a flicker of hope that he wouldn't ask what she thought he was about to ask. "Why won't you call me Benedict?"

"I told you, it's too familiar."

"Hmm." He raised her hand and brushed his lips against the inside of her wrist, but his eyes remained fixed on her face. "Would you call me Benedict if I asked you to marry me?"

"That seems an extreme step to take merely to hear me say your Christian name."

"What would your answer be, if I asked you to marry me and call me by that name for the rest of your life?"

"I wish you wouldn't," she said before she could think of a better way to put it.

He froze. Several seconds ticked by, the trees rustling in the rising wind. "Sebastian Vane is ruined," he said at last, his voice tinged with concern. "Surely you've heard the rumors about him. If you're betting your happiness on him—"

"That would be my risk, wouldn't it?" This time when she pulled, he let go of her hand.

"Are you refusing me for him?" Lord Atherton sounded somewhat shocked.

"No," she said. "Because he hasn't asked me anything. I am refusing because I don't care for you the way I hope to care for my future husband."

He stared at her in amazement. "Forgive my plain speaking, but—are you certain about that? We get on so well together. I've never enjoyed another lady's company as much as I do yours. I thought you felt the same.

Surely you know how advantageous our marriage would be. Your father has already blessed the match! Do you think he'll be so quick to bless a union between his daughter and a bitter, reclusive man on the brink of ruin, a man suspected of murder and thievery? For God's sake, Abigail, surely you're not so foolish and sentimental as that."

She could stand it if he listed his advantages; she could stand it if his pride was wounded and his family snubbed her forever. But she couldn't stand to hear him disparage Sebastian that way. "He is *not* bitter, or reclusive," she snapped. "The rumors are just that— idle chatter with no substance to them, only animosity. He's shunned by your father largely out of guilt, because your father took advantage of old Mr. Vane's illness to loot the Montrose Hill estate. Don't you dare deny it," she warned him as he rocked back on his heels and scowled. "Eighty acres of land for less than fifty pounds? And then he only offered to sell it back for more than five thousand pounds?"

"There was more to it," he began.

"What?" Abigail asked bluntly. "Do you think I didn't notice every little cut your father made at him last night? Mr. Vane was invited to Stratford Court as a guest, yet your father treated him as a leper. I'm tired of hearing vague whispers of terrible deeds when no one seems to have a shred of convincing evidence, let alone proof. And you were once his friend." She spread her hands in amazement as his face grew dark. "Have you proof he killed his father? Or stole anything?"

Lord Atherton said nothing. A muscle in his jaw twitched.

"Ask yourself how advantageous a husband you would be if your estate dwindled to a few acres around a heavily mortgaged house. Ask yourself how many young ladies would simper and sigh over your attentions if there were rumors in town that you were possessed by devils. Ask yourself how dashing you would be without an income, without the use of your sword arm, without your father's title easing your way in every part of life. And then ask yourself how you would bear up under the lies and suspicions heaped upon you by people who were once your friends."

He was staring at her in shock. Her fury relented, and she put one hand on his arm. "I don't blame you for what your father did," she said more calmly. "I do like you a great deal, my lord. You are right, marrying you would be very advantageous. You're handsome and charming and I enjoy your visits enormously . . . but I don't love you, and that's why I cannot accept your proposal."

"You're refusing me for him," he repeated, but not with the same heat as before.

She shook her head. "I would refuse you in any event. We might get along well enough as husband and wife, but I want more out of marriage—and I suspect you would, too, eventually."

"And that is your final decision." He sounded numb.

"Yes."

He nodded. "I see." Somewhat jerkily, he made a stiff bow. He took a few steps back toward the garden, then paused and glanced over his shoulder at her. "Miss Weston . . . You may not understand everything that happened between my father and Mr. Vane, but . . . you may be right about Vane. There is no proof that I know of that he killed his father." He gave her a quietly wry look. "I wish you every happiness with him." And before she could say a word, he turned and walked away, his boots crunching on the path.

Abigail's shoulders sagged in relief. Thank goodness that was over. It could have been much worse; why, if her parents knew how she'd shouted at him . . .

The thought seemed to echo in her mind for a moment as the import sank in. Her parents. Lord Atherton had spoken to her father last night. Her father had blessed his suit. Papa had no doubt rushed to tell Mama to begin planning a wedding. That must be why Mama had kept her close all day; they had expected him to call and propose. Both her parents would be eagerly waiting to congratulate her. If Lord Atherton went back to the house and told them she had refused him . . .

Abigail's breath grew short. Surely he wouldn't. Lord Atherton was a gentleman . . . but he was also taken off guard and hurt by her answer, and he had only to reveal a few key details of her reply to horrify Papa.

She looked toward the house in dismay. How could she just walk back there and smile as if nothing had happened?

Sebastian. Had she refused Lord Atherton for him? She couldn't say that, because she certainly didn't have Sebastian, either, but . . . But he had her heart. How could she marry another man when she would always wish for him?

Without thinking she raised her eyes toward Montrose Hill. She couldn't see it from here, but she knew what it looked like, faded pink brick and ivy, alone on the hill. She was desperate to know if he was well after last night. If only he had come to see her today instead of Lord Atherton. If only he were here now, to tell her he loved her and wanted to marry her, and that everything would turn out well.

Thunder rumbled above. The sky had grown darker since she'd come out, deepening to an almost violet hue. Dimly she thought she should go back to the house, but her heart and mind strained not toward home, but toward Sebastian. And before she was aware of making any decision at all, she picked up her skirts and plunged into the woods, up the hill.

Chapter 21

Sebastian's knee wasn't broken. The fall had torn his skin and Mrs. Jones had gasped over the amount of blood inside his boot, but once she'd cleaned him up and splinted the joint, the pain began to subside. She brought him a cup of strong tea when he was thoroughly bandaged, and Sebastian didn't complain about the drop of laudanum he could taste in it. Tonight he couldn't deny the desire for a little oblivion.

In the morning he took stock of his situation. For the first time in years he felt a sense of urgency. Benedict was set on winning Abigail, and Sebastian didn't intend to yield the field for a moment longer than necessary. When the Joneses tried to give up their half day off, he told them to go. Mrs. Jones frowned and gave him a stern lecture about staying in bed, but they went. And as soon as they disappeared down the path toward town, Sebastian threw off his bedclothes and got dressed.

He was under no illusion about his disadvantages. For the first time in a long time, he envied Benedict his health, his fortune, his status. But by God, he loved Abigail. A man of action—the man he used to be— would stride into her house, propriety be damned, and ask her to marry him. A few persuasive kisses would be employed. If he could get her alone, and she encouraged him, more than kisses might occur.

Boris was waiting by the door. Sebastian tried to close him in, but Boris began baying at the door, alternating his deep, fearsome bark with pleading little whines that might have come from a dog one-tenth his size. Sebastian cursed under his breath but went back. The Joneses wouldn't be back for hours, and there was no one in the house who could let him out.

"If you have an ounce of gratitude in you, you'll come with me and help persuade her to live with us," he told the dog, who burst out of the house like an inmate being released from prison. "*Abigail*, Boris. Abigail who always has cheese for you. Your favorite person in all the world."

Boris gave a joyful woof and bounded off toward the woods, tail thrashing happily. Sebastian shook his head and continued on his way. Not for the first time he wished he kept a horse. Mounted, he could be there in a matter of minutes. On foot it would take him close to an hour. He spent the walk planning every word he would say, and hoped Mr. Weston would be at home.

To his relief, the gentleman was, and greeted him politely. "Vane. How do you do, sir?"

"Very well, sir. Thank you for seeing me."

"Come, sit. I trust you've recovered from your indisposition last night."

The splint and bandages were clear through his trouser leg, but Sebastian nodded. "I must thank you for allowing Miss Penelope to let Adam help me home."

"No trouble at all," said Weston graciously. "Delighted to be of assistance."

He drew a deep breath. "I have come to ask permission to court your daughter Abigail."

Weston was already shaking his head. "Vane, you're a good neighbor. But I have to tell you that my daughter may very likely be engaged by now."

"Benedict Lennox intends to ask her," confirmed Sebastian even though the words made his fist clench. "Has she said she will accept him?"

The older man looked startled. "Atherton told you that?"

"At Stratford Court last evening."

Weston blinked. "I see. Indeed. He asked my blessing on his suit, and I gave it. I believe he plans to speak to Abigail today."

"If he's already proposed and she's accepted, I will wish them great happiness and be on my way. However . . ." Sebastian flexed his hands. "If he hasn't proposed, or if she hasn't accepted, I would like your permission, sir."

Mr. Weston leaned back in his chair. "Forgive my blunt speaking, Vane, but . . . why should I?"

"I love your daughter very much."

"Ah." Weston grimaced. "I'm afraid . . . I'm afraid I cannot."

He'd been braced for that. "I understand you may be reluctant because of my financial state. In your place, I would be suspicious as well. I can provide for a wife; I've recently come into some money that will enable me to retire a good portion of my debt."

"Oh? How much?" asked Weston evenly.

"A little more than four thousand pounds, from my uncle who died in India."

Weston's eyes narrowed. "India."

Sebastian nodded. "I was in Bristol just a week ago seeing the solicitor about the inheritance."

Mr. Weston got up and walked to the window, where he folded his arms and stared outside.

"I know there are other reasons for doubting me," Sebastian went on. "Let me explain the rumors about my father—"

"It's not because of those," interrupted Weston. "I think you should take my answer and not press, Vane."

He was thrown off kilter by that. Everyone wanted to know about those rumors. He'd never told anyone except Abigail the full story. "Then why, sir?"

Weston's glance held a shade of pity. "It won't serve anything. I hate to accuse a man—indeed, I think many of the rumors about you are grossly exaggerated. But there is one I cannot discount; the source is unimpeachable, and with my daughter's future at stake, I won't chance it. I'm sorry."

Sebastian stared. Not the accusation of murder? What, then? "I believe my father's lunacy was caused by scientific research he conducted, not his blood. He was an inventor, experimenting with metals and solutions—"

"Vane, please," said Weston, shaking his head.

He had trouble controlling his breathing. "Then why?" Weston frowned at his demand, and he tried to soften it. "I would like to know why."

Weston's jaw firmed. He came back to his desk and sat down. "Very well. I expected to see you here at some point, asking for my daughter. I'm no fool, Vane; I presume you've met Abby walking in the woods a time or two. She's a tenderhearted girl, inclined to see the best in people. I could see in her face when you called that she was smitten. So I went into town and made some inquiries. I know you've been paying off debts recently, hinting to your creditors of a sudden flush of funds, in sudden possession of ready money after years of barely making payments. That's all well and good; there are a number of explanations."

"I inherited the funds," he repeated. "I have letters from my uncle's solicitor."

"But letters can be forged, can't they?" Weston held up one hand. "I make no accusation, and I don't believe every rumor I hear—most of them are nonsense—but one story did catch my ear. Your father sold off a great deal of property while you were with Wellington's army, and it left you in a very bad way when your father disappeared. Without a body, the estate couldn't go to probate, which left everything tied up, didn't it?"

Sebastian closed his eyes.

"That's why I doubt you killed him," Weston added, a touch kindlier. "At least not deliberately. No real benefit to a missing man, is there? But not long afterward, a good sum of money disappeared from Stratford Court."

Stratford. Sebastian wished the earl had simply broken his knee last night. "I did not steal that money," he said, softly but clearly.

"Four thousand guineas," said Weston as if he hadn't heard. "Curiously close to the sum you . . . inherited, just at the moment you might have felt the desire to improve your respectability. Understand, I make no accusations. But I dislike such dangerous coincidences. My daughter has a very handsome dowry. Paying out four thousand on old debts would be a very worthy investment for a man on the brink of gaining ten times that amount."

Slowly, stiffly, he forced himself up from the chair. His hands were numb, and his heart felt dead. "I appreciate your candor." Each word was ice cold on his lips. "I am not a thief. Whatever happened to Lord Stratford's money, I had nothing to do with it. And I would count myself the most fortunate man in the world to marry your daughter without a farthing in dowry."

"I'm sorry, Vane," said Weston once more, driving the final stake through his hopes.

He gave a jerky nod and turned toward the door. He took a step and almost fell before realizing he'd forgotten to retrieve his cane. He fumbled for it, then bowed and left, barely able to see in front of him.

No. Weston's reply echoed through his mind like the slamming of a door. *No.* Forbidden even to ask Abigail to marry him. *No.* Distrusted as a thief because he'd tried to use his inheritance—his divine stroke of bloody good fortune—to make himself more acceptable as a husband. *No.* He was damned sure that Stratford would have had him arrested years ago if there'd been a hint of proof he'd stolen that money. Instead the earl had done something far worse: cost him the only girl he had ever loved . . .

He staggered into the wall as he reached the hall. With curiously steady hands he pulled at his cravat, short of breath. Would he be allowed to see Abigail again? Wildly he thought of the grotto—they could meet there, whether her parents approved or not . . . But that would be fleeting. He would know it was doomed. Hadn't he told himself that the first time he saw her?

"Mr. Vane!" He started. Penelope Weston beckoned him across the hall. Slowly he obeyed her summons, crossing the room to the small antechamber she ducked into. "Are you here to see Abigail?"

"I would like to." He had no idea what he would say to her.

She beamed. "Brilliant! Your timing is exquisite. Lord Atherton just left." She was brimming with glee. "In quite a different mood than when he arrived, I must say. He was all smiles and flattery before, but after a private talk with Abby, he strode out of here as if the place were on fire. That augurs well, don't you think?"

Part of him leapt in jubilation that she'd disappointed Benedict. At least he wouldn't have to suffer that misery. "Where is she?"

"In the garden still, I expect. Lord Atherton walked off with her but came back alone, and then he hurried his sister into the carriage and left." She led the way to the garden, and pointed off to the north. "Lord Atherton came from that way, near the Fragrant Walk."

"I know where it is." On impulse he caught her hand and pressed it. "I'm in your debt, Miss Weston."

"Make my sister deliriously happy, and all debts are paid." She waved him off.

He limped around the formal garden, along the kitchen wall where he'd kissed her just a few days ago, and toward the Fragrant Walk. There was no sign of Abigail. He peered into the woods, but saw nothing. A fat raindrop hit his face; for the first time he realized how dark the sky had become. A storm was rolling up the Thames. He hesitated. Abigail had probably gone into the house, and he should go home before the downpour.

Cursing himself, he went back to Hart House. To his relief, Penelope was still at hand. "Has she come back inside?" he asked. "I didn't see her."

"I don't think so," she said in surprise. "Let me check."

He waited at the back of the hall, by the garden door. When Penelope returned several minutes later, she was frowning. "She's not in her room, and her maid hasn't seen her. Neither has Thomson. She's not with our mother, either."

"Is there anywhere else she might go?" Thunder growled in the distance. "It's threatening to storm."

Penelope hesitated. "She's very fond of walking in the woods."

He strode through the door back onto the terrace and glanced at the sky again. "In the rain?"

"It's not raining . . . yet . . ."

"Surely she wouldn't," he murmured, letting his eyes roam up Montrose Hill. He'd never realized how visible his home was from Hart House.

"You don't know my sister if you think she wouldn't," said Penelope, breaking into his thoughts. "She seems so proper and responsible, but Abigail usually manages to get what she wants."

A slow smile curved his mouth. If she wanted him, he meant to see that she got him. He couldn't change Mr. Weston's mind, but perhaps . . . perhaps Abigail could. "Thank you, Miss Penelope." He started toward the wood.

"Pen," she called after him. He glanced back and she shrugged. "I hope we'll be on family terms soon." She grinned and raised one hand. "Good luck, Sebastian."

Sebastian strode back through the gardens and down the Fragrant Walk, breathing deeply of the fragrance that would always remind him of her. He cut into the woods, forgetting everything he knew about how dangerous they could be in the dark. Ben had left, looking grim, without taking leave of his host. Abigail had remained outside, alone, and not been seen since. Sebastian had no grounds for his suspicion that she had gone looking for him, but he walked as quickly as his leg would allow.

By the time he reached his house, he was beginning to worry. The sky was deep purple now, growing darker by the moment as thunder cracked and streaks of lightning lit the roiling clouds. She could be lost in the woods. Perhaps she hadn't meant to come see him; perhaps she'd only meant to clear her thoughts in the quiet of the trees. His blood ran cold. Perhaps she'd gone to the grotto, which would be damned near impossible to find in the rain, even with a lantern. He'd just been so set on the thought—the hope—that she might have come to him, he hadn't taken the time to rule out those other possibilities.

What an idiot. Cursing himself, he limped across the ragged grass. He needed a lantern and his greatcoat, for she'd probably be chilled to the bone. First the grotto, then the usual paths where he had met her. If she wasn't there, he would return to Hart House and get Weston's servants to come out with him. He'd search the whole wood until she was found, storm be damned.

Something caught his eye as he neared the house. There was a movement in the woods, and then, to his intense relief, Abigail emerged from the trees, a look of deep uncertainty on her face. She raised one hand, and he saw Boris's big black head butting her arm. She stopped and turned to the dog, bending down to him and patting his ears. Sebastian had no trouble recognizing his dog's expression, even in the fading light: bliss.

"Good dog," he muttered. "*Damned* good dog." Then he raised his voice. "Abigail!"

She turned toward him, and the hesitation on her face vanished. In the blink of an eye, Sebastian's heart went from pounding with apprehension to throbbing with hope. He took a step in her direction, and she ran at him, holding up her green skirt. He dropped his cane and caught her in both arms, inhaling a harsh breath of elation at the feel of her against him again.

"Oh, Sebastian," she gasped against his chest. "I worried so when you disappeared last night, and Penelope said you were avoiding me—"

"Even when I wanted to avoid you, I couldn't." He tipped up her chin until she met his eyes. "I was just at Hart House, hoping it wasn't too late."

Her bosom heaved with every breath she took. "Too late for what?"

He gazed into her eyes, those starry eyes that had bewitched him from the start. "To tell you I adore you. I tried to deny it, and then I tried to ignore it, and now it seems like the only truth I know. I love you, Abigail Weston."

Her smile was glorious. "Lord Atherton proposed to me today."

"What did you tell him?" he asked in a low voice, tensing in spite of himself. Penelope could have been completely wrong, after all . . .

"No," she exclaimed with a little burst of disbelieving laughter. "I told him no! And he—and he—" She stopped, staring pleadingly at him.

"What did he do?" Sebastian felt the sudden urge to go pound Ben into the dirt.

"He asked . . . if I was rejecting him for you," she whispered. "I told him of course not, because you hadn't asked me anything, and yet . . . I think I rejected him because I was hoping so desperately you *would* ask me . . . because I am in love with you, and I could never marry him when I would always want you instead."

His heart soared. "And you came here to tell me that?"

She nodded.

All the glory of heaven seemed to shine on him. Sebastian thought he heard angels singing. A smile curved his mouth. "I wasn't going to Hart House merely to tell you I love you. I want you to choose me over Ben, whether I deserve it or not."

"I already did," she said softly. "Weeks ago."

His fingers tightened on her arms as the joyful glow receded. "But I spoke to your father today. I asked his permission to marry you—"

"Yes," she cried, straining toward him.

He held her at bay. "He refused, darling."

"Bother him!" Her smile was blinding with happiness. "He'll change his mind after I talk to him."

Sebastian knew he should doubt. Thomas Weston had been firm in his denial. But her reply was everything he'd hoped to hear; her confidence swept aside his worry, and recklessly he believed. He kissed her hungrily. "Marry me, Abigail," he breathed against her lips.

"Yes," she whispered, winding her arms around his neck. "Yes, yes, *yes*."

They might have stood there kissing for an hour, but the storm chose that moment to break. Icy drops of rain pelted down, swelling to a downpour in a matter of seconds. Abigail shrieked with laughter, Sebastian cursed, and they ran for the house, hand in hand. By the time he managed to get the door open and let them in, her hair hung in dripping locks and his neck was soaked where the water had run down his coat collar. Boris trotted past them and gave a great shake, sending water everywhere.

"Boris!" He wiped his face as Abigail laughed again. "I'm sorry, I'm not prepared for visitors," he said, belatedly realizing how rough his home was. The fire was laid in the grate, but not lit until absolutely necessary. The furniture was old and threadbare, the floors scuffed. He could make her a cup of tea, but there was no milk, no cake, no biscuits.

"I didn't come for tea." Her eyes shone. "I consider myself at home."

He grinned. "You are."

She pulled a few pins from her hair and shook her head, sending wet curls tumbling down her back. "Perhaps you could read to me?"

Sebastian went very still. "What would you like to hear?"

Beautiful color bloomed in her cheeks. "I think you know . . ."

Rain lashed the windows. It might last an hour or all night. A man of honor would resist. A man of conscience would remember her father's very definite refusal. But Sebastian was done with all that. He wanted Abigail; he wanted to marry her. Making love to her would satisfy the first driving desire, and almost surely lead to the latter. For once in his cursed life, he was going to get what he wanted, scruples be damned.

"I do," he murmured, and led her up the stairs.

Chapter 22

Abigail knew she was being wicked, and she didn't care.

She firmly blocked all thought of her parents or Lord Atherton from her mind. Her initial urge to run had indeed come out of her desire to avoid facing them, but as soon as the quiet of the trees enveloped her, she knew where she was going. Or rather, she knew where she wanted to go—getting there proved a challenge. She'd almost gasped in relief when Boris came bounding through the bracken toward her, his tail wagging in greeting. As if he'd been looking for her, he began nudging her up the hill, and before she knew it the pink brick of Montrose House appeared through the trees.

Now she was here, where she longed to be—where she belonged. Sebastian only let go of her hand when he had to kneel down and stir up the fire. His bedchamber was plain and bare. A worn leather armchair, a table, a chest of drawers, a blanket near the hearth that was clearly Boris's. And a bed.

The sight of the last gave her a moment of pause. She wasn't nervous, precisely, but suddenly she wished she knew better what to expect. Devoted readings of *50 Ways to Sin* had given her some ideas, but they felt wildly insufficient now. She wasn't really like Lady Constance. What if Sebastian thought she was actually that uninhibited and wild?

She closed her eyes and told herself not to be silly. Sebastian was far better than Constance's lovers; he was alive and real and he was in love with her, ready to make love to her. In the grotto and in the woods, he'd known just the right touch, just how far to take her down the road to ruin. He knew she hadn't much experience, and it hadn't stopped him from showing her a world of pleasure she'd never dreamt of before, and he'd made her feel adored while he did it. Her heart skipped a beat at the memory, and she opened her eyes, her moment of shyness evaporating.

Sebastian was watching her. "Uncertain?" he asked. "I won't do a thing you don't want me to do."

Abigail smiled. "I know. I trust you." She caught sight of something then, and blushed. "You kept it!"

He nodded, his eyes never leaving her face. "Of course I did. It made me think of you."

Her blush deepened. She picked up the item in question, the issue of *50 Ways to Sin* where Constance pleasured herself, wearing a blindfold, while her mysterious lover watched. "You mentioned it in the grotto."

One corner of his mouth crooked. "I had trouble thinking of anything else in the grotto. When the candle went out, I thought God had sent yet another plague to torture me."

"What do you mean?" she whispered.

"Constance called her blindness very freeing." He started toward her. "I have to say, I believed her. I never would have kissed you that first time if not for the darkness."

"Never?" She arched one brow.

"Well." He gave her his sinful half smile. "Not that day."

"Sometimes I feel I owe a debt to Lady Constance." She picked up the wicked pamphlet and opened it, choosing a passage at random. " 'In my admittedly debauched adventures, I had never felt such longing. The absence of sight only made my skin more sensitive to his touch; my ears more attuned to his breathing,' " she read aloud. "Perhaps we should put out the lamp . . ."

Sebastian crossed the room and took the pamphlet from her hands. "Enough. I don't need a story to give me ideas." He turned and tossed the pamphlet onto the fire. "I could write my own series, and not mention half of the thoughts and desires you've inspired."

"Really?" Abigail tore her eyes off the burning pamphlet. "You would write one?"

He grinned. "Only for you, my love." He touched her wrist. "Dearest Abigail," he began. His fingers trailed up her arm. "There is much I have longed to tell you since we met. I daresay you would blush to hear most of it"—she smothered a laugh, and he grinned—"but someday I hope to show you."

"I like this story." She started to turn as he moved behind her, but Sebastian stayed her with one hand on her hip.

"You should," he whispered, brushing her damp hair gently over one shoulder. "It is an ode to your beauty, your charm, your compassion. Where was I? Ah." He pressed a lingering kiss on her nape. "You have haunted my dreams since the night we met. You burst into my life like a comet, dazzling my eyes and heart. Still, not even I was mad enough to think you would ever turn to me . . ."

"You were never mad." Abigail shivered. He was

unlacing her dress, slowly and deliberately. She could feel every tug on the lace, every fractional loosening of the bodice. Her hands were in fists at her sides as he prolonged the torment.

"Not in the way everyone thought," he muttered before resuming his tale. "If being near you drove me mad, it was a madness I would happily embrace. Not being near you was a torment I could not long endure." He eased the bodice forward and Abigail let it slip down her arms.

He inhaled a ragged breath. "God in heaven." He smoothed his hands over her shoulders, down her arms, pushing the dress off. Abigail let her head fall back as his lips skimmed over her neck. His fingers plucked at the ribbon of her chemise, tied in a bow between her breasts. "So lovely," he murmured, his breath hot against her skin. "So perfect."

"And impatient!" She tugged her arms free of her sleeves and put her hands over his to yank at the ribbon. She wanted the shift off, so she could feel his skin against hers.

This time Sebastian didn't protest. He shoved down the loosened shift and cupped his hands over her breasts, first lightly, then firmly, drawing her solidly against him. A shudder ran through him. "Abigail," he whispered, his voice raw with longing.

She twisted in his arms. "I love you," she breathed, stretching up to kiss him.

He returned the kiss with fervor. With one arm, he held her tightly to him. With the other hand, he made short work of her stays' lacing. Barely taking his mouth from hers, he divested her of one piece of clothing after another.

Her heart raced. With each layer of fabric that came

off, her flesh seemed to grow more tender, more sensitive. By the time she was left in just her shift and stockings, she felt feverish, burning on the inside while shivers rippled over her skin as if a chill wind blew on her. She reached for him instinctively.

"Cold?" He folded her into his arms even as he continued nuzzling her ear.

"Not really." She slid her hands up his chest, feeling the hard thump of his heart, and toyed with the end of his cravat. "I've never seen a man's bare chest before . . ."

He paused. "Would you like to?"

Her face warmed, but Abigail nodded. Without a word Sebastian shrugged out of his coat and yanked loose the knot of his cravat. Feeling very brazen and bold, Abigail began undoing the buttons of his waistcoat, and within minutes it was on the floor, along with the long crumpled cravat. Taking one more long look at her, he undid the button at his throat and pulled the shirt over his head.

"Oh my," whispered Abigail, transfixed. His chest was a shade paler than his face, with a light sprinkling of dark hair. He was lean, but sculpted with muscles like she'd seen on statues. Her gaze caught on his arm as he tossed the shirt aside. Goodness, he looked so strong without the shirt, and her fingers itched to touch him. "You're beautiful," she said helplessly. "Not a wreck of a man at all . . ."

"You haven't seen my knee yet. But I truly was wrecked." He took her hand and laid it on his breastbone, right over his heart. "Until you salvaged me up and brought me back to life."

"I did no such thing," she said in a low voice. "You had locked yourself away, and you were the one who decided to cast off your solitude."

"But only because of you, darling," he replied. "Only you could have lured me. I don't mean you gave me life; you made me want to live. I cannot tell you what vibrancy and happiness you breathed into me, whereas I have nothing to offer you—"

"Stop." She laid her palms on his chest, marveling at how warm he was. "You understand me. We're alike, you and I—if I were in your place, I would have reacted much the same way you did, to all the injustices you endured. We are both inclined to be solitary creatures, and yet we both want someone at our side. Someone who will appreciate a long-lost grotto, or a treasured book." She darted a glance up at him through her eyelashes. "Someone who understands our improper curiosities and desires . . ."

The muscles under her hands tensed. His eyes reflected the fire. "Indeed." He wound one finger in the trailing ribbon from her shift. "My only desire is to show you every wicked sort of pleasure you crave." The shift slipped off her shoulders at his gentle but relentless pull.

"How do you know I crave wicked pleasures?" She backed up, stepping out of the fallen shift. He raised one brow, and she blushed. "I'm not Lady Constance, you know."

"I know." He caught her in his arms. "You want love, as well as wicked pleasures." He kissed her, and Abigail thought she would melt from the heady combination of love and passion in that kiss. His tongue played over hers, teasing, demanding, seducing. She barely noticed when he lifted her off the floor and carried her to the bed.

A riot of images and words passed through her brain as he laid her on the mattress and stripped off his trousers and boots. Then she looked at him, as bare as she was now, and everything vanished from her head. He was beautiful—his chest and arms taut with muscle, his legs lean and strong. A white bandage circled his left knee, but he diverted her attention from it by leaning over her for another kiss. This time his tongue thrust into her mouth, and Abigail moaned, realizing it was an imitation of things to come.

He moved onto the bed, lowering himself above her. One hand tangled in her hair as he kissed her, harder and more demanding. She moved beneath him, writhing restlessly as he cupped her breast, his thumb teasing her nipple to aching readiness. There seemed no good place to put her hands, so she simply wound her arms around his neck and held on, reveling in the drowning delight of his kiss. When he turned his head away, she protested.

"I've only begun," he rasped, sliding his weight down her. "Let me kiss you everywhere . . ."

She could only make an incoherent sound of assent as he applied his lips to her sensitized nipples. His fingers wandered all over her skin, from the notch at the base of her throat down her ribs and across her hip. As he had done in the woods, Sebastian held her as he wanted her; when she made to clasp his head to her bosom, he spread her arms wide and ravished her breasts until she was whimpering for release. She didn't even notice that he'd eased her legs apart until he slid farther down, nestling his chest between her knees. Ignoring her gasp of shock, he boldly ran his fingers down her cleft, opening her to his gaze.

Abigail raised her head, blushing with discomfort even as her body seemed to swell and ignite with heat. The taut hunger in Sebastian's eyes quelled her urge

to speak, though, and she only watched him in rapt silence as he dipped his head and pressed a lingering
kiss there.

"So soft," he whispered, stroking her lightly. "So
lovely." He circled and caressed, just as he'd done in
the woods, and Abigail's hips moved on their own. A
dark smile of satisfaction touched his lips. "So passionate." He pushed one finger inside her, and her belly
contracted. Abigail gulped for breath, dazed and mesmerized. He glanced up and met her gaze, then slowly
he pushed another finger inside her.

She fell back on the pillows, her spine flexing of its
own accord. Leisurely he slid his fingers in and out,
teasing that spot of intense feeling without pause. She
gripped the bedclothes; her wits scattered. A storm was
gathering inside her, a feverish anxiety for release. Her
legs twitched and trembled, and when Sebastian lowered his mouth again, licking and swirling his tongue
where his fingers had wrought such frenzy, she almost
screamed.

"God, Abigail . . ." He rose up on his knees and
settled her legs around his waist. "I don't want to hurt
you . . ."

She thrashed her head from side to side. "Don't
stop!"

He shuddered and shifted, and then she felt him
press against her. He stroked her again, and she jerked
in response, forcing him deeper. Abigail's imagination
ran wild, picturing his flesh parting hers, their bodies
melding into each other, the twain becoming one. Sebastian sucked in his breath and pushed again. She
barely felt the sting as he thrust home.

"I know," he said in a strangled voice. "Just . . . Let
me . . ." He grasped her hips as he began rocking back

and forth, tiny, sharp motions than made her moan. "Like that . . ." He sounded as breathless and tense as she felt. His fingers settled on that spot again, and stroked in time with his thrusts.

The end came abruptly, a sudden rush of heat through her veins. It wasn't her first climax—he had brought her to one that day in the woods—but Abigail had never felt anything like this one. The blood roared in her ears; the fullness of him lodged inside her seemed to amplify the waves of release pounding through her veins. She came with a cry, clutching for him, wanting him to feel the same unbearable pleasure.

"Yes," he panted, holding her hips against him. "Abby . . . darling . . ." He toppled forward, falling to his elbows. This time when he thrust, her eyes flew open. His head was thrown back, his teeth gritted. Slowly he pulled his hips back, then drove forward, the very picture of a man caught in ecstasy. Abigail managed to get her arm around his waist before he moved again, and again, before he rested his forehead against hers and gasped and shuddered. Dimly she felt him pulse inside her—although her entire body seemed to be pulsing at the moment—and then finally go still.

"That's . . . That's the way I want passion," she managed to say. Her muscles still quivered.

Sebastian's fierce expression melted away, and a lazy smile curved his mouth. "You shall have it that way as often as you desire."

She giggled and hugged him close. He kissed her, then turned onto his side, taking her with him. With his head on her shoulder and his arms around her, Abigail had never in her life felt so contented. "I love you," she whispered, brimming with happiness.

His lips touched her brow. "I adore you."

"I think Constance wants both, too," she whispered, idly running her fingers through his hair.

He didn't stir. "Hmm?"

"Love and passion," she clarified. "She's always in search of something—adventure, variety, excitement—but she'd never truly satisfied with what she finds, even when she declares it surpassed all her hopes. Her lovers please her, but none of them touch her heart."

"She seems more in pursuit of passion than love." He shifted, settling himself more comfortably around her. Abigail nestled into his embrace.

"Perhaps." She stared up at the shadows of flames flickering on the ceiling. "I suppose it's easier to find."

Sebastian was quiet for a moment, then he raised himself up on one elbow. "It is, but passion alone is rarely enough. Perhaps Lady Constance is too quick to accept the momentary passions offered to her—although I expect that's what makes her stories so alluring to young ladies." She gasped in mock affront. He grinned, the gleam of his teeth barely visible. "Isn't that why you read them?"

"Well—somewhat," she allowed. He nodded and made a self-satisfied sound in his throat, and she swatted his shoulder. "It's impossible for a man to understand. Young ladies aren't supposed to know anything about passion, or pleasure. It's wicked for a girl to wish a man would kiss her, but the man is expected to have a vast experience of passion so he can teach his wife. But . . . it doesn't always happen that way, does it? There are a great many unhappy marriages in London. Young ladies aren't the only ones who read Constance's stories."

"I don't intend to miss one from now on."

She laughed. "Because you're also in search of passion?"

"No." He eased back down beside her, laying his head on her shoulder. "I've found both love and passion. I intend to purchase a subscription because the stories delight and arouse the wanton woman I plan to marry, and her pleasure is my pleasure."

Abigail blushed but didn't deny it. "That's why I think Constance wants love. Passion alone is arousing, but without love, it's only fleeting."

"I hope she finds it," mumbled Sebastian. "It's the bloody best feeling in the world." His arms tightened around her for a moment before she felt him relax into sleep.

"I hope so, too," she whispered, feeling unspeakably benevolent toward all of humanity. She brushed her lips against Sebastian's forehead once more, then slept.

Chapter 23

He came awake with a jerk, lurching upright in bed. For a moment his heart thudded painfully; what had woken him?

A soft noise brought him back to his senses. He looked down, hardly daring to believe it was true. Abigail was still here, still in his bed, still gloriously bare except for the linens and blankets. He could see one slim shoulder peeking out, and reverently Sebastian folded the blanket over it. God, she was beautiful. He would be content to lie here all day just looking at her . . .

A muffled pounding interrupted his thoughts. This time he recognized it. Someone was hammering on the front door, and he had a terrible suspicion who. Reluctantly he slid from the bed and pulled on his clothes.

Abigail stirred. "What is it?" she whispered without opening her eyes.

Sebastian tucked his shirt into his trousers and reached for his boots. "I believe your father is attempting to break down my door." She frowned as if she didn't understand his words. "Wake up, darling." He leaned down and kissed her shoulder, bare once more. "Abigail."

She took a deep breath before opening her eyes and blinking up at him. Sebastian's heart seemed to swell. "He's not going to be pleased."

He almost laughed. "Probably not," Sebastian agreed, but still smiling. He couldn't seem to stop, even though he was possibly about to be shot.

Abigail gave a gusty sigh and threw off the blankets. "I'd better go talk to him."

"I'll speak to him," murmured Sebastian, although he made no move to go. Abigail was walking around his bedchamber, completely naked, and he didn't think he could look away to save his life.

She pulled her chemise over her head and tied it. "I know how he gets. Papa likes to be in control, and he gets very annoyed whenever someone outmaneuvers him." She began fussing with her stays.

Sebastian limped around the bed to help her. "I daresay he'll be more than annoyed this morning. He did tell me quite firmly that I couldn't have you."

She turned in his arms. "But—"

"But I don't intend to be denied again." He kissed her. "You're mine now."

Her smile was glorious. "And you're mine." She stepped back and reached for her dress. "Papa will come around. He always does. Don't be put off by his bluster."

Sebastian laughed. The pounding on the door had woken Boris, and his deep barking echoed through the house. "I can face anything for you, my love."

His cane was missing, no doubt still lying in the grass where he'd dropped it to catch Abigail. He barely felt the pain in his knee as he limped downstairs, though. Boris calmed down a little at his approach, and Sebastian ordered him up the stairs before opening the door. Sure enough, Thomas Weston stood on his doorstep looking like a man bent on murder. "Is my daughter here?"

Sebastian tensed unconsciously. "Yes."

"Prove it."

"I'm here, Papa." Abigail stepped close to his side. Her gown was buttoned slightly awry, and her hair streamed down her back in loose waves, but her voice was clear and calm. She slipped her hand into his. "Won't you come in?"

"I will not." He glared at Sebastian again. "I thought better of you than this, Vane."

"If you're angry at him because I'm here, you mustn't be," replied Abigail. "He had no idea."

"But he bloody well took advantage, didn't he?" growled her father.

"I meant only to take my leave of her, after we spoke yesterday," Sebastian said evenly. "Her sister directed me to the garden, but she wasn't there. The storm was about to break, and I feared she might have gone into the woods, which aren't safe in the rain. I came here to get a lantern and search—"

"And he found me." She gazed up at him almost in wonder, her eyes glowing with happiness. Sebastian was helpless against that look. "Papa, I came here on my own. But I was wrong to worry you, and should have left a note."

Weston seemed deprived of speech. He closed his eyes, ran one hand over his face, and exhaled as if the motion physically pained him. "That's all you can apologize for, not leaving a note?"

"I apologize as well, sir." Sebastian pressed her hand as she started to speak. "I should have sent word that she was safe."

"You should have sent her home!" Weston pointed at his daughter. "You. Come here. I want a word with you."

Abigail meshed her fingers more firmly with Sebastian's. "You can speak to me in front of Sebastian. I have nothing to hide from him."

"No?" He raised one brow. "And can he say the same? Did he tell you he called on me yesterday? And that I explicitly told him my answer was no?" His wrathful gaze turned back on Sebastian. "Or perhaps he forgot."

"I told him *my* answer was yes," she retorted.

"Abigail—"

"Papa, I am not going to marry Lord Atherton," she went on. Her voice was still firm, but Sebastian could feel her hand tremble in his. "He asked me yesterday, and I told him I couldn't."

"And would you give that same reply if this scoundrel hadn't been waiting in the wings?"

Sebastian's temper stirred. He hadn't been waiting; he'd been trying to make his best effort to persuade Weston. Asking for a man's daughter in marriage simply because he wanted her with a raw, ungovernable passion hadn't seemed like a winning strategy, so he'd shored up his finances, forced himself to rejoin society, and restrained himself from making love to Abigail. Well—until last night. And now he'd discover if that had been a brilliant checkmate or a fatal error.

But he sensed the man was acting out of true paternal concern, so he said nothing. Abigail, though, colored up like a rose. "I am going to marry *this scoundrel*," she snapped at her father, "and you'd better not even think of blustering about it! I wouldn't have married

Lord Atherton in any event because I just don't want to spend the rest of my days with him."

Weston didn't move for a moment. "Very well. So be it. I won't make you marry the man. But I will keep you from marrying this one."

"Now, Papa," Abigail began, but her father didn't let her.

"Perhaps I've indulged you too much, Abigail. I promised to show consideration for your wishes and desires. But I did my own investigation, unblinded by infatuation, and I cannot allow it."

"Why not?" she cried. "What good reason do you have?"

Weston's face turned dull red. His eyes glittered with fury as he shot one more glare at Sebastian. "He's a thief, my dear. Lord Stratford told me in confidence. He stole four thousand guineas from the earl, after threatening to make Stratford suffer because of a piece of property his lordship had bought from Michael Vane. And now, when he has a chance at an heiress, he's miraculously 'inherited' four thousand pounds."

"If his lordship had any proof of that charge, I'd have been in prison these past seven years," said Sebastian through white lips. "It's not true. My uncle's solicitor in Bristol can prove the inheritance."

Weston shook his head. "A solicitor would be just the person to help disguise and conceal the money, then announce a very timely and convenient 'inheritance.'"

"Papa, you're being unreasonable!" Abigail exclaimed. "Think about it for a while—I know you had such hopes when Lord Atherton called on me, but I hope you wanted me to marry for love, not just a title!"

"I want you to marry well," he said with icy finality. "And Sebastian Vane is not a wise choice. I won't risk your future on him."

No. He refused to listen to the echo of Weston's denial yesterday. Abigail said she loved him. Sebastian loved her more than he'd ever thought a man could love a woman, and he was a long way from giving up. But Abigail's hand was so tight around his, he could hardly feel his own fingers. Weston looked angry enough to hurt someone.

Sebastian raised her hand to his lips. Even if Abigail was right, her father needed some time to calm his temper. "Perhaps you should go with him, darling."

Tears glimmered in her eyes. "I won't."

"Just for now," Sebastian murmured, softly enough that Weston couldn't hear him.

"You damned well better," growled her father. "Now, Abigail."

She whipped around to glare at him. "I have to fetch my shoes. They're upstairs. In the bedroom." She hurried off, swiping at her eyes.

When Abigail came back downstairs, Boris trotted at her heels as if they were setting out on a walk. At the door, she lavished a multitude of pets and kisses on the dog's head until Boris heaved a sigh of happiness. When she glanced up at him again, Sebastian understood that she was giving his dog the farewell she couldn't give him. "Good-bye," she whispered. "For now."

In spite of himself he smiled. "Good-bye, love."

She followed her father to the waiting gig. Boris scrambled to his feet to follow her, and Sebastian stopped him with a curt command. Thomas Weston, grim-faced, never looked at him again, but Sebastian could see Abigail's face turned back until they vanished down the rutted, muddy drive.

Boris nudged his hand, startling him out of his reverie. "Yes, I know," he muttered, his mind racing. Weston had handed him a chance to make everything right. The man believed him a thief, not a murderer. He was found wanting because of missing money, not his missing father. Sebastian had always discounted the rumors of theft because he truly believed Stratford had blamed him out of spite after their furious confrontation. Sebastian had all but called him a swindler, and a man like the earl would repay that insult tenfold. But even he didn't think the earl would create the entire story out of thin air. Some money must have gone missing, and Stratford merely seized the opportunity to darken his name a little more.

He drew a deep breath. It seemed impossible that he would discover anything now, after so many years. No one at Stratford Court would receive him, let alone jump to help him. Proving that he wasn't a thief was as improbable as proving that he hadn't killed his father.

But somehow he had to do just that.

Unknowingly, Abigail had reached the exact same conclusion. She refused to look at her father as he drove them home in frosty silence. When they reached Hart House, she ran upstairs to her room and pushed a bureau in front of the door. Mama knocked, Papa pounded, and Penelope pleaded at the keyhole; she ignored them all.

Papa said Sebastian was too risky to wager her future happiness on. She thought otherwise, and she meant to

prove it. She paced her room, wishing they'd lived in
Richmond longer. She needed information and didn't
know how to get it. She needed to know more about
the stolen money before she could prove someone—
anyone—other than Sebastian had been responsible.

Because she loved him. She knew he hadn't done
it, just as she knew he was the only man for her. Papa
was wrong about him, and once she proved it, he would
have no choice. Abigail refused to admit any other possibility. She just needed a plan.

After several hours she had made little progress. She
knew frustratingly little. When Penelope brought a tray
of dinner, Abigail let her in, both for the food and for
her sister's help.

"My goodness, Abby!" Penelope whisked through
the door with eyes as wide as saucers. "I thought Papa
would tear the house down when you were gone! And
now you're back, he's still in a terrible temper!"

"If he'd been calm and sensible, there would have
been no need for that," she said coldly. "Pen, I need
help."

"Right." Her sister set down the tray and nodded,
rapt. "How?"

"We have to prove Sebastian didn't steal four thousand guineas from Lord Stratford seven years ago."

Penelope kept nodding. "How?"

"I have no idea."

"Well, that's not a good start."

Abigail threw herself on her bed with a moan. "I
know."

"What *do* you know?"

Abigail pointed at her desk. "I made a list, in order."

Penelope read it in silence. "Not much, I see."

"No."

There was a long silence.

"We need to ask someone," said Penelope. "Someone who was here at the time, who might know firsthand."

Abigail covered her eyes. "I thought of that. Lord Atherton would probably know, but he won't be eager to help me. I—I turned him down, Pen."

"Good for you," muttered her sister. "But I meant Lady Samantha."

"Do you think she'd tell us anything?" Abigail was doubtful. "I suspect no one at Stratford Court will be much help. You saw how they treated Sebastian."

"But Lady Samantha thought better of him than most, and she was friendly and kind even before her brother arrived. She lives at Stratford Court, so she would at least know the details of the stolen money."

"But her father might not even let her talk to us, once Lord Atherton . . ."

Penelope snorted. "Do you think he intends to go around telling everyone you laughed in his face? He thinks too highly of himself, that one. I expect he'll scurry back to London and say he was never in love with you anyway."

She blinked. "You really hate him."

Her sister flipped one hand. "Let's call on Lady Samantha; she did invite us the other night, and if we both go, she might be persuaded to tell us."

It still sounded unlikely to Abigail, but she had no other ideas. She nodded. "Let's go tomorrow."

Whether her parents hoped she was reconsidering Atherton's proposal or for some other reason, they were allowed to go. Adam drove them all the way around town and over the bridge, a longer journey than the ferry. Abigail's nerves were drawn tight by the time they were shown out to join Lady Samantha in the exquisite Stratford topiary garden.

"Miss Weston. Miss Penelope." With a strained smile she greeted them. "I'm not terribly surprised to see you."

Abigail's face warmed; had Lord Atherton told her? "We—we have a particular reason for calling today—"

Samantha held up one hand. "Yes, I know."

Abigail exchanged a wary glance with her sister. "You do?"

The other girl nodded, a quick jerky motion. "I had a letter this morning." She started walking, her head lowered and her eyes trained on the path. "I don't know what to do about it."

Penelope motioned her to go, so Abigail fell in step with their hostess. "I only hope to ask a few questions."

Samantha nodded. "About the missing money. I know." She drew a crumpled letter from her pocket and held it out.

Abigail smoothed it open so her sister could see it, too. She caught her breath as she recognized Sebastian's handwriting:

My dear Lady Samantha,

I may be the last person you wish to hear from at this moment, but I pray you won't throw this on the fire unread. I must beg your help. For years I have been reluctant to stir up trouble with your family, for reasons you know well. But now I stand in danger of losing everything I hold dear if I cannot prove myself innocent of stealing from your father. You must know as well as I that it would have been impossible for me to have

done so, just as you know why and how such a
rumor would have begun in the first place. Your
last note to me hinted at something; would you
tell me anything you know that might help me
clear my name? I will understand if you refuse,
but I would be eternally in your debt if you could
look past our estrangement to the memory of our
childhood affection for each other.

Your servant,
S. Vane

Your last note to me. Abigail mouthed the words questioningly at her sister, who shrugged. She folded the letter and handed it back. "Yes, it's about Mr. Vane. It appears he and I had the same thought."

Her smile was wistful. "You're in love with him, aren't you? And he with you."

Slowly Abigail nodded.

Samantha sighed. "My brother told me he asked you to marry him, and that you refused."

Again Abigail nodded.

"He also said that he thought you wouldn't have him because of Mr. Vane." She studied Abigail. "Is that so?"

"I said no to your brother's very flattering proposal because I don't love him the way he deserves to be loved," Abigail began, but Lady Samantha held up one hand.

"I know." Her smile was a little sad. "I could tell. I—I was sorry, I must admit; I would have liked having you for a sister."

"And I you," Abigail said impulsively, then bit her lip.

"Then you were right. Benedict hated losing at anything to him, but if you love Sebastian instead . . ." She spread her hands.

It was the first time she'd ever heard anyone else call him by name. Abigail heard Penelope's quiet gasp beside her. Somehow that steadied her nerve. "I do," she said simply.

Samantha's shoulders slumped a little. Her eyes closed. "He deserves to be loved."

There was no reply one could make to that.

Samantha looked up again, staring into the distance. "It makes it easier for me to decide. I'll tell you what I know, which may not be enough to help—"

"Samantha!"

They all jumped at the harsh exclamation. Lord Atherton was striding toward them, his face set. He stopped beside his sister, stony-faced. "Miss Weston. Miss Penelope. I beg your pardon, but I must have a word with my sister."

"No, Ben, not now," she said, resisting his attempt to take her arm. "I'm perfectly fine."

"Just come with me a moment, please, Samantha—"

"I am speaking to the Misses Weston!"

Atherton gave them a frustrated glance, then lowered his voice. "I heard about the letter—it should never have been given to you."

"I'm glad," she said with a sudden flare of spirit. "It should have been sent, and delivered, years ago!" She took his hand. "Walk with us, Ben. I was just about to tell the Weston ladies a story."

He glanced again at Abigail and Penelope. "They don't want to involve themselves in our affairs. I have it from Miss Weston's own lips."

"This is a different matter," said Penelope boldly. "What are you afraid of?"

"What gives you the right to ask?" he retorted.

"What makes you think Samantha knows anything?"

"Because she was at Montrose Hill the night Michael Vane disappeared," said Abigail softly, watching Samantha pale. Lord Atherton made a sharp motion with one hand, then went still. "As were you, my lord. I suspect you both know more than you've said, and have let an innocent man suffer."

"I want to tell them, Ben." Samantha touched his arm. "It's all right."

His mouth thinned. He looked at each of them in turn, then swept out one hand. "As you wish. Lead on, Samantha."

"I should begin by confessing I was desperately in love with Sebastian when I was a girl." Samantha ignored her brother's scowl. "It was many years ago, before the war. He was . . ." A smile illuminated her face in a way that made Abigail's stomach clench. "He was wonderful," Samantha said wistfully. "Dashing, strong, clever in a quiet, sly way. He and Benedict were closer than brothers; I can't remember when they weren't signaling each other with lanterns or swimming the river to share some caper. And the sad thing is . . . it's my fault they aren't still friends today."

"Not true," muttered her brother.

"I cried so bitterly when he went into the army, but I was certain he would return to marry me. I was only twelve or thirteen. He was nineteen, and doubtless thought of me as a child. But my belief remained unshaken, and by the time he did come home, I had persuaded myself that he would fall desperately in love when he saw how I'd grown up." She paused. "Unfortunately, things had changed for him. He was terribly wounded. His father's mind had broken, and Mr. Vane had done some shocking things. He—he sold a large piece of property to my father. He sold some of his other property to others, but the parcel my father bought was the best: the acreage that lay along the river. Without it, Montrose House was cut off from the water. And even worse, my father bought it for almost nothing."

She stopped again, biting her lip, and a note of apology entered her voice. "My father is a demanding man. He drives himself very hard, and he expects others to do the same. I suppose he thought Mr. Vane deserved to lose his land, with his wits gone. They had never been friendly," she hastened to add. "Only Ben and Sebastian were. But Sebastian obviously felt that friendship ought to have weighed a little in his father's favor. He came to Stratford Court, on crutches with his leg in splints, and asked my father to reverse the sale. I don't know precisely what happened . . ."

Atherton's face might have been carved of stone. Abigail remembered Sebastian's description; a shouting match, ending with curses and a slammed door. The earl had mocked him, asked if his wits had also fled, and offered to sell back the land—including the parcel that held Eleanor Vane's grave—for several times what he'd paid.

"But anyone could see Sebastian was in a fury when he left. He even argued with Ben. My father was in a foul temper, too, and rode off to London soon after. I was a fool," Samantha went on, her voice growing softer. "I still thought he would marry me, even when he told me—he *told* me—he wouldn't be a good husband. If I had been less headstrong, I would have understood that he was telling me he didn't love me. Instead I only saw that his father had ruined his fortune, leaving Sebastian penniless, and that he blamed my father. In truth . . . in truth, I blamed my father, too. My father would never let me marry a penniless gentleman, which flew in the face of my determination to marry Sebastian."

"Samantha," said her brother desperately. "Stop. None of this matters. You were a girl—it was so long ago . . ."

"I wanted to mend everything," she said, fixing a reproachful look on him. "My father had just sold a very valuable painting, and the buyer had paid him in guineas. I don't remember how I knew this, but I knew the chest of coins was in my father's study. I decided it would make things fair if I gave that money back to the Vanes."

Her brother swore, very quietly, and pulled away from her. Samantha went on, inexorably, while Abigail and Penelope listened in rapt dismay. "My father was still away, so one night I took the money. I—I put it in a leather satchel and took it across the river. Ben had told me years before how best to get across in the punt, and I went to Montrose Hill. My original plan had been to give it to Sebastian, but I reconsidered; he would never take it. I would give it to Mr. Vane, then, and explain that he must give it to Sebastian and tell him it was a hidden savings. Then the Vanes wouldn't be destitute, and everything would be fine."

"Didn't you worry about your father's reaction?" asked Penelope. Abigail jumped at her sister's voice; she'd been so caught up in Samantha's tale, listening with growing alarm and elation as various mysteries resolved themselves.

Samantha blushed. "I did, but not much. He had recently sacked his valet, and I persuaded myself he would blame the valet. I never dreamed . . ."

Atherton cursed again and pinched the bridge of his nose. Abigail didn't say anything. It seemed fairly obvious to her what would have happened, but Samantha had already admitted she was young and headstrong then. "So you took the money," she murmured.

"I did. I took it to Montrose Hill and found a way into the house. It was late, and everyone was asleep. I found Mr. Vane's room—" She cringed. "It was locked. That ought to have warned me, you're probably thinking. It should have. But I was set on my plan, and the key was right there by the door, so I let myself in. Old Mr. Vane . . . He had been a very kindly gentleman. When I came into his room, he called me Eleanor and kissed my hand. I corrected him, and I remember he touched his brow and said, 'Of course, pretty little Samantha. I remember you now.'" She looked at them pleadingly. "He seemed like himself; he seemed to know me. I explained why I had come, and he nodded. He understood! He took the money and promised he would make everything right. He kissed my brow and scolded me for coming so late at night. He even walked me out of the house himself and cautioned me to be careful. I— I thought he was recovering . . ." Her voice faltered and died.

Abigail closed her eyes, heartsick. That explained how Michael Vane had escaped. Sebastian hadn't forgotten to lock the door that night. But then . . . "When did you realize things had gone wrong?" she asked.

"Not for a while. My brother was very attentive, keeping me from hearing anything. I sent Sebastian a note, explaining that I had found a solution to his problems and begging him to call on me, but he never came. Finally I asked Ben, and that's when I heard Mr. Vane had disappeared. I didn't hear the rumor that Sebastian had killed him for a few more days, and by then my father had come home. He discovered the money missing and—" She stopped. For a moment her face crumpled in anguish. "I know you blamed Sebastian," she said to her brother. "I knew it, and I was too much a coward to admit it was I. Now—now I think you must have suspected me all along. Now I think you were trying to conceal my guilt. I never told, but you always knew when I was telling tales. You shouldn't have done it, Ben."

Atherton looked heartsick at her gentle condemnation. "I didn't know you took the money. I thought you'd merely tried to run off with him."

"But what happened to old Mr. Vane?" Penelope ventured.

Samantha shook her head. "I have no idea. He was well and lucid when I left him that night, I swear it."

Abigail's elation was tempered. Samantha's confession exonerated Sebastian only of stealing the money. The whispers of murder were even worse. Now that she was set on clearing his name, she wanted to do it completely, not just the reason her father cited. "Thank you for telling us," she said. "I have to tell Sebastian, you know."

Samantha nodded. "I want you to. See? I don't even have the courage to face him myself. But you really love him," she said wistfully. "I long ago realized my love was mere infatuation. I never had the strength to stand up for him the way you have. And he never really loved me . . . as I think he does you. He came to Stratford Court again for you, and he danced with you. He hasn't dined with anyone in Richmond for years, nor danced since before the war. I would like him to be happy, and since I contributed to his ruin, I should do something to help him."

"Will you tell your father, too?"

Her face as pale as snow, Samantha gave a tiny nod. "Somehow." She looked away. "When you tell Sebastian, let him know I'm desperately sorry."

"Thank you, Lady Samantha," said Abigail fervently. "From the bottom of my heart."

Samantha gave her a pained smile. "Good day, Miss Weston. And good luck."

"I'll walk you out," muttered her brother. Abigail followed him, glancing back to see Samantha once more walking slowly through the garden, head bowed.

"Will your father be furious at her?" asked Penelope. Atherton's mouth was set, his eyes hard. "Yes."

"But surely you're glad the truth has come out," Penelope persisted. "Surely you can't abide a man taking the blame for another's crime, even if that someone is your sister."

"You have no idea what you're talking about."

Penelope's face turned dull pink. Abigail made a sharp motion at her; she had no interest in a quarrel with Lord Atherton. But her sister ignored her. "Perhaps you ought to help clear Sebastian's name, too, since you helped to muddy it."

"I did nothing but take my father's word," he said thinly. "Vane never denied it. Samantha may have taken the money, but it was never found; curious, don't you think? Who's to say Vane didn't find it and keep it, knowing no one would be able to prove he'd been at Stratford Court? I daresay a sack of guineas would have been very tempting."

Penelope nodded. "That's right. Just because he got the girl you wanted, he must be a lying opportunist."

"Penelope!" Abigail seized her sister's arm, white with fury. "*Stop. Talking!*"

"No harm done, Miss Weston." Atherton's voice had

never been so cold or remote. "He's misled others besides your sister."

Abigail took a deep breath, clinging to her poise. "Thank you for your help, my lord. I know you were reluctant to give it, but I appreciate it deeply."

For a moment his eyes softened as he looked at her. Abigail gazed steadily back. Finally he nodded once and pushed open the door in the garden wall, revealing Adam walking the horses while he waited for them. "Good-bye, Miss Weston."

Chapter 24

Abigail barely listened to her sister rant about Lord Atherton's behavior. He'd acted to protect his sister, but now the story was out. She had part of what she needed: Sebastian hadn't taken the money. But she didn't believe for a moment Atherton's charge that he might have found it and kept it. That meant the money had disappeared along with Michael Vane. If they could find it, Sebastian could return it to Lord Stratford. Coupled with his daughter's confession, the earl would have no choice but to exonerate Sebastian. Her heart jumped at the prospect. That would put her father's objections to rest forever.

But where would Michael Vane have hidden the money? From what she'd seen of the house, it seemed unlikely Sebastian wouldn't have found it there, with all the floors and walls bare. He'd searched the grounds, too, and would have noticed a freshly dug hole. But there were acres of woods, with infinitely many places to hide a satchel of guineas. Any random tree trunk could have offered a spot.

Except . . . Michael Vane had been lucid when Samantha saw him. He knew it was money she gave him, to help Sebastian. Would he have thrown it into a hole in the ground? She frowned. Perhaps. There was no way to know how long his lucidity might have lasted. Sebastian said he'd sold everything because he feared the devil was after his money.

"What are you going to do next?" Penelope's question roused her.

"I have to tell Sebastian."

"And then?" her sister prodded. "How are you going to find the money? You know that's the only way Lord Stratford will admit he was wrong."

"You're right, and once again, I have no idea." She stared furiously out the window. "Where would old Mr. Vane put it?"

"Sebastian's guess is probably the best."

And she'd been forbidden to see him again. Abigail thought some more. "We'll have to sneak out and go see him."

"Brilliant!" Penelope's eyes gleamed. "Tonight?"

She couldn't bear to wait. Her parents were already upset with her, so she had nothing to lose. "Yes."

She racked her brains all day for ideas. The list of places to look was pitifully short: the house, the river, the woods. Short, and as vast as the Arabian Desert. Unfortunately, Penelope was right: only Sebastian would really know where to start, and she wouldn't see him until tonight. Both her parents were at home, although she knew they had accepted an invitation to dine at the Huntleys' tonight. She crossed her fingers they would go as planned.

Mama tapped at her door late that afternoon. "Are you feeling better, dearest?"

"I'm in perfect health."

Her mother's face was shadowed with worry. "Abby, you'll understand one day. When you've met a fine gentleman without any of these troubles, you'll be glad your father acted as he did."

She would not, but she refused to provoke her mother. She lifted one shoulder.

"Well, I daresay a few nights of quiet will do you good," said Mama after a moment of silence. "Papa and I dine with the Huntleys tonight. I'll send Marie to tend you." She crossed the room and leaned down to kiss her on the forehead. "We do want you to be happy, dearest."

Abigail nodded. She knew that, just as she knew she could be happiest with Sebastian. Hopefully her parents would realize that soon.

When her mother had gone, Abigail curled up in the window seat to watch the sun sink beyond the curve of the river. She laid the cameo pendant on the sill and paged through *The Children of the Abbey*, hoping for some inspiration.

And astonishingly, they provided some.

She found Penelope in the drawing room. "I have an idea."

Her sister threw aside her magazine and leapt from her chair. "A good one?"

Abigail's heart pounded. "Perhaps." Perhaps not, but she chose to ignore that. "Are you still coming?"

"Of course! I just have to do one thing—don't you dare leave without me!" Penelope bolted out of the room.

It was a brisk night. Abigail put on a warm pelisse and bonnet before meeting her sister in the garden. A quick stop in the stable provided a lantern, and Abigail had borrowed James's compass, which she was careful to read while she could still see Montrose House. She had a feeling she'd wandered in circles before Boris found her and led her there last time, and she didn't have hours to waste tonight.

"Abby, will you tell me where the grotto is?" Penelope asked as they walked.

"Why?"

Her sister shrugged. "Curiosity."

Abigail wondered if Sebastian had left the rug and cushions there. But she also remembered the glass mosaic, and the thrill of finding it. "It's just past the Fragrant Walk, down the hill. I expect there was once a path leading to it, but Sebastian cleared the brush away. It's not difficult to find now."

Penelope nodded. "Thank you."

"I didn't know you wanted to see it," she began, but Penelope waved one hand.

"Oh! I just wondered. It might come in handy to know."

It might. If her parents persisted, it might be the only place she could meet Sebastian. Perhaps she shouldn't have told Penelope . . . But she looked at her sister's face, determined and fearless as they strode through a darkening forest to try to clear Sebastian's name, and decided that was ludicrous. She trusted Penelope.

They reached Montrose Hill at the same time Boris found them. He gave a happy bark and bounded over, tail wagging. Penelope stopped dead, but Abigail laughed and let him lick her hands and face before rewarding him with a piece of ham she'd filched from her dinner plate. And then Sebastian was there, obviously setting out for his evening walk. He swept her into his arms without a word. Abigail burrowed into his beloved form, heedless of her sister watching or Boris nosing at her pockets for more treats.

"I didn't think I'd see you again for an age," he whispered, his lips light on her earlobe.

"It *has* been an age, to my mind."

He gave a low laugh and released her. "What are you doing here?" He included Penelope in his question.

"We're here to find the stolen money," Penelope told him.

Abigail nodded. "If my father won't consent because he fears you're a thief, we'll just have to prove you aren't."

Sebastian looked startled, then his lips quirked. "I had the same thought. Unfortunately, I've pondered it for seven years with no luck. And after so long . . ."

"Well, we know who took the money: Lady Samantha."

Sebastian stared. "How—?"

"We went to see her today. She was glad to confess, I think. She got your note and said she didn't know what to do, but in the end she told us." Abigail repeated everything she could remember from Samantha's confession.

Sebastian's jaw was clenched by the end, and he stared toward the river. "So she really was here. I didn't think she could have been, but . . . she let my father out." Abigail remembered him blaming himself for not locking the door that night, and felt a foolish burst of gratitude that she'd managed to lift that one bit of guilt from his shoulders.

"What was her last note to you?" piped up Penelope. "Your letter mentioned it."

He gave a humorless half smile. "She wrote to say she'd found a solution to my problem and would I please call on her. Of course I never went—I wouldn't have been allowed to see her in any event. Her brother made that clear enough." He glanced over his shoulder as the sound of hoofbeats thudded down the drive. "Speak of the devil."

Benedict Lennox, Lord Atherton, swung down from his horse and glared at them. "Searching hard already, I see."

"What brings you to Montrose Hill?" asked Sebastian. Boris growled at the newcomer, and Abigail noted Sebastian did nothing to stay the dog.

Atherton shot a black look at Penelope. "A bribe."

Penelope just smiled, coy and sweet.

"I think we can manage well enough on our own," said Sebastian coolly. This time he wasn't making any effort to hide his dislike. "Go home, Ben."

Atherton's answering grin was fierce. "Let's have a look for the money first, Bastian."

Boris's growl grew louder.

"I'm glad for any help," declared Abigail, reaching down to scratch the dog's ears. "Lord Atherton, thank you for coming. It's very decent of you."

"Not really," said Sebastian under his breath.

"I look forward to returning Lord Stratford's funds so he can put a public end to that ridiculous rumor," Abigail went on firmly. "I have an idea where we should look: the mausoleum."

Sebastian shook his head. "I searched there that night. I follow your logic, but I searched everywhere. He wasn't there."

"But you were looking for your father, not a leather satchel full of guineas," she argued. "Have you been there since?"

He hesitated. "No."

Because it was now on Lord Stratford's land. She turned to Atherton in triumph. "Have we your permission to go there?"

"By all means." He knotted his horse's reins. "Let's be done with it."

Sebastian hesitated, then shrugged. He muttered something about lanterns and headed toward the stables. Abigail took the chance to speak to Lord Atherton. Her former suitor was occupied with tending his horse, and didn't look at her. "Thank you," she said softly.

"I've not done anything yet."

"But you came." She reached out to touch his arm, then stopped. "I'm sorry—"

"Samantha is set on confessing to our father," he said brusquely. "If the money is returned at the same time, he won't be as angry."

She blinked. "Will he punish her?"

"Yes."

Oh dear. "Will he hurt her?" she asked hesitantly.

Atherton shrugged. "Some. Not much. I, on the other hand, expect to be horsewhipped. Are we ready to go yet?"

Sebastian came back, lanterns glowing in his hands. "It's a good distance."

"How fortunate I have no other engagements this evening," returned Atherton. He held out his hand, and after a pause Sebastian gave him a lantern. "Lead on, Vane."

They were a mostly quiet party as they walked. Sebastian thought this was the most quixotic endeavor imaginable. Like Abigail, he, too, had arrived at the idea that Samantha might know something. He'd written to her, hoping against hope she would tell him. The story Abigail related staggered him, although it fit. Once he allowed it was possible for Samantha to have been there that night—and he still found it incredible that she had—a host of possibilities opened up. Her story almost made him hopeful for a moment; if his father had been lucid that night, maybe he hadn't fallen into the river and drowned, or wandered into the woods and died of hunger. Maybe he'd kept enough shreds of sanity to have planned an escape, perhaps thought of something that might save him . . .

But that was a remote possibility. Sebastian hadn't seen more than a handful of lucid moments in his father's last several months. He had combed these woods, not for one night but for months, searching for any sign of his father. True, he hadn't been looking for a satchel of coins, and he had to remind himself that's what they were seeking tonight, not Michael Vane. He couldn't stop himself from instinctively keeping his eyes open for the green cloak and straw hat that had disappeared with his father, even though he knew he wouldn't see them.

They spied the mausoleum after a half hour's walk, almost lost to the growth of the woods. It was down the hill, quite steeply in some places, and more than once he almost lost his footing. His knee was still tender from the fall at Stratford Court. Having Abigail's hand in his steadied him, and as the ornate stone chapel came in sight beneath its disguise of vines, he felt a bit of hope stir.

"What made you think of this?"

Her face was beautiful and pale in the darkening woods. "The book you gave me. It was so old, thirty years or more, but so well kept. He loved her, didn't he?"

Sebastian remembered his father sleeping with

a threadbare nightgown wrapped around his arm. "Dearly."

"At first I assumed you had kept it so, but you were a boy, and then a soldier. *He* must have cared for it. It wasn't a fine book at all, but it was filled with notes in her handwriting. I see why he would have kept it so carefully. It was a little piece of her."

That was true. Michael Vane had burned most of his own books in his fits, but nothing from the little shelf that held his wife's things.

"And I expected you would have searched here before, but you hadn't been here in years, since it was no longer your property," she continued. "I—I don't know that anything will be here. Perhaps it's a completely mad idea. But I thought it wouldn't hurt to have a look."

He smiled. "It's a brilliant idea. I should have thought of it myself." Perhaps he would have—but perhaps not. As much as he'd longed to clear his name, there hadn't been anything jolting him into action until Thomas Weston's refusal. Even if this didn't succeed— even if nothing succeeded—Sebastian would be glad he'd tried, with Abigail.

"It doesn't look promising." Benedict stopped and surveyed the chapel. The steps were completely covered in moss and bracken, and a fallen tree had narrowly missed the leaded roof.

"We've crawled through worse." Sebastian handed his lantern to Abigail and began clearing the tangle of plants away. It made him think of the grotto, and how he'd cleaned it for her. After a moment Benedict joined him in silence until they had a narrow path up the steps. Gingerly Sebastian balanced on the top, crumbling step and pulled back the bolt holding the outer door closed.

It opened with a loud, rusty groan, then stuck in the grit. Benedict stepped up and put his shoulder to it, and they heaved the door open.

Abigail and Penelope squeezed up between them until all four were pressed against the inner gate, which was locked. They held the lanterns aloft and Penelope sneezed as they peered into the gloom beyond.

It was as black as pitch in the crypt. As his eyes adjusted, Sebastian tried to make out his mother's bier at the back. He dimly remembered her funeral, when the crypt had been opened last. He'd cried and cried until he fell asleep in a corner and was almost forgotten. With a flash of memory he felt his father's arms scooping him up, warm and strong, Michael Vane's familiar voice stark with relief at finding him.

But there was nothing else. No leather satchel sat invitingly on the center sarcophagus, which really concealed the stair leading to the underground crypt. Sebastian told himself not to be dismayed; it had been a slim chance. But his heart felt as though it had turned to lead, and he rested his head against the bars.

"I wish we could go in," whispered Abigail. "Hold the lantern a little to the right, please." She pressed her face to the gate, making it rattle. "I think I see something . . ."

He raised his head. "What?"

She screwed up her face in frustration. "I can't tell. It's too dark."

"What do you think it is?" demanded her sister. "Let me look!" Abigail stepped aside to let her wiggle into place. Sebastian slid his arm around her waist, tucking her snugly against him. Absently he took a deep breath with his face against her temple; her hair smelled like roses. It made the disappointment a little less.

Penelope squirmed and pressed against the bars for several minutes, trying to get a better view. At her urging, Benedict edged around her to hold his lantern aloft. She squinted for a few minutes. "Yes, I think you're right, Abby! There's something behind the sarcophagus!"

"But what?" asked Benedict. "We'd have to break in to have a better look, so please don't say it's a dead rat."

"It looks like . . ." She stretched onto her toes. "It looks like a shoe."

Benedict looked at him, eyebrows raised. Sebastian let go of Abigail and drew his knife. "I've no objection to breaking the lock. Do you?"

Benedict shook his head. "None at all." He helped Abigail and Penelope move out of the way as Sebastian slid the blade of his hunting knife between the bars above the lock. "Ready? Now!" Benedict pulled hard on the gate as Sebastian drove his weight against the knife handle, using the bars as a fulcrum. The bars squealed, then with a loud snap, the rusted metal gave way. Benedict almost flew backward down the steps as the gate swung open.

Some sense made Sebastian throw up a hand to stop the ladies from rushing inside. "Let us make sure it's safe," he said, taking his lantern back from Abigail. In the glow of the light, her eyes were huge and dark as she nodded soberly. Benedict took another lantern, and together they stepped inside.

The crypt wasn't long, barely twenty feet. Three columns of biers lined the walls, the names of long-dead Vanes etched in their sides, but so covered with dust and cobwebs, the names were illegible. The ornate sarcophagus filled the center, with only a narrow aisle on each side. Sebastian took the left side, Benedict the right. Just as they used to do, all those years ago.

"There is something," said Benedict as they reached the sarcophagus. "There—in the back—"

Sebastian heard his voice catch at the same moment his lantern light reached around the corner. "Stop," he ordered. "Do not come in," he shouted at the ladies, who had started forward at Benedict's exclamation. He looked at his old friend. "Take them out," he said. "Now, Ben."

Benedict, looking as though he would be ill, obeyed.

Sebastian barely heard their worried questions. He took a step, and then another. He held his breath. He'd seen bodies before, even skeletal ones. Battlefield graves were notorious for opening in the first heavy rain. But he'd never seen his father's, and the sight nearly made him fall to his knees.

Michael Vane hadn't fallen in the river, or into a hole in the ground. He'd made it to the crypt and curled up next to his beloved Eleanor's tomb, where he still lay. His straw hat had disintegrated, and his green cloak was eaten away in gaping holes. But the ragged iron-gray hair still had the wave in front, just as Sebastian remembered. And clutched in the exposed bones of his arms was a leather satchel.

"Sebastian?" Abigail's voice rang with worry. "What's there?"

He lowered himself to the floor and stared in numb sorrow at his father's remains. "My father. And, I believe, the money."

Chapter 25

Lord Atherton made Abigail and Penelope go out of the mausoleum entirely. He looked a little green, and Abigail felt very thankful he'd stopped them before they could see what was there. Sebastian remained inside.

To distract herself she asked her sister, "What bribe did you offer Lord Atherton to get him to come tonight?"

"Oh. I thought he owed it to Sebastian, after the dinner party . . . I promised to tell him where the grotto is if he came and helped." Penelope gave a faltering smile. "It worked."

"Ah." She'd better tell Sebastian to remove the rug and cushions before they gave anyone the wrong idea. Or rather, the right idea.

Lord Atherton had gone back up the steps but not inside. He swung the heavy outer door closed, then open again. She edged a little closer. "What are you doing?"

"I wondered how he'd got locked in." From the inside of the door he slid the bolt out. "I didn't think there'd be one on the inside." He glanced at the gate, still ajar. "I suppose Mr. Vane had keys to that."

Penelope joined her. "What a terrible way to die," she murmured. "Alone in that little crypt."

He'd wanted to die. He'd told Sebastian so—and when his son refused to help him, Michael found a way. Perhaps it had even been how he wanted to die: next to his beloved wife, without staining his son's conscience. Wordlessly Abigail groped for her sister's hand.

It was full dark by the time Sebastian emerged. His coat was covered in dust and his limp seemed worse than ever, but he carried a large leather sack in his arms. He closed the gate gently, even though it swung open an inch because of bent bars, and then he closed the outer door and slid the bolt home. He handed the sack to Benedict.

"I didn't count it," he said quietly, "but it's guineas."

Benedict was motionless. "I'm sorry."

Sebastian just looked at him. He turned to Abigail, who went into his arms, ignoring the grime and dirt covering his coat. He made a motion to stop her, then simply let her slide beneath the coat to embrace him, her head against his chest where only she could hear how ragged his breath was.

"He looked peaceful," he said, his voice a little hoarse. "He must have come here after I searched— there was so much ground to cover. If only I'd come back and looked again . . ."

She tightened her arms around him. "It's done. Who knows what he was thinking, but he must have come here on purpose." That inner bolt, and the locked gate, lingered in her mind. Michael Vane hadn't wanted to be found.

"Let's go." Benedict sounded greatly subdued. He had the satchel hefted under one arm. "Let's go, Sebastian."

Sebastian raised his head at the sound of his name. For a long moment he and Benedict just stared at each other, then he looked down at Abigail again. She nodded hopefully. It was time to go, and to let the world know how wrong they'd been about him.

Even in the dim light of Penelope's lantern, she could see his mouth curve into a weary smile. "Yes. Let's go home."

Sebastian arrived at Hart House early the next morning, before Abigail had even finished dressing. The previous evening's events had left her wide awake until the small hours of the morning, and then she'd slept later than usual. The first she learned of his arrival was when her sister burst through her door as her maid was pinning up her hair. "Sebastian is here!"

"What? How do you know?" Abigail leapt from her chair, ignoring Betsy's squawk about her hair.

"Milo started barking, so I went to look." Penelope beamed at her. "Aren't you going to see him?"

"Yes, I am." She seized the hairpin from the startled maid, rammed it into her hair, and flew out the door and down the stairs.

Thomson was standing guard outside her father's study. "I'm sorry, Miss Weston, you're not to go in."

"Just let me knock."

"Nor to knock."

Penelope skidded up beside her just as the study door opened to reveal Papa, his face set in a furious glower. "Abigail, come here. *Only* Abigail," he growled as Penelope tried to follow. She gave her sister an apologetic glance before slipping past her father into the study.

"I ought to whip your backside for sneaking off last night." Papa stalked back to his chair. "What the devil were you thinking?"

She rushed to sit beside Sebastian on the sofa. "I love him, Papa. You said I couldn't marry him because you thought he was a thief, so we had to prove otherwise."

"What if you'd been wrong?"

She smiled at Sebastian. He grinned back. Abigail's heart soared; she'd never seen him look so happy. "I knew I wasn't."

"Your father agrees, now that he's read Lord Stratford's letter." Sebastian turned to her father again. "Have you any other objections, Mr. Weston?"

"Lord Stratford—?"

Papa grumbled something under his breath. He handed Abigail a page from his desk.

Dear Sir,
 I must correct a false impression you may have formed the other night when we spoke. I am absolutely persuaded that Sebastian Vane had no part in any theft from Stratford Court.
                                        Stratford

She raised hopeful eyes to her father. He glared broodingly at her for a moment, then sighed, dragging one hand over his face. "This is the moment where I have to admit I was wrong and you were right, isn't it?"

"Have you any other objection, Mr. Weston?" repeated Sebastian. His hand was in a fist on his knee, and he looked as tense as a bowstring.

Papa sighed. He glanced away and shook his head,

then he turned back to Abigail. The ire faded from his face until he looked a little sad. "Only that I'm going to miss her terribly."

Abigail gasped, and jumped up to throw her arms around his neck. "Thank you, Papa!" She whirled around and threw herself into Sebastian's arms. He had risen when she did, and he caught her easily.

"Give me a moment to leave the room," said Papa dryly as he got to his feet. "But I will be right outside the door. Bear it in mind, Vane."

Sebastian was kissing her before the door had latched. For a moment there was nothing but the two of them, clinging to each other without anything to divide them again.

"Stratford's letter?" she asked some time later, when her hair had come undone from its pins and his jacket was wildly askew.

He grinned. "I'm as astonished as you are! Benedict sent it early this morning and asked me to deliver it. Somehow he guessed I'd come here . . ." He tipped up her chin and kissed her again until Abigail almost forgot what he'd been saying. "He sent another letter as well," he added, his merriment fading. "From my father. It was inside the satchel. He must have written it, planning to leave it for me, and then become confused, or changed his mind. He . . . He said he was going to join my mother and leave me in peace. If he'd left it behind that night, I might have found him in time—"

She put her finger on his lips. "Don't. It can't be changed now. You must forgive yourself."

He nodded. Gently he took her hand, turning it so he could press his lips to the pulse in her wrist. "I'd much rather think of the future."

"Which will be . . . ?" she prompted, her heart skipping a beat at the way his sleepy eyes glowed, and his mouth curved up on one side.

"A wedding." He kissed her. "A marriage." He kissed her again. "A lifetime with you."

She sighed and linked her hands behind his neck. "Just the way it was meant to be."

Next month, don't miss these exciting new love stories only from Avon Books

Kiss of Wrath by Sandra Hill

It's been centuries since Mordr the Berserker was turned into a Viking vampire angel and now he has a new assignment: protect lust-worthy Miranda Hart. Miranda needs a miracle to keep her late cousin's five children safe from her cousin's dangerous husband. But Miranda wants nothing to do with a hunk who claims to be a Viking. Together they must decide if they fit in each other's worlds . . . before their enemies close in.

All I Want Is You by Toni Blake

Christy Knight thinks maybe it's time for her to leave Destiny, Ohio, and find a guy who's smart, sexy, and solvent. Her rugged handyman neighbor fits the bill. Jack DuVall hasn't been entirely honest—he's not really a handyman and he's not broke, but he finds gorgeous, feisty Christy irresistible. When secrets are exposed, the seaside town of Coral Cove could be the perfect place to find a red-hot destiny of their own.

The Once and Future Duchess by Sophia Nash

After a debauched bachelor party, the Prince Regent demands that the Duke of Candover be brought to heel— and he believes Isabelle Tremont, the Duchess of March, is the lady up to the challenge. For Candover, there's no shortage of other candidates, but if he and Isabelle can put aside pride and duty, then a love once denied might be their destiny.

REL 0514

TEN THINGS I LOVE ABOUT YOU

978-0-06-149189-4

If the elderly Earl of Newbury dies without an heir, his detested nephew Sebastian inherits everything. Newbury decides that Annabel Winslow is the answer to his problems. But the thought of marrying the earl makes Annabel's skin crawl, even though the union would save her family from ruin. Perhaps the earl's machinations will leave him out in the cold and spur a love match instead?

JUST LIKE HEAVEN

978-0-06-149190-0

Marcus Holroyd has promised his best friend, David Smythe-Smith, that he'll look out for David's sister, Honoria. Not an easy task when Honoria sets off for Cambridge determined to marry by the end of the season. When her advances are spurned can Marcus swoop in and steal her heart?

A NIGHT LIKE THIS

978-0-06-207290-0

Daniel Smythe-Smith vows to pursue the mysterious young governess Anne Wynter, even if that means spending his days with a ten-year-old who thinks she's a unicorn. And after years of dodging unwanted advances, the oh-so-dashing Earl of Winstead is the first man to truly tempt Anne.

*G*ive in to your Impulses!

These unforgettable stories only take a second to buy and give you hours of reading pleasure!

Go to *www.AvonImpulse.com* and see what we have to offer.

Available wherever e-books are sold.

AVON

IMP 081